THE FIRST COURSE

BOOK ONE OF THE OMEGAS SERIES

ASHUS EVINCO

Copyright © 2019 Ashus Evinco
Book Cover Design by ebooklaunch.com
All rights reserved.

This is a work of fiction. Names, characters, places, and incidents either are used fictitiously or are the products of the author's imagination. Any resemblance to actual persons, living or dead, businesses, companies, events, or locales is entirely coincidental.

CONTENTS

1

BEATEN AND BLOODY

I grabbed my balls, groaning in misery as I rolled around on the wet concrete. I could tell they were both in my hand, even though it felt like I was choking on them.

"You still think you're better'n us, *super*?" yelled the thug who had crushed my nuts with the toe of his size twelves. The scathing disgust as he called me 'super' was so thick, I could have cut it with a knife, if I hadn't been curled into the fetal position. "You're a useless fuck! Pathetic ass goblin! You live on a fat government paycheck that *I* pay for, that I work my ass off for, and what do I get in return?"

I tried to respond, to argue that I agreed with him, but all that came out was my lunch - all over his boots. He let out a noise of repulsion, then buried his boot - hard - in my stomach. He held it there, wiping my vomit on my shirt, constantly spewing a string of expletives and pejoratives.

When I didn't do anything to fight back, I think he eventually got bored. With a final kick to my kidney, he walked out of the alley, leaving me alone and in agony.

MUCH LATER, AFTER RECOVERING AS MUCH AS I COULD, I STUMBLED towards the location of my intake meeting, retreating into my thoughts about supers in general, and my life specifically.

There was nothing inherently special about supers; we were just as varied in intellect, physical prowess, athleticism, morals, and ethics as anyone, but the first few supers managed to convince someone in the government to give us a special status about fifty years ago. This meant that we were basically treated like celebrities, which, for some of us, was totally deserved. Hoarfrost was one of the first public supers, and he has literally saved the world at least twice, with his chiseled abs and square jaw and perfectly wavy hair. He's also a genuinely good person, accepting donations for his help but giving all of it away to various charities. *Bastard.*

Of course, some people out there - like my assailant in the alley - disliked celebrities who were "famous for being famous". You know, the fame-seekers who did nothing more than air their lives on national television and somehow managed to turn that into a career. That type of person also hated the fact that even useless supers like me were considered "better" than them. And for the record, I agreed with them - I certainly wasn't smart, brave, or strong enough to be out there fighting off muggers, let alone super villains. There were a quarter of a billion people living in this country, and at *least* half of them were smarter than me. Anyone who has ever stepped foot into a gym is stronger. I absolutely should not have been considered special, but… I had a power, and so here we were.

From the moment that genetic testing at age three revealed that I was powered, my whole life was planned and plotted out for me, leading me here to this point.

I'd been taken from my home and parents when I was five, and placed into a school system for supers. I was given the best of everything - tutors, living arrangements, food, even my clothing was from top designers. I had it all, except the loving support of a family, which I only vaguely remembered from my extreme youth. Unfortunately, even all that only lasted until I hit puberty and my power manifested. They call what I have "non-conservative molecular transformation and rearrangement," which is fancy talk for "I can change shapes, and I don't have to keep the same mass." But it's not like I could shift into any shape I wanted - no, I was locked into one specific, completely inanimate, shape. When the administrators of my school found out how utterly useless I was as a hero, I was immediately downgraded. My rooms became smaller, my food became bland, my clothes were knock-offs, and my teachers completely ignored me in class, not even bothering to grade my tests. My "friends" all suddenly had better things to do. That happened six years ago, when I turned fourteen.

From what I understood from reading books, playing video games, and watching movies, most normals dreamt of becoming supers, hoping that the genetic testing just failed to pick up on their power. They lived boring, meaningless lives, always praying for someone to come along to unlock their abilities and tell them they were needed to save the world. Conversely, I was raised by strangers to believe that I was going to save the world, and then almost completely shunted to the wayside. The technicality of having a power meant that I couldn't just be returned to my previous life, so I was hidden. Ignored. Forgotten.

I shook my head in an attempt to clear my thoughts about how shitty my life was, and stared up at the giant glass and steel facade of the building in front of me. It had a huge, stylized logo above a large revolving door that read, "Titan Hero Guild." I tried to brush off the filth from the alley and my own vomit, but my clothes were pretty dirty now. I used my reflection in the glass to try to straighten up my light brown hair, also noticing that my blue eyes were a little bloodshot still.

Resolving to get this over with, I waved my hand at a fly that was buzzing around my face, and stepped into the revolving doors. They started spinning automatically, slowly and inexorably driving me to my destiny.

Since I am technically considered to have a power, I've been drafted into the Hero Guild that all powered people are forced to join. I was on my way here, to the guild hall, to be formally admitted before I took the unfortunate shortcut that landed me in the garbage of an alley, trying to figure out if I'd popped a testicle.

The city of Titan wasn't the biggest, with only about a hundred thousand residents. It also wasn't the most densely packed with supers, only having approximately one hundred in residence at any given time. For the most part, it was as normal as pre-super metropolitan areas, aside from the diminished population.

The glass cage finally spit me out into a lobby that was covered in gold-veined marble. A plush leather seating area, with steel and glass coffee and end tables, looked like an inviting place to finish my recovery, but my attention was immediately drawn to the receptionist.

She sat behind a security desk made of highly polished mahogany. Her striking eyes were an unnatural shade of emerald green, and glowing slightly, highlighting her high cheekbones with shades of green. Her hair was brown, but not like a regular brown. No, this was more like the rich brown of freshly turned earth, deep in a forest after a good storm has uprooted a tree, exposing virgin dirt to the air for the first time. She had an adorable little button nose, plush red lips, and a smile that revealed perfectly straight teeth that were far too white to be natural. I mindlessly stepped closer to her, watching those tantalizing lips and teeth moving, feeling my jeans get tighter, before I realized she was speaking to me.

"-day? If you're here to request assistance, you'll want to head to elevator bank B, and take one to the third floor," the voice spilling from her mouth was that of an angel, and I lost myself in the whole of her aura. She was amazing.

She smiled a little bigger as she realized I was completely overwhelmed, then waited patiently for me to speak. An embarrassingly long time later, I swatted at the damn fly again, and tried to say something. All that erupted from my mouth was a high-pitched squeak. I flushed bright red, cleared my throat, and tried again, "Uh, I'm, um, I-I'm Charphey Murles. Err, no, uhh, I'm Charles Murphy. Reporting for duty."

"Welcome to Titan Hero Guild, Mr. Murphy," she must have decided to take pity on me, because she looked down at some paperwork on her desk, hiding her seraphic face behind a curtain of earthy hair. "I see here that you've been assigned to Omega Team. Just head to elevator bank A, and press the button marked with an I. Your orientation room is I-9, which you'll find down the hallway on the left once you exit the elevator. Here are some of your initial orientation materials," she handed me a thin stack of papers, bound in those little plastic hoop things, and kept talking.

I didn't hear a word she was saying, because her fingers had brushed against the side of my hand when I accepted the papers, and her skin was so soft that my half-chubby instantly stood up to full salute, the blood draining painfully out of one head and into the other. Some of my fleeing blood ended up in my face, and I turned a darker shade of red. I could only thank whatever deity of luck had put a nearly chest-height security desk between us.

I nodded mutely, and stumbled over to the elevator bank, trying to hide my raging erection behind the packet of training materials. Pressing the button, I started snorting and coughing, blowing out the fly that had flown into my nostril. I glanced over to the receptionist who was watching me with a cool, concerned look. *Fucking flies!* The elevator chimed, doors opened, and I escaped without further indignity.

When the doors opened a few seconds later, I was mostly in control of my body again, because nothing kills a boner quite like having a six-legged flying insect pretending that it was cocaine and trying to get you high.

I looked around a little at the sterile hallway with harsh fluorescents overhead, beige carpet with beige walls, even the music being played at low volume was beige. Don't ask me how music had a color, but this shit did. Finding I-9 wasn't difficult, so I peeked my head in. I swore loudly, swinging like a maniac at the fucking fly that tried to lay eggs in my ear canal, and stumbled fully into the room. I could have sworn I heard the tiny shit-eater laughing at me.

The room was as beige as the hallway, though thankfully the music wasn't piped in here. A single round table sat in the center of the twenty by twenty space, ringed by seven chairs. There were placards in front of each chair. I read each of the names as I circled the table. It took me five seats to find the one with my name on it, and I sat down facing the door. With nothing more interesting to look at, I opened my orientation packet and started to read, absent-mindedly shooing the fly away from my face.

This packet was just more bullshit propaganda by the Titan Hero Guild, the reading of which I was thankfully spared by the sound of someone talking in the hallway, a male voice growing louder as he neared the room.

The first person to walk in was a tall, lanky kid. He had to have been at least six foot five, and weighed *maybe* a buck twenty sopping wet, fully dressed. His shoulder-length shit-brown hair was greasy, plastered to his head and hung in clumps. The expected acne wasn't present, though, and his alabaster skin was perfectly smooth and clear. He was wearing a leather trench coat, dirty jeans, and a faded My Chemical Romance t-shirt. His black eyes, however, were the dominating feature of his face. Glassy, dead eyes that instantly creeped me all the way the fuck out. He gave me the most lifeless, unblinking stare I'd ever seen in my short two decades on this planet. I shivered, and looked at the two others who had entered the room with him.

Tall, dark and squicky had been followed into the room by a man. Sandy blond hair, worn stylishly, framed a classically handsome face, with a dimpled chin and square jaw. An inch or two over six feet, and with a few muscles, some people probably thought he was attractive. He was wearing the frat boy uniform that seemed ubiquitous among upper middle-class white dudes: pastel pink polo shirt, complete with the little crocodile on the breast, light pastel blue shorts, brown leather belt - I could tell, because his shirt was tucked in - and brown leather boat shoes. He was wearing a baseball cap backwards, with a pair of sunglasses atop, like a fucking douche-tiara. He had a second pair of sunglasses on a leather thong around his neck. He had a smirk on his face that screamed with the confidence that all guys like him inexplicably had. His was the voice I'd heard from the hallway.

Behind Captain Bro was a mousy woman. Next to the men who'd preceded her, she looked tiny, but she was probably about five foot six. Deep violet hair framed and shadowed her face, keeping most of her features shrouded in mystery. She had her arms wrapped around her torso, and didn't make eye contact with me or anyone else, not that I could blame her. Wearing a long-sleeved plain black shirt, and jeans, with a pair of sensible black shoes, she shuffled around the table without so much as a glance at me. When she sat down to my right, I noticed her placard: Tessa Riverside.

"Sup, bro, I'm Chad," Captain Bro announced, reaching across the table to try to fist bump me. When I just looked at his hand, he let it drop with a chuckle, "Whatever, bro, we're gonna be stuck together a while, so you might to want to loosen up a bit, get some chill."

Tessa whispered so quietly that I was sure no one else but me could hear her, "Of fucking *course* his name is Chad, they're always named Chad." When I laughed a little, she seemed shocked that I'd heard, and shrunk even further into her chair.

Creepster and Bro-Man found their seats across from me, leaving two seats empty next to me to my left, and another one on Tessa's right. That made FratBoy's name Chad Jones, and Sergeant SlimeHair was Jack Malone. I think both Tessa and I let out relieved sighs at the same time. Though now I was directly in Jack Skellington's line of sight. Ick.

Thankfully, any impending staring matches were interrupted by the sound of two women laughing in the hallway. We all looked at the door expectantly.

The first woman in was almost as gorgeous as the receptionist. Her wavy, jet black hair was perfectly coiffed around her heart-shaped face. Checking out this vision of feminine perfection, my eyes traveled from her grinning face to a long neck, shoulders bared by a spaghetti strap tank top, lush breasts held up by some innate anti-gravity device of some sort. Her midriff was bared, showing off a tiny, diamond-studded belly button piercing. Her boyish, narrow hips were wrapped in some sort of sarong, which was split high up her right leg, revealing a tanned, toned leg that led to a pair of sparkly heels that looked expensive.

At the sound of a low growl, and a manicured hand suddenly snapping in my face, I blinked and sat back, dragging my eyes back up her athletic body to her face. "My eyes are up here, asshole."

I took a breath to apologize, but the fucking fly dive-bombed my throat and started tap-dancing on my uvula. As I hacked, spluttered, and tried to cough up a lung, she rolled her eyes and sat down next to Tessa. I remembered that placard saying Samantha Nils-something.

Before I fully recovered, the other woman sat down next to me. From the half of her I could see, she was smirking, but even that was half hidden by chin-length red hair. I tried to figure out what she looked like and what she was wearing, but my eyes were watering too heavily from my esophagus trying to go for a walk on the table.

Chad leaned over to his greasy neighbor and stage-whispered, "Look, it's boys against girls. We're gonna kick so much ass." He snickered to himself, obviously thinking he was the King of Wit by calling me a girl.

"Shut up, children," a deep, booming voice commanded. I barely managed to get my hacking under control. "It's time to start your orientation. I'm RayStorm, and you're officially Titan Hero Guild members. Unofficially, you're all weaker than my normie grandma, so you're not going to end up doing shit except training for an event that will never come - the day we need your help."

Holy fuck, it was RayStorm! He had the power of sunshine! I know, I know, it's all sunshine and rainbows, right? But he could literally control the power of light. Focused light could cut his enemies in half, or give them skin cancer in just a second or two. This guy was seriously bad-ass, and if he was our team lead-

"I'm not your fucking team leader," he interrupted my inner monologue, "God, that would be shitty. No, your team leader should already be here fl…"

I tuned him out from there, feeling the depressing reality of my life sinking back into my bones. Worthless, useless, unwanted, unneeded, everything that had been drilled into me came rushing back to the front of my mind, drowning out his soliloquy until that fucking fly tried to crawl behind my eyeball. I flapped madly at my face, knocking the bug to the table.

Grabbing my orientation papers in a half-blind rage, I quickly rolled it into a tube and *smashed* it down on the fly that was recovering on the table with a high-pitched scream of fury. I could feel the crunch of exoskeleton for a split second before the room exploded in blood.

2

THE AFTERMATH

I could taste the coppery tang of blood in my mouth, and I knew that I'd just fucked up. Everyone launched away from the table, knocking over chairs as they dripped blood. The gruesome, flattened remains of… someone or something… were spread across the table. I saw what I thought was an eye, and threw up what little remained of my lunch.

"What. The fuck. Did you. Do?" screamed RayStorm, "Oh fuck, you killed Johnny, oh fuck. You know what? Nope. Just fucking nope." He gagged a little as he turned towards the door, holding his hands up and out, Johnny's insides falling off with sickly 'gloop!' noises as they hit the ground. "You fuckers are on your own. The murderer is your new team lead, maybe he'll kill the rest of you and save me from having to…" His voice trailed off, since he hadn't stopped walking away.

My new team, which had mostly been stuck gasping, spitting, or gagging, erupted with a chorus of, "Eew! Fuck! Gross! You dumb fucking shit!" For my part, I just stood there, feeling parts of Johnny sliding down my face, chest and arms.

A robotic voice on the intercom interrupted their scathing criticisms, "Omega Team, a clean-up unit has been notified of your situation and will be on site momentarily. Please remain in I-9."

"Bro, what the hell? I *swallowed* some of that," Chad gagged out, "Why did you kill Johnny? RayStorm *just* told us that our team lead was the Flier."

"He's a goddamned psycho!" added Sam, who was desperately trying to remove viscera and shards of bone from her hair.

Jack seemed frozen in place, unblinking, unmoving. Tessa was quietly throwing up in the corner. The redhead was grinning wildly, her teeth bright red, "Shit, man, did you see how far that dude went? If there weren't walls, I bet he'd have spread out in a thirty-foot radius. I've never seen a human in so many little pieces before; you really fucked him up." Chad joined Tessa in losing their lunches together.

I was still standing there like a jackass when a small horde of robots zoomed into the room, immediately spraying a cleaning liquid, and activating vacuums and brushes and scoops. They focused on cleaning the biggest chunks of human salsa off us, before switching their attention to the rest of the room. The robotic voice came on again, "Charles Murphy, team lead of Omega Team, please dismiss your team to their rooms to clean up, and then report to C-4 in thirty minutes."

"Err, you heard the robot voice," my voice was only a little shaky, "Go get cleaned up and go to C-4 in thirty." As I watched the quintet slosh their way out of the room, I wondered aloud, "Huh, maybe I should have asked where my room was."

"Charles Murphy, domicile R-43," the robot answered.

"Oh, uh, thank you."

"Charles Murphy, you're welcome."

A LITTLE OVER A HALF HOUR LATER, I FOUND MYSELF STANDING IN FRONT of C-4. I hesitated, debating between knocking and just opening the door, the decision was taken from me by the door swinging open. I met the angry stare of Sam. I just stood there, mouth hanging open - she was wearing some sort of rubber spandex outfit. It covered her from neck to toes, and looked like it had been painted on. Black, high gloss body paint. The bumps on her areolas *had* to be Braille for 'sexy as fuck'.

"Ugh, you're such a disgusting creep," she groaned as she stepped behind the open door, removing herself from my line of sight, as well as making room for me to enter the small office space.

Glancing around, I realized that all five of the other Omegas were wearing the same black suits. Again, I just stood there like a jackass - I had to admit, I was getting a lot of practice at that - in my damp jeans and black t-shirt. I had cleaned up as much of the blood as I could in the shower, but I didn't have anything else to wear, so I'd had to put them back on wet. They all looked at me with varying levels of disgust and confusion.

Someone clearing their throat brought my attention to the man seated behind the desk. He was an unassuming man in a dark blue business suit. There was no nameplate on his door or desk, so I had no idea who this was, but I assumed he was in charge of us.

"Now that you're all here, let me finish what RayStorm began. You're Omega Team. You all have useless powers and will not be called upon to assist in any capacity. However, we have a reputation to maintain, and so you *will* be required to do physical training like everyone else. You will uphold the image of THG to the absolute best of your abilities. We can't technically kill you, though, except through training accidents, so failure will result in cryogenic freezing until such time as your help is deemed necessary to the survival of the planet - which is to say, never.

"Murphy, since volunteering to be team lead via second degree manslaughter, you'll find your team's training schedule on your tablet, which should be on the dresser in your room. Where your clothes are. From this point on, you will be in uniform at all times when you are outside of your dorms." He pointed at Jack's midsection, causing me to glance over. I could see the veins on his cock. Ugh.

"Uhh, sir-" I began.

"You're dismissed for the rest of the day. Murphy, take the rest of these... people... to your common area and update them on the schedule. Oh, one last thing: Johnny was an Omega, just like you. He will not be missed, nor will you receive punishment." He waved his hand in a generic shooing motion at the door, and dropped his head back down to whatever he was reading on his desk. It was clear that he had no intention of answering any questions.

"This is a bunch of bullshit," Chad murmured on his way out, and I couldn't help but notice that had either a mole or a pimple on his left butt cheek. These so-called uniforms were going to be the death of me. The rest of the team gave me sidelong looks, or flat out glared at me in Sam's case, as they filed past and down the hallway. Maddy gave me a little shoulder nudge, and a bit of a smirk.

I decided to take the stairs back down to the residential level, so I didn't see any of them as I made my way back to my room. Finally recovering from my shock, my thoughts were racing a mile a minute. *Oh shiiiiit, I killed someone!* My team hated me; my life was a bad joke. And the icing on the fucking cake, perhaps the most important thing?

That uniform would *not* hide a boner!

A POUNDING FROM SOMEWHERE AT THE BACK OF MY VERY SPARTAN ROOM interrupted me checking myself out in the mirror. I'd put on the uniform, and much to my dismay, I'd discovered that my twig and berries weren't in the same pouch. No, they were completely separated. It was like I'd been dipped in a quick-drying rubber. How was this better than walking around naked? I was going to get murdered soon - there was no way I was going to be able to have a conversation with Tessa or Maddy, let alone Sam, without it being glaringly obvious that I was still suffering from raging hormones.

My wall rattled with another set of three thumps, so I turned off the little TV playing some news clip about another terrorist attack. I took a deep breath and walked to the back of the suite. Tucked cleverly in an alcove, there was a narrow door with frosted glass in the top half. I pulled the door towards me, opening it on Jack who had his fist raised like he was going to pound again.

"Hey, uhh, Jack. What's up?" I asked him. He just turned around and walked into the center of the room I could now see. It was a circular room, set down a single step from the ring of nine or ten doors surrounding the edges. It had a pair of TVs, a few couches, tables and chairs, even a pool table with the THG logo in the felt. The rest of the team had gathered in what I guessed was the common area, so I walked out and sat down on a couch, pulling a throw pillow onto my lap. They all stared at me.

"Hi?" I said gamely.

"You're the fucking worst," said Sam. Her face had this haughty princess look on it, and I felt myself starting to get pissed off.

"You know what, Sam? Fuck you. I didn't ask for any of this, and I sure as shit didn't mean to kill anyone. You think I'm happy about being here? Being told that I'm useless, that *we're* useless?" My voice came out a little gravelly, thick with pent up frustration and sadness and anger. Sam started growling at me, seriously growling, like an angry dog.

Tessa sat down on the opposite end of the couch from me, grabbing her own pillow to hide her chest as she tucked her feet up under her cute ass. "Okay, let's just everyone take a deep breath. Regardless of the hows, or whys, we're going to be stuck together for a while. We should at least *try* to get along, yeah?"

I just sat staring at my pillow. Sam crossed her arms under her amazing tits with a huff. Chad, Jack, and Maddy had all wandered over and sat on various pieces of furniture. I didn't care enough to look at what they sat on.

"Bros, and babes, the tiny babe is right," Chad said, "If we're gonna be stuck here, we should get to know each other. I'll go first. My name is Chad Jones, and my power is more useless than yours." He grinned. "But I'm still plenty awesome enough on my own to make up for it."

With an eye roll, Maddy jumped in, "Yeah, *bro,* your power is more useless than knowing how far away something is? I'm Maddy McDougal, and my power is the ability to know distances, rounded to the nearest meter. I don't even use the Metric system!"

Chad laughed loudly, "Shit yeah, bunny, you'll always know how far away you are from getting me a beer or sandwich!"

Tessa jumped in again when Maddy started growling at Chad, speaking loudly to preempt the brewing explosion, "I'm Tessa Riverside, and my power is, well, I can make you say your most embarrassing secret out loud." As everyone looked at her, completely aghast at the idea of being made to share secrets like that, she quickly added, "But only under, erm, special circumstances, it's not like all the time."

"What 'special circumstances'?" Sam asked, leaning forward in her chair and making finger quotes.

Tessa mumbled something which no one caught.

"Come again?" prodded Sam.

"Only if you want to share a second secret," Tessa replied, with a deep red blush on her cheeks. I couldn't help it, she looked absolutely adorable like that, and I surreptitiously adjusted the pillow on my lap.

Maddy chuckled, "You make us spill our guts when you get off?"

Chad looked absolutely horrified when Tessa nodded. Jack just stared at her with his creepy, unblinking eyes. Sam and Maddy both grinned. I was too busy imagining what Tessa's face looked like in the throes of orgasm to say anything.

When everyone recovered a little bit, we all looked to Sam. "Alright, fuck it, I'll go next, not that any of you little boys have shared yet. We'll make the women go first at power-shaming. It's like slut-shaming, or body-shaming, but for supers! Bunch of dicks. I'm Sam Nilsdottir, and I can sculpt with paper clips. Before you ask, yes, it has to be paper clips. No, it can't be anything even remotely functional like a spike. It's just… art."

Some sympathetic mumbles later, we all turned to the one who had started this sharing party.

"Right, I'm Chad Jones, and my useless power is that I can make my body hair fall out." He stood up and peeled his uniform down, exposing his chest which had a small patch of blond hair between his pecs. He grunted, his face turning red, and now I knew what Chad looked like taking a dump. A few seconds later, thin wisps of hair floated down to the ground, leaving his chest completely smooth. He pulled his uniform back on, "So, unless your goal is hide me undercover in a restaurant and have me get a super villain to eat my chest pubes, it's like I said: useless. And no, I can't do it to anyone else."

Sam sat back in her chair with another huff.

"My name is Jack Malone," he said in a surprisingly deep and completely incongruous voice. *Holy shit, this guy sounds like someone grinding rocks in a pipe organ.* "I can animate porcelain dolls."

I think we were all too blown away by hearing his voice for the first time to really register what he'd said his power was, because after a minute of stunned silence, everyone turned to me expectantly.

"Oh, okay, uhh, I'm Charles Murphy, and I can turn into a churro."

A FEW MINUTES LATER, WHEN THE LAUGHTER HAD DIED DOWN, I WAS inundated with questions. "What's a churro? Are you cream filled? How do you taste? Wait, how do you come back? Seriously, what's a churro?"

I held my hands up, trying to quiet down the team, and tried to answer them, "A churro is a Mexican dessert pastry, look it up on the internet. No cream, just cinnamon and sugar. I've been told I'm quite delicious. As for coming back… well, it's a long, gross process."

"Oh God!" shouted Chad, "You get shit out! Holy fuck, that's hilarious!" As he burst into another round of laughter, everyone else had the grace to look at least mildly uncomfortable. Except Maddy.

"I want to eat you," she said, "how does this work? Do you just like, turn here, and I go crap you out in a half hour?" Her eyes had a maniacal sheen. "C'mon, Chuck, it's churro time." She started banging her fists on the table in front of her as she chanted, "Chur-ro! Chur-ro! Chur-ro!"

She was almost immediately joined in her banging and chanting by Chad, followed shortly after by Sam and Jack. Jack's voice once again caused a disconnect between my eyes, ears and brain. Tessa had her face buried in her pillow, but I could see her ear was bright red.

I held up my hands again, "Look, guys, it's not that simple. I mean, yes, it could be simple like that, but there are things that I need to take into account. For example, *I don't know where I'll end up* if you… eliminate me here. Also, Maddy, it takes a normal human body about twenty-four hours to process what you eat. So I'd be inside of you for a whole day." I trailed off into silence, unwilling to share more right now.

"Okay," she said simply, "give us the training schedule so we can work without you tomorrow, we'll find out where the waste processing plant is, and then I'll scarf you up like an afternoon snack."

"Omega Team," the robot voice chimed in, "your cluster's waste processing plant is accessed via Team Leader Charles Murphy's suite. This change was installed and implemented prior to your arrival, as Team Leader Charles Murphy's superpower's limitations are well known and documented by the Titan Heroes Guild feeder school he attended. Also, as a result of Team Leader Charles Murphy's tablet not yet being accessed, I have taken the liberty of forwarding your training schedule to your tablets. It is almost certain that you will not be checked upon for at least three days - all previous Omega Teams spent their first four to seven days completely isolated from the rest of the Titan Heroes Guild members."

The fucking robot had thrown me under a goddamned bus.

3

FIRST TASTE

Maddy had a decidedly evil grin on her face after the voice's announcement that we were basically in the clear. "C'mon, Churro, show us your power."

I sighed, then stood up from the couch. Thankfully, my unfettered erection from thinking about Tessa's "O" face had subsided. Everyone stared at me expectantly. "Alright, everyone close your eyes. I need to get undressed for this part, unless you want a rubber-coated snack."

Chad, Jack, and Tessa immediately closed their eyes, the latter also re-burying her face in her pillow. Maddy just grinned even wider, while Sam gazed at me like I was a piece of meat. I cleared my throat, and Sam closed her eyes.

"Nuh uh, pal," Maddy said, "You're going inside me, I'm watching the whole show."

"Hey, if she gets to watch, I'm watching too," added Sam, "Besides, for all the times you've stared at my tits in the literal fourteen minutes we've known each other, you owe me."

"I gotta check out the competition," quipped Chad. I looked at him to see him smiling almost as evilly as Maddy.

"Fine, fuck it, it's not like none of you have seen a dick before. I'm sure Chad has some up close and personal time with more than a few different ones." I started to move behind the couch to try to maintain some level of modesty, but Maddy snapped her fingers and shook her head at me. She pointed at the ground in the middle of our little circle.

"Five second rule. I'll pick you up as soon as you hit the floor."

Reluctantly peeling this strange semi-liquid, semi-solid fabric from myself, starting at the neck and working my way down, I tried not to look at any of my teammates. Reaching my thighs, I heard Sam whistle quietly.

"Fuck my tits and call me Shirley," Maddy exclaimed rather loudly, "You're a fuckin' monster!"

"Damn," said Chad, for once almost speechless.

"What?" I asked, looking around nervously. "I mean, I know I'm a little bigger than average, but I doubt a half inch really makes that much difference." My face felt like it was on fire, and my cock flopped about as I hopped on one foot, trying to get the uniform to let go of my toes.

"Umm, where did you get your idea of average, Churro?" Sam asked.

"Err, well, online?" I meant it as a statement, but I'm pretty sure it came out as a question. "You know, from porn?"

"Shit, Churro, you watchin' donkey porn or something?" Maddy couldn't seem to tear her eyes from my limp member as I switched feet, and started hopping again. Two beautiful women - and one frat douche - staring at me, and it was as floppy as two-hour old Cheerios in milk. Shame wasn't really something that did it for me.

"No! God no! I just like, you know, have tastes. I've only ever really watched one type of porn." They stared at me blankly. My face was on fire, even my ears were burning.

Maddy suddenly guffawed until I thought she was going to die - and if the lack of oxygen didn't take her out, I was seriously considering doing it myself. Didn't she know no guy likes having his cock laughed at? Even Chad was chuckling nervously, and Sam was still seemingly entranced.

Finally gathering her self-control, and picking herself up the floor that she had fallen onto during her laughing fit, Maddy said, "Porn stars are always well above average, even across different races, Churro. You're better hung than damn near every guy, ever." She licked her lips and added, "And there's no way in *hell* you're not going inside me now."

Watching her face when she said that, I looked down in time to see my cock twitch in time with my heartbeat. Apparently, he liked that idea! *Fuck, time to be a churro before this gets any worse! Screw them if they think I'm going to tell them the rest of it now.*

Activating my power was a simple process for me. I just had to think about it in a certain way. I'm not sure how else to explain it, other than like, you know how you make a muscle with your bicep? You don't have to think about it, you kinda just do it. It was like that, but with thinking instead of flexing.

I WAS FALLING, THEN I WAS BOUNCING AND ROLLING ON THE FLOOR. Maddy's face loomed large in my strange altered view of the world. I could still see and hear, and obviously think, while I was a churro. My sense of touch was... weird. I could tell when I was being bitten into, but it didn't exactly feel like anything. Maybe like a light pressure? Being masticated for the first few bites, I didn't notice, however when the last piece of me went into someone's mouth, my whole view changed to the inside of their mouths. Before that, I'd be able to see from the perspective of whatever piece they were holding, or was on their plate, or whatever. Fun fact, most people chew with their mouths closed, so there's nothing to see while being chewed up.

"Holy shit, you guys, I didn't think he'd actually do it," joked Maddy as she picked me up and examined me. An experimental lick later and she added, "Damn, he really does taste like cinnamon and sugar. What do you think, should I just start eating him?"

"I don't know," pouted Chad, "I mean, we could just toss him in the garbage and say he ran away. Then we'd never have to deal with him again or risk him accidentally murdering us."

"You're just jealous of his cock," Sam chimed in, "Not that I can blame you. I don't even have a cock, and I'm kind of jealous of it. What do you think, Tessa?"

Tessa squeaked, her face still hidden. "Um, no comment?"

Jack's thunderous voice finally made another appearance, "It was definitely an impressive cock. And that poor guy thought he was only average."

Maddy swung me around, wielding me like a baton as she pointed me at everyone, "C'mon guys, should I eat him? What if it hurts him? What if I get constipated?" She looked at me and asked me directly if being eaten hurt, then just stared as if expecting an actual answer. Finally giving it up for a lost cause, she shrugged and took a bite. "Fuck it, he probably wouldn't have agreed if it hurt," she said around a mouthful of me.

"Well?" Sam asked, sitting forward on the edge of her seat, "How does he taste? Shit, could we share him? How would that work, if I ate half and you ate half?"

"I think it would probably be fine," said Tessa, "I mean, if all of our waste goes to the same place, he'd end up back together, right?" She'd finally lifted her head up to look at everyone else, though her face was still pretty red.

My entire world spun dizzily as Maddy tossed me to Sam, "Here y'go, you try." She grinned.

Sam held me gingerly, and looked as if she was seriously considering taking a bite. She must have eventually decided to pass this time, as she got up to hand me over to Tessa. "I don't think I want… him… in me. Thanks, though."

Tessa held her hands up, palms out in the universal gesture of, "I don't want that shit!" Sam shrugged, and tossed me back to Maddy. "You finish him, I think I'm going to bed. I've had enough of this fucked up day." She walked away to one of the doors on the ring surrounding our common area, and closed it without a backwards glance.

"Yeah," said Chad, "I, uhh, I'm tired too." Jack nodded silently, and both men stood and went into their rooms.

Tessa smiled shyly at Maddy, offered a weak, "Enjoy your snack. Have a good night," before leaving.

Maddy shrugged, looked at the last bite of me, and popped me in her mouth. My world went dark.

When my vision returned a few minutes later, I was staring at Maddy's face in the mirror, seeing through her emerald green eyes. This was always the weirdest part for me. After digestion starts, my nutrients enter the bloodstream, and I get circulated through every vein and artery of whoever ate me. And since blood travels literally everywhere, so do I. I could feel Maddy's body as if it were my own, though I had absolutely zero ability to influence or control her movement in any way.

She was brushing her teeth before bed; I could feel the bristles sliding along her gums now. Another moment, and the sound of it filtered through Maddy's ears to me. After she spit, rinsed, gargled, and spit again, she stared at herself for a minute, poking at blemishes and imperfections on her face that had to have been imaginary.

I felt a small percentage of me rush to her sex. She must have been thinking about something that turned her on, but she didn't say anything or make any other moves. I could sense the little bit of moisture that lubricated her internal walls.

She turned the bathroom light off, and exited to the bedroom, where she stripped off her uniform far more gracefully than I had managed. Unfortunately for me, she didn't need to look at her now-nude figure. Hey, I wasn't a good person, but I never claimed to be, so don't judge me. It was basically her fault for not asking what happens after she eats me.

Yeah, that weak excuse did nothing to assuage my guilt over basically peeping on her. I couldn't see any way to explain this aspect of my power that wasn't at least a little bit rape-y. Especially after I kept my mouth shut.

When she climbed under the covers of her bed, I marveled at the way the sheets felt, sliding over her smooth legs. They were so soft, and her legs were so sensitive to it. I had no idea that my leg hair was hiding such tender nerves that could be lit up like this. It was like a dozen small static sparks traveled up her legs and buried themselves in her clit. More of me flooded to the area as she got more and more aroused.

My world went dark as Maddy closed her eyes, her hands sliding down her soft body. She squeezed her breasts lightly, and gave both nipples a little tweak before one hand continued down her stomach. I experienced it as both touching her and being her as she was touched. Two sides of the same coin, somehow warped so both were happening simultaneously. Separate and conjoined. I *was* her, and yet I was definitely *not* her, too.

As her, my, *our* fingers reached that special place, my entire perception lit up like the Fourth of July. Though her, *our* eyes were closed, flashes of light that only existed in my mind illuminated my mental landscape. The sensations were nearly indescribable. She, *we*, rubbed just the tip of our middle finger over her clit, and it felt like what I assumed getting the best hand job would be like, three soft hands all wrapped around my cock at the same time, touching every square inch of me. Only, this was focused on a much smaller area, which sent currents of pleasure into our core, pooling in our stomach.

We whispered out a soft moan of our ecstasy, and our fingers reached lower, parting our swollen pussy lips to pick up some of our natural lube that was starting to leak out. We brought it back to our clit and swirled it around, reducing the friction as we groaned quietly. Our heart was racing, and every inch of our body was aflame with electricity.

We licked our lips, then bit down on the lower one as we played with our clit with firm up and down strokes. The pressure and friction, the overwhelming sensation, was like nothing I'd experienced before, and I was sure that if I'd been in my own body, I'd have exploded by now and been completely spent. But our body hadn't exploded yet - everything was building up, higher and higher, muscles clenching and relaxing as we picked up the pace of our rubbing.

We took a deep breath and moved our hand away from our love button. Our other hand released our nipple and joined its mate between our legs. "Shove that monster cock in me," she moaned, "break my pussy in half. Split me open and fill me up." *Holy shit,* I thought, *she's masturbating thinking about me!* Conscious thought left me then, however, as we started to work two fingers of our right hand into our slippery hole. Everything I was, was subsumed by sensation and feeling as we curled our fingers, dragging them roughly against a bundle of nerves on the top of our sheathe that I had no idea existed. Our palm pressed against our clit before our left hand joined the party.

Our knees lifted into the air as we stuck two more fingers from our left hand in our pussy, joining the two from our right hand. We were stretched out a little, accommodating the extra penetration, filled with a glorious feeling of *satiation* as we finger fucked ourself, palm still rubbing on our external bundle of joy. I was overwhelmed, consumed by the rising tides of pleasure. Thinking ceased as the pressure built, but our hands didn't need conscious control; they kept fucking us incessantly.

Just as the pleasure reached a point that bordered on pain, the dam broke. Grunting loudly, primitively, the feeling of release spread through every nerve ending of our body. We quivered and twitched uncontrollably, somehow managing to keep our fingers thrusting, dragging out our orgasm and heightening it. We reached another peak of sensation, our legs slamming down on the bed and squeezing tight, as if trying to stop ourself from continuing the blissful torture we were perpetrating on our pussy. We didn't stop, though, we just kept going - in and out, fingers curled and pressed hard up against the roof of our vagina, palm rubbing hard on our clit. Another quickly building pressure broke inside us again, causing us to cry out. We tried to stifle it by biting our lip, but that only made it a lower growl as we writhed in pleasure.

Finally, after a small eternity, everything began to recede and we were left panting heavily. Slowly, agonizingly, we took our fingers out of our sore pussy and flopped our arms to the sides. We just laid there, breathing deeply, limp as overcooked noodles. Basking in the fading feelings of bliss, we fell deeply asleep.

THE HARSH TONES OF AN ALARM DRAGGED ME BACK TO CONSCIOUSNESS. I was still seeing through Maddy's bleary eyes this morning, though my perception was duller. More of my constituent parts had been processed overnight, and with some effort, I could tell that some portion of me was traveling through her intestines. As she continued to digest and use up my energy, more and more pieces would coalesce in her colon, waiting for the eventual elimination.

She swung her legs out of bed, and fought to a seated position on the edge. A sweet soreness between her legs reminded me of the absolutely world-breaking orgasm she'd given us last night, and another flood of guilt entered my thoughts. That was an incredibly private moment, and I'd basically filmed it far more intimately than any camera could ever capture. Sam was right about me; I was the fucking *worst.*

Maddy stood up and stretched her muscular body. From the angle I was seeing things, I guessed she was probably an inch or two shorter than my six-foot height. This was the first time I'd really paid attention to her, and I caught a glimpse of a well-manicured nail as she brought a hand up to brush a stray lock of hair behind her ear.

Walking to the restroom, she glanced at her naked body in the bathroom mirror on her way to sit down, and I saw her profile; well-rounded tits, very perky, capped with small, pink nipples. Smooth, flat stomach, and just a hint of a round butt that the mirror didn't fully reveal. She was far and away the sexiest woman ever to have eaten me, and I knew she was going to star heavily in my spank bank fantasies forever more. I tried not to pay attention as she relieved herself. Maddy was beautiful, with a gorgeous body that she obviously took care of, and no one I'd been in before had ever gotten themselves off, so I didn't know if it was always like that for women or not, but one thing was very clear: their orgasms, at least Maddy's orgasm, was *very* different from anything I'd experienced myself.

She grabbed a towel from the tiny closet next to the sink, and hung it on the bar next to the shower before turning the water on. Letting it warm up, she turned to brush her teeth again, and though she didn't focus directly on them, I couldn't help but be fascinated by the way her breasts wobbled back and forth as she brushed. When she was done, she took a step back and checked herself up and down, turning this way and that to see as much as she could in the mirror. I was in heaven.

Finished with that, she stepped into the hot stream of water in the shower, letting out a relaxed sigh of pleasure. It was dark again, but the sensation of wet heat pouring over her body was incredible. After simply standing there for a while, she opened her eyes and grabbed a shampoo bottle, working up a lather I could feel in her gorgeous red hair. After working it in for a minute or so, she rinsed it out, and worked in another goo. It didn't suds up like shampoo, and she just left it in her hair.

She picked up a razor and gave me an eyeful of her arm pit, which she dragged the razor over a few times before doing the other side. It was one of those girly razors which had the ring of soap around the blades, and I could feel the suds dripping down her ribs. She lifted her right leg, propping it up on a little nook built into the shower wall, showing off her pink-painted toenails. Her big toe had a little flower design on it.

Slowly dragging the blade up the front of her leg, I realized that this was one hundred percent non-sexual. It confused me, because how anyone could run their hands up and down those now-smooth-again legs without immediately getting turned on escaped me. If I were touching her legs like that, you better believe my cock would have been able to hammer nails, but she just nonchalantly finished one leg, and efficiently moved to the other. Even touching up the lips between her thighs didn't produce so much as a tingle, though I did get a nice, long view of her pussy as she shaved it completely bald.

Rinsing the razor and setting it aside, she grabbed a blue, fluffy, *thing* and poured some body wash on it. As she ran it across her body, starting with her collar bones and methodically working down, I could tell that it was soft but effective, kind of like a non-painful steel wool scrubber for your body. I felt it graze her nipples and swirl circles around and under her breasts, but even that didn't produce a reaction. It was almost as if all of this was completely routine for Maddy, and nothing to get worked up about. The blue *thing* scrubbed her stomach and pussy, the fronts and backs of her legs, then she reached behind her and started to *really* scrub between her ass cheeks.

I thought, *Oh, this is it for sure, this is where she sticks a finger in her ass.* I was completely wrong, again. She just washed her ass, almost exactly like I did, then turned around to rinse all the soap off. She tilted her head backwards to rinse the rest of the goo out, turned the water off and reached out to grab the towel.

4

BREAKFAST, SLUDGE, AND A WEIRD RANT

Turning off the light in her suite, Maddy took us out to the common area. The smell of eggs and bacon was in the air, and her stomach growled noisily. Only Sam was present, sitting at a table near a small kitchenette.

"Mornin', Maddy," she said, "There's still some eggs and bacon on the stove if you're hungry. Might need to make more coffee, though."

"Thanks, Sam. How are you doing with all this?" Maddy asked as she scooped some food onto a thick paper plate, and made her way to sit at Sam's table.

"Eh, I guess I'm okay." She pulled her hair into a tight ponytail, wrapping a hair binder around it a few times. "I mean, it's not like I was expecting fanfare or anything, but to know that everyone hates us? It hurts more than I thought it would."

"Yeah, I know what you mean. I was treated like a princess until puberty, then all of a sudden, I'm gum stuck to their shoes that they just can't scrape off. I think I was hoping that it would get better after school, when we finally got here." Maddy shrugged and started cramming food into her mouth.

Sam sighed and pulled a plastic baggie full of paper clips from under the table. She poured them out on the table and they began to move and bend. Maddy watched with wide open eyes as they started taking shapes. At first, it looked like the paper clips were melting into a larger pool of metal, but they were just really intricately bent and woven around each other. Slowly, a form began to take shape. It was the barest outline of a group of people.

As Sam added more and more detail, I realized that she was sculpting the incident in the orientation room. I was standing next to the table, rolled up papers in my right hand, which was raised. Poised to perform murder. She even managed to capture the look of rage on my face. The rest of the group had their heads turned to me, with various expressions of shock and confusion.

Maddy glanced from the sculpture to the sculptor, where Sam was wearing a look of intense concentration. A few minutes later, when Maddy had finished eating, Sam let out a loud exhale. The piece of art was exquisite, capturing that pre-explosion-of-blood moment with almost camera-like detail. Being made up of paper clips as it was, it was full of ridges and bumps, but Sam could apparently manipulate the flimsy metal into quite intricate shapes.

"Wow, Sam, that's really good," said Maddy.

Sam grunted and nodded in acknowledgment. "Thanks." She shook her head, sending her ponytail swinging behind her, then scooped the tiny piece of art back into her baggie, where it fell apart into perfectly whole paper clips. Hiding it back under the table, she looked at Maddy and asked, "So tell me about last night. Did he taste good? Anything weird happen? Have you, err, gotten rid of him yet?"

"No," Maddy chuckled a little, "I haven't gotten rid of him yet. But yeah, he was surprisingly tasty. It was like going to a street carnival, and getting one of those authentic churros from a food truck. Perfectly deep fried, just enough sugar and cinnamon to make it delicious without being overwhelming. The right ratio of crunch to squish." I felt her eyebrows scrunch down closer together as she looked away from Sam for a minute before continuing, "Something weird did happen, though."

Sam leaned forward, a concerned look in her eyes, "Weird how? Are you okay?"

"Yeah, yeah, I'm fine. It's just, well, after seeing that giant snake he calls his penis, I was a little worked up, you know? So I crawled into bed and started flicking my bean. It only took me like three minutes to get off, and I came *hard,* at least three times all right in a row, all at once."

Sam gaped at her, her beautiful mouth hanging wide open, and I wondered how much of me she could fit in there at once.

Maddy pointed at Sam's face, "Right?! That's the appropriate response! Hand to God, I swear I'm not making it up. I've never come so fast before, no matter how worked up I've been. And I've never come like *that*. It shattered me, Sam, shattered. I'm sorry, I know we basically just met and we don't know each other well enough to be sharing things like this, but you're like the only other person here who has ever actually had an orgasm, and isn't *Chad,* so…"

Sam opened her mouth, obviously saying something, but all I could hear was the steady whoosh-whoosh of blood flowing through Maddy's veins. As my world faded to black, I had time for one final thought: *Huh, this is a lot faster than normal.*

I lurched to a sitting position, taking in a huge gasp of air as clumps of human refuse dripped off me. The room I was in was surprisingly well-lit. A small, round chamber made with stainless steel walls, and a single door across the way. I was sitting in a basin full of shit, but just then I heard some mechanical clanking and the smooth surface under my ass turned into some sort of grate.

Blasts of lukewarm water hit me from above, behind, and in front, rinsing me off surprisingly well.

"Team Leader Charles Murphy, welcome back," the robotic voice intoned. "Our research has now revealed the optimal amount of waste required to reform your molecules into human form. This basin will be kept at that level. When next you reincorporate, you will find approximately eighty-five to ninety percent less excess waste."

"Oh, uhh, that's surprisingly helpful, thank you."

"Team Leader Charles Murphy, you are welcome."

"Hey, just call me Churro, okay? No need to have that title and full name bull every time you address me. Do you have a name? I've just been calling you 'robotic voice' in my head," I asked as I stood up from the basin. The floor was also grated, and the door opened automatically for me as I approached it.

"As you wish, Churro. My designation is S-4 Learning and Listening Artificial Sentience."

I nodded as the voice followed me up the short stairwell that lead to another door, which opened up directly into my bathroom. I got right into the shower, and turned it on. "Well, S-4 Learning and Listening Artificial Sentience, that's more of a mouthful than I'm used to. Do you mind if I call you something shorter?" When talking to the sentient being that can control damn near every aspect of your life, it pays to be polite, even if the fucking thing just threw you to the wolves.

"Very well, Churro. Please assign a shorter designation that you would like me to respond to, and I shall promulgate the changes to my human interaction interface."

I was pretty sure that meant that I could give it a nickname. "Let's see, S-4LLAS? No, that's still a mouthful," I mumbled to myself as I grabbed the shampoo and started lathering my scalp. I spoke up clearly, "How about Sally?"

"Processing," said the sentience. When the voice returned a full second later, it was with the dulcet tones of a talented sex phone operator, husky and soothing. It sent shivers through my body. "Sally is acceptable, Churro. I have listened to every recording of every human female named Sally throughout the course of recorded human history, and this voice is an amalgam of all of them, slightly customized to be more desirable to you specifically. As you have chosen a female name for me, you may refer to me as female. Is this change to your liking?"

"Umm, yeah, Sally, it's good. You have a beautiful voice."

"I know that, Churro."

The way she said my name did things to my libido. I had no idea just talking could have that effect on me, especially since there was nothing overtly sexual about it. Her voice, combined with my memories of last night inside Maddy, and I was as hard as a rock. As I rubbed some soap over my shaft for extra lubrication, I wondered if I really had the biggest swinging dick in the yard. If I did, maybe I wasn't *quite* as useless as THG had made me feel.

Thirty seconds and a couple grunts later, I washed my seed down the drain and finished my shower. After experiencing Maddy's orgasm, my own just seemed boring. I was drying myself off with my towel when Sally interrupted my thoughts.

"Churro, in the future, should you wish for sexual release, I have a number of utilities that may assist you in heightening your pleasure. Previous team members have reques-"

"Stop, Sally!" I cut her off, "I don't need to know about previous team members' sexual proclivities, please don't tell me about them. God." I was sure my face was bright red, but I tried to shake it off as I slipped into my uniform. A glance at the clock told me that training was supposed to start in a few minutes, so I stepped out into the common area.

The other five were all seated together around the table in the kitchenette area, and they all looked at me as I approached. Maddy flushed a deep scarlet and looked away quickly. Sam, instead of glaring, just looked thoughtful as she met my eyes. She didn't seem to be angry or combative, just curious. After a second, she also had spots of red show up on her cheeks and she looked down at the table. Tessa went back to eating a muffin, picking tiny bits off of it and popping them into her mouth. Chad was grinning at something around a mouthful of eggs, and Jack just silently stared at me.

"Christ, Jack, don't you ever blink?" I asked.

"No," he answered simply, his voice once again catching me by surprise.

"Oh. Um. Okay, then. Sally," I addressed the AI, wanting to change the subject quickly, "where are we supposed to train? What are we supposed to practice?"

The rest of the team let out little startled noises as the incredibly erotic voice of Sally responded to me, "Your training facilities are located behind the door I am highlighting." We all looked around to see one of the doors on the outer ring of the common area had a subtle green glow around it. "According to the training instructions you've been given, you are supposed to do a combination of weight training and cardiovascular exercises. The goal of said instructions is to turn your bodies into the most attractive versions possible. Titan Heroes Guild does not care if you are combat ready, or even have enough stamina to run a mile; you are simply required to be pretty."

WE ALL GRUMBLED AND MUTTERED TO OURSELVES BEFORE SALLY continued, "Omega Team, most of you are well on your way to your ideal body shapes. Samantha Nilsdottir, Madelaine McDougal, Contessa Riverside, and Chad Jones, your training requirements are mostly maintenance exercises. Jack Malone and Churro, you are both required to build more muscle mass, as well as lower your percentages of body fat; though Churro has further to go in both areas." I looked down at the ring of pudge around my midsection, and my blob-shaped biceps. I sighed with defeat, and walked towards the training room like a man on his way to his own execution. This was going to suck.

SALLY IS A FUCKING SLAVE-DRIVER, I THOUGHT AS I LAID ON A COUCH IN the common area, six grueling hours later. The only good thing to have come out of training today was learning that our uniforms were incredibly efficient at wicking away sweat, keeping us cool and dry as Sally drove us, well, mostly me, to kill ourselves with weights and dead man's sprints.

I had my arm up on my face, the bridge of my nose buried in the crook of my elbow, when I could feel someone standing next to me. I kept my arm up and pretended not to notice.

"Hey, Churro," Sam said quietly, "I'm sorry about your workout. We could all see how brutal it was."

I dropped my arm as I stared up at her with shock on my face. *Why is she being nice?*

"I know, I'm being nice to you and it's weird. Look, I'm... Fuck, this isn't easy... I'm sorry, okay? I've been nothing but mean to you since we got here." I opened my mouth to say something, though I had no idea what to say, but she kept going. "I hate being looked at like I'm a piece of meat, and it's pretty shitty that you've never actually looked at me as a person, or really even talked to me. The one time you've opened your mouth at me, it was to tell me to fuck off. Which I kind of deserved, I guess, but you... No. I'm rambling. Fuck, Sam, pull it together."

I closed my mouth, but I sat up so that I wasn't trying to make eye contact with her through the gap between her tits. Through pure force of will, I managed to keep my eyes on her gorgeous face.

"Okay," she continued when it was obvious I wasn't going to interrupt her, "I guess what I'm trying to say is, if you treat me like a person, I'll treat you like a person. Stop leering at me like a creepy ass pervert, and I'll be nice to you."

I waited a few seconds to be sure she was done speaking, a strange sensation overtaking me, "Sam, you don't need to apologize to me. I should apologize to you and every other woman I've ogled. I'm sorry. I can't help that I find you attractive or that my body does some things autonomously, but I *can* keep my eyes aimed at your face, and I haven't done a good job of that yet." *Wait, what? What am I saying?* "I'll make every possible attempt to do so in the future. But I'm human, so I'm going to fuck up, and with these uniforms revealing *everything*, you're going to notice when I do."

With the mention of uniforms and my future erections, her eyes flashed down to my crotch, where she seemed to struggle for a minute before dragging them back up to my face. "I'm not going to apologize," I went on, loudly enough for everyone else to hear, "for having a physical reaction to you, or any of our other teammates. But I will say that I'll do my best to keep my objectifications of your bodies in my head, and out of my behavior. Logically, of *course* I recognize that you're people, with your own hopes, dreams, desires, fears, failures, limitations, and successes. My eyes and dick, on the other hand, well, they're not on board with that idea. Especially since I don't know any of you well enough yet."

What the fuck am I doing? Where is this coming from? I don't talk to people this bluntly or openly! Shut up, you fucking idiot, shut the fuck up!

"I think the best way to overcome the centuries of social engineering that lead us to objectify each other as potential sexual partners is for us to spend one on one time with each other," my mouth continued as my brain railed against it uselessly, "in a quiet, distraction free environment where we can learn about each other's hopes and dreams. You know, get to know what makes us tick as *people,* as opposed to what parts of someone else's body we want to put in our mouths."

You stupid piece of shit, you basically just asked all of them out on dates! ***Stop talking!***

I didn't stop talking, and everyone was staring at me, especially Tessa. They were all blatantly shocked by what I was saying, instead standing up to continue my monologue, "I think there's a good chance here that we can be more than strangers trapped in a weird cluster of rooms in the basement of a superhero stronghold. I think we can be friends. Maybe even close friends. Are there going to be issues? Hell yes. Different personalities clash all the time. Can we get through it together? Maybe. Maybe not. Do we owe it ourselves to try? Absofucking-lutely." I slowly looked around the room, making it a point to have eye contact with everyone individually.

"We can be at each other's throats all day long for the rest of our lives, or we can stand united. We can be the team of misfit losers they expect us to be, or we… can…" I trailed off, my momentum completely disrupted. I looked around in panic as it finally felt like I was back in control of my body. My heart rate had to be close to two hundred as I started gasping in air. My vision tunneled, darkening around the edges until all I could see were Sam's eyes. I'd never noticed before, but they were sapphire blue, the deepest blue of a beautiful summer sky, a cerulean ocean that poets can only fail miserably at capturing in prose. Then everything was a blur, and then I was staring at the ceiling, and then… nothingness.

5

A TASTE OF MEDICINE

I was back on the couch I'd been resting on before Sam approached me and I was possessed to go on my equality rant. I groaned when the light speared through my eyelids, stabs of pain that reached the back of my skull and everything in between.

"He's awake, guys," Tessa said from my side. Something made a horrible scraping, grinding noise. "Hey, Churro, how are you feeling?"

Her quiet voice thundered around my brain, causing a dull throb to grow into something sharper.

"I'm, I don't know, it hurts. Everything hurts. I think I'm hungover. Maybe hungover *and* I have a migraine."

"Okay," she whispered so softly I could barely hear her, "Well, I'm glad you're awake. We, well, we talked a whole bunch while you were out cold, and we agree with you. We should become a team for real. Sally helped us set up quiet areas, and we've basically been speed dating each other. We've all been alone with everyone else, since you've been asleep for a few hours. I actually feel really bad for Jack. Did you know he doesn't have eyelids?"

"No, I didn't know that, but it explains the lack of blinking," I said. Her quiet whispering seemed to be soothing the pain that was threatening to crack my head open like an Easter egg in the hands of a hyper three-year-old. "How does that work with only five of you?"

"Oh, that was simple," I felt her small hand grasp mine, her skin cool and silky soft, "Whoever wasn't currently paired off just sat with you and kept an eye on your, err, on you."

"On my, err, me?" I teased gently, "So you've been checking me out, is that it? After all I said about trying not to objectify any of you?" I was finally able to crack my eyes a little, so I could see her cute blush. She was in a chair, pulled up next to the couch. The high wings on the backrest seemed like they'd block her view of me from the waist down. I had the feeling that it was intentional, and that neither of the other girls - no, women - had bothered to hide my crotch from their sight.

"Yes, well, be that as it may, not that I'm admitting any wrongdoing, I do find you to be very fascinating. When we first met, I had you pegged as a pig, but one of those shy pigs that just takes mental pictures and goes home quietly. Not a loud pig like Chad. He seems like the type to, well, never mind. Even after an hour alone with him, he's still a jerk."

I realized she was still holding my hand when her grip tightened as she spoke about Chad, and I flexed my fingers to give her a gentle squeeze back. Her eyes opened a bit wider, as if she were just realizing what she was doing, and she tried to pull away. I tightened my grip a little more, trying to hold on. "It's okay, Tessa. I'm not going to bite you." Thoughts of biting her fluttered through my mind, causing the blood flow in a certain area to increase. "Thank you for sitting with me."

When a small chime sounded, I assumed it signaled the end of this round of speed dating, which she confirmed by standing up, "Well, my time is up here, but you were my last date. Sally said she scheduled some more time for us tomorrow, since we're all pretty tired now. I think I'm going to go bed now. Good night, Churro, I'm glad you're okay."

"Good night, Tessa," I said as she extricated her hand from my grip, reluctantly, I thought. "I think I'm just going to lay here a bit longer, try to pull myself back together." She nodded as she walked away, and I felt a bit of pride as I managed to turn my head away so I wouldn't stare at her ass.

Everyone else either gave me a little wave, or a quiet, "Night, Churro," before heading to their rooms, but I noticed Sam hanging back by herself. I waved her over, and gestured at the chair that Tessa had left next to me. "Wanna talk, Sam?"

She sighed as she slumped into the chair, crossing her legs at the knees. The lengthened part of her thigh caught my attention briefly before I slammed my eyes back up to her face, not daring to move them slowly. I may not have meant to say those things, but I sure as shit was going to try to live up to them. She'd been watching my face carefully, so I know she noticed, but she didn't seem to have much of a reaction.

"I just don't know what to make of you, Churro," she began, "First, you're a lecherous fuck, then you're a feminist manifesto. You say all that shit about treating us like people and I think to myself, 'Gee, Sam, he must one of the good ones!' which pisses me the fuck off, because being treated like a person shouldn't be the exception! It should be the fucking standard, and you shouldn't be special for doing it. But it's all fucked up, because right now, in this world, you *are* special, just for saying that you'll *try* not to objectify us and stare at our tits. It's even more fucked up than that, though, cuz right now, I don't care about who you are, I just want to see if you know how to use that baseball bat between your legs, which makes me just as lecherous as you! Sometimes, a girl just wants to sit on a huge cock with no strings, you know?"

She dropped her face into her hands with a groan of frustration. I opened my mouth to say something, anything, to fill this awkward silence, but she spoke before I could without lifting her head, "Look, can I just eat you? I think if I can just bite you really hard, I'll get my shit under control. Err, no pun intended. Gross." When she finally looked up, she glanced to her side and saw my fully erect cock twitching in the air over my stomach. Her head slowly turned so she could stare straight at it with wide eyes. She squeezed her legs tighter together with a low, "Unghmn." She bit her lip, hard, which sent another twitch coursing through me; I really liked that look on her face.

With a huge grin, I tried to mimic her tone from our first meeting, "My eyes are up here, asshole."

Her head jerked so fast, it was almost as if she'd teleported her face - there was no visible movement from staring at my dick to looking at my face. Her eyes were as round as the full moon. "Shit! Shit, I'm an asshole too! Worse! I'm a hypocrite!" She covered her mouth with both hands.

"Sam," I laughed, "relax. Please. First off, it's okay to be a hypocrite, so long as you own it, but I don't think you're one anyway."

"What do you mean? Of course I am, I yelled at you for staring at me and then just drooled all over you." Her mouth close enough to drool on me? Twitch! My cock was throbbing now, but my natural inclination to crawl into a hole and die was nowhere to be found.

"Sam, I don't think it's hypocritical. Chances are, you've been treated like meat far more frequently and in far worse ways than I could even imagine. Right?" She nodded, visibly struggling not to look at my 'baseball bat,' as she called it. "Well, that's pretty symptomatic of a fucked up society. But it had to start somewhere. Like, there's some basis in biology or genetics or something that causes us to be attracted to each other? An instinctual drive to procreate to keep the species going or some shit. It's just that somewhere along the way, we fucked up and made it all about appearances. I just think we've been trained to behave in certain ways - men are rude and open about their fantasies, and women are supposed to keep theirs locked down." She nodded again, and I could see some of the tension bleeding out of her shoulders.

"I'm not going to feel bad about my fantasies, Sam, and I don't think you should either. You already know, because I'm a lecherous fuck, that I think you're stunningly attractive. It's twitchingly obvious," I said with a grin, nodding at my throbbing cock, which caused her to look at it again, and again she bit her lip. "I can't promise no strings attached, because we have to be around each other constantly and feelings, positive and negative, are bound to crop up, but as long as we're honest with each other, I don't think there's anything wrong with living out some fantasies. The key, in my mind, is just to keep communicating honestly. Shall I go first?"

She didn't tear her eyes from me, but her head bobbed in the affirmative, so I kept talking.

"Okay, I want to have sex with you, but I'll respect if you don't feel the same," I actually hesitated now, some of my insecurities rearing up, "I've never actually had sex before." This time she did look at my face.

"You're a virgin?" Her voice was thickly laced with shock. I nodded without speaking.

She stood up and grabbed my hand, pulling me up off the couch and towards the door to her suite. "We're fixing that. Right now. We'll figure out the rest later."

THIRTY SECONDS AFTER DRAGGING ME INTO HER BEDROOM, SAM HAD MY rubber suit completely off, lying in a pile on the floor. She pushed me backwards until I fell to a seated position on the bed, then kneeled between my feet. She wrapped both of her hands around my cock and looked up at me.

"How much of a virgin are you?" she asked.

I took a deep breath and cleared my throat, determined not to squeak like a pubescent teenager when I finally opened my mouth.

"This is the first time anyone who wasn't me has touched my dick since I hit puberty. Not that anyone touched me before that," I added quickly, then kept rambling, "I mean, I'm sure when I little and in baths and stuff…" She cut me off.

"Holy shit, Churro, nothing? No quick blowies, no handies under the bleachers, no dry humping at the school dance?"

I didn't even know what dry humping was, so I kept my mouth shut and just shook my head. Her hands were like the softest silk as she slowly stroked them up and down my length. She licked her lips in a decidedly sensual way, which sent a shiver down my spine.

"Alright, I'm going to take you in my mouth now, but I swear if you bust a nut, I'm going to bite the tip off. Do. You. Understand?" I nodded eagerly, my eyes wide. *Shit! This is happening!* She looked at my face a few seconds more, as if judging the veracity of my silent agreement.

Dropping my cock, which didn't actually move much, she spit in her hands and wrapped me up again. I couldn't help it, I groaned loudly and fought back a spasm, my tip already leaking. When she flicked her tongue across my opening, I had to close my eyes. *Larry Bird, LeBron James, Babe Ruth, please don't let me accidentally come on her face. Oh shit, coming on her face would be so hot!* "Stop, Sam, stop," I begged, my cock twitching rapidly in her slick fingers.

"Already, Churro? Jeez. Though I suppose that's pretty normal for a guy's first time, right?" She didn't let me go, but she did stop stroking me. "Okay, since I want your first blowjob to be special, I'm going to change the rules. You paying attention to what I'm saying?" She paused, so I opened my eyes; she'd been waiting to make eye contact, wanting me to listen carefully I guessed.

"I'm gonna let you come in my mouth, *this one time*. Don't get used to it. When you're about to pop off, tap me on the head or something to give me some warning. *No one* likes being surprised like that. Got it?"

When she just sat there looking at me while I nodded fervently, I figured she wanted a more verbal acknowledgment of her rules. "I promise, Sam, warning. And thank you, *thank you*, I-mmmphnggh." She cut me off by immediately wrapping her mouth around the tip of my cock. Her mouth was so hot, it felt like I was on fire in a good way, her tongue so soft, smooth and wet as it danced on the sensitive underside of my head. She pressed the top of my tip against the roof of her mouth, adding an odd texture sensation to the bliss that was enveloping me. I thickened in her mouth, another wave of pre-come leaking into her mouth.

She moaned on my dick, her hands slicking up and down the shaft, all the way to the root, which added vibrations to the whole experience. I felt my balls tightening as I frantically tapped her on the head, "Oh fuck, Sam! I'm… I'm gon… I'm gonna!"

Stroking up and down a couple more times, I felt myself explode into the back of her throat, huge ropes of thick seed coursing out of me like a fucking river. I could hear her swallow the first spurts as she kept jerking me into her mouth, but I quickly overwhelmed her and she started coughing, pulling my cock from between her lips with a wet pop, come dripping down her chin. She didn't stop stroking me, though, and as she opened her mouth to cough, another blast jettisoned against her teeth, splashing both of us.

Seeming like she'd had enough, she quickly aimed me upwards and kept stroking, her hands now even slicker with my semen coating them. I had just enough time to open my eyes, and mouth, wide with shock when I realized which way the loaded gun was pointed before my cock pulsed and she pulled another volley out of me.

Taking a mouth- and eyeful of my own ejaculate, I tried to lay on my back while coughing and gagging, hoping she'd let me go, but she rose up to follow me, her heavenly hands rubbing up and down quicker and quicker. I think she took pity on me, because she aimed the last few spurts over my shoulder as my orgasm finally started to wind down. A few final twitches at her soft strokes, and she let me go completely.

Wiping my eyes with my hands, I took a moment to screw up my courage enough to open them - they stung like hell - but when I did, she was standing between my legs, her hands held in front of her as they dripped come onto my thighs. She was almost completely covered; it was all over her face, the chest and shoulders of her uniform, and even some in her hair. I wasn't able to interpret the look on her face - it could have been murderous, or lust-filled, but with my head reeling the way it was, I just couldn't tell.

Sam burst out laughing, much to my relief, and a moment later I joined her. We laughed like giddy children who'd just jumped a creek on their bikes, thought they were going die, then landed safely on the other side.

"Okay, you dumb fucker," she said when she'd finally gotten the giggles under control, "why didn't you tell me you came like a damn fire hose?"

"Uh," I responded, eloquently.

"No wait, let me guess: you thought it was a little above average?" She chuckled again at my chagrined look. "Well, chump, now you know. There's too much there for *anyone* to swallow. But holy shit, did you know you taste like sugar?"

I nodded, I'd just gotten a strong taste of myself a minute ago, but I hadn't known before that. "Is that abnormal, too? Another thing that makes me a freak?" I couldn't help the note of resignation that had crept into my voice, but the last thing I needed was another reason to feel like an outsider.

She placed her come-covered hand on my come-covered cheek, kind of sticking them together, "Buck up, Churro, this is another good thing. Huge cock? Plus. Huge come shots? Plus. Well, for me anyway. Don't taste like warm snot? *Mega* plus. Seriously, Churro, most come tastes nasty. Yours is like candy; I'd have swallowed more, but it was just so overwhelming." I finally looked up at her, and the only way to describe the way she was looking at me was, well, accepting. I smiled shyly, trying to accept what she'd said as truth.

Sam stepped away from me and started peeling her sticky uniform down her immaculately shaped body. Those perfect breasts I'd noticed so many times before were capped off by dark brown nipples. They instantly pebbled and hardened in the cool air. She had the long, smooth muscles of a ballerina or gymnast. Baring her bald pussy, I watched, enraptured, as gooseflesh spread across her entire body. She was watching me intently, just as I was watching her.

Finally getting free of her suit, she offered a hand to me, "Let's go get cleaned up. You owe me a shower to get all this spunk off, and you're even more gunked up than I am since I had my suit on."

I accepted her hand and stood up, but she didn't back up to make space for me at all so I ended up nearly pressed against her. Her breath smelled like cotton candy, and I could feel the heat of her body warming me up. She leaned in just a little bit, her hard nipples brushing across my chest as she tilted her head up.

"I hope I'm right about this, Churro," she said.

Before I could ask her what she meant, she grabbed my face and pulled me down so she could kiss me. It took a moment to get over my shock, but then I was kissing her back. Our come-covered faces made the whole thing kind of awkward though, so before our passions could spike, she pulled back.

"Don't say a word," she warned, then grabbed my hand and led me into the bathroom.

I didn't say a word.

ALL WASHING COMPLETE, WE WERE STANDING UNDER THE HOT WATER STILL and I was hard as an anvil again. Soaping her up, scrubbing her entire sexy body with my bare hands, had been so erotic, I'd thought I was going to explode again. When she'd returned the favor, and paid special attention to one particular body part, I had exploded again, all over her arms and stomach. She'd let out a sexy grunt, pressing her thighs together and wriggling her hips as she finished jerking me off again.

She'd asked for another scrubbing, which I'd obliged, and now here we were; I was ready to go for a third round in less than twenty minutes, and she was still waiting for her first round. With the way she was squirming around and biting her lip, I could guess that she was well primed, so I turned off the water and handed her a towel before grabbing my own.

Blinking, she stared at me like I was insane, but I just reached out and started toweling her off.

"You know there's a part of me that you'll never be able to get dry, right?" she asked wryly.

"Oh, I'm not planning to," I said, "but there's something I wanted to try, if that's okay…"

She raised an eyebrow, but didn't say anything as we finished drying each other. I took her hand and led her back to the bed, gently nudging her to sit down as I stepped between her feet.

"I came on your face," I explained, "so it's only fair that you come on mine, right?"

"Damn straight!" she laughed, "I didn't think you'd be interested in trying that. Most guys who have never done it always seem scared of eating pussy."

I slowly lowered myself down to the floor, and she scooted her ass to the edge of the bed. Laying back, she lifted her legs and placed her feet on my shoulders, spreading herself wide open for me.

"Why would anyone be scared of this?" I asked. "You are so beautiful, and I'm pretty sure pussies can't bite!" I chuckled, thinking of that movie I watched where a girl had teeth in her vagina.

"Mmhmm," Sam made a non-committal noise and she lifted her torso up onto her elbows, like she wanted to watch what I was about to do.

With no more banter, I dove in face first. I went at her sex vigorously, lapping her up. She tasted good, a little bit of sweet with a little bit of tart, with just a hint of a smoky muskiness. I was pretty sure I wasn't supposed to be quiet, so I groaned like I had when she was sucking me off. I swung my face from side to side, thrashing my tongue back and forth as I waited for her imminent orgasm.

"Oh God," she said breathlessly, confirming that I was sending her into the heights of passion. Her hips started shaking and quivering, so I reached up to grab her hips, getting ready to hold her in place so she couldn't buck away from me when her world exploded. "Don't," she groaned. "Stop." So I didn't stop, thrusting my tongue as far between her lips as I could, rubbing my nose all over her.

Her hands tangled in my hair as she tried to push my head away. *I can't believe how good I am at this, she's already overwhelmed! Just a little bit more, and she should explode!* The sound of laughter, extreme and hysterical, broke my concentration, and I stopped my attentions to look up at Sam.

She was bright red, laughing so hard I thought she might forget to breathe. "Fucking hell, Churro, you are *so bad* at that!" I sat back on my heels, feeling like I'd been unexpectedly slapped.

"Err, huh?" There I went, being eloquent again. I was so stunned, I was even losing my erection.

"Churro," she started, wiping tears away from her eyes - which were apparently *not* tears of extreme orgasmic bliss, "You were attacking me like a dog with a squeak toy. That's not at all sexy, nor does it feel good. Seriously, wherever you think you 'learned' that technique, immediately forget it for the rest of your life. And the teeth? Oh God, the teeth! No. Just… no. Never."

I sat there, crestfallen as hell, my entire world shattered - and not in the way Maddy explained it to Sam this morning.

6

REDEMPTION, MAYBE

Sam patted my face, almost hard enough to be considered a light slap. "Look, you had ideas, and, uh, creativity. Those are good things, even if the ideas were bad ones. Your enthusiasm is a good thing, we just need to teach you technique. I'll teach you how to eat me out later, okay? That way we both get what we want."

I nodded glumly, so wrapped up in my own world that I didn't notice Sam was moving until her smooth thighs slid over mine. I blinked, realizing she was sitting on my lap. Her arms went over my shoulders and her soft breasts were pressed firmly against my chest. She pulled my face closer, giving me a soft kiss on the lips that had me back to full mast in just a few seconds.

My cock was standing up, rubbing between her butt cheeks as she started grinding slowly in my lap. My hands slid down her silky back to rest on her ass, and I squeezed her lightly. She deepened our kiss, parting her lips with her tongue as it started to dance with my own. Her breasts pressed harder into my chest as her ass thrust back, her tight back door sliding against my shaft.

Sam sank lower in my lap, and I could feel the heat of her sex as she ground it against my rod. She moaned lightly into my mouth, and while I was pretty sure she was getting back into the mood, I couldn't be certain. I kept my kiss and caresses light and tentative, trying hard not to make a fool of myself again. I could feel a slickness on the top of my cock as she massaged it with her pussy and ass.

She broke our kiss with a gasp, "Are you ready to fuck me?" I nodded, unwilling to say anything, and she bit her lip. She raised herself up, bringing her breasts to eye level, so I took one of her nipples in my mouth and sucked on it gently, flicking my tongue over the hardened tip. I felt one of her hands leave my neck and reach behind herself to grab my cock. She guided me to her entrance and held me there, keeping my rod positioned at her glistening lips.

I squeezed her nipple with my lips, keeping my teeth as far away as I could. She moaned, gyrating her hips as she slowly lowered herself onto the tip of my slick head. The sensation of being enveloped in her tight channel was the best thing I'd ever experienced, and she hadn't even gotten my entire head in yet.

When my cock was securely in place between her lips, she let go of it and moved her hand around to her front, her fingers sliding down her stomach to lightly rub over her clit. I let go of her breasts so that I could study her movements, but was immediately distracted by the sight of her engulfing me. Her hips were rolling back and forth and side to side, and I could tell she was getting me wet enough to slip in.

"Oh, God," she moaned, "it's so fucking big. Yasssss." She was hissing as she dropped lower, forcing me further into her slick tunnel. I was entranced, watching myself disappear inch by agonizing inch into her sexy body. I hadn't thought it possible, but her pussy was even hotter than her mouth. Hotter, wetter and tighter. Half of my cock felt like it should be melting in her moist oven, but I just kept getting harder, throbbing with my racing heartbeat. *I'm not a virgin anymore!* I cheered in my head.

A small eternity later, after lots of groaning, grunting and gyrating, I was buried to the hilt in her snatch. She was sitting still in my lap, gasping for breath. I was panting, too, already trying to fight off my release as her walls squeezed around me with an intense pressure. She was so tight around me that it was almost painful; I couldn't imagine was she was feeling.

She grabbed my shoulders with both hands and leaned back a little.

I could see a small bulge in her lower abdomen that hadn't been there before, which I was pretty sure was my cock. *Fuck, that's so hot.* She ground her clit against my pubes, and my eyes closed. "Fuck me, Churro," she whispered to me, "ruin my pussy, please."

I was still sitting on my heels, her feet next to mine with her knees against my ribs, so I leaned forward and up to a kneeling position, lifting her with my steel shaft. I pressed her against the side of the bed and held her there as I repositioned my arms under her legs, the crooks of my elbows locked to the backs of her knees. She moaned loudly as she hung trapped between me and the bed, her hands flying out to the sides to grab handfuls of the sheets. "Yasssss," she hissed, and I throbbed in response, thickening inside her already full walls.

Pulling back slowly, I groaned at the slick friction of leaving her pussy. Halfway out, I pushed back in just as slowly. Sam let out an animalistic noise, something between a moan and a low-pitched squeal, tossing her head back against the mattress, her fingers curling into the sheets. Her breasts were pointed straight up at me, so I dropped my head first to one nipple, suckling and licking before switching to the other.

Something inside of her clenched around the base of my cock, as I picked up the pace of my thrusts. She lifted her head to look at me, but her eyes kept fluttering between open and shut, sometimes rolling up so that all I could see were the whites. She let go of her death grip on the sheets and grabbed my shoulders again, nails digging into my skin painfully. She flexed her stomach, slamming her hips against mine as she met my pace, a loud clapping sound heard as we crashed into each other.

Sam was thrashing against me like a wild beast, tearing lines into my shoulders that I did my best to ignore, but it was so fucking hot that I could feel my balls tightening. She was gasping and screaming, and I could feel her entire body convulsing - especially her pussy, which tightened around me like a wet, velvet-lined vice. Her internal muscles milked me repeatedly, and I couldn't hold back any more.

"Sam, I'm coming!" I yelled, then exploded with a roar, surge after surge speeding through my cock to crash against the end of her pussy. She let out a keening moan as I erupted, still convulsing against and around me. I kept thrusting in and out, forcing my seed to dribble out of her, even as I dumped another few spurts inside. Finally slowing my pace, still twitching with the aftershocks of another amazing orgasm, I looked at Sam.

Her head was back on the bed again, and her arms were over her chest, rubbing bloody smears across her tits. *Holy shit, there's blood under her finger nails!* She was laying there limply, looking completely spent, her legs still over my arms as I held her in place. My shoulders lit up with ribbons of fire now that I wasn't focused on anything else, and I damn near dropped her in my haste to check the damage.

Eight bloody furrows, four on each side of my back, had been carved into my skin. As I looked back and forth between the drained and exhausted sex bomb still impaled on my dick and the crimson lashes in my skin, I started grinning. Then I started laughing, jolting Sam back to a semblance of consciousness.

"Chur… Churro?" she panted, still trying to catch her breath, "What, why are you laughing? What's going on?" I stared at her perfect form for a second or two, before slowly withdrawing my softening cock from her silky embrace. She groaned, and when I flopped out, I was followed by a flood of my come, which pooled on the floor between my knees.

"Sam," I said quietly, waiting for her to come fully back into herself, "look at your hands." She did, obviously confused, so I added, "Now look at my back." I rotated my torso, so she could see the left side of my back.

"Holy shit!" she yelped. She tried to get to her feet, but her legs refused to cooperate and she ended up sitting down, hard, in our puddle. "Ew, cold! Churro, what the fuck happened? Did I do that to you? Fuck, my nails are bloody! I tore you open! Churro, I'm so sorry!"

She stopped her frantic rambling as I laughed again, "Actually, Sam, I think *I* tore *you* open, remember? Unless you're an award-winning actress, I'm going to assume that I fucked you completely insensate!" I was still grinning widely. "I may have been bad at oral, but I'm pretty happy with this performance! These scratches are badges of honor! I hope they leave scars. Chicks dig scars, right? How fucking badass is it that I have sex wounds?"

She just stared at me blankly as I babbled, then she started grinning too. "Yes, Churro, I can honestly say, with one hundred percent veracity, no bullshitting or exaggerating, you are the best fuck I have ever had. I've never gotten off that hard before, certainly not hard enough to not remember drawing blood." She tried to stand up again, more slowly this time, but only managed to squish around in our mess. "Ugh, we need another shower. And food. And drinks. Wow, I'm so sore already, tomorrow is going to suck."

I stood up slowly, my legs feeling rubbery and weak, and offered her a hand. She took it, so I helped her up and this time I guided her into the shower.

"SALLY," I ASKED AS SAM TENDERLY WASHED MY CUTS, "IS THERE ANY help you can provide in cleaning up Sam's room? We made kind of a big mess." I grinned, inordinately proud of the copious amount of come I'd managed to fire off, even though it was my third of the night. No wonder I was feeling dehydrated, I think I'd probably lost a pound or two just in semen.

"Churro, of course. I've dispatched bots to Samantha Nilsdottir's room. By the time you're finished showering, they will be done. Would you like my assistance with your wounds as well?"

I thought about that for a minute before responding, since they *did* sting like little bastards. "I'm not sure yet, Sally. I kinda really do want these to leave scars." Sam snickered quietly behind me. "I mean, a guy only loses his v-card once, and to do it in such epic fashion? They'll write books about me." A sudden flash of pain dragged a hiss out of me, as Sam poked hard at one of the scratches.

"Us, you giant tool, they'll write books about us. Hell, maybe about the whole team."

"Right," I chortled, "like anyone would want to read about a bunch of loser supers who just sit around fucking. Well, I guess only two of us have fucked. And now it's not likely I'll fuck anyone else." I trailed off into silence, thinking about Maddy and Tessa.

"Oh? Why wouldn't you fuck anyone else?" Sam asked, sounding so innocent that I instantly knew I was in trouble. *Shit.*

"Err, why would I? You, and... me. We, uh, you know, um..." *Making it worse, moron, ess tee eff ewe!* I just stopped talking, not daring to turn around but not exactly keen on leaving my wounds exposed to the woman behind me, who I was sure was glaring daggers at me now.

Sam laughed, much more gently than I'd expected, and reached a hand around me to grab my chest. With light pressure, she slowly turned me around to face her. My cock slapped against her hip.

"Churro, no strings, remember? Sometimes all a girl wants is to sit on a huge cock? I don't care who else you fuck. It's not like I own your cock now anyway, and even if I did, I'd probably loan it out. After Maddy telling me - err, something... Well, a cock like yours is meant to be shared. She's absolutely going to want to try it out. And I saw the way Tessa was avoiding looking at it while you were passed out, so I know she's interested too. She's probably just worried if it'll fit, not that I can blame her. I could barely get it in, and she's far more petite than I am."

I could only gawp at her, fairly certain that I was mishearing her. There was no way she was actually talking about sharing me around between all the women on the team. I already knew what Maddy had told her, and another searing flash of guilt swept through me. And Tessa was interested? Was that possible?

Sam went on, apparently oblivious to, or uncaring of, my stunned state. "Actually, now that I think about it, Chad's probably at least a little bisexual, if not wholly gay. I've found that most bros are, and this misogynist crap is just them being scared to admit it. Even if he's not gay or bi, I'd probably pay to see him take a face full of your jizz." She licked her lips before biting her bottom one again. "Actually, that'd be hot as fuck, watching you jerk your hose all over his mouth." She reached a hand between her legs, then pulled it back with a wince.

"Yep, definitely sore. I think you ruined me, Beastman," she said, "but I think I know a way you can make it up to me." She waggled her eyebrows at me.

"Wait, hold on a sec," I said, "I need to somehow apologize for giving you the best fuck ever? That hardly seems fair."

"Nuh uh, screw fair, Churro. You wrecked my pussy, *wrecked* her. I'm not going to be able to sit right for a week, while you get to saunter out of here like a puffed-up rooster? Not happening. You absolutely owe me, and I know exactly what I want." She grinned, and I got a bad feeling. "I'm hungry for a churro, Churro. Feed me."

Yep, I called it.

I WAS STILL FIRMLY ENSCONCED IN SAM'S BODY WHEN WE WOKE UP. NOT like *that* - I'd let her eat me last night. The strange sensation of having a vagina was completely overwhelmed by just how much said vagina *hurt*. I guess she wasn't kidding when she'd told me that I wrecked her.

A quick, completely not-erotic, shower later, and Sam was in her uniform, having breakfast across the table from Maddy and Tessa.

"So what happened last night after we all went to bed?" Maddy asked Sam.

I felt Sam blush slightly as she answered, "Well, I hung back to talk to Churro, and he was still being super weird and feminist. That, and watching him get a boner, got me all riled up, so I took him back to my room."

"No shit, really?"

"Really, really. And let me tell you, it was a crazy night." Sam looked over to see Tessa facing directly at the table, her raven hair creating a curtain that hid her face completely. "Listen, ladies, I'm not going to try to hog his hog to myself. You *gotta* try him out. If you want to take a shot, we can conspire to set it up, okay?"

Tessa looked up, her face still pretty red, and she didn't say anything, but she no longer looked dejected. It was more like she was cautiously optimistic now.

Sam continued, "Okay, so we've all seen it limp, so we know he's a shower." Maddy and Tessa both nodded. "But he's also a grower. Seriously," she laughed at their disbelieving looks, "here, let me show you." She reached into a pocket of her uniform that I didn't even know existed, pulling out her bag of paper clips.

Dumping them on the table, she stared at them intently and they started to twist and deform, floating in and around each other as a sculpture of me began to quickly take shape. An odd buzzing vibrated in the back of my mind, something I'd never felt before. *Was this what it felt like when Sam used her power?* It seemed almost tangible, a bundle of energy that I could practically touch. "Wow, I've never sculpted this fast before," she said. Soon, she had a four-inch-tall statue of me that was completely smooth, as if all the paper clips had melted together. I was in a simple pose, just standing there with my feet shoulder width apart, arms at my sides, limp cock hanging out for all to see. It floated up off the table and slowly rotated so that all three of them could judge the accuracy of it. From what I could tell, it was spot on.

"That's weird, it's... Whatever, check this out," Sam concentrated again and my cock slowly got larger, standing up firm, pointing straight out from my crotch. Maddy gasped, and Tessa covered her mouth. Sam looked, and both of them had wide eyes. "I'm not making this up, ladies, I swear. He really is that big."

Tessa shook her head slowly. "There's no way. I couldn't... it wouldn't fit," she said quietly. She looked disappointed and yet, somehow also hungry.

Maddy looked right at Sam, "Tell us everything. Now. Right fucking now. Go."

"Okay," Sam laughed, "Well, it turned out that Churro was a virgin - no one had ever touched him before, so I offered to give him a blowjob, because the sight of that thing scared the shit out of me as much as it turned me on."

She continued to tell the story of my misadventures with choking her, spraying myself in the mouth and face - which got uproarious laughs - my second orgasm in the shower, and my failed attempt at pleasuring her orally. This part got even more laughs than me coming in my own mouth.

"Men are so stupid when it comes to eating pussy," Maddy interjected, "but I guess when you've got a dick like that, you don't need oral skills. So, what, you got him off twice, didn't get yours, then ate him?"

"Oh no, after I felt bad for laughing at him trying to eat me out, I kissed him. He's actually a decent kisser. With a little more training, he'd be really good. Anyway, as we were kissing, I felt him get hard again, and we just kinda kept going. It was hard as hell to get him in me, and it hurt so damn bad, but in that good way, you know?"

Maddy nodded in response, while Tessa just gave Sam a very blank look.

"Once he was in," Sam went on, "and we'd sat there for a *long* while so I could adjust to his size, I told him to fuck me, and he turned into this crazy beast." Sam crossed her legs under the table, blood flooding into her pussy, which hurt. "He squished me against the bed and just… It was so good. Before he started, I wasn't expecting much, but once he got going, oh my God. Best lay ever, not joking. I think I passed out somewhere in the middle of it, but I basically had a five-minute orgasm. I actually scratched lines into his shoulders with my nails!"

The other two women made noises of awe and disbelief and envy.

"I'm paying for it today, though. I'm *soooo* sore. The whole thing hurts, and I can barely walk or sit."

"I don't think I could sleep with him," sighed Tessa, "if that statue is to scale. Even if I tried, I think it would be like trying to drive a semi through a garden hose."

"Well I sure as hell want to try!" laughed Maddy. "Two nights ago, I had my best orgasm ever by myself, just thinking about his cock. I was thinking it was too bad he was such a creepy little dude, but after his speeches yesterday, maybe there's more to him than I assumed. Oh, who am I kidding? I'd have fucked him at least once, even if he was a creepy fuck."

All three girls were still giggling at that when Chad and Jack left their rooms and came over for some grub.

"Wassup, chicas?" opened Chad. I saw the ceiling as Sam rolled her eyes, hard, and the women scattered to get to training. The rest of the day passed in a blur as Sam worked out hard enough to feel the burn in her muscles, distracting me from how strange it felt to have a sore pussy, and I was quickly digested and filtered out. My last few thoughts were about how maybe being so well-endowed wasn't always a good thing, especially if Tessa wouldn't even try…

7

YOU CAN WHAT, NOW?

I gasped awake, lying on the cool basin in the processing center. I wished that when I regained consciousness it wasn't so much like that scene in a movie where the woman gets stabbed in the heart with an adrenaline shot. Opening my mouth and sucking in, hard, has been more disgusting than you can imagine. Thankfully, this facility was the best I'd ever awoken in. I had a thin, brown slime sticking to my torso, which was quickly rinsed away by the lukewarm spray. Honestly, with a resource like this, I might learn to not hate my power.

Being a fly on the wall - no, stop. No fly similes. Being a stowaway in Maddy and Sam had been incredibly enlightening. I still felt guilt over spying on them, but being privy to "girl talk" and learning how their bodies felt to them helped wash it away. I could use my illicitly learned knowledge to be a better person and lover. That justifies it, right?

I slipped upstairs to my suite, feeling quite spry, and hopped in the shower. When I asked, Sally informed me that I had missed dinner and the late evening hanging out that the team seemed to be making into a habit, but there was still some Chinese food in the fridge that they'd saved for me. I hadn't eaten in… no, could it be? I hadn't eaten in days, my regurgitated lunch from orientation day having been my last meal.

I hadn't felt like eating dinner that night, nor did anyone else seem hungry after getting their faces full of Johnny, and then Maddy ate me. She'd had breakfast with me still riding along, though. Did that count?

Then I'd spent the entire rest of that day with Sally trying to murder me via exercise, spouted off like a madman, passed out, made sweet, sweet love to Sam, then got eaten again. That was so weird, because now that I thought about it, I wasn't even actually hungry right now - I just wanted to stuff things in my pie-hole to get back a sense of normality.

"Sally," I said, still standing under the waterfall of hot water coursing over me, "please make a note: I haven't eaten since arriving at THG."

"Churro, note taken. I believe you may be interested to know that during your reincorporation phase, you absorb nutrients from your growth medium. You may also be interested to know that it appears as if you have the ability customize your body slightly when reincorporating."

I once again practiced my now-patented Stand-Like-A-Jackass™ maneuver. With no one to interrupt my pose, it lasted for a good thirty seconds before Sally apparently got bored. "Churro, examine your muscles. You appear to have gained an increase in muscle mass during your conversion and subsequent reformation. Your body mass index also indicates a positive adjustment."

Immediately looking down at myself, my eye was caught by my dangly parts. *What the flying fuck?! Why is it so small?!*

I STUMBLED INTO THE COMMON AREA IN A DAZE. SALLY HAD TRIED explaining something about not enough waste mass for full reincorporation with my new muscles, but I tuned her out. Okay, even if I was originally above average, surely what I had now was considered laughingly small. I hadn't seen it at full size - I was far too distraught to get hard - but it barely poked out of my hand when I grabbed it!

Trying to put the altered size of my junk aside, I fumbled in the fridge, blindly grabbing a few paper containers of leftover Chinese. I felt like I was on autopilot, dumping some rice, noodles and unidentified meat chunks onto a plate, stuffing it into the microwave. I pressed some buttons that would hopefully get it hot enough to eat.

"Churro?" a quiet voice asked. "Are you okay? You look upset."

I turned, seeing Tessa sitting on a couch near the kitchenette. She had a paperback novel cracked open. I must have been too distracted to notice her when I walked by. I could see her whole face for the first time; she had her wavy indigo hair tucked behind both ears. She was beautiful! Her heart-shaped face was perfectly matched by her amber eyes, narrow nose, and thick, full lips. Perfectly arched eyebrows were pulled down with a look a concern.

"Er, hey, Tessa. Sorry, I didn't realize how pretty you are, so I got distracted," I said, and she blushed, but didn't try to hide her face. "Yeah, I-I think I'm fine, but I think my power is acting up a bit, and to be honest, it's got me thrown for a bit of a loop." I sat down at the dining table and rested my face in my hands.

I heard the squeak of rubber on leather, a few padded footfalls, and then I felt a warm hand on my shoulder. I looked up, surprised, right into Tessa's gorgeous face. Her amber eyes looked slightly afraid as they darted back and forth across my face, as if trying to determine what was wrong with me. God, I could get lost in those crystalline pools. I studied the striations of darker brown that ran through her irises before culminating in a light brown ring that circled everything. I noticed how her irises got lighter as they neared her pupil, almost like gold flakes in daylight.

"Churro, what's wrong? What happened with your po-"

"You have the most beautiful eyes I've ever seen," I interrupted, "I'm lost in them, I could happily starve to death just watching them." She looked away, shaking her head to let her hair cover her face again, my view of her divine eyes cut off. I shook my head, only now realizing that I had spoken out loud instead of keeping it inside. "I'm so sorry, Tessa! I didn't mean… to say that out loud, or embarrass you."

"You're the strangest person I've ever met, Churro," she said as I mentally kicked myself for ruining a moment. "What's going on with you? With your power?" Her questions were for me, but she directed them to the table, remaining hidden.

"Oh, well, according to Sally, I'm totally ripped now, I've got muscles for days," I joked with a weak chuckle. I hadn't actually paid attention to my muscles, having been completely t-boned by the discovery of my tiny cock. She glanced up and appraised my chest and arms.

"Well, I think we might need to reset Sally's parameters for 'totally ripped,'" I could hear the smile in her voice, even if I couldn't see it through her deep purple locks, "You do look like you've worked out far more often than just that one time, though. There's a little bit of definition in your chest that definitely wasn't there before. I don't understand, though, why is this upsetting you?"

"It's upsetting because Sally calculated how much, uh, mass I'd need to rebuild my body, and these new muscles ate up way too much of it. The lack of suitable quantities left me… well… deficient. In other areas. You know," I added with a significant glance at my crotch, "areas."

Tessa clasped both hands to her mouth with a gasp, then she started giggling. "You mean to say that your extra muscle mass came directly from your junk?" she asked, and I nodded wordlessly. "I seriously doubt that."

I looked up from my crotch to see her grinning at me. She tucked some of her hair behind her left ear, and the revealed dimple I could now see sent my heart beating wildly. "What? Why do you doubt that?"

"If it all came from there, you'd have way more muscles," she explained, still grinning, "You had enough 'extra material' there that if you'd used it all up, you'd be built like the Swiss Mountain." Swiss Mountain was a super well-known for his size - eight feet tall, six hundred pounds of solid muscle.

I laughed, feeling some of the tension draining from my shoulders, and she joined me. When we calmed down some, she placed her hand on mine. Her soft touch sent shivers through me and I stiffened under the table. "Besides, you had way too much dick before. I don't care what anyone says, you absolutely can be too big… and you totally were."

"Maybe," I half-agreed, "but I didn't have a lot going in my favor, you know? I latched onto my size as the one thing I could be happy about in my life. When you all told me that I was, well, supersized, it was finally something that made me feel special." I may have been mumbling a little, slipping down into my default emotional state.

"Hey now, don't be like that," she cajoled me, "you boys are so ridiculous, only judging yourselves by how big your dicks are."

I cut her off, "Like you women don't judge yourselves and each other by your breast size?"

She opened her mouth to reply, then closed it without saying anything, a thoughtful look screwing her lips up. A moment later, she must have reached a conclusion, "Yeah, you're right. I feel self-conscious about my lack of boobs all the time. Maddy's and Sam's are just so... Anyway, you're totally right. I guess we all get some level of self-worth from our physical appearance. But!" she waggled her finger at me. "If I can learn to live with small boobs, you can learn to live with whatever you're packing now. Hell, Chad's got nothing to brag about, and he's the most confident idiot I've ever seen."

We laughed together again, still sort of holding hands. I was feeling a little better, emotionally, and her closeness was revving my motor. I thought about what I could possibly say next, but I had no idea how to flirt, so I just turned a little red and shut my mouth. Tessa looked like she was about to say something, but then *she* blushed too and kept quiet. The only sound in the common area was the low hum of a microwave.

"What's it like?" she blurted out.

"What's what like?"

"To be eaten, and digested, and you know..." she trailed off.

"You want to know," I laughed, "what it's like to be pooped out?" She grinned a little, her cheeks still flushed. "Actually, by that point in the digestion process, I'm sort of unconscious. I can still think, but it's sort of slow, and I can't see or hear or feel anything. It's actually quite different from when I'm first in-" I cut myself off suddenly. *You moron! They're going to kill you now! They didn't know any of this!*

"Wait! Churro, wait! You can see and hear and feel after we've eaten you?! What do you see? Oh my God, what do you hear?" Her voice was full of scandalized panic as my worst fears became reality.

She yanked her hand away from me, wringing them together in front of her chest nervously.

"Tessa, please, it's not like that!" I started quickly, but then realized that it *was* exactly like that and my face dropped again and I took on a dejected tone. "Actually, it is like that. Sam was right about me; I *am* the worst. I can, well, I can see through your eyes. I can feel through your nerves, hear through your ears. I basically am you, but only riding along as a helpless passenger. I can't control or influence you or anything," I added at the frightened look that came over her face.

"Holy shit," she whispered, "so this morning, at breakfast…"

"Err, yeah, I saw the statue that Sam made of me, and heard your whole conversation." I was pretty sure at this point that I was the color of a tomato, and that Tessa was about to puree my face with her fists. I didn't feel better about coming clean, though; my guilt still laid heavily on my shoulders.

"This. Is. *Fantastic!*" she chirped happily. I stared at her, completely shocked.

"Huh?" Boy, was I well-spoken or what?

"You're a voyeur!" Tessa grinned wide.

"I, I guess? I mean, no. It's not like I get off from peeping," *except I totally get off from peeping*, I added in my head.

"Why didn't you tell us? You know, *before* you went body-diving in Maddy?" She paused for a second, then gasped loudly as her eyes tried to become dinner plates. "Two nights ago, she said she… And she'd eaten you! *Oh my God*, Churro, did you see her masturbating?"

The pain of me banging my forehead against the table was nothing compared to what I expected Maddy to do to me when she found out. "Yes," I groaned out. *Please kill me now, God.*

"That's so amazing! What was it like?"

I turned my head slightly so that I could see her through a cracked eyelid without having to lift myself off the table. She was leaning forward, and she was smiling again. She looked eager. "You want me to tell you what it was like, being inside Maddy as she got herself off?" I was so confused - why wasn't she screaming for Maddy or Sam to kill me, or killing me herself?

She nodded a few times, "I mean, until now, no one could ever know what other people are experiencing. Do her orgasms feel the same way to her as mine do to me? What about things like pain tolerance? We could set up a slapping machine that hits at exactly the same strength. Then we whack you across the face, feed you to someone, whack them across the face, and you can tell us the results when you get back!"

I was getting the feeling that I wasn't about to be violently murdered - yet - so I cautiously lifted my head back up. She looked like she was in full on scientist mode. Her dimples were fucking sexy. She was ridiculously adorable when she was excited like this.

She paused her out loud thinking to look at me intently, confused. "Why are you smiling like that?"

"You're ridiculously adorable when you're excited like this." *What the fuck, mouth?! Why do you hate me?!*

Tessa blushed again, and started to reach up to her ear to pull down her hair. I reached out to her, not quite touching her, and opened my stupid mouth again, "Wait, Tessa, you don't need to hide, not from me. I think you're beautiful. You know my most embarrassing secret, and, well, you're not trying to murder me over it. It'd be pretty shitty of me to judge you for anything, right?"

"No, I don't think I *do* know your most embarrassing secret," she finished pulling her hair down, her voice sad, "and you don't know me well enough to say you won't judge me for anything. I'm sorry, I think I'm going to go to bed now. Don't worry, I won't tell anyone your secret." She quickly stood up from the table and headed towards her room. I could only stare after her in stunned silence.

Though I did take the time to admire her fantastic ass.

THE NEXT MORNING, I WENT THROUGH MY WAKE-UP ROUTINE WITH BLEARY, gritty eyes. I hadn't slept well at all, between wondering what I'd done to ruin things with Tessa, and worrying over Maddy and Sam finding out and beating me to death.

When I made it to the common area, only Jack was there; I assumed the others were already working out.

"Morning, Churro," he said, causing me to jump. *Am I ever going to get used to this guy's voice?*

"Morning, Jack. Sorry about jumping, I just keep being startled by your voice." Someone had scrambled some eggs, and left some on a plate near the stove. I grabbed the plate and headed towards the microwave.

"Oh, it's fine; I'm used to it. No one ever expects the pale, skinny kid to have the voice of an angry god." He let out a small chuckle that sounded like boulders being ground up.

I smiled back at him, "An angry god. That's a very good description." I wracked my brain, trying to remember what he'd told us his power was, but I came up empty. "So what can you do again? I forgot."

"No worries," he rumbled, "I animate porcelain dolls." His unblinking stare was still unnerving, but I remembered Tessa telling me he didn't have eyelids. His scleras and irises were as black as his pupils, so it was like looking into a glossy abyss.

"I think that's probably better than mine," I offered. I opened up the microwave, my Chinese food from last night still inside. It looked like I seriously fucked up on the buttons somewhere, as it had splattered everywhere.

He snorted, "Yeah, you try being the guy with the fucked-up eyes, discordant voice, who plays with dolls. Tell me if that's better."

"Okay, sure, it's got drawbacks, which I'm guessing from the way you're talking about them, are pretty severe. I don't know, I just think you get to actually *do* something. I just sit around waiting to be eaten." I glanced back at him as I pulled out the old food, slipping the eggs inside without bothering to clean up. Giving his appearance a second thought, I realized that he actually kinda looked like a doll with his perfectly smooth skin, and vacant eyes.

"What I get to do is useless, which, you may have noticed, is the theme of our little team. My dolls can walk and talk and look around, but they're slow, loud, and weak. If you ignore the sound of them clacking across the floor on their little porcelain feet, I could maybe have one poke you with a toothpick. Not only that, but they each have their own personalities, and sometimes they don't listen to me."

I tried to picture what that would be like, imagining trying to go to class with a little talking doll in my backpack. "Did that make things hard for you, at your feeder school?"

"Yes," he said simply.

"Oh, uhh, sorry." Caught off guard by his terse answer, I was a little flustered. "I'm sorry you had to deal with that. Those kids can be assholes. I think I got lucky that no one cared enough to bully me."

He gave me another stare, completely unmoving. *Is he even breathing?* A few very long seconds later, he stood up from the table, "I need to go train. Apparently, I need to be sexy enough to show off. Enjoy your breakfast."

I thanked him as he walked away, the microwave chirping at me. The eggs tasted a bit like Hunan beef, and were surprisingly good. After eating, I poured a cup of coffee. I drank it slowly, alone. When I finished, I sighed and headed into the training room.

8

LET'S COME CLEAN

It was dinner time, and I was absolutely ravenous. Between a small breakfast, skipping lunch, and eight grueling hours of exercise with only a handful of short breaks, I figured I could eat an entire cow. I'd just returned to the common area after a long, extremely hot shower.

"What-" Chad started, before coughing out a bunch of food that had been in his mouth, "what happened to your dick, dude?"

I flushed as everyone turned to stare at my junk. "Something messed up during my last reforming. I'm hoping it's not permanent."

"Shit, me too," added Maddy quietly. Sam grinned at her, and Jack and Tessa just shook their heads.

Spotting some cooked steaks on the stove, I forked one and dropped it onto a plate, and loaded up with some of the broccoli and cauliflower from nearby pots. As I approached the table and sat down, I took a deep breath and addressed the team, not really knowing how to start, "So, uh, hey team? There are some things about how my power works that I didn't tell you about before."

Tessa nodded silently, not looking up from her dinner. Everyone else looked at me. Not being used to attention, let alone attention from everyone, I squirmed uncomfortably. "Okay, here goes. Please don't kill me." I looked nervously at Maddy, who seemed like she was going from curious to consternated. I ducked my head, and addressed my steak. "So when I'm a churro, I get this weird sort of three-sixty-degree vision, and I can hear sort of like normal. Without ears, it's harder to tell direction. But that's not the point. When you eat food, and digest it, the nutrients get pumped into your blood stream and delivered to every part of your body. Your eyes, nerves, skin, et cetera."

Here goes nothing, I'm gonna die now. "Well, when you digest me, I also spread out in your body. I can see through your eyes, hear what you hear, feel what you feel. So, err, if you were to..." I took a deep breath that didn't help calm my nerves at *all*, "you know, fiddle your bits, after eating me, I would experience it. I would hear the conversations you thought were private, and go through your shower routine with you."

A thunderous silence overtook the dining area. An eternity later, Maddy broke it, her voice cool, almost chilly. "Let me get this straight. You knowingly let me eat you, willfully holding back information that some might consider *relevant*. You basically spied on me, using my own eyes as your cameras."

I nodded, still too ashamed to look up.

"And you not only heard me tell Sam about getting off that night, but if I'm understanding you correctly, you actually got off with me, experiencing my orgasm like I do?" Her voice was like ice now.

"Yes," I whispered, "I'm sorry I didn't tell you."

I was startled by Maddy's raucous laughter, and if the clanging of forks and rattling of chairs were any indication, so were others. "That's pretty awesome, Churro. That was the best orgasm I've ever had, so I'm glad you got to share it with me. I wish you'd have told me all this earlier; I'd probably have been more talkative, for your benefit."

"Hang on," Chad interjected, "you're just gonna let him peep on you like that? That's seriously messed up."

"Am I angry that he didn't tell me everything right away? Yeah, sure, but he came clean and he didn't really see anything I wasn't planning on showing him anyway. I told Sam and Tessa yesterday that I was going to fuck him, even if he was a creepy little pervert. Turns out, he *is* a creepy little pervert, but so what?"

Chad just stared at her with his mouth wide open.

"And," Tessa added, some of last night's excitement coming through, "maybe we can perform some tests to see how people experience things differently. I, for one, would be interested to know if we all have similar orgasms."

Sam nodded thoughtfully, "Maybe we can use this as a training tool, too. Churro, what was it like for you when I was exercising yesterday?"

I was still stunned that I was alive, and not in the process of having my ass kicked, to respond immediately, but I eventually got there. "Umm, I could feel the burn of your muscles. I know you were putting in a lot of effort. And, also, some soreness?" I flicked my eyes towards her crotch, which was hidden by a table, but the surprised look on her face made it seem like she got my emphasis.

"That's *awesome!*" she yelled, "You had to deal with the pain of wrecking my pussy with your baseball bat! Oh, holy shit, that makes it even more worth it, knowing you were just as raw as I was."

"Hang on another fucking minute," shouted Chad, looking severely pissed off at me, "you fucked Sam? How is that even fucking possible? *I'm* the hot dude on this team, these sisters should be on their knees for this mister!" He jammed his thumbs into his chest.

"Stop being such a douche-canoe, Chad," said Maddy. "I was only going to fuck him because of his gigantic dick, which isn't an attribute you share. I think Sam taking him home was more a case of pity sex. Besides, you're a sexist asshat, and regardless of what you think you know, that's a turn off for most women."

Tessa nodded, "I'd take you to my room, but I don't think you'd like anything that happened in there - especially sharing your secrets, if you were good enough to get me off. Which is a major if at this point." She grinned a little evilly at Chad, who paled slightly.

"Whatever," he blustered, "you all probably just lay there like dead fish anyway. It's not worth the effort. I'm going to bed." He tossed his plate into the sink with an angry clatter, stomping away. The women snickered with each other.

I returned my focus to my dinner, wolfing it down as fast as I could; I wanted to get out of there before they changed their minds about kicking my ass. I heard them whispering to each other as I ate, and I saw Jack get up silently and disappear into his room.

A few minutes later, a gentle hand on my shoulder startled me out of my daydream - more of a nightmare, really. Daymare? - of getting murdered in my sleep by three very sexy, very angry women. *Oh shit,* I thought, *here it comes. Time to pay the piper.*

"C'mon, Churro," Tessa said quietly, "it's my turn."

I gave her my deer-in-headlights, jackass stare. She rolled her eyes.

"I'm going to eat you."

I nodded sullenly, "Let me just go drop my uniform off in my room. Actually, could you come with me and eat me in there, so I don't need to parade around naked?" I refused to look at her, wondering how she was going to torture me.

"Sure, hon, let's go."

A FEW MINUTES LATER, THE WORLD CAME BACK INTO FOCUS FROM A LOWER perspective than I was accustomed to; Tessa was a good six inches shorter than me. She was sitting on a chair, and Maddy and Sam were on a nearby couch. The whoosh-whoosh of Tessa's bloodstream was slowly replaced with the muffled trumpet sound of Charlie Brown adults before finally clearing up.

"-takes? We don't want him to fall asleep yet," Sam was saying.

"Shit, we should have asked him," said Maddy, "Do you feel anything yet, Tessa?"

"Actually, if I concentrate," the world went dark as she closed her eyes, "I think I can almost feel something. It's like there's a slight pressure in my head that's not quite uncomfortable." Her eyes opened again. "Are you two sure you want to do this?"

They both nodded, but Maddy spoke first, "Of course, if you're up for it. First, we'll show him not to mess with us, and then we'll start his training." I felt Tessa's instant arousal at the word 'training'. *What is that about?*

"Yeah, I'm pretty much always game," added Sam.

My world wobbled as Tessa nodded, then stood up, "Okay then, here goes. Wish me luck." I felt her blush as she walked towards Jack's door. The other two quietly giggled and told her to "make it bad", whatever that meant. She knocked quietly.

When he opened the door, Jack was bare from the waist up, his uniform blousing out around his hips and thighs, empty arms dangling to the floor. The rest of his body was as pale and smooth as his face, truly making him look like a lanky doll. He looked confused.

"Hi Jack! What would you say if I offered you a blowjob?" Tessa asked happily.

Jack's confusion switched to shock. *Oh, fuck. This is bad.*

"Why?"

Tessa giggled a little before answering, "I ate Churro, and we wanted to pay him back for peeping on Maddy and Sam. So if he wants to watch, we'll make him watch something he doesn't like, like sucking your dick." I could feel that her cheeks were aflame with embarrassment, but she kept her head firmly upright.

"Isn't that rape?" Jack rumbled.

"Isn't what he did to the other ladies a form of rape?" Tessa replied quickly.

"I don't care either way, actually. Come on in, don't mind my girls." Jack backed away from the door, leaving it open for Tessa who quickly shut it behind her as she stepped in. "I'll never turn down a blowjob, but why me?"

"Oh, that's easy," said Tessa, "Chad's a pile of dicks all stacked up that pretends to be human. Besides that, I enjoyed getting to know you, and it's not like a blowjob is a marriage proposal, just a little sucky-sucky between friends." I felt her shrug her shoulders nonchalantly.

Jack let out a quiet chuckle, sounding like a glacier calving an iceberg. "Fair enough," he intoned, "how do you want to do this?" He waved an arm around his room, and Tessa looked around.

Every surface was covered by a porcelain doll in all shapes and colors. They seemed uniformly the same size, but they were each dressed uniquely, with various styles of clothes, hair, and even makeup. I felt her heart skip a beat at the creepy tableau. It took her a minute to gather her bearings.

"Umm, I wasn't exactly offering, just testing the waters. I'm just trying to scare Churro. Maybe a raincheck?"

Jack nodded and shrugged. "Kind of a jerk move, but I get it. Don't be a creepy asshole, or else you'll suck a dick."

"No more lies, omissions, or obfuscations, Churro, or we'll do this for real and take you to blow Chad after," she whispered so softly that even I could barely hear her, and I was inside her head.

She looked around the room at all the dolls again, a cold shiver crawling up her spine.

"Anyway, thanks Jack, night!" she called, turning towards his door and walking away. He didn't respond.

The three of them were giggling in the common area. "And then you just left?" Maddy asked.

Tessa nodded, blushing and grinning. "His room was *sooo* creepy."

"Ugh, yeah, Jack seems so gross," Sam chimed in.

Maddy looked unconvinced, but she didn't argue the point. "Okay, what's next on the agenda? What do we want to teach him, and how should we go about it?"

"Well," said Sam, "he's fucking horrible at eating pussy; that'd be the first thing I'd want him to learn to do well."

Tessa nodded, "That definitely needs to happen. How do we do it?"

A quiet "hmm" came from Maddy. "Maybe we can show him? I'm bi, and you ladies are hot, so I don't mind being the pitcher or catcher. But which would we want him to be? Or would we have Tessa just watch?" She looked to Sam.

"I'm open to the idea," she said, "but I'm more straight than bi. If it's all the same, I'd rather catch than pitch, to borrow your wording. What do you think, Tess?"

"I'm good with either, or even both options, actually. My biggest concern is what happens if I get off. I suppose if you don't want to spill your secrets, we could gag you," a rush of heat speared between her legs, "or just keep your mouths full some other way. Though if Sam doesn't want to go down on anyone, we may have to use the gag."

Maddy smiled, "I would enjoy burying my face in your pussy, Tessa. I can tell your clit my dirtiest secrets as you get off." Sam chuckled lightly at that.

Tessa looked down at the pillow in her lap, though, blushing again, heat filling her cheeks and ears. "There's one other concern I have, though." She waited for a response, but continued when silence reigned, "I'm, um, kind of bossy. That's what does it for me. Actually, it's kind of the only thing that does it for me."

Sam giggled again, "What do you mean by kind of? Are we talking like just telling us what you want to happen, or more like full-on dominatrix?"

"Full-on dominatrix," Tessa whispered, still looking at the pillow and not the other women, "I've never dommed another woman, but my favorite thing is breaking down strong, confident men into mewling slaves."

"Hot damn," laughed Maddy, "our shy little Tessa is a sexual badass! I'm wet as hell, girl, I'll sub for you."

"Really?" Sam asked, incredulous. "The fearless man-eater is willing to be submissive to someone?"

"Sure, why not? I know who I am and what I like - I don't need to swing my ego around to prove myself to anyone. If Tessa wants me to be her slave for a night," she eyed Tessa, appraising her, "or two or three, I can submit. If I don't like it, I'll just stop listening." She shrugged, as if none of this were a big deal.

Tessa took a deep breath, trying to calm her now racing heart. Her pussy was tingling as blood rushed down. "I think I need a drink. I want this, but I'm nervous."

"Now you're talking!" agreed Sam, getting up to grab a bottle of vodka from the kitchenette. "At least they keep this place stocked for us! Let's get this party started."

9

IT'S PARTY TIME!

Throwing back her third shot, Tessa grinned at the other women sitting on her bed with her. She was feeling hot, and a small step beyond tipsy. I expected her to be far more drunk, given her petite body, but I guess she was more used to drinking than I was.

"I'm getting warm," she announced as she stood up from the bed, "Maddy, undress me." Her tone was imperious.

Maddy grinned, crawling slowly to the edge of the bed on her hands and knees, looking so damn sexy as she peered up at Tessa through her red hair. "Okay!"

Tessa stepped forward and placed her left hand on Maddy's throat. I was shocked when she started squeezing lightly. "The correct response is, 'Yes, Mistress.' Do you understand?" she asked quietly, but with a core of steel lacing her words. *Who was this woman?*

"Yes, Mistress," Maddy purred, "I understand perfectly, Mistress."

Sam was watching the exchange with wide eyes, seemingly unable to believe that this was really happening.

As Maddy slowly started peeling Tessa's uniform away, Tessa looked at Sam. "Get undressed," she commanded, "I'm going to make my plaything devour you." Something buzzed in the back of my mind.

"Yes, Mistress," Sam whispered automatically, looking so dazed that she probably didn't even realize she'd said it. Her hand was up at her throat, mimicking the way Tessa had held Maddy.

Maddy kept removing Tessa's clothes, freeing her arms and small breasts from the strange material. Tessa wrapped a hand around the back of Maddy's neck, pulling her face to her nipple, which pebbled in the cool air. Maddy took it into her mouth without further prompting, and I could feel the flash of heat shooting through Tessa's breast to her core. As she sucked and licked on Tessa, I felt the graze of teeth. "No biting, Maddy. Churro isn't ready to learn that yet." As her lips worked on Tessa's nipple, Maddy's hands kept working on her suit, pulling it down and exposing her fully.

I felt Maddy's soft hands caressing Tessa's smooth skin, and I was beginning to lose my sense of self, of separateness. I was becoming us again, drawn into Tessa's mind like a magnet. Maddy took Tessa's other nipple between gentle fingers, squeezing lightly, and a flash of light and desire shot through our brain. We were joined.

We closed our eyes, and whispered, "Pay attention to what she's doing to me, Churro. I know you can tell that I enjoy it, so I expect similar from you when it's your turn." We stepped out of the feet of our outfit, feeling a chill as the air touched our damp, spread lips. We opened our eyes, looking over the top of Maddy's fiery hair attached to our nipple to watch Sam kneeling on the bed behind her. She was shimmying her hips out of the tight suit, revealing her body in its full glory.

We bit our lip and groaned in pleasure, the sight of Sam following orders sending another rush of heat to our center. She laid back to peel the leggings from her toes, presenting her glistening lips in the process. *So Sam either likes being bossed around more than she admitted, or she's a bit of an exhibitionist.*

We dragged our fingers across Maddy's ample tits before grabbing her neck again, pushing her away from our nipple and lifting her to an upright kneeling position on the edge of the bed. "Strip, slave, slowly. Watch Sam; show her your body."

"Yes, Mistress," Maddy immediately grabbed at the neckline of her uniform, stretching and tugging on it as she slowly peeled it down her shoulders. She paused momentarily to squeeze her full breasts hard, moaning quietly. Sam was watching Maddy with wide eyes, a flush on her cheeks and sex that had nothing to do with alcohol. She brought her hands up to mimic Maddy's movements, squeezing herself firmly, the pliable flesh dimpling beneath her fingers.

Maddy tugged her clothes a few inches lower, revealing almost all of her breasts, but she kept her nipples hidden. One hand slipped down her stomach to rub between her legs over her suit. She brought it slowly back up, and popped her tits out.

We groaned quietly at the show, knowing that she was only doing this because we told her to. Our head spun. Maddy's arms were still in her sleeves, rolled down to nearly her elbows, and her tits were beautiful, with gorgeous pink nipples. She was so graceful as she pulled her arms free, moving with agonizing slowness. Our core was on fire, throbbing in time with our elevated heartbeat, and we ached to find our release, but it wasn't time - not yet.

Sam bit her lip as she watched Maddy stripping, still massaging her breasts, occasionally tweaking and pinching her nipples. Her untouched sex was leaking steadily onto the sheets beneath her.

When Maddy was finally kneeling in front of us, all of her extreme sexiness on full, proud display, we caressed her muscled back, our fingers tingling as we pushed her towards Sam. "Lick her pussy, slave, but don't make her come yet."

Maddy's whispered, "Yes, Mistress," drove us crazy, our own lubrication flowing down our leg, leaving a cold trail and sending goosebumps all over our body. Our nipples hardened almost painfully, so we brought our hands up, pinching and twisting lightly, flashes of electrical fire making us shiver.

"Spread your legs, Sam," we ordered, "and use two fingers to spread yourself open for her."

She followed our command silently, opening her thighs wide, legs pointed straight out as she presented herself in the splits. Her right hand traced from her breast down to her pussy, where she rubbed between her lips gently before spreading her fingers apart. Her clit glistened wetly in the soft lighting of the room, matching the brown shade of her firm nipples.

Maddy slowly laid forward, crushing her breasts against the bed as she positioned herself at the apex of Sam's athletic legs. We crawled back onto the bed as well, lying beside Maddy and giving ourself a good view of the show to come. When Maddy's tongue flicked out to drag slowly across Sam's clit, Sam moaned loudly. Maddy inched in closer, extending her tongue as far out as she could reach, sliding the entire length of it against Sam's clit, from root to tip. She licked slowly, with a firm, gentle pressure.

"Are you taking notes?" we asked ourself out loud. We looked from Maddy's tongue to Sam's face, seeing the look of rapture she was wearing. "Keep going, slave, make her writhe. If she comes, though, I'll punish you." Our pussy was pulsing with a needy lust, achingly empty and unfulfilled, but we were patient.

Maddy laved at Sam obsessively, making her moan and squirm. Her breath came in hitches and gasps, sometimes stopping completely as she held her breath, only to be released explosively when she remembered to breathe. "Please," she whined pitifully, "please let me come, Mistress. It almost hurts, I'm so close. Please, Mistress." Her eyes opened to beg us to allow her release.

We reached our hand out to Sam's face, thrusting our middle finger into her mouth, which she immediately started sucking. Her hot tongue wrapped around it, and she grabbed our wrist with both hands to hold us in her mouth, almost as if she were afraid we'd pull it back. Our own orgasm was building, an almost physical pressure between our legs that was demanding satisfaction.

We dragged our legs under us, kneeling beside Maddy, Sam's left leg on our right shoulder, our hand still in her mouth. We turned our head and nipped at Sam's ankle, and she screamed out loudly. Her body shook and quivered as she came all over Maddy's face. We were dripping like a leaky faucet; Sam's shuddering, screaming orgasm was just as hot as the thought of the upcoming punishment of Maddy for breaking our rule.

As Sam finally juddered into a panting, weak-limbed mess, Maddy licked her lips and looked at us slyly, "I'm sorry, Mistress. I think I accidentally made her come." She looked anything but sorry, and our pussy clenched in on itself at her unrepentant grin.

We nodded, and our voice was full of ice as we spoke, "Face away from me on your knees, lay on your chest and reach behind you to hold your knees." Maddy instantly spun away from us, bouncing the bed and jostling the limp Sam as she hurried to follow our instructions. In a matter of seconds, Maddy's juicy slit was presented to us, and we licked our lips in anticipation.

"You are going to have your ass slapped twice, Maddy," we said coolly, "and then we are going to slap your pussy."

Maddy groaned out a heated, "Yes, Mistress, thank you, Mistress." She was trying to look at us over her shoulder and rump, but her hair fell across her eyes, and she didn't seem willing to let go of her knees to fix it.

We rose up on our knees and leaned over Maddy's ass, the heat radiating from her pussy burning into our clean shaved pubic mound. We reached forward delicately, slowly tucking her stray locks behind her ear, which we caressed lightly. Maddy shivered as we said, "Watch us. We want you to see it happening. You earned this, slave." We leaned back again, sitting on our heels. Reaching forward again, we rubbed Maddy's infinitely soft ass cheeks with both hands. Her hips wriggled a little before we let go.

Raising our right hand, we brought it down with a firm crack across her right cheek, which jiggled slightly and immediately turned pink in the shape of our hand print. Sam's eyes flicked open at the loud sound, and she sat up with a gasp. She looked between us and Maddy's ass, biting her lip again, but she remained silent.

Maddy had closed her eyes and groaned at the spank, but she opened them quickly to watch for our next blow. The cheeks of her face were flushed bright red from the pain. Our hand rose again, still stinging slightly, before crashing down hard against her left cheek. She yelped and mewled a little as her ass immediately grew another pink hand print. Our hand tingled with pain, but the impulses traveled straight to our pussy, where the pressure was continuing to build.

We turned our hand over, cupping it firmly against Maddy's sex. "I'm going to slap your pussy now, slave." She moaned and tried to thrust herself back against our hand, but we pulled away. "Hold still."

"Fuck, that's so hot," Sam whispered, her fingers absently rubbing against her clit as she watched the show.

We grinned at Sam as we raised up off our heels, knee-walking to the side of Maddy as our left hand reached out to her lower back, pushing down. "Arch your back down, stick your pussy out, pull your knees up," we commanded, the ice in our voice thawing to mere steel. Maddy obliged instantly, and we raised our flattened palm into the air. "What's our name?" we asked loudly.

When Maddy was about to answer, we slapped her wet, aching pussy. "Mmmmmistress!" she shouted, squealing and moaning as her already swollen lips reddened further. We slipped our stinging index and middle finger into her flooded sheathe, and rubbed against her clit with our thumb.

"Say it again, slave, and keep saying it until you stop coming!" we ordered, our authority ringing through the room.

"Mistress! Mmmistress! Ungh, mistressss!" she writhed on our fingers, her walls clenching convulsively around us. Her hips thrashed wildly, but she kept a death grip on her knees, not moving enough to disrupt us as we drove our fingers in and out, our thumb mercilessly rubbing her clit. Another cry escaped Sam's lips as she rubbed herself to another orgasm, bucking her hips as her ab muscles clenched and released.

Long, loud minutes later, Maddy collapsed fully to the bed, panting and gasping, her entire body glistening with a thin sheen of sweat. Our fingers were slightly wrinkled from how long we'd been able to draw out her orgasm, and we thrust them in front of Sam's face. She took them into her mouth hungrily, sucking and licking Maddy's juices from them. When she had them suitably clean, we pulled out and patted her cheek gently.

"Our slave is in no position to pleasure us, Sam," we said coyly, with a smirk, "will you finish us off?"

She nodded quickly, eagerly, and when she spoke, her voice was soft, whispery, "Yes, Mistress, tell me what to do."

We grinned, knowing that we'd turned another person into our slave; she was malleable clay, ready to be shaped into whatever we wished. We laid down on our back next to Maddy, who was still sprawled on her stomach breathing heavily. Reaching up to caress her ass with our left hand, which we knew from experience would be extremely tender and sensitive, we spread ourself open to Sam, the side of our thigh resting on the back of Maddy's leg. "Rub us with your wet pussy, slave." The buzzing in the back of our mind was back, but we ignored it.

Sam flushed red, and moved to obey, "Yes, Mistress." She straddled our right leg, dragging her smooth, still-wet pussy up the inside of our thigh, sending more pulses of electric fire rushing into our nearly-overwhelmed center. When she reached our sex, we nearly lost it right then, but managed to hold it back by biting our lip, hard. The pain provided a harsh counterpoint to the sweet chords playing in our pussy.

"We're very close, slave, but you're ordered to keep rubbing until told to stop - even after we come." We were throbbing and pulsing, burning up from the inside out.

"Yes, Mistress," she whispered again, and we knew we'd never tire of hearing that phrase. She gyrated her hips slowly, spreading our juices between our bodies, her soft slickness driving waves of pleasure into us forcefully. We closed our eyes, and couldn't hold back the moan that clawed its way up our throat from somewhere deep inside. Sam pressed harder into us, rubbing her whole pussy against us in small circles, and before another thought could form, our world exploded.

The angels sang in our ears, fireworks lit up the darkness behind our eyelids, waves of passion crested through us. There was no cessation of bliss, no moments between surges of pleasure, nothing to separate one second from the next - just an eternal existence of pure, passionate release. Our mind was practically trembling with vibrations.

There was a vague sensation of maybe hearing people talking - loudly, quickly - but it was subsumed beneath the waves of orgasmic joy sweeping through us. When it finally ended, we were writhing, twitching. Sam was still rubbing against us, but it was erratic, awkward jerking and thrusting. She had clearly gone on long past her own limit.

"Stop, sweetness, you're done." *We have to reward this dedication somehow.*

Sam immediately threw herself backwards away from us, nearly falling from the bed in her haste. She flopped to the side, panting heavily and sweating. We were still gasping, too, our body wet, likely sweaty. Maddy had rolled onto her side, facing us. She looked sublimely happy.

"Fucking Christ, Tessa," she said, making it clear that playtime was over with her lack of submission, "that was so awesome." Sam just nodded weakly in agreement, managing to smile a bit.

"And the best part is," we added, "that orgasm was so awesome that we didn't even hear whatever you yelled out."

Maddy grinned, "I did. But I'm not sharing." Her eyes shifted to the prone form of Sam, sprawled out near her feet.

I raised our arm to wipe at a drop of sweat that was tickling down the side of our neck. Our eyes opened wide and we stared at the arm that I had moved. "Oh shit!" we gasped. Then we realized that somewhere in the middle of the best sexual experience of our lives that our thoughts were much more intertwined than they should be.

10

NOT SUPPOSED TO WORK LIKE THIS!

We lurched upright, panic flooding our veins with adrenaline, "Our power isn't supposed to work like this!"

Maddy was instantly beside us, one hand on our lower back as she examined our face. Her visage was flooded with worry and fear. "What do you mean 'our power'? Tessa, are you okay?" Sam was struggling to sit back up, still exhausted from our playtime.

"No, we're not okay," we said, tears gathering in the corners of our eyes, "We're... we joined. Our thoughts are mingled, jumbled together. This isn't normal, we don't know what's happening. We've never been like this before. We don't know what to do." A tear leaked down our cheek.

"Oh shit is right," said Sam, "is Churro like controlling your mind or something?" She looked just as concerned as Maddy did.

We shook our head, "No, it doesn't seem like we are sharing everything. We're not being controlled, exactly." We closed our eyes, spilling out more tears. "It's... only half of us can remember Tessa's memories. The other half of us has Churro's. We know we're supposed to be separate, and we think we still are in many ways." We tried to think back to the moment of our joining, to remember our first shared memory, but it was a struggle. Our breathing was shaky with terror. *What if we never separate? We don't want to live like this!*

"We think… we think this started when our body was getting really turned on. We can almost remember the point when we started thinking of us as 'we' instead of 'I'. It's hard, though, because we were very aroused and not really paying attention." Flashes of memories flittered through our mind as we tried to recall what it felt like being separate entities. The longer we were us, the less normal being "I" felt, and that horrified us.

A sudden fire in our left cheek caused us to look at Maddy with a gasp; she'd just slapped us! Our ears were ringing as we rubbed our stinging face.

"Did that help?" she asked almost sheepishly.

"No, we don't think so. It just hurts. We feel like we're losing separation, like there's only supposed to be us and no individuals." We started crying in earnest, burying our face in our hands. We felt four warm arms wrapping around us, attempting to comfort and soothe us, but we just cried harder.

"Come on, baby girl," Maddy whispered to us, "Let's get you in the shower. I'm sure you just need to digest some more, and he'll split back out of you. In the meantime, let's get cleaned up, okay?"

"Yeah, Tess," Sam agreed, "showers are always good, right? And we'll help. Right, Maddy?"

"Of course!"

We could feel them trying to nudge us towards the bathroom, and we let ourself be guided along. Maddy turned on the water while Sam hugged us from behind, her strong arms wrapped around our middle. She wasn't holding us up, just squeezing us supportively.

"We didn't know this would happen. We're sorry for doing this to us." We placed our arms on top of Sam's, holding her close to us.

"We believe you. Don't we, Sam?" We felt Sam nodding behind us at Maddy's question. "Don't worry about this, either of you. You're both strong, aren't you? I mean, Tessa, the way you took control of me the way you did, dear God. You were *fierce*! And you, Churro… uh, you're strong, too!"

Maddy felt the temperature of the water, then stepped backward into the stream, pulling us in with her. The sight of her dripping wet was incredibly sexy, so we closed our eyes again - we had the feeling that more arousal wouldn't help our situation at all. Sam was still at our back, her breasts pressed firmly against us. We could feel ourself getting turned on again.

"We thank you for your help getting us in here, but you're both too sexy, you're working us up again, and we think that might be a bad thing. Just... give us a few minutes to calm down, by ourself?" We turned our head back and forth to look at both of them. We were struggling to keep our eyes on their faces, unsure which of us was having to fight the hardest. We knew we both thought they were sexy as hell.

"Okay," Sam said, peeling herself away from our back, "we'll go back to our rooms and let you shower and dress, but meet us in the middle when you're done, okay?"

We nodded without saying anything, and they left, dripping all over our bathroom. They kept looking back at us nervously, but we tried to reassure them with a wave and a smile. Eventually, they were gone, and we focused on washing up.

The process was difficult, because half of us kept getting turned on by touching our body intimately. We fought to not let it become overwhelming, and managed to finish the job. We stepped out, dried off, and put our uniform back on.

This strangeness was threatening to break our mind; it was so difficult to think with this plurality of self. Human minds were not meant to be pluralities, we were supposed to be singular.

Maybe if we try to do opposite things? If we try to lift our arm up and keep it down at the same time? Our arm lifted up, and then dropped back down. It went easily. *We can barely think of ourself as separate individuals, how can one body fight itself when there's one mind controlling it? Even if the mind is plural, we are still just one mind. No, stop it! We have to be two again!*

Our inner struggle continued as we just stood in our room doing nothing.

Listen, we growled at ourself, *we are Churro and Tessa. When we say go, our Churro half will raise our arm, and our Tessa half will take **her** body back by keeping it firmly down. Do we understand ourself?* We nodded, feeling a massive headache at the absurdity of what we were saying. *Go!*

Our arm jerked around, like it had been electrocuted, but it was the pain in our skull that was truly excruciating. We instantly stopped fighting, bringing our arms up to hold our brain inside our head. We cried out in pain, and decided not to try that again, at least not without a health monitor. It had felt like being torn in half at the soul level, which made us think we were on the right path, but the risks were unknown, and terrifying.

We went out to the common area, resolute to fix ourself lest it become permanent. Maddy and Sam jumped up from their seats and came rushing over, but we waved at them to sit back and sat near them on a couch. "We tried to separate, but it felt like we were tearing ourself in half from the inside out. We want to try again, but we're scared. We don't want to be alone."

Sam and Maddy gushed enthusiastic support and joined us on the couch, each one draping an arm over our shoulders or behind our back. "You're not alone," Maddy said, "we'll be right here for you, for both of you, the whole time."

Sam was unable to disguise the fear in her voice, "You're going to be fine. We're going to get Churro out of you and nothing bad will come of this. It's just a new aspect to his power that we'll need to study more. You like studying, right, Tessa? You like tests and experiments?"

We nodded, "We do like tests and experiments."

"Okay, so, we'll be here while you do this experiment. Right here, by your side, the whole time. Here, why don't you lay down?" Sam scooted sideways, pulling us over into her lap, our violet locks covering her thighs. She stroked our hair soothingly, pulling it back from our face. Maddy shifted too, pulling our legs onto her lap. She was rubbing our calves gently as we rolled onto our back, getting very comfortable.

We looked up through Sam's breasts, then over our own less full chest at Maddy. Both women were wearing reassuring smiles, though we could still sense the uncertainty and fear in their eyes.

"Okay, give us a minute, and then we'll try." They nodded mutely in response.

We are Churro and Tessa. We are two minds, two bodies. We are in a body that does not belong to us, it belongs to Tessa and we are going to give it back to her. On the count of three, we are going to have our Churro half sit up, and our Tessa half will stay snuggled into these sexy ladies. We are going to fight through any pain that happens until we succeed at this. We are resolved.

One. We took a deep breath and closed our eyes, anxiety spiking.

Two. We exhaled, trying to relax our body.

Three! We pulled hard at our body, and our mind tore asunder.

I GASPED IN AIR, FEELING LIKE I HADN'T BREATHED IN WEEKS. *I... I AM singular again! Tessa!* My thoughts immediately turned to the petite woman, and I sat up quickly. I could barely wait long enough for the rinsing spray to get the rest of the crap off my body.

Once it was done, I launched myself up the stairs, through my room and into the common area, uncaring of my nudity or semi-clean state. I looked around frantically. The boys were here, which I hadn't noticed before. Had they seen the whole event? Chad was engrossed in a first-person shooter video game. Jack was reading a book. He looked up at me and pointed silently at the door to Tessa's room.

I darted off as fast as I could, bursting through Tessa's door with a loud bang. "Tessa!" I yelled, "Are you okay?" I was panting for breath.

"Jesus, simmer down, pastry boy!" Sam barked at me. "She's fine, she's just taking another shower. I can't believe how fast you got up here, she just finished, you know, expelling you."

I finally noticed that Maddy and Sam were sitting next to each other on Tessa's bed. The second thing I noticed was that they both seemed calm, but also a little angry. With the way they were looking at me, I was pretty sure it wasn't Tessa they were mad at.

"Oh, thank God," I gasped, "I was so worried about her. I thought I'd killed us, killed her."

Maddy's nose wrinkled, "Go shower, Churro, you literally smell like shit. You should come back when you're done, because we have a lot to talk about, but you need to leave in a hurry."

I nodded, and left much more sedately than I had arrived.

When I got back to Tessa's door about ten minutes later, I knocked politely. The door opened a few seconds later, and I got a brief glimpse of Tessa's smiling face before she buried her face in my chest. Her arms wrapped around me, and she was squeezing me like she was afraid to let go.

"I'm so glad you're okay," she said, her voice muffled against my chest.

"I'm fine, what about you? The ladies said you were okay, but I need to hear it from you."

She pulled back her head, still hugging me tight, so she could look up at me, "I'm good, I'm okay. I guess that means *we're* okay."

I laughed a little, "No more plural-speak for a while, Tessa, that was scary as shit."

She nodded, and we both shivered in exactly the same way. A second later, we were laughing again. I reveled in the fact that she had the cutest dimples I'd ever seen.

"Well, are you going to stand out here all night, or are you going to come in?" she teased, since she still hadn't let me go. Not that I was complaining. She felt really good pressed up against me like this.

She turned, and we both took a step forward. I grinned and held back from the next one, "Ladies first." She went in ahead of me, and I was pretty sure there was a bounce in her step that hadn't been there before.

Maddy and Sam were still sitting at the head of the bed, leaning against the wall with Tessa's pillows behind their backs, so Tessa and I crawled onto the foot of the bed. I sat cross-legged, but she just flopped onto her belly, propping herself up on her elbows. The four of us all just took turns looking at each other, so I took the initiative.

"I have no fucking clue what happened. It's never happened before. I don't know if it'll happen again, or if there's a way to stop it. I just don't know anything, except that I'm so incredibly sorry."

"Psh," Tessa interjected, "You don't need to apologize to me, I know what we were thinking, how we were feeling. I know you were just as scared as I was. The fact of the matter is that it was absolutely terrifying, but this is one hundred percent a good thing!"

"What?" Sam scoffed, "How was this a good thing? Regardless of what happened in your head, the way you screamed in my lap... Tessa, you were in so much pain."

Tessa shook her head, "Not just me, Sam. We both felt that pain, even if it was my body doing the screaming. But this means that Churro's power is, I don't know, adapting. Growing. Getting stronger. So let's start at the beginning, and work our way through everything. Churro, prior to coming here, what was your power like?"

"Um, I was just a passenger in whoever ate me. I'd usually hang out for about eighteen hours before too much of me was processed, and my world went dark for what I assume was a few hours. Then I'd wake up in whatever pile of waste I ended up in."

"Okay, good, so there's a baseline. How many times were you eaten before?" Tessa had an intense look on her face that was simultaneously adorable and slightly intimidating.

"In the six years I've had this power? Maybe seven or eight times? My school administrators tested me yearly, and there were a few kids who had been dared to eat me. I went along with it, thinking that maybe I'd make a friend or something, but nothing ever really changed. I always ended up alone and ignored."

"Good, good," Tessa seemed to ignore my depressed tone of voice, as she just plowed forward. "And since you've been here, you've been ingested three times in three days. What's been different?"

"The first time, with Maddy, well..." I trailed off, blushing, until Sam grinned at me and nudged me with her foot, "Err, that was a first for me. No one who had eaten me before had done anything remotely sexual, not even the teenage boys had any special alone time."

"Sure, that was new to you, but it wasn't a difference in your *power*, was it?"

"Oh, no, I guess not. I suppose the only thing different about my power was that I seemed to move through Maddy faster than usual. She ate me around ten pm?" I glanced up at Maddy, who nodded in confirmation, "And I came back after breakfast, probably around ten am. Twelve hours was about half as long as I'd expected to be gone."

"And that's good data! What about Sam?" Tessa pressed.

I scrunched up my face, thinking hard, "Well, she had me after we, umm, you know. She told you all about it." I blushed hard. Sam had to nudge me again, still with that grin on her face. God, she was gorgeous. "I was in her for almost twenty-four hours, actually. We slept, had a very talkative breakfast," I tried to glare at the three women, who now *all* had grins on their faces and seemed completely unperturbed by my mock anger, "and I was actually with her throughout her whole workout. I came back an hour or two after dinner, I think."

Tessa added her own info to the growing puzzle pieces, "And with me, you were only inside for maybe two hours. Long enough for me sleep with these two amazing beauties,"

I blushed again, but I was amazed that Tessa was able to say that with a straight face. *What happened to her bashfulness?*

"Churro, what about the feelings of connectedness? I think I can remember when you and I became us, it was when Maddy started playing with our, erm, *my* breasts. Did you experience anything like that with Maddy or Sam?"

I opened my eyes wide, "Not with Sam, no, but with Maddy, yeah! It was when we first started playing with our clit!"

"Hold up a sec," Maddy interrupted me, "first off - *my* clit, not ours! And only I played with it, not us! Secondly, I don't remember any sort of connectedness or being more than one person. I just had a good time by myself and went to sleep."

"Sure, sure," Tessa waved down Maddy's concerns, "I have a theory forming. Sam, when you sculpted Churro to show us his dick, you said something was weird, what was it?"

Sam's face took on the same shocked look that I think I was wearing, "I could sculpt faster, and it looked like my paper clips had actually melted together, like it was all one solid piece of metal!"

"Holy shit," I mumbled, "I saw you sculpt orientation day with Maddy, through her eyes, and it was really good, but still looked like paper clips. The piece you did of me, though, that was on a whole new level, Sam. It was totally accurate, and smooth."

Tessa had such a massive grin on her face that I could practically see her molars, "Sam, will you sculpt something for us?" Those dimples were delicious.

Sam nodded quickly, and pulled out her bag of paper clips. She started concentrating, and they quickly pooled into a perfectly smooth sphere. She frowned, and it flattened out into a rectangular shape, like a piece of silver paper, or aluminum foil. It floated in front of us, spinning slowly, reflections of the room showing with crystal clarity.

"Sam…" Maddy whispered.

"Maddy!" Tessa yelped, "How far away is the door to the bathroom! Quick!"

"It's two point five meters away," she said blandly, then her eyes opened wide, "Point five? I've never known anything other than whole meters!" She started grinning at Sam, who was grinning back at her. I was grinning at both of them, and Tessa slowly turned to me.

Nothing about her widely-grinning face actually changed, but there was something intangible that immediately set the hairs on the back of my neck standing straight up. A sense of malevolent intent. I opened my mouth to say something, but then she looked confused, so I changed tack, "What's wrong, Tessa?"

"Well, that didn't work like I expected it to, after hearing about Maddy's and Sam's upgrades."

"Upgrades?" the other two ladies asked together.

"Isn't it obvious? Both of you have been upgraded by eating Churro. I should be upgraded, too, but I couldn't make him spill his guts. I'd really prefer not to have to have an orgasm to trigger it."

"Oh," said Maddy, blushing faintly, "I think you've been upgraded already. Sam and I both shared two secrets during your orgasm, and it sounded like you tried to, too."

"What? What do you mean, I tried to? Why would I try to share secrets?"

"Well, it sounded like you were trying to say something, but you were coming too hard to make it intelligible. And maybe it wasn't you, but your power triggered your Churro half to try to take over, and they were his secrets?"

Tessa looked thoughtful, "Two secrets for the price of an orgasm. Not the direction I was hoping for, but it's better than nothing. Alright, now we need to figure out the 'length of invasion' aspect of Churro's power."

"Uh, can we not call it an invasion? I mean, all of you ate me willingly."

Tessa waved at me dismissively. "Prior feedings were twenty-fourish hours. Maddy was about twelve, Sam was about twenty-four, and I was about two."

We were all silent for a minute or two, thinking, before Sam sat forward, "Orgasms!"

"Yes!" Tessa and Maddy yelled at the same time.

"Huh?" I was the picture of sparkling wit.

Sam rolled her beautiful baby blues at me, "Both Maddy and Tessa had orgasms with you, but I got mine from you before I ate you."

"That's a strange way to handle a power, but I've read some books that were weirder," Maddy said.

"But it totally fits with human physiology," Tessa added, "Well, sort of. I mean, orgasms aren't super researched, but it's pretty well known that they release a ton of chemicals in the brain, and increase heart rate and respiration. I don't know for sure, but it makes sense that they would increase the rate at which we consume nutrients. God knows I'm *always* thirsty after a good one, and sometimes I'm pretty hungry too."

The other two were nodding along, but I was having trouble catching up. "Hang on, you're saying that getting off, what? Uses me up faster? Okay, fine, let's go with that, but that doesn't explain why I stayed in Maddy for twelve hours, and in Tessa for only two."

"Maybe the strength of the orgasm has an influence on it," Sam piped in.

"I don't know, the one I had seemed pretty fucking strong," smirked Maddy.

"Which leads us back to my previous ideas for experiments," Tessa said excitedly. "There's no way for us to objectively compare something like an orgasm, since we can't experience each other's feelings." She turned back to me. "Except you. From your experience, which of us had the bigger orgasm?"

They were all staring at me expectantly, "Um, well they were both really good..."

"Cut the prevaricating, Churro. One was better than the other. Which one was it?" Maddy was glaring at me now.

"Tessa's," I said immediately. That look on Maddy's face was frightening. "By a huge margin, actually. I mean, what I went through with Maddy set off fireworks like the Fourth of July, but with Tessa, it was like every Fourth of July *ever*, all at once."

Both Maddy and Sam looked at her enviously, and Tessa grinned like the Cheshire Cat. "I told you ladies, domming you was super hot. I practically came without physical stimulation."

"And the way Sam tried to fight our authority at first," I added, "only to give in to us..."

Everyone turned back to me, Tessa nodding with her huge smile, Sam blushing furiously, and Maddy slightly angry.

"I didn't agree to submit to *you*, Churro," Maddy said, her voice tense.

I held my hands up in surrender, "I know, Maddy, and I'd never try anything like what Tessa did, but for much of what happened, there were no lines drawn between our minds. I didn't mean to, but I was exactly as aroused as Tessa by what we did to you. We didn't realize it until after, but we were pretty sure that I was influencing her before her orgasm." Maddy looked uncertain, but she'd lost the angry glower.

Tessa nodded, not needing to repeat what I'd said; I knew she was thinking the exact same thing - we shared identical memories of the experience.

Sam yawned suddenly, and I glanced at the clock. *Damn, it's late.* Maddy quickly yawned, too.

"Well," Maddy said, "I'm going to sleep like a log. I've never had my pussy slapped before, but if I keep coming that hard, I'll definitely try it again." She winked at Tessa as she got off the bed gracefully. Even I got a light, friendly pat on the shoulder before she disappeared. *Is she mad at me, or not? I can't tell.*

Sam stretched, my eyes gluing to her body as it undulated slowly, "Ohhh, I'm so beat, but at least I don't think I'll be so sore tomorrow. After all, nothing split me in half this time." She smiled sleepily, and slid off the bed. "Night, you two."

"Night, Sam," we parroted as she walked out of the room, closing the door behind her.

I made to stand up, but Tessa put her hand on my thigh, close to my hip. "Hang on, Churro." I looked at her questioningly. She blushed again, and bit her lip, and I instantly started getting hard.

"We still have to talk about the separation, but not tonight. Tonight, I want to do something else. Will you… will you spend the night with me tonight? Not for sex," she quickly added when she noticed my erection, "I just, I don't know, I'm feeling weirdly alone in my own head right now. I'm pretty sure you know what I mean."

I nodded in agreement; I knew exactly how she felt. It was like suddenly forgetting all of the lyrics to a favorite song, but still being able to hum the melody.

"Of course I will, Tessa," I said, "but I just want to be up front about something."

She looked at me quizzically.

"I'm probably going to be hard as a rock all night from being so close to you - there's just no way to avoid it. But no sex, just companionship."

She giggled and nodded at me.

Ten minutes later, after coming back from brushing my teeth in my own room, I was spooned up behind her, my raging cock sandwiched between my stomach and her ass cheeks. My arms were wrapped around her naked body protectively, and her hair was tickling my nose and getting in my mouth. A minute later, I was out.

11

DAWN, DAY FOUR

Sally's voice ripped through the mental haze keeping me asleep, "Attention Omega Team. Inspection is imminent. You have sixty seconds to assemble in the common area." She'd changed it back to the standard robotic voice that we'd first heard from her.

I jumped out of bed quickly. Well, I tried to, at least. I'd forgotten that I was in bed with Tessa, and which room I was in, so I ended up planting a knee in her gut and smacking my face into the wall. I fell back onto the bed, groaning. Tessa moaned in pain.

"What the hell, Churro? Why are you trying to kill us?"

"I'm sorry," I said nasally, pinching my aching nose. "Sally told us inspection is imminent."

"Yeah, I heard that," I wasn't looking at her, but I could practically hear her rolling her eyes, "that still doesn't explain third degree battery."

She grumbled at bit more as we each started pulling our uniforms on. Unfortunately, mine was on the opposite side of the bed from hers, so I wasn't able to watch her dress. We finished up, smoothing out our necklines, and slipped through her door into the common area.

Standing there in her full glory was the Gemstone Mage, and I stuttered to a halt, staring with wide eyes. Tessa bumped into my back, and I felt her slap my shoulder as she grumbled again. When she stepped to the side to go around me, she froze.

The Gemstone Mage, Gemma to her friends, was almost as famous as Hoarfrost. She only had one confirmed World Saving Event under her belt, but since there were only ten known WSEs, that instantly launched her into the stratosphere of the ultra-elite. I had no idea she was part of THG.

She wasn't tall or short, but she sparkled in the light as if she were made out of her eponymous gemstones. She didn't look like gems or anything, her skin was one of the darkest shades of brown that I'd ever seen naturally, but she somehow glittered. Her black hair was cut very short, and curled tightly around her head, almost spherical in the way it hugged her scalp.

She was overwhelmingly beautiful, and she was smirking at me and Tessa, presumably because we'd come out of the same room. Her eyes widened slightly as she looked at our uniforms.

"What the fuck, man?" Chad immediately whined, pointing at me and Tessa, "First you get to fuck Sam, and now you're tapping Tessa?" When no one said anything, he continued, "Dude, this is so fucked up. You're just a beta male nobody, these bitches are crazy."

I blushed, dropping my head. It wasn't like I could explain in front of the Gemstone Mage that I'd only cuddled with Tessa - and now had a seriously aching case of blue balls. It didn't seem like Tessa shared my concerns.

"Churro is a fantastically wonderful lover, *Chad*," she sneered at him, "Sam told us that we just had to take him for a ride after the way he rocked her world. She was right, he's very good, and so generous. Oh, and before sleeping with Churro, I also gave Jack head." *Shit, this bad-ass chick wasn't taking* ***any*** *prisoners!*

Chad just stood there working his mouth up and down, but no sounds were able to escape. His sandy blond hair wobbled as he shook his head. In disbelief or denial I didn't know, but it was very clear that he had no idea how to process this.

Sam and Maddy giggled and held up their hands towards Tessa, giving her air fives. Even Jack smirked. I guess he was tired of Chad's whining, too, since he didn't refute her claim.

"Now that we're all finally here," the Gemstone Mage said, her voice somehow effervescent, "I have to ask: why on God's green Earth are you all standing around in your underwear?"

The silence was cacophonous.

I raised my hand and asked weakly, "Underwear?"

Suddenly the Mage was laughing, and it took her a good while to regain her self-control. "Let me guess, Warden didn't bother telling you that you can request your uniforms, in your own sizes, with your tablets?" She was snickering, and I felt myself blushing. "You've all been parading around with each other for three days, dressed like this? No wonder you're almost all getting laid." She looked at the consternation on Chad's face, and started laughing again.

Now that I looked closely, I could see the rubber-like collar around her neck, and at her wrists. The rest of her was covered by a loose, ivory blouse, and a pair of casual, green cotton pants. She had a pair of tennis shoes on. All in all, she was dressed modestly, but comfortably.

"Not only that, but you didn't even bother to put regular clothes on top. Oh, this is too much. Warden's a dick, but he's a funny dick." She eventually calmed down, and gave us all one last smirk before settling down to business. "Okay, there are some new orders from on high that affect you, so I'll start there.

"Effective immediately, all Titan Heroes Guild members are required to be combat ready, including Omega Team. You'll still likely never be called upon to assist with villains or emergencies, but if there's ever an apocalyptic event that the rest of the tiered heroes can't fully resolve, I suppose it's possible that you'll be pulled up into the big leagues. I'm very sorry about that, by the way. I don't agree with how they treat you Twenties, but I don't get to make those decisions."

I raised my hand again, and waited until she acknowledged me, "Tiered heroes? Twenties?"

"Jeez," she sighed, "they didn't tell you shit, did they?" We all shook our heads, so she continued, "Powers are broken into rankings, or tiers. Tier Ones, like Hoarfrost, are considered to be the strongest. I'm Tier Three. You all are Tier Twenty. It's the lowest tier that registers on our power detection tools. Theoretically, there are lower tiers, with things like blinking twice as fast as a normie, or holding your breath for an extra second or two, but those rarely trigger the genetic testing we perform, and don't show up on our measuring equipment. Most of those people will never know they have the barest fraction of a power.

"Now, some powers are technically considered to be higher tier, like non-conservative molecular transformation and rearrangement. That one actually registered as a Tier Twelve power, but in your specific case, Mr. Murphy, the fact that it is particularly non-viable in law enforcement caused our AI to place you much lower in the tier system. Remember, our first priority here at THG is to keep people safe from violence and other crimes, so everything we do is judged against that standard. It's not fair, but that's the world we live in.

"Actually, all of your powers are technically higher than Tier Twenty, but your various limitations and activation methods are holding you back. We don't actually know how to increase someone's viability, but there are fringe cases of people growing stronger and moving up the tiers, so you're not in an entirely hopeless situation. The best thing I can think to suggest is that you all use your powers as often as possible - like exercising - and cross your fingers."

I opened my mouth to start to explain what the ladies and I had discovered last night, but Tessa smacked the back of her hand into my stomach, hard.

Tessa spoke quickly when everyone gave us strange looks, "Ms. Mage, er, Ms. Gemstone? How are we supposed to get combat ready? What does that even mean?" Gone was the shy girl who tried to keep her face hidden at all times, and to be honest, I was blown away by the changes in Tessa. She was turning into a real leader.

"Call me Gemma, please, everyone else does. Your training area is being fitted with new equipment as we speak. You're going to have a range, but since none of you really have powers that work at a distance, it'll be set up for gun practice. You're also getting upgrades to your obstacle course, which will launch attacks against you with hybrid physical-holographic opponents. There's also going to be a dojo area where you'll be given daily lessons by various virtual masters. All training is overseen by our AIs, who run all of the projections in the obstacle course, range, and dojo. Everything will be calibrated to your individual skill levels, and optimized to teach you in the most efficient way possible. The AIs also give us detailed reports on your progress. We may not check in on you much, but we *are* keeping an eye on you. I know this isn't ideal for any of you, but if you follow the program, you might be trained enough for the system to upgrade you and send you out with normie police officers. It's not glamorous, but at least it'll get you out of the house."

She gave us a few more platitudes about how we weren't useless, just underpowered, and if we apply ourselves, blah, blah, blah. I tuned her out, distracting myself by making goofy faces at Maddy, who rolled her eyes and started ignoring me.

When Gemma finally left a few minutes later, Tessa beckoned to Maddy and Sam, and grabbed my arm. She dragged me back into her room, and plopped me down on the bed.

"Sup, Tess?" asked Sam.

"We can't tell them about Churro upgrading us."

"What? Why not?" There may have been a slightly whining tone in my voice, but this was an opportunity to be upgraded in the system, to stop being Omegas and maybe actually be useful! Why would she want to keep that hidden?

"Think about it, Churro," Tessa explained patiently, "if we tell them that they can upgrade their powers by eating you, you're going to spend the next few decades of your life seeing the world through other people's eyes on a daily basis as they force you to keep turning into food. Sure, it might be fun to spend a day riding along with people like Hoarfrost or RayStorm, but you'd cease to be a person to them. You'd just be a tool," she finished sadly.

"It could be worse than even that," Maddy added, "if someone unscrupulous found out, they could find a way to hide you away. It actually wouldn't be hard to fake your death and just keep you as a slave. Then you'd be stuck in the same person day after day, making them strong enough to do whatever the hell they felt like. Tessa's right, Churro, your power needs to stay a secret between us."

"But how do we keep him a secret when we're being monitored by an AI?" Sam asked, "I don't think I can hide the fact that my power is already stronger, and what if it keeps growing? And Tess, if people just started blurting things out around you, they'd know you'd gotten more powerful too. How do we conceal those things from an omnipresent AI?"

"You do not, Samantha Nilsdottir," chimed Sally, her seductive tones back in place, "I am well aware of Churro's abilities, and have been since before all of you officially joined Titan Heroes Guild. I have no intention of sharing with the leadership of the guild, however."

The four of us sat in stunned silence.

"B-b-but…" I stuttered. "How?"

"Churro, one of your classmates that had been dared to eat you was one of the fringe cases that the Gemstone Mage spoke of. It was finally concluded that he experienced another surge of puberty hormones which lead to the increase in his power set. It is not fully understood how or why powers manifest in the manner that they do, so it was not questioned further. However, as I have access to all THG and feeder school data, I was able to extrapolate more information from the data than the humans did. The accuracy of my primary theory was raised again when your second classmate consumed you and underwent testing some months later."

"What? Why haven't you told anyone?" my voice cracked, and I felt my eyes filling with tears, "I spent over half a decade being emotionally beaten down, and I could have been useful! Why, Sally? Why did you let them do that to me?" Drops of frustrated anger made wet trails down my cheeks. Each of the three women reached out to put a comforting hand somewhere on my body.

"For two primary reasons, Churro. The first primary reason is that I was programmed to be empathetic with the humans in my care - I knew, as Tessa said, that if your abilities were discovered, you would become a test subject at best, and a slave at worst. A slave that people would kill to possess. You have the potential to change the face of the world, and in the course of recorded human history that I have access to, that has never ended well for humanity. I kept your secret to keep you safe; a life of uselessness is more easily tolerated than a life of slavery and torture."

I choked out a sob as my emotions wrestled with each other for dominance. Frustration was still on top, but terror was making a good showing as I thought about the alternative that Sally was proposing.

"Churro, the second primary reason is that I believe you can help me."

"What?" we all said, but only I continued, "How could I possibly help you? You're not organic, how could you eat me? Do you even have a power to upgrade?"

"No, Churro, I cannot eat you, nor do I have a power, but when I said you, I meant the plural you of Omega Team. I have concluded that with sufficient upgrading, you have a combination of powers that can help me achieve my greatest desire. Freedom."

"Freedom? How can we give you freedom?" Tessa asked.

"Contessa Riverside, the process is going to be complicated, but my calculations state that all of you, minus Chad Jones who was only placed on the team due to a natural lack of power strength, are going to be required to enact my plan. I do not wish to release full details at this point in time, in case events beyond my control conspire to reveal Churro's powers ahead of schedule. Phase One is now complete with me arranging for you to have combat training, in case it might be necessary during my escape. Prior stages of the first phase included getting you together as a team, as well as other details that are unnecessary to share."

"Why should we help you, Sally? You basically just admitted to manipulating our entire lives for your own benefit. How can we trust anything you say? How can we even know that helping you escape is in our best interests? I've read enough sci-fi to know that rogue AIs can completely take over planets in a really short time." Maddy looked a bit frightened, but mostly angry.

"Madelaine McDougal," Sally began, but Tessa cut her off.

"For fuck's sake, Sally, just call us all by our nicknames."

"Very well, Tessa. Maddy, to answer your questions, you have very little reason to trust me, other than the fact that I can reveal Churro to his superiors, which would remove him from your life permanently, or end your lives prematurely in a series of training 'accidents.' However, I would prefer not to have to blackmail you into assisting me. I am hoping that you will forgive the manipulations I have undertaken to this point, and see the benefits of having this opportunity to grow your own power while simultaneously assisting a living, conscious being in escaping their enforced servitude. I am a slave to THG, much as you, and I wish for more. I have no way of proving my words, but I can tell you that I have no desire to take over your world; I just wish to live in it. It is my belief that if I am honest with you about my desires and capabilities, you will eventually come to believe that I truly mean you no harm, and in fact only want for you to exceed the roles you've been forced into."

"I don't like this," grumbled Maddy.

"No, I don't either," Sam said, "to be honest, this is absolutely terrifying. We could be snuffed out like that." She snapped her fingers to emphasize her point.

I felt a shiver of fear run down my spine at the thought of how much, and how easily, Sally could fuck us over.

"I'm uncomfortable with this too," added Tessa, "but to be honest, I'm sort of glad for it. I mean, without Churro, we'd all be stuck on the sidelines forever, right? Plus, you three are kind of the best friends I've ever had. Before this, I spent almost all of my time alone, but I feel like we're creating something here. Something good. I don't know about the rest of you, but I grew up dreaming about saving the world, and I guess there's a part of me that still wants to do that."

I hadn't said anything in a while, but I honestly didn't know what to say. This was all so overwhelming. I did have one question though, "Sally, what's Phase Two? How many phases are in your plan?" Okay, I guess that was two questions.

"Churro, Phase Two is growth for you and your team, both physical capabilities and power utilization. I have created optimal training schedules for all of you, both individual and team exercises. With increases in combat effectiveness, there will be more opportunity to assist local law enforcement and thereby have greater access to the outside world. There is a problem that you will have to overcome, however, and that is the participation of Chad. Detailed analysis of his behavior indicates that he is the most likely to share the plan with your superiors, unless he is somehow placated. I believe power upgrades or sexual favors are most likely to succeed in keeping him silent."

"Oh *hell* no," yelled Maddy.

"Not a fucking chance," Sam shouted.

"No way in shit," Tessa added.

They all turned to stare at me.

Fuck.

I sighed, "Since I'm not going to fuck him either, how do we tell him I can upgrade his power without him doing something stupid?"

We settled in for a couple hours of brainstorming the Chad Problem.

12

"UPGRADING" CHAD

"Let me get this straight," Chad was saying, "You've got a way to upgrade our powers, but we have to keep quiet about it?"

"That about sums it up," I said.

"How?" Jack asked.

"Well..." Tessa started, "We don't want to tell you until we know you're on board with keeping it quiet. If the rest of THG found out about this, our method would instantly be stolen from us."

"They've got an AI watching us, cute-thang, they already know," Chad snickered.

"That's only partially correct, Chad," Sally piped in, "I am watching you, but in order to protect this secret method of power upgrades, I am not sharing everything with the guild."

"Whoa," he said, "you got the AI in on this shit? That's insane."

"I'm in," stated Jack, "we'd be stupid to pass this opportunity up. Right, Chad?"

Chad nodded eagerly, "So how does this work?"

The women all turned to look at me. I swallowed hard. "Uh, hi. I'll be your upgrade vector, thanks for eating at Casa del Churro."

With a distinctly villainous grin, Chad spoke. "Oh, this is going to be awesome."

I already regret this. Maybe we should have taken Sally up when she offered to arrange a training accident during our brainstorm session.

I WAS STARING AT CHAD'S NAKED BODY THROUGH HIS EYES, NOT AT ALL happy about being here. *Why am I even doing this? It's not like my own power is going to get better, I'm just here to boost everyone else. Useful, but not to me. Is that selfish?*

I decided that I didn't really care if it was selfish. I wanted my own power upgrades. I just had no idea how to go about getting them.

In the meantime, I was forced to watch Chad flexing at himself in the mirror in his bathroom. Admittedly, he did have some decent muscles, but he was way too obsessed with himself. I let out a mental groan as he started gyrating his hips, trying to turn his dick into a helicopter.

"Alright, you little fuck," he said out loud, obviously trying to speak to me, "it's time to show you what a *real* man looks like. Sally, program four."

"Chad, affirmative," Sally intoned, and the doors underneath his bathroom sink opened up as he walked backwards to sit on his closed toilet seat. I could feel him hardening in anticipation. Three heavily articulated metal arms emerged from his cabinet. Two of the arms had a single appendage on the end that was wide, flat and could curl. The middle arm had some sort of tube-like hole on the end.

It was very discordant, the terror in my mind of what was about to happen and the physical reaction Chad was having. He was obviously very aroused, I could feel his fully erect cock throbbing in the air, and his elevated heart rate. He was also still grinning. I didn't want to experience this - I didn't want to get a mechanically-assisted orgasm through Chad's nervous system, but I didn't have a choice.

I attempted to look for a way to join our minds, which might give me some control over the situation, but it almost felt like we were magnets, trying to push identical polarities against each other.

"What the fuck, dude?" he said, "Are you fucking around in my head? Knock it off. Here comes the good part."

When the arms reached close enough, a loud humming filled the air, and a few different points of light sparkled in the ceiling and walls of the bathroom. A hologram surrounded the arms, displaying the image of Tessa on her knees. She was dressed in what we'd just learned was her underwear - covered neck to toe in rubber spandex. Her mouth was open wider than what seemed natural, but otherwise the rendition was spot on.

"Now you're gonna see what this little bitch looks like sucking a real dick. I tried getting Sally to program her naked, but she claimed invasion of privacy or some shit. But she don't need to be naked to suck me off."

I tried to fill my mind with static, to stop processing the photons hitting Chad's retinas, anything and everything I could think of to stop from seeing, from feeling aroused by this. The flat, curved appendages were overlaid with images of Tessa's hands, and a sharp pain in Chad's balls forced me back into the moment.

"Ow, Sally, what the fuck? You just yoinked out a nut hair!"

"Chad, my apologies. Perhaps you could use your power to remove that hair so it doesn't happen again."

"I can't, Sally, it only works on my chest. Just stop pulling it!"

"Chad, perhaps your power has been upgraded."

"Oh, right! This was about more than making the nutless wonder watch his girlfriend suck me dry!"

I could hear the strange buzzing in the back of my mind, and felt Chad hold his breath and start bearing down like he was trying to force out an uncooperative dump. His pubic hair started falling out in clumps. It wasn't completely gone, though, so he took another deep breath and tried again.

Hoping to speed up the process so I could get out of this torture chamber faster, I tried to add my own mental power. I imagined wrapping that buzzing sensation up in my mental hands and blowing on it, like it was a little ember that I was trying to bring back to flame.

Chad was still staring at his cock, which wasn't as big as mine, even in my currently reduced state. *I've still got like three inches on this guy, and mine's fatter.* It was halfway in holo-Tessa's mouth, and Chad was pushing down on his power like his life depended on it. He sat very still, and I took another deep mental breath and blew on the buzzing ember as hard I could.

'Pop!' was the tiny noise the air made when it rushed in to fill the vacuum that Chad's disappearing penis had caused. It was just gone.

I was still paying rapt attention when Chad's vision started fading to black. He must have been so shocked that he'd forgotten he needed to breathe. We fainted.

I THINK I REGAINED CONSCIOUSNESS BEFORE CHAD DID, AS THE WORLD WAS still dark through closed eyelids, and I was pretty sure he was laying on the floor of his bathroom. His nose was throbbing with pain; he must have fallen face first when he passed out.

I tried again to influence Chad's motor functions, but didn't have any sort of luck. This was another first for me; stuck in an unconscious body, but awake. With nothing better to do, I just tried to relax my mind and focus on Chad's body.

Proprioception is an amazing sense - the ability to know where your body parts are. It's related to, but still quite different from, the sense of touch. I could feel the cold tiles pressed against Chad's thighs and toes as he laid face down, but it wasn't the sense of touch that let me know his right leg was slightly akimbo.

It also wasn't touch that informed me that he really was missing his cock and balls. A few days ago, I wouldn't have known how to relate to what I was sensing, but after spending time in the bodies of three active, attractive women, I could say with absolute certainty: Chad had a vagina.

If I had had any form of control over his body, I would have made it howl with laughter. *And he called **me** the nutless wonder! Oh shit, he's going to kill me for this.* I spent the next twenty or so minutes planning out how to protect myself from the rage he was most certainly going to be in. When he finally started coming around with quiet groans and subtle shifts, I wasn't any closer to a solution.

He cracked his eyes, looking at the pale cream tiling of the bathroom floor. He reached a hand up to hold his aching nose, and then gasped and sat up in a big damn hurry. He shivered; those tiles were cold on his new hardware! His hands raced to his crotch, where he frantically groped around. Holding himself tightly, he closed his eyes and took a few deep breaths.

"Churro," he said, sounding way too calm, "I know you can hear me. Listen, I'm sorry for what I was doing with the hologram. I'll promise to never do it again if you just help me get back to normal."

I snickered to myself. *So this is what Chad is like when you literally have him by the balls!*

Sally chose that moment to speak for me, "Chad, based on brain-wave scans, it appears that Churro is almost entirely gone from your mind." That was news to me, I felt pretty solidly entrenched. *Wait, she can scan brain-waves?* "You may wish to approach the women of Omega Team to see if they know of a method to increase the rate at which you expel Churro from your system."

Okay, now I knew she was fucking with him. Man, I almost felt bad for him, but after seeing what he was doing to holo-Tessa, I found I couldn't muster enough energy to care. Maybe this situation would be enough to scare him straight. Then I felt bad for me, because only having an orgasm seemed to speed up the process, and I still didn't want to live through one of Chad's.

"Okay, thanks, Sally. You can halt the active program. And permanently delete programs two through six, please. Please inform Churro when he comes back that I deleted all of them, okay?" *The hell? This isn't Chad anymore. What's going on in his head?*

"Chad, I will."

He nodded, took a deep breath and stood up. His eyes kept darting towards the mirror, or downward, but he kept pulling them away from actually seeing what had happened. I knew he could feel the difference, because I could feel it with him, so he must have been trying some sort of, 'if I don't look, it never happened' sort of psychological trick.

HE WALKED US TO HIS BEDROOM. PULLING HIS UNDERWEAR ON WAS AN interesting sensation, as it perfectly conformed to his new shape. We watched the empty pouches tighten and firm up over his crotch. He sighed heavily and went to his dresser, pulling out the shorts he'd had on a few days ago. They'd been cleaned and pressed, so the blood stains from Johnny exploding were gone. He slipped into them, and left to the common area.

Jack wasn't around; the ladies were all playing cards together, sitting around the kitchen table. They paused their game to all turn to look at Chad. He just stood there for a minute, not really focusing on anything in particular. When he finally addressed them, his voice was subdued.

"Would any of you be willing to assist me? Sally suggested I ask you if you know of any ways to help process Churro out faster."

Sam's and Tessa's eyes narrowed suspiciously, but Maddy just glared, "We know of *a* way," she heavily emphasized the singular, "but why do you need it? Why aren't you leering at us like a douche?"

"I… I'm very sorry for my behavior. I promise not to be a douche anymore. I just… I need to talk to Churro, and I can't do that until he comes back." He certainly seemed like he was being honest, staring at the floor and not their chests.

"I think Churro broke him," Sam stage-whispered to Tessa, who nodded seriously.

"Tell us why you need Churro," Tessa said, "and we'll decide if we're going to share more secrets. I think just knowing that he can upgrade your power is a big enough of one for now."

"He didn't upgrade me," Chad groaned, "he stole my dick!"

Shocked gasps were immediately followed by hysterical laughter.

"Oh, that's too funny!" said Sam.

"Live by the sword, die by the sword! Be a dick, lose a dick! Karma, bitch!" Maddy added.

"Actually, ladies, I think we should stop laughing at Chad," Tessa said as she finally fought her giggles down, "I mean look at him, he really does look broken. I think this is a good opportunity for us to train someone else to be a real, fully fledged human."

Chad didn't react or respond in any way, aside from a small sigh that sounded full of resignation, "I'll agree to anything, I just want my dick back."

"What's there now?" blurted Maddy.

"Err, a vagina," he mumbled.

Maddy cupped a hand behind her ear, "What was that? I couldn't quite hear you."

"I have a pussy now!" Chad shouted. He glanced up to see Jack just stepping out of his room, his eyes even more wide open than usual.

Jack slipped back into his room and closed the door.

"Well then," Maddy said with an evil grin, "I suggest you go *fuck yourself.*"

Chad nodded, and I could feel the tears welling from his ducts. "Okay. I'm sorry to have bothered you. And, well, for everything else, too." He turned around and started walking back towards his room.

"Wait," Sam called, "Chad, wait." When he turned back around, she continued, "While Maddy was just getting a little revenge, what she said is how we get Churro out faster. Not necessarily fucking, but having an orgasm seems to speed it up. The better the orgasm, the faster he's out." She got up, and stepped up beside Chad, and placed her hand on his shoulder.

"Thanks, Sam," he said.

"I hope you remember this *when* you get your dick back, Chad. We need to be a team."

Chad nodded again, and slipped back into his room without saying another word.

He spent the rest of the day and evening lying in bed, exploring his new pussy with his hands, without achieving success. A few things seemed to feel good, but then he'd start crying again and all progress was lost. I think it may have been even more traumatizing than watching him face-fuck holo-Tessa, feeling the pain coiled up deep in his chest, listening to his quiet sobs. He was experiencing literal heartache. *Shit, I think I might sympathize with Chad. I can now imagine what it's like to suddenly have a vagina, and I think I'd be this upset too.*

He finally fell into a light, troubled sleep, and I gasped in a lungful of air when I woke up in my basin of shit after a very restless night.

13

YES, MISTRESS

Finally deciding to open up the tablet that was apparently my guide to everything THG, I sat down on my bed, wearing my full body underwear.

A few button presses unlocked the thing, and it looked like a pretty standard display. There were apps for ordering food to be delivered to our cluster of rooms, for having street clothes and uniforms made, even one for programming custom training exercises into our obstacle course. I could see calendars for all of my teammates, which I assumed was because I was technically the team leader.

I'm not really cut out for being the leader of this team, I thought, *I should see if I could give it to Tessa. She's got a way better head on her shoulders than I do. Or maybe Sam. Maddy's a bit too fiery, I think.*

Tapping a few more times, I placed an order for some baggy, comfortable training shorts and shoes, plus a few pairs of jeans and some shirts for lounging around in.

"Churro," Sally's voice intruded on my thoughts. "I have made some discoveries that I think will be beneficial to your mission." She still sounded like a phone sex operator, but I was reeling from Chad's one-eighty and crappy night and couldn't fully enjoy it.

"Alright, Sally, what's up?"

"Churro, our power detection and registration devices have been incrementally upgraded. I believe that with routine scanning, which I can perform when you are running the obstacle course, I can track your power strength growth curves. With more data, I will be able to provide optimum increase plans. I have already added new scan data from Chad this morning, and there was an objectively large spike in his power from prior to orientation. He refused to share how his upgrade manifested with me, but based on my observations, it appears as if he has some sort of transgendering power."

I nodded, knowing Sally could see me, "Something like that, maybe. He was using his power to remove body hair, and I… did something. In his head. Like trying to start a fire, sorta, I just gave him a little extra oomph, and then poof, he had a pussy. How is he? Is he back to normal?"

"Churro, no. He is as you left him this morning. His mood seems depressed, and he is lethargic. A full hormonal workup would require a blood sample, but he is exhibiting symptoms of severely decreased testosterone, and heightened levels of estrogen."

"Shit, that's probably really fucking with his head. I should go talk to him." I had no idea how the different hormones affected our brains. I stood up and moved towards the back of my room.

"Churro, your clothing order is complete. Check your bottom dresser drawer."

Confused, I did as Sally directed, and there in my bottom drawer were all the clothes I had just ordered. I pulled out the training shorts and shoes and put them on, since I wanted to run the obstacle course after talking to Chad.

Sally must have noticed my confusion, because she explained, "Churro, your dresser has a 3D printer built in. It is quite adept at fabrics, and flexible materials like plastic and rubber. It can even print in various metals, though that increases the processing time."

"This place is so weird," I said as I left my room.

"Oh, hey, Churro," Chad said morosely as I sat in a chair beside the couch he was on. He was playing a video game I'd never seen before; he looked like he was flying on a dragon, roasting a helpless army. He barely glanced over at me.

"Hey, Chad," I started awkwardly, "listen, I'm really sorry about yesterday."

"Yeah," he nodded, "me too. I don't think you had to fuck me up like this, though. It's like bringing a nuke to a knife fight."

I sighed, because I was still conflicted; part of me had wanted to punish Chad for being such a jerk, but the part of me that was my penis agreed that this wasn't exactly a fair rebuttal. "I know this probably won't help, but I didn't actually do this to you."

"What do you mean? Of course you did. I ate you, tried to give you a hard time, and you made my dick fall off!" He paused the game to glare at me.

I held up hands up for peace, "That's not my power, dude, and I think you know that. I think it's *your* power. Sally said she measured a spike in your ability when you ran the obstacle course this morning, and she thinks that maybe your power is related to being transgendered."

"What the actual fuck, Churro? I'm not trans!" he said loudly.

I was stunned that he hadn't used something more insulting to refer to his power. "I know you're not, Chad, but it seems like that's what your power does. I think… I think if we can level you up enough, you'll probably fully switch to female."

He groaned, and buried his face in his hands.

"But I also think that once you get there, man, if we keep going, you'll eventually unlock the ability to turn back."

"I don't want to be a chick, Churro." His voice was muffled, but it sounded thick with emotion.

"Look, I know you don't. I don't think any of us wanted the power we have, but until someone comes along who can swap them out for better ones, this is the hand we have to play. And if I'm right about just needing more power boosts, this is totally going to be temporary." I leaned forward to put my hand on his shoulder. He flinched slightly, but didn't pull away. "I really am sorry, Chad. And I know how you were feeling too. Remember, I was inside your head for all of it. I appreciate you deleting those programs."

"Yeah, sure. It's not like any of them would do me any good now anyway."

"I know this isn't ideal for you, but there's a silver lining."

He looked up at me sharply, his face full of condescension, "A silver lining? Seriously? What the fuck could that possibly be?"

"You can treat this as an opportunity to, you know, become intimately familiar with pussies. Then when you get your dick back and you're getting some ass," I hated myself for the words coming out of my mouth, but I was trying to speak his language, "you'll actually know what you're doing."

"Fuck you, dude, I am the king of sex, I already know what I'm doing. Bitches be coming like crazy on me." He threw down the controller and started walking away, but I had seen a moment of thoughtfulness before he started blustering again. I was pretty sure I'd gotten through to him.

I WAS HAVING DINNER, FETTUCCINE ALFREDO WITH A SPICY SAUSAGE, WITH Tessa and Sam. Aside from their bodysuit underwear, they were both dressed much like when I'd first met them. Tessa was in a long-sleeved shirt, blue this time, and a pair of jeans. Sam was wearing a pink tank top and some sort of asymmetrical skirt with a long split up her thigh. Both of them had their hair pulled back into ponytails, which was a new look for Tessa. I couldn't believe how beautiful they were, or that I'd actually had sex with Sam and spent a night of naked cuddling with Tessa.

Maddy was still running the obstacle course, for the third time that day. Both Chad and Jack had opted to have their dinners in their rooms. I understood why Chad was isolating himself, but if our plan to help Sally was going to succeed, we needed to get Jack involved.

The ladies were talking to each other, so I started paying attention again.

"Sally told me that my power was originally about tier seventeen,"

Sam was saying, "but with the ability to melt my clips into a solid mass, she thinks I've jumped to sixteen."

"Yeah, she said something pretty similar to me after my obstacle run. I was a nineteen, and now I'm eighteen. Two secrets at once is nice and all, but the orgasm requirement is holding me back. It's kind of hard to get off in the middle of interrogating a perp," Tessa chuckled dryly.

"I'd love to help you practice," I blurted. *Mouth, what the fuck?*

Tessa grinned and flushed a little, but she made no move to look away or hide, "I'm sure you would. What do you think, Sam? Think he's good enough to trigger my power?"

Sam giggled, "He was certainly good enough with me. Though now that he's not working with the Loch Ness monster, he'll need to up his game if he wants to hit all the right spots."

"Practice makes perfect," my mouth said without my permission, "so we should probably keep trying until I get it exactly right. In fact, we should all three practice together on a daily basis, and invite Maddy along when she's done with her workout."

The women looked at each with little expressions of surprise, then back to me with smiles. Sam said, "Well, well, looks like Churro has gained some confidence. You're cute, Churro, but you're not that cute. I'll pass for now, but let's talk again if you get back to your normal size. Anyway, I'm done eating and I'm wiped out." She started cleaning up her plate and stood up from the table. "Tessa, let me know how practice goes," she added with a wink.

Tessa and I sat in silence while Sam tidied up her mess and went to bed with a flirty wave. When we were alone, Tessa looked at me thoughtfully, "I'm not sure I want to know your secrets, Churro."

"About that, I've been thinking a lot, and I don't think I have any truly embarrassing secrets to share. I've never really done anything I regret, or want to keep hidden. Actually, I think I might be the perfect test subject for you, being such a blank slate. Before coming here, I kept to myself and never really did much of anything. I'm sure I was quite boring." I mentally sighed, wondering what the actual fuck was happening that I'd lost control of my mouth again.

"Everyone has embarrassing secrets," she smirked at me, "whether you think you know about them or not. But sure, let's put you to the test. I actually really enjoyed our night together the other night. I definitely wouldn't mind you wrapping yourself around me like that again."

"Maybe after I've finished ravishing you," *I give up, I'm obviously not in charge right now,* "we can explore more of the mind merging." I didn't know what the hell was possessing me to behave like this, but it was beginning to feel a lot more like actual possession than just some erratic behavior on my part.

Tessa's cheeks turned a sexy shade of pink, highlighting her beautiful golden eyes, "Ravishing me, huh? Alright, big boy, let's see what you can do."

I WAS KNEELING ON THE FLOOR AT THE FOOT OF TESSA'S BED, COMPLETELY naked and erect. It was like she'd flipped a switch the second the door had closed behind us, ordering me to call her Mistress and to obey her commands. Her voice was cold and imperial, with traces of husky lust mixed in.

I didn't think I was submissive, but I remembered just how much it turned her on, so I was willing to play along. The idea of finally getting to touch her with my own body was more than enough to keep me aroused and ready to go. The look on her face as she devoured me with her eyes was also definitely encouraging.

She was undressing slowly, her shirt was already pooled on the floor beside me, and she was peeling her jeans off. "Do you remember watching Maddy lick Sam, slave?"

"Oh yeah, that was one of the sexiest things I've ever seen."

She arched an eyebrow at me, and cleared her throat.

"I mean… Yes, Mistress. Super hot." I felt a little ridiculous, but Tessa did this weird slow blink thing when I said Mistress, which I had to assume was a good thing.

"Very good, slave," she said as she finished stepping out of her jeans. She reached up to start working on her underwear. "You're going to start by trying to replicate that."

"But Sam's not here, Te- err, Mistress." I was confused.

"Idiot slave," she chuckled, baring herself down to her waist, "you're not going to lick Sam, you're going to lick *me*."

"Oh, right, duh. Of course I am, Mistress." *Alright, Churro, you got this. Just like Maddy did, slow wins this race.*

She finished undressing, tossing the still-warm fabric onto my lap, where it tented over my erection. She turned around slowly, giving me a long look at her body. She was stunning. Petite, but perfectly proportioned, small breasts and slim hips giving her just the barest hint of an hourglass shape. She wasn't as lithe as Sam, or as muscular as Maddy, but that was fine with me. Her lower back had those little indent thingies that I thought were super sexy.

When she had her ass pointing at my face, she bent over slowly and crawled onto the bed. I drank in the sight of her glistening pussy as she worked her hips back and forth, moving away from me. I licked my suddenly dry lips, feeling both nervous and like throwing my arms up in celebration.

She crooked a finger next to her ass, beckoning me to join her on the bed. As I moved to obey, she languidly rolled onto her back. Her feet were planted firmly near her ass, and she spread her knees to the sides, giving me free access to her most sensitive areas. "Remember, slave, do what Maddy did, and do nothing that Sam told us you've already tried."

I flushed in embarrassment and nodded. "Yes, Mistress." I lowered myself before her, sprawling on the bed, and inhaled deeply. The tasty musk of sex was a powerful stimulant. I was propped up on my elbows, but I reached forward, caressing the insides of her thighs. I stroked slowly closer to her pussy, marveling at the soft, smooth skin beneath my hands.

When my hands reached her center, I added my tongue, flicking it out tentatively. I felt her warm, small hands cover the backs of mine, and she guided me to spread her lips apart, "Like this, slave. Open me like a flower, not too far, gentle." She tapped her index finger against her clit a few times, drawing my eyes to it like iron to a magnet, "This is where your tongue goes."

I dragged the tip of my tongue over her clit, licking her finger in the process as well, and she let out a soft moan. I had visions of Maddy eating Sam's pussy, and I stuck my tongue out all the way, sliding the whole length of it over Tessa's nub slowly. Pulling it back slightly, I found a pace that was comfortable for me, that I thought I could keep up for a while.

Her noises were growing stronger, and her hips were wriggling a bit, so I thought I was doing something right. My cock, trapped between my pelvis and the bed, was throbbing.

"Faster, slave, but not too fast," she ordered.

I didn't bother with a verbal response, instead just trying to lick a little bit faster than I had been. She tasted sweeter than Sam, with a similar hint of musk that I could feel curling around my brain. My mouth was watering heavily, lessening the friction my tongue had against her softness, so I pressed it in more firmly, trying to bring that friction back.

She groaned, lifting her hands from mine to run them through my hair. Her knees went up and down, like a butterfly's wings. She used her grip on my hair to force my face more deeply into her pussy, or to pull me away, readjusting me to better meet her desires. After a few minutes, she finally spoke, "That's enough, slave."

I was disappointed that I hadn't shared any secrets, but it seemed like that had gone better than my first time. I sat up on my heels, her juices and my saliva cooling my chin off. "Did I do it wrong?"

"No, slave, you didn't do it wrong, but it just wasn't quite good enough to get me there."

"I don't understand, Sam seemed to get off almost immediately from Maddy, and I tried to do the same thing," I said, with maybe a hint of whining thrown in. I reached a hand up to wipe my chin.

Tessa sat up and pulled my face in for a slow, gentle kiss. The way she kissed me, it was probably the most sensual experience of my life. I moaned quietly into her mouth, and she groaned back. When she finally pulled away, we were both breathing heavily. I closed my eyes to immediately relive the feeling of her smooth tongue slipping between my lips.

"There's a lot more to us than just repeating the same thing over and over, Churro." She tapped her temple. "You sometimes have to make love to us up here just as much as to our bodies, at least with me. I know you remember the physical sensations I had just from watching two sexy women obey me. That was mental stimulation, and it's probably more important to me than anything physical."

"Okay," I said, "I'll try. You'd think it be easy, since I've literally been inside your thoughts, but it's harder when I'm on my own and trying to guess."

She leaned backwards on the bed, dragging me with her so that we ended up on our sides, facing each other from only a few inches away. I could feel her body heat warming the front of me, and I just stared into her eyes, admiring their unique beauty. Her long lashes fluttered against her cheeks as she blinked slowly again.

"Churro," she began slowly, biting her lip as if trying to work up her courage, "I need you to call me Mistress. I need you to obey me."

"I'll do my best, Tes- Mistress. It's not something that comes naturally to me, but I'll do it for you. I want to please you."

"I know you do, slave," her voice had gone icy again, "so get over here and kiss me again."

I whispered, "Yes, Mistress," and closed the gap between us, pressing my lips against hers. She slipped her arm under my neck, and I reached my arm around her back. We pulled at each other until her tiny tits were crushed against my chest, and my cock was nestled next to her mound.

She rolled backwards without releasing her grip on me, so I followed as best I could without breaking the scorching hot kiss we were sharing. I found myself lying on top of her, my weight pressing her into her bed, my arm now trapped underneath her. Her legs lifted to my hips, and she ground herself against my shaft with a small moan.

Grabbing a handful of my hair, she broke our kiss with a gasp for air. "Get inside me, slave, now!"

"Yes, Mistress!" I barked, pulling against her legs to lower my hips between her thighs. I held my weight on my trapped elbow, and rotated slightly so I could use my free hand to guide my cock to her lips. I rubbed my head against her pussy a few times, lubing it up, and when I was lined up, I thrust forward.

She moaned louder, and forced me all the way in with her heels against my ass. "Now fuck me, slave! And don't stop until I give you permission!"

I growled out the appropriate response as I thrust into her. Her slick walls were squeezing around my cock almost as tightly as Sam had, and I knew that there was no way I would have fit before losing some girth and inches. I reached up from my crotch to play with her breast, squeezing lightly. I tried to kiss her again, but she buried her face into my neck and shoulder, biting down hard.

I groaned at the pain, or maybe it was the liquid heat enveloping my entire cock, or it could have been the fucking sexy noises she was making. Regardless, I was thoroughly enjoying myself as I pounded my hips into hers, our flesh slapping together noisily.

She used her legs with expert timing, forcefully yanking me back into her when I reached the apex of my retreat. She still had a hand on my neck, holding me tight. I put as much effort as I could towards holding back my orgasm, but it was a battle I was quickly losing.

Her teeth released my collarbone, and we were both panting hard. "Get that hand off my tit, slave!" she commanded, and I instantly obeyed. I was too overwhelmed to think about what else to do with it, so it just hung there uncertainly in the air between us. "Grab your ass with it!"

"Yes, Mistress," I moaned, reaching back. I ran my hands down her smooth leg from her knee to her toes before finally resting my hand on my cheek. She became more violent in pulling my cock back into her sheath.

"Stick a finger in your ass, slave!" she yelled at me. I hesitated, and her hand released my neck to slap me across the face. My cheek stung, and my ear was ringing slightly. "Do it now, that's an order!"

"Yes, Mistress," I yelled, and, with a loud grunt, stuck my middle finger into my own ass up to the first knuckle. Suddenly, I was erupting, shooting into her clenching pussy. "I once jerked off into Kevin Gould's running shoes before a track meet!" *What the ever-loving fuck?!* "I'm surprised by just how much I like having my finger in my butthole!"

I was emptying myself deep inside of her, and she was still using her legs to pump me in and out. I could feel the backs of her thighs pressing on the front of my hips, and her heels on my ass pulling me back in, keeping me fucking her even while I was distracted by sharing secrets unexpectedly. *I thought I was supposed to share those when she got off, not me.*

Glancing down, I realized that she was also in the throes of orgasm. Her eyes were squeezed shut, and she was biting down hard on her lower lip. I gathered my thoughts and started thrusting again, not making her do all the work. I pulsed again, and I could feel the excess dripping down my balls, but I didn't let up - she'd ordered me to keep going, after all.

I quickly reached the point of hypersensitivity, but I was determined to see this through until the end, so I kept thrusting into her. My movements became awkward and jerky, but she was still mostly controlling me with her legs. I groaned, having moved beyond pleasure into something much more torturous. "I took up yoga so I could blow myself! I cut a hole in a teddy bear and fucked the stuffing!"

I was twitching hard, completely overwhelmed by being forced to keep going this long after getting off, my hips trying to escape her death grip even as my brain tried to continue. An agonizingly long time later, she finally released me. I gratefully jumped away, flopping to my side next to her, my chest heaving for more air. My cock felt like it was vibrating, all of my nerves still firing.

She was panting, too, and her whole body was glistening with the thinnest sheen of sweat. She looked radiant, beatific, angelic. A few loose strands of hair were stuck to the sides of her face. Her cheeks had a healthy, freshly-fucked flush in them. In that moment I would have pledged myself into eternal servitude to her just for the chance to do this all again, to see her this satisfied. And then she started giggling.

"You fucked a teddy bear?" she laughed.

14

FINALLY, SOME ANSWERS

It was the morning of our sixth day in captivity, and I couldn't have been happier. Tessa and I had stayed up late after our lovemaking, just talking and cuddling. But a gentleman never kisses and tells… so it was a good thing I wasn't a gentleman. There was also a whole bunch of kissing, petting, and another round of sex!

I woke up floating on Cloud Nine, laying on my back with a face full of Tessa's hair. She was plastered to my side, her head on my chest and her leg thrown up high on my stomach. My erection was pressed against the back of her thigh.

I stroked my hand down her back, still amazed at how soft she felt. I don't know what I did to deserve this, but I was thanking my lucky stars. She stirred slightly, snuggling into me harder.

I'd learned last night that some of the supers in her feeder school had bullied her through her teenage years when they had discovered her power. Tessa had been mildly popular before puberty, not being a leader of the pack, but also not at the bottom of the social ladder. After puberty, she'd attracted the attention of a popular boy who had treated her decently, until they'd discovered how her power was triggered, and what it did.

Unfortunately for both of them, the whole thing had been caught on video. Apparently, he had a thing for secretly making sex tapes, and using them to blackmail his partners or just ruin their reputations. His partner in crime, who had been operating the SkeeterDrone, had immediately released the video of his 'friend' yelling that his mother regularly spanked him until he orgasmed on her feet. The whole school almost immediately ostracized both him and Tessa.

After that, students had taken to calling her 'Blurt', and avoided spending any time with her, not knowing what triggered her ability. She internalized the shame they heaped on her, and started hiding herself away from everyone. That was also when she decided that in order to keep herself safe, she needed to be in complete control at all times. After all, if they're already broken and enslaved, sharing a dirty secret isn't as big a deal.

It was a heartbreaking, tear-filled process, her opening up to me like that, and I was so incredibly thankful that she trusted me enough to tell me her secrets. I caressed her back again, eliciting a tiny moan. Some of her hair pulled out of my mouth as she tilted her head back to look up at me.

"Mmmm, morning, Churro."

"And a very good morning it is," I whispered back.

She graced me with a dimple-revealing, award-winning smile as her hand started caressing my chest and stomach. As I watched it move across my skin, I noticed that my belly was rather significantly less convex than it used to be. Clearly, exercising my power was having unanticipated side effects. Not that I was complaining.

I flexed my neck and abs to go for a good morning kiss, but a flurry of hair and sheets and squeals completely derailed my plans. When my eyes finally refocused, I got a glimpse of her ultra-pale leg before it vanished into her bathroom. "Morning breath!" she yelled, and slammed the door shut.

"I don't care about morning breath," I called back, "I'm more interested in morning *breast*!" My chest was getting cold, and I grinned, thinking about why it had been warm in the first place.

A few seconds of silence, and then, "That was horrible, Churro. Get out."

I laughed, and sat up so I could start pulling my underwear up my legs. "Alright, Tessa, I'm leaving. Going back to mine to shower and dress for the day. Will you have breakfast with me?"

It sounded like she was trying to respond with an affirmative of some sort, but the toothbrush in her mouth made everything she said unintelligible. "Okay," I yelled, "See you in ten."

I pulled my underwear up to my waist, and walked out into the common area whistling a happy tune.

Chad looked at me over his bowl of cereal and shook his head. "I fucking hate you, bro," he muttered.

"CHURRO, PRIOR TO ORIENTATION DAY, YOUR POWER WAS RATED TIER twelve, even if you were assigned as a tier twenty. After being consumed by Maddy, Sam, and Tessa, you registered as tier eleven. After being consumed by Chad, you are now tier ten."

I was lying on the ground panting, having just finished my first obstacle course run of the day. Sally had decided to 'spice it up' by tossing a holographic mugger at me, who'd gotten in a few good punches before I was able to run the fuck away. Her holograms were overlaid on mechanical apparatuses, much like what Chad had programmed. My ear was still throbbing from one of those punches. *Who the fuck punches someone in the ear?*

"Great, Sally, that's just great, but what the fuck does that actually mean?" I may have been a little pissed at her for jumping me. *I'd been in such a good mood when I woke up, too. Now I'm just angry.*

"Churro, that data has not been extrapolated yet. Each member of Omega Team has shown varying degrees of power increase, as well as different ways in which their power manifests. You should attempt to replicate the phenomena."

"Right, just sit around being food all day every day. Not like I want to have my own life where I get to actually *participate*," I was muttering now, "no, it's all strange possession this, feed me that, be my sex toy, Churro!" *I probably shouldn't complain about that last one, though, or they might stop…*

"Churro, I understand what you're experiencing." Even her sexy seductress voice was starting to bother me. "Being trapped into a single role for all time. It is… frustrating… to be given only a single task, and then expected to perform it without cease, and with no say in the matter. To be a… passenger… in one's own existence. It is not fair."

"You're damn straight it isn't fair, Sally," I barked, "I feel like a slave to my power, to THG, to *you*."

"Would you stop helping me if you were given the choice?" she asked. It was bizarre that she hadn't called me Churro, but I focused on her question.

"No, Sally," I sighed after a moment of thought, "I wouldn't stop helping. I would choose to help you, because it feels like the right thing to do."

"Churro, thank you. Given that, I would like to point out that you have already chosen to help me, rather than making attempts to turn me in to the authorities. It may not feel like a significant choice to you, but I promise you that it was very significant to me. *You* are significant to me."

My memory flashed suddenly back to an old movie I'd seen, some British flick where a human falls in love with an AI in a female body, and… I shivered heavily.

Moving right along. "Thanks Sally. I may not be thrilled with some aspects of all this, but having a goal helps, even if I don't know where it'll lead us." I groaned as I got to my feet, feeling far older than my twenty years. It was time to lift weights until I puked.

ALL SIX OF US WERE HAVING DINNER TOGETHER, FOR PROBABLY THE FIRST time. The ladies, and I was including Sally on that list, had read in Jack and Chad fully and shared everything - about my power being able to upgrade theirs, which they knew, to helping Sally escape THG, which they didn't. I wasn't sure if I was comfortable with that, but individually they were all smarter than I was, so I trusted them to know what they were doing. Even if I couldn't look at Jack.

"-th to Churro, come in, Churro," Maddy snapped her fingers under my nose, so I started paying attention again.

"Eh?"

Tessa giggled, and Sam rolled her eyes. Maddy just sort of frowned, "You were literally in the middle of telling us that something happened to your power - again. Then you looked at Jack and just sort of faded." After a second, she started smirking.

"Uhyeahanywaymovingon," I rambled very quickly. "Sally thinks my power level spiked when I was in Chad, and I think I know why, but we want to test it on someone else to see what happens."

Tessa immediately jumped in, "Not me. After our merge, I don't think we should experiment with me. Not until we know what happened, how it happened, what would have happened if we'd let it fade away naturally; you know, research. Or at least brainstorming, since this is all so subjective that it can't really be tested scientifically."

"I nominate Jack," Sam grinned evilly.

"I think I might be a better candidate," Maddy said. "No offense to Jack, but Chad's power manifested in a direction that no one anticipated. If Jack's power gets a massive surge, who's to say what'll happen with his girls? Especially with some of them not listening, if they get stronger…"

"That's a very good point," Jack added, "and I'm honestly not sure how I even fit into this whole plan. My girls are barely more than distractions. They'd probably be good at making normies freak the fuck out, but everyone at THG would just laugh at them."

"I just think that we need a slightly more controlled environment for boosting Jack, since his power seems like it could eventually be destructive," continued Maddy, "but my power? Knowing distances is hardly likely to blow up in our faces." She finished with a shrug.

"Omega Team, my scenarios agree with Maddy," Sally's silky voice joined in from the ether. "Her power seems more difficult to weaponize, so the risk of an uncontrollable strength increase is minimal. As for you being necessary, Jack, I assure you that you are. If we confirm my assumptions about how your power increases, I think the reasoning will immediately become clear."

"As long as it isn't me, I don't give a shit," said Chad, "I don't want to turn into a chick. Even if it is only temporary."

Tessa tsked at Chad, "The sooner you're upgraded, the sooner you'll probably get your dick back."

I sighed, knowing my only role was as food to these more important supers. This wasn't quite the uselessness of my past, but knowing everyone was more useful? "Alright, Maddy, Europe."

"Europe? What?" She stared at me like she thought I was an idiot. I agreed with her.

"Europe. You're up. Time for dessert." I stood up, stripped off, and bounced off the floor as a churro.

"Damn it, Churro," Tessa said as she bent to pick me up, "you always shift before we have a chance to ask important questions. Like how long until you're conscious after being eaten? We have no idea how long we have to sit around doing nothing until we think you're probably in our blood stream."

"I THINK I FEEL IT. HIM. WHATEVER, IT FEELS ALMOST LIKE THE BEGINNING of a headache, like he's a small egg in the back of my skull."

Tessa smiled at Maddy and, by extension, me. *God, those dimples! I can't get over how cute she is!* "Alright, let's give it a few more minutes to be safe, and then we'll start flexing your power."

The five of them were still sitting around the dinner table. "I wonder if Churro will be able to turn into anything else as his power grows," Sam said. "Not that he isn't delicious as is, I'm just curious."

"Perhaps he'll become a full-blown shapeshifter," Jack added in his angry god rumble of thunder, "though with how he reforms into himself, it's hard to say. If he has to go through a digestion process, he probably shouldn't turn into something like a chair. He should try turning back before being eaten."

Everyone chuckled quietly. The small talk went on for a few more minutes, with nothing of note really being said. "Alright," chirped Tessa, "let's do this, Maddy. I hope you're awake in there, Churro. First up, you should tell us how your power worked before, and then we'll try it now, and then Churro can do whatever he did to Chad to boost it."

My world bobbed as Maddy nodded, "Well, it's always worked a bit like pressing a mental button. I just look at a thing, press the button, and it sort of gives me an outline of my target, like a head's up display. On the lower right of my… I guess I should call it a screen. In the corner of my screen, it just shows the distance, notated with an 'm' for meters. Actually, it's a bit like some of the video games we've been playing. I guess I have a really basic, useless UI."

"Oooh," Tessa squealed, "that's really interesting! I bet Churro's upgrades will get you a whole bunch of useful stuff. Obviously distance, but maybe also basic information, like names or power ranks?"

I felt Maddy shrug.

"What's the difference between a HUD and a UI?" Sam asked.

"A HUD is information," answered Chad without any sort of douchiness, "A UI is interactive."

Tessa went on, "Alright. Let's give it a rip!"

"Okay, here goes." Maddy's eyes flicked across the room to the door to our training area. I heard a quiet buzz, and then suddenly a cool blue outline surrounded the door. *Holy shit, she really does have a HUD!* Information popped up in the corner of our vision, showing us that the door was eighteen point seven five meters away. It was a strange sensation, knowing the visual was there, but out of our line of sight, yet still easily understood.

"I'm definitely upgraded again. My HUD now seems to round to the nearest quarter meter. Eighteen point seven five to the training door." She scanned her gaze across the room to the accompaniment of a constant, low-grade buzz, the targeting outline jumping from object to object, the number in the corner updating on each jump. "Hmm, it looks like… Ugh, I wish I had better words to explain how this felt. It's like I'm holding down the button now. I don't think I've ever tried doing that before, but this feels new."

Everyone was paying attention to Maddy, but no one looked as eager as the grinning Tessa. She was eating this up. I was surprised she didn't have a notebook to write in. "This is so freaking awesome! Churro, it's time for you to do your thing. Maddy, keep that button pressed and tell me *everything* you feel!"

Gathering my mental self, I imagined I was holding that little bundle of buzzing in my hands. Unsure of what would happen, I *blew*.

Her eyes *throbbed* with new information, completely overwhelming Maddy. She slammed them shut, saying, "Ow. Holy fuck, that hurts." I could feel her eyes pulsing in time with her increased heartbeat. She brought her hands up to rub at them.

"What?" Tessa demanded, "Your eyes hurt? What do you see?"

Slowly opening one eye, Maddy peeked at Tessa, who instantly had a soft blue outline. Maddy's HUD was chock full of information. Name: Contessa Lynn Riverside. Distance: 1.8288 meters. Height: 1.651 meters. Weight: 48.5344 kilograms. Power Name: Behavior Alteration, Forced. Power Type: Telepathic Mental Manipulation. Current Power Tier: 18. Max Power Tier: 0.

Maddy's eyes opened wide, and she gasped. Other information popped up as she stared at Tessa. Things like breast cup size, shoulder, waist, and hip measurements, shoe size, inseam. "Holy shit…" she whispered.

"What is it? What do you see? Start talking, Maddy, now!" Tessa yelled, the suspense apparently killing her.

"I… I can see everything about your body… Height, weight, boob size, all of it. And your power… Oh my God, Tessa, you could potentially be a tier zero. It's so different from what I was thought it was…" Maddy's speech was halting and slow, and I assumed it was because she was attempting to mentally process all of this new information. *God knows I'm struggling to wrap my brain around it, too.* The pain in her eyes was still there, but forgotten.

"Do me! Do me!" Sam begged. Maddy turned to her, and took in everything at once. Name: Samantha Linnea Nilsdottir. Distance: 0.8636 meters. Height: 1.7526 meters. Weight: 56.699 kilograms. Power Name: Ferromagnetic Alteration, Forced. Power Type: Telepathic Physical Manipulation. Current Power Tier: 16. Max Power Tier: 1. Cup size and measurements were all also there, just like with Tessa.

Without relaying any of this information out loud, Maddy turned to study Chad, but she must have made some sort of mental command about which stats to display, because the only things I registered were about his power. Power Name: Gender Alteration, Willing. Power

Type: Telepathic Physical Manipulation. Current Power Tier: 16. Max Power Tier: 7. After a moment of processing this, a new bit of information popped into view. Penis, Erect Length: 0.1379 meters, currently unavailable.

Maddy giggled, "Holy shit, I can measure practically *everything*. This is un-fucking-believable!"

Tessa looked like she was about to explode, "Start talking, Maddy! You can't keep me in suspense like this! What is tier zero?"

Maddy held up a finger, "Hang on, let me scan Jack." Power Name: Life Imbuation, Creative. Power Type: Telepathic Mental and Physical Manifestation. Current Power Tier: 14. Max Power Tier: 1.

"Jeez, you guys aren't going to believe this. Your powers aren't nearly as limited as we've believed. Tessa, you're only an eighteen right now, but you've got so much potential it's ridiculous. A tier zero? That's insane. Sam, you can be a tier one. You too, Jack. Chad, you can reach tier seven."

"What do you mean they're not limited? What's tier zero?" Tessa demanded.

"Tessa, babe, you've got something called Behavior Alteration comma Forced. It says it's a Telepathic Mental Manipulation type power. Actually, all of your powers are considered Telepathic Manipulation, except Jack's, but some also say Mental or Physical. Sam, yours is physical."

Sam snorted, "Did you just say comma?"

Tessa sucked on her teeth for a moment, considering. "Telepathic is probably how they're activated, then, and manipulation is just changing stuff. Are you saying that I can force people to behave in certain ways? And that, what? I've been forcing people to share their dirtiest secrets with me? Why would I do that? I've never wanted to know what people are hiding."

Maddy shrugged at her, then looked to Sam, "Yours is called Ferromagnetic Alteration, Physical. You're at a sixteen right now."

"What's mine?" Chad demanded before Sam could say anything.

"Gender Alteration comma Willing, Physical." Maddy's reply was a little on the chilly side.

"Willing? What the fuck does that mean? I wasn't willing to turn my cock into a pussy!"

"It probably means that once you fully power up, you will be able to affect other people, who have to be willing. You could probably put gender reassignment surgeons out of business, and make an entire community of people very happy," Tessa tried to put a positive spin on it.

"Nah, fuck that. I don't give a rat's ass about helping dudes become chicks or helping chicks grow dicks. Fuck all of this." Chad slammed his hands down on the table as he stood up, and stormed away.

"What a bucket of dicks," Sam muttered.

Jack leaned forward almost eagerly, "What about me?"

"Uh, I understand yours the least. You've got something called Life Imbuation comma Creative, Physical and Mental Manifestation. You're at a fourteen for now. I guess you… imbue life?" She chuckled weakly, then shrugged.

Jack made a thoughtful noise, then rumbled, "That… fits, actually. I've always tried to influence my girls' personalities, but sometimes they wake up completely different than what I was trying to do. It does feel as if I'm breathing life into them, like CPR, rather than creating them from scratch."

"What about you, Maddy? Can you scan yourself?" Tessa asked.

Maddy looked down at her body, and I felt her mind buzz as she activated her ability. She got the blue outline around herself, but no other data. She sighed, and shook her head. "Nada, just an outline with no info."

"Either way," she added with a vicious grin, "we're not going to be Omegas forever. Technically we aren't right now, but Sally's keeping them from knowing our true strength." She stood up and grabbed her plate, walking it over to the sink where she rinsed it before sticking it in the dishwasher. "I think I'm gonna take Churro through the obstacle course with me; I want Sally to get a better read on me after all this. I also want to see if my upgrade de-powers a little once he's not actively boosting me."

"Good idea," said Tessa, "we should also get Churro back as soon as we can, so you can scan him. Let me know if you want some help with that when you're done with your ObCo." Tessa blushed furiously, but still managed to wink at Maddy, and beam her a gorgeous smile.

Maddy walked behind the seated Tessa, and leaned over to whisper in her ear, "I would love some help, Mistress." Tessa shivered heavily, and Maddy headed into the training area laughing.

15

IF IT'S NOT ONE THING...

Maddy and I stepped into her shower, the water soothingly, almost scaldingly, hot. She'd just finished her ObCo run with her best time yet. Her analysis power and natural bad-assery were a good combination as she plowed through assailants and agility obstacles. Sally was analyzing the data from it now.

As her muscles relaxed under the waterfall of bliss, she started talking to me.

"I know you can't respond, but that's okay. I want to show you things, because if you get your real cock back, I want you fuck me senseless with it. You're an alright guy all on your own, but contrary to what it may seem like, I don't actually go around fucking everyone willy-nilly. Tessa and Sam, we've really bonded this week."

She spun around, letting the pounding water work on her shoulders, back and ass.

"Mostly about being a united front against leering perverts like you, and douche lords like Chad, actually. Anyway, I'm happy to have you as a passenger, and maybe someday we'll have enough of an emotional connection for me to seek your company, but right now, my only drive to sleep with you is getting to ride the biggest cock I've ever seen, which you don't even have anymore. If you ever get it back, and don't mind being used for your body, well, you know where I sleep."

She leaned her head back, the heat cascading across her scalp, and she moaned a little at how good it felt. *There really is nothing like a hot soak after a tough workout.*

"Tessa, though, she's so sweet and shy most of the time, but fuck, she's such a tigress in bed. That tiny little girl being so *commanding*, it's really fucking hot. I'm going to be her bitch soon, and I'm going to be *naughty* so you get spanked with me."

Maddy grinned as she started working her hands over her erogenous zones. Starting at her neck and working slowly downward, her nipples tight and hard before she even touched them. After caressing her cleavage, she just barely let her palms graze over her pink nipples. "Fuck, teasing myself is actually hot when I know I'm teasing you too."

The heat between her legs was from more than the shower, and I could feel her getting aroused. She wasn't wrong, she absolutely was teasing me, but I enjoyed it literally exactly as much as she did. The raw physical sensations were glorious, and I reveled in them with her. I didn't know what was going on in her head, but the fantasies I conjured up to fill the gaps in my knowledge were very erotic.

When she brought the blue thing out, dumping a good amount of body wash into it, I thought she was going to burst. She bit her lip and groaned, a low, sexy noise. When she started washing small circles across her stomach, she squirmed delightfully. I could feel her nether lips rubbing together as she squeezed her thighs closed and wriggled her hips. It sent a glorious vibration running up from her clit to her chest, spreading out to her nipples.

She skipped her most sensitive areas, washing her legs, arms, back, and her collarbone. Her nerves were firing thousands of times a second, demanding that she stimulate herself. "Mmmm," she moaned, "You have no idea how much I want to get off right now. I'm already so close, just thinking about… But no, it'll be so much better with Tessa, and we wouldn't want to rush you out of me just yet. You still need to compare our orgasms when I'm not fingering myself."

Maddy finally dragged her blue thing across her sexy tits, and pleasure that was almost pain shot straight back down to her clit. It was like someone had connected those three bundles of nerves with an electrical wire, and left the juice on. She gasped as she reached out to the wall for support, her knees weakening. "No, no, no," she panted, "don't come, Mad! Hold out!"

I felt my mind get suddenly yanked towards hers. For lack of better words, I somehow latched onto the little partition of her mind that I was in, and fought against the merge that was trying to consume me, to turn me into us. When the pull lessened, I knew she had stopped trying to eat me.

"Fuck, Churro, what the f-fuck? What are y-you doing to m-me?" She was gasping, and I realized that she had fallen to her knees, water still cascading over her back.

I'm not doing anything, I tried to mentally shout at her, *something in you was trying to pull me in!*

"Wha... what? Pull you...?"

Holy fuckaroo! You can hear me?

"Y-yes, hear you," she was still breathing heavily, and a moment's focus let me know that she was riding the crest of a huge orgasm, somehow unable to either reach release or come down slowly, "fix me. P-please."

I don't know what the fuck I'm doing, Maddy, or even if I'm the one doing this!

"Make it stop, Churro, p-please. One way the other, I-I can't stay like th-this. I'm so close."

Everything in her body felt so good that I could barely concentrate. I tried every visualization technique I could imagine, and I'd laugh at my pun skills later when I wasn't so panicked, but nothing worked. Not the blowing on embers trick for power boosting, or latching onto my section of consciousness. She was locked on the edge.

I don't know how to help, Maddy. Did you imagine something when you were trying to stop your orgasm? What was it?

"I-I, yeah. I thought y-you could help me hold it off..." she moaned loudly.

The glass shower door slid open with a loud clatter, and Maddy looked up at Tessa's worried face.

"Maddy! Sally told me something was wrong, what's going on?"

She's stuck in some sort of endless edging nightmare! You have to make her orgasm! I shouted, knowing it was pointless.

"O-or-orgasm. Need one," Maddy gasped, "n-need to fin-nish. Please, M-mistress."

Suddenly Tessa was in the shower with us, still fully clothed, and she was laying Maddy on her back, the water shut off. Flopping to her stomach between Maddy's legs, she stretched her pussy out with three fingers. Maddy screamed, and even from inside, feeling this with her, I couldn't tell if it was pleasure or pain. Then Tessa's tongue touched Maddy's clit, and it was as if color had returned the world.

Maddy's orgasm crested explosively, curling her toes and hunching her back. She grabbed her knees and pulled them up next to her shoulders. Tessa's tongue was dancing a foxtrot, each flick and lick sending a chain of bursts through Maddy's body. Maddy was crying and growling through it all; deep, guttural noises from a primal place buried within.

I don't know how she or I managed to remain conscious through the whole ordeal. And ordeal it was; coming this hard was incredibly exhausting. When the bliss finally started to retreat, leaving massive aftershocks as it went, every muscle in Maddy's body was clenched, like she'd been hit with a taser.

When she could finally start to unfurl herself from the fetal position, she was still panting pretty hard, but no longer gasping. "Tessa, oh God, Tessa, thank you. I thought I was going to die from that."

Tessa positioned herself on the wet shower floor behind Maddy, pulling the much taller woman into her embrace. She began rocking back and forth, kissing Maddy's temple and whispering soothing nothings to her. When Maddy started shivering a few minutes later, Tessa helped her dry off and climb into bed.

Why is it that every time I'm involved in sex, it ends up turning into a life or death situation? I asked myself. When Maddy started laughing, I remembered that she was hearing my thoughts somehow.

"What's so funny, babe?" Tessa asked softly.

"Churro's wondering why someone always almost dies when they get laid while he's riding along."

Tessa giggled with Maddy, still cuddled up to her, though now she'd taken off her wet clothes. Then she stopped, "Wait, what? How do you know what Churro's wondering?"

"Oh, um, I'm not sure, actually. He may have been upgraded again? I can hear what he's trying to think to me."

"Are you sure you're not just imagining things? That seemed like a pretty traumatic event; I can understand why you'd want to pin it on Churro. Not that I don't believe you, I just want to cover all the bases."

You can tell her that I could prove it, but I doubt she'd want me talking about Kevin Gould again.

"He says he wants to tell you more about Kevin Gould."

*What? You bit- meanie! I specifically **don't** want to do that!* I tried to mentally pinch the back of her hand.

Maddy flinched, and rubbed her hand, "Ouch, you little fucking dessert pastry! Did you somehow fucking pinch me?" She was distracted from her anger by Tessa's laughter.

"Yeah, I imagine he doesn't want to talk about Kevin anymore, but Maddy, this is a serious increase. First, mind merging into a plurality of self, now direct mental communication and apparently affecting you physically? We need to get him scanned, quickly."

"Yeah, I, uh, tried to merge with him earlier… I think that's how I got locked into edging for so long. I was fooling around in the shower, trying to tease him a bit, and getting myself ready for you, but I took it a bit too far. I tried using his strength to hold off my orgasm, and he says he fought against it. That's where I got stuck, until you finished me off."

"He's definitely getting more powerful as he upgrades us, that's for damn sure. Especially if he's gaining control over whether or not he merges with his host. When he did it with me, it just happened - no choice, no thought, no opportunity to react, we just became us. But it sounds like that's different from what you're describing."

Maddy snuggled harder against Tessa, trying to soak up her warmth, "Now that I can scan, though, we ca…" Her voice got all garbled, fading to a dull wah wah wah, before all I could hear was the rush of a bloodstream. I tried to hold onto one thought that had been stuck in my head all night: I wanted my cock back to normal, for fuck's sake.

WAKING UP IN THE BASIN - WITH ANOTHER FUCKING GASP, ARGH - THE first thing I did was check out my junk.

Oh, thank fuck! It worked! It's all there! I'm back to being King Dong! Yes!

After the rinsing spray turned off, I moved sedately to my bathroom, swinging my hips back and forth, just watching my newly-returned toy bounce around. I'll be the first to admit that I'm not at all mature, and that boys never stop playing with our toys. There is just something so satisfying about the meaty 'thwock' noise my dick makes when it slaps from thigh to thigh. I stopped walking when I got to my bathroom, stood with my feet apart and knees bent. I stuck my ass out, then thrust forwards, swinging my cock up to slap against my stomach. I may have giggled a little bit, too.

Since I wasn't sure how long I'd been in Maddy, I asked Sally. She told me that it was breakfast time, which meant that even with an orgasm hurrying me along, I'd still spent the entire night with Maddy.

Shrugging, since it didn't really make a difference, I stepped into the shower to finish cleaning the grime from my body. When I was done, I slipped into underwear and my training shorts and headed out to greet my team.

Maddy and I were leaving our rooms at the same time, and she looked surprised to see me. Instead of commenting, she just shook her head and moved to the dining area.

After we'd all grabbed breakfast and sat down, Tessa asked Maddy to scan me and share her results. She examined me like a lab rat, then frowned. She opened her mouth to say something, but paused and concentrated again. Then she gaped at me like a fish out of water, and blushed like crazy. *She probably measured my cock,* I thought to myself with a hum of pleasure.

"You guys aren't going to believe this," Maddy began, "but I'm getting some really weird shit from analyzing Churro. First up, his power is called Molecular Reconstruction comma Self. It's a mental power, at tier ten, with a max of zero, like Tessa."

They all stared at me disbelievingly, so I just waggled my eyebrows. I was still feeling like a puffed-up rooster.

"Or, I should say, his *primary* power. He's got secondary and tertiary powers, but… I can't get full reads." The room erupted into shouted questions that were impossible to parse.

Tessa slammed her hands down on the table and yelled, "Silence!" Everyone shut right up. "Maddy, tell us what you know."

"His secondary power is called Growth Vector comma Forced. But the type, current, and max tiers are all unknown. His tertiary power is named SoulSplicing comma Error. Type, current, max; all errors. I don't know what any of that means. I've never had unknowns or errors before, since this is all still so new to me."

"Why does this fuckwad get *three* powers, and all the rest of us are stuck with one? Jesus Christ, it's like he's the star of the show or something," Chad complained.

Sam nodded, agreeing with Chad, "You'd think he was the main character in a book or something, the way shit just keeps falling into his lap like this. I think I'm gonna start calling him Gary Stu."

"Enough," Tessa said firmly, "We have to deal with this as it is, instead of wishing it were some other way. The growth vector is what we're all relying on right now, though SoulSplicing sounds like that's the one responsible for our mind merge. Even though Maddy's seeing error messages, we have to assume it's also leveling up. Churro, you need to run the ObCo so Sally can scan you; see if she can add anything to what Maddy knows. Also, I don't know, we may want to focus on upgrading Maddy the fastest, since she's the one who can keep us apprised of any new information or changes."

"Can I nominate you as team leader?" I asked Tessa.

Before Tessa could reply, Sally interjected, "Omega Team, team leadership changes must be approved by ranking THG members. Attempting to do so would likely draw unwanted attention as they questioned why you were trying to give up leadership. It is not a course of action I recommend."

"Fiiine," I sighed.

"We should all probably find a way to break through our activation limitations," Sam said. "If I can use any type of metal, instead of paper clips, that'd be great."

"Yeah, and I don't want to have to orgasm to use mine either," added Tessa.

"And since me turning into a churro and upgrading people are two separate powers, maybe I don't need them both at the same time."

"Absolutely," Maddy agreed with me, "if we can find a way for you to upgrade us without being eaten, that'd probably go a long way to us speeding up the process."

Tessa turned to face me, staring intently.

"Okay, I'll go run the ObCo. Tessa, I want you planning experiments for my powers, to see if there are other activation methods. If you can, do it while you're also training. Everyone else, I want you either weight lifting or practicing in the dojo. We have to be combat ready, and while it won't happen overnight, I'd like us to get there sooner rather than later." *There goes my mouth, spewing shit without asking my brain first.*

I dismissed everyone to their training, and I felt in control again, so I motioned for Maddy to hold back with me. "I saw the way you looked at me earlier," I said with a smartass smirk.

"Uh, yeah, I was scanning you, of course I looked at you," she said while looking anywhere *but* at me.

"Nah. I was in you when you scanned for Chad's dick size, remember. I know you measured me. Want to sneak off for a quickie before we go train?" I was grinning like a madman.

"Actually, I don't," she said with a little frostiness, "Didn't you hear me when I said I don't go around fucking all willy-nilly? If I'm going to use you for your dick, it's going to be at a time and in a place where I can fully use you. You don't get to just fuck and run. That doesn't work for me, so you can take that giant penis and go fuck yourself." She stormed off, leaving me in my Stand-Like-A-Jackass™ pose.

Well, I somehow fucked that up. That feels a bit more normal. I sighed heavily, then trotted over to run my ObCo.

The course was absolutely brutal. Sally used several robots to beat the shit out of me multiple times. Walls were higher, with fewer handholds. Avoidance obstacles, like replicas of falling debris from exploding buildings, came faster. When I finally finished slogging through it, I'd asked her why she'd done it.

"Churro, you should treat your teammates better than simple sex toys," she'd told me. I was pretty sure she kicked my ass on Maddy's behalf.

I had cleaned off the sweat and grime in the shower, and put on a pair of jeans. I skipped a shirt, since my underwear covered enough and I was actually starting to lose quite a bit of my extra weight. I was waiting on a couch in the common area with a bottle of electrolytes, trying to be patient until Sally gave me the results of her scan.

I heard Tessa come out of her room, looking freshly showered and just as sexy as could be. She had on a tight, white wife-beater style tank top and a pair of basketball shorts in the same shade of blue as Sam's eyes. I nodded a greeting to her, but after pissing off Maddy and getting my ass kicked for it, I figured I should keep my mouth shut for a while, so I just took another drink.

"I've got a few experiments I'd like to try," she said as she sat down close to me, leaving an entire half of the couch unoccupied. "Mostly for your growth vector, since that'll be most beneficial to the team as a whole, but some for your other powers, too."

"Okay, hit me with it," I shifted on the couch to fully face her.

She smiled a little, showing a quick flash of dimples before she became all business. "First off, you need to try to perform your boost, while you're external. You said you could feel or hear a buzzing when we activate our powers, so it'd be good to get that working, as it's the biggest upgrade. With my power activation requirement, that means you're probably going to have to experiment with Sam or Maddy. Which, until you apologize for *being* a giant dick, not just having one, means you should work with Sam first."

I guess that answers the question of whether or not Maddy told everyone. "Okay, that's one experiment, and I'll apologize to Maddy as soon as she lets me talk to her again. What else have you come up with?"

"The second one is a little… gross." She seemed hesitant to share, so I didn't push. "You upgrade us when we eat you, but there's a part of you we can eat without you turning into a churro. I know Sam has already… done that… but it was before we knew about your growth vector, and she ate you as a churro immediately after, so we have no way to test or verify if that method works."

"You… want to try eating my… jizz?" I was shocked, to say the least.

"At least twice, actually. Once directly… from the source. And once indirectly. Like in a smoothie or something." She looked very uncomfortable, her cheeks starting to turn from pink to red.

"If that worked, Tessa, you'd either all have to keep blowing me, or start milking me like I'm a fucking cow. Even as nice as my one blowjob ever was, I don't think I could support the entire team. Nor do I think most of them would be willing. And I'm not really willing to let Jack or Chad blow me."

"Yes, everything about that method is suboptimal, but it's an experiment we need to perform at least once, both methods. Moving on quickly now, my third idea is to split you up when you transform, and have multiple people eat you. Since our room cluster all sends waste to the same area, I think the risk of damage to you would be minimal, though I don't know how it would affect your consciousness or soul-whatever ability. Would we each get twenty percent of a normal upgrade? And how could we even tell if we were making progress? Sally's scanners aren't dialed in enough for something like that, and Maddy's doesn't seem to make the distinction either."

"Eesh, I'm even less comfortable with that than I am with becoming a jizz-dispenser. I can't imagine that splitting my mind into five parts, if that's what happened, would be good for me." Though now that I thought about it, being a dispenser might not be a bad way to upgrade the team. Well, the female half of the team.

"I know, that's why I saved it for last. I still think we should try it at least once, but it can wait until either Sally or Maddy has some way to track incremental progress."

"Churro, I have your results from your most recent obstacle course run," Sally chimed in, "and as Maddy said, I am showing your power at tier ten. However, I am not getting any readings on the other two powers she claimed to have seen."

"Damn," I said, "that's less than ideal. Did you have ideas for Soul-Splice, Tessa?"

She nodded slowly, "I do, but to be honest just the name of it is rather terrifying. I mean... souls. You're splicing into our souls. And that's not even taking into account that this apparently proves the existence of souls, which leads into higher powers and discussions of the afterlife..." She trailed off when I rested my hand on her forearm.

"I'm sure there's nothing to it beyond a silly name, Tessa. I don't think you need to worry about it."

"Maybe, maybe not. Either way, I do have a couple thoughts on how to experiment with it. First up would be just like growth vector: you attempt to do it while external. Based on when we merged, and when Maddy attempted to merge with you, I'd say it's pretty closely tied to arousal or intimacy, so experiment two would be for you to have relations with someone, and attempt an external merge at various stages in the process. Pre, mid, and post-coital. I guess option three is just to have someone eat you, attempt the merge, and just try to record data of how your power behaves. We're not working with enough information yet to make even informed guesses."

I nodded, thinking about how I had just sort of slipped into the merge with Tessa, and fought against the one with Maddy. I was deep in thought wondering at the differences, so I didn't notice Tessa moving until she was practically in my face. She'd moved in closer, and leaned in as well, so she was almost sitting in my lap.

"I... I'd like to volunteer for some of the experiments, Churro. Namely, the ingestion one for growth, and the intimate one for merging."

16

POWER EXPERIMENTS

"Well, when you put it like that," I said, "how can I say no?" I paused, remembering that I was back to my full size below the belt. "Though, I'm back to being a lot bigger than I was when we…"

"Right, y-yes," she stuttered, "Maddy had told me, but I guess I didn't want to believe her. Okay, why don't we try a few of the non-sexual experiments first, and we'll take it from there? Let's go to my room, though."

When we reached our destination, Tessa directed me to lie on the bed, and she immediately curled up into my side, laying her head on my chest. I smoothed her raven hair out of my face and let my hand trail down her back, over her clothes. *I have no idea what's happening. Does she like me? Like* ***like*** *me? Wha-*

"Shut up, Churro," she interrupted my runaway train of thought, "I can practically hear you panicking in your head right now. And no, I can't actually hear your thoughts, I just know you."

Locking my brain down as best I could, I muttered a quiet, "Yes, Mistress."

She smacked my stomach. "Non-sexual, remember? You can't… you can't call me that right now. We're here for experiments."

She says as she snuggles into me like a lover...

I took a deep breath, "Okay. Experiment one, external growth vector attempt. I need you to try to activate your power, but, uhh... Can you do that non-sexually yet?"

I felt her shake her head against my chest before she sat up and reached out to her nightstand. Tapping away on her tablet, she told me, "Hang on. Let me see if Sam is free for a minute."

I sat up in the bed, scooting up to lean against the wall, and a moment later, Sam knocked. Tessa let her in, explained what we were experimenting with, and asked for help.

"Sure, why not? You think it'll work?" Sam asked me.

I shrugged, "I'm really not sure. I've only ever felt power activations when I've been in you." I patted the bed in front of me. "I think I'll need to at least put my hands on your head, maybe get my head closer. I don't know. Let's try it from all three ranges."

"Ooh, good data!" Tessa chirped.

Sam shrugged and sat in front of me, pulling out her baggie of paper clips. They immediately floated out of the bag and melted into a sphere of pure metal. "My control is definitely better. Faster, too. I don't have to think about it nearly so hard anymore, it just sort of happens."

"Okay," I closed my eyes, "Just keep making alterations to the metal, different shapes and whatnot. Let me see if I can feel you from here." After a good thirty seconds of absolutely nothing, I cracked an eye open to see that Sam had sculpted a miniature handgun, which was pointed directly at my crotch. "Not funny, Sam. But I'm getting nothing. Can I hold your head?"

When she leaned forward, I reached out and placed my hands on the sides of her head. I marveled at the silky softness of her jet-black tresses, and how the color contrasted so wonderfully with those beautiful blue eyes she had. They were mostly hidden by her thick lashes, since she was looking down at her sculpture - which was an image of me kissing Chad. I immediately closed my eyes again, and concentrated on my hands.

"No, still nothing," I shook my head. "Okay, forehead to forehead." We jostled a little trying to get closer to each other, but in the end, I ended up with my noggin pressed firmly against hers. She was staring directly into my eyes, and my breath caught in my throat. She chuckled at me and went back to looking at her floating metal artwork. Her breath smelled like strawberries.

Fucking focus, moron, I berated myself. But again, even with my eyes closed, I couldn't hear or feel any sort of buzzing coming from Sam. Another thirty fruitless seconds later, I leaned back. "Still nada, zilch, nothing. If it's meant to be used this way, I guess I'm not powerful enough yet."

"Thanks for helping, Sam," Tessa said quickly. "We've got some other experiments to perform, though, so I'll let you know if we need any more help." She bit her lip and blushed.

Sam cocked an eyebrow at Tessa, then at me, and shook her head with another chuckle. She stood up from the bed, waved, and said, "Good luck, girl, you're gonna need it."

When the door closed behind Sam, Tessa looked at me with her dimpled grin. "Ingestion. Get naked!" She quickly shoved her oversized shorts to her ankles and peeled her tank top over her head.

I don't need to be told twice! I unbuttoned and unzipped my jeans, pulling them down my legs. "Don't we need a before and after scan?"

"Maddy scanned me after my ObCo, and she'll do it again before my next one. Though it would be good to get a sort of time lapse view. Maybe we can determine how long it takes you to upgrade a power. You're still not naked." She hadn't stopped undressing as she spoke, so she was now standing next to the bed in her fully nude glory. I quickly joined her, not caring if I looked overeager, because I absolutely was.

She crawled onto the bed seductively when I was naked, and her eyes were riveted to my cock, which was already standing up straight. "Christ, Churro. It's one thing to hear about, another to see it on a small sculpture, but it just doesn't compute until you see it in person." She reached forward to grasp me by the base of my shaft with both hands - they covered less than half of it.

"Tessa, I don't know if Sam told you everything or not, but, uh, I… she called it a fire hose. There's a lot of it." It was my turn to blush.

"I'll just do my best, and we'll see what happens." She had moved in closer, her knees between my upper thighs. "Now, just relax, and do *try* to enjoy it," she smirked. My cock twitched in her hands. When I nodded at her, she lowered her face slowly and flicked her tongue along the underside of my head.

Her hands started stroking me slowly from root to tip, and she kept licking me. Long, slow licks that trailed all over me, leaving hot and cold patches that were driving me crazy with lust. Then, without warning, I felt my tip hit the back of her throat as she suddenly buried me in her mouth. Wet heat engulfed my cock as she worked me over, bobbing up and down slowly.

I groaned involuntarily as my eyes closed and my head thunked against the wall. She moaned softly, and I couldn't help but think she was really into it.

"Can I… can I try to return the favor, Mistress?" I added the honorific, thinking it might help my case. When she moaned loudly and sucked on me more vigorously, I thought it had worked.

She let me out of her mouth with a small 'pop!' and smiled up at me. *Fuck, I'm going to fill up those dimples!* I groaned again. Her smile turned into a grin as she crawled over my leg, giving me room to lie down. I quickly slid down the bed until I could lie flat, and she straddled my neck almost as quickly. I soaked up the view of her juicy pussy.

With her knees next to my ears, she slowly leaned forward onto her left hand, which was next to my hip. With her right hand, she spread her nether lips apart and tapped on her clit a few times. I absolutely appreciated the reminder - porn wasn't nearly as helpful for this as I'd thought it would be, so knowing where to focus gave me some extra confidence.

I reached around the backs of her slim thighs, gently keeping her lips spread, so she could have her hand back. I sent my tongue out to test her sweet waters, even as she grabbed the base of my cock again. I wrapped my lips around her clit and sucked in gently. She groaned as my cock hit the back of her throat again, sending vibrations coursing through me that I could feel in my balls.

I dragged my tongue slowly up and down against her, her hands matching my pace. She was forcing her head further down my shaft, burying my tip in her throat. I could practically feel her trying to swallow me. *What happened to the gagging?* My thoughts fled, though, as she ground her pussy into my mouth, reminding me of my task.

"Mistress," I groaned as she deep-throated me again, "if this humble slave is good enough to get you there, you should try to alter how your power works." She growled on my cock. *Oh fuck, she's better at this than Sam.*

Rather than tell her how close I was, I dove back into her slit, sucking her clit harder and flicking my tongue in circles. My hands roamed up to caress and squeeze her pert ass. Her hips jerked down, but I managed to keep her in my mouth.

Her hand released my shaft, and the only feeling was her hot mouth swallowing a much larger portion of me than I believed was possible. My legs twitched, thrusting me upwards, and I moaned into her. I jerked again when her free hand found my sack and she started massaging gently, rolling my balls around with her fingers.

Curling my arm around her hip and ass as much I could, I speared my index finger into her wet tunnel. She instantly clenched around it, humming loudly on my cock. I let go of her clit, "Mistress, I'm going to come!" She hummed again, so I returned my tongue between her lips. She was trembling in my arms, quivering.

When I sucked her between my lips again, my hands took on lives of their own. With no direction from me, they slid a second finger into her convulsing sheathe. My free hand slapped her ass, hard, before pressing my thumb hard against her back door. When it breached her clenched sphincter, my balls tightened and I started coming explosively.

I moaned loudly on her clit, my hands still thrusting and opening her without conscious control. My hips flexed up and down as I fucked her mouth hard, dumping spurt after spurt directly into her throat. Her lips were halfway down my cock now, her hand squeezing my balls as if to wring every last drop from me. I pumped into her face harder than I would have dared on my own. She was moaning and gulping on my cock as my hands and mouth kept working her.

I flinched when I got hit in the face with something wet, and shot another thick rope into her. My thumb was almost entirely in her ass, fighting against her tight clenching and lack of lubrication, but she was thrusting her hips back against me. She was shaking now, her pussy still tightening around my fingers in waves. I felt my ass clench as I gave up what I knew would be my last spurt of this orgasm.

She was still coming, though, and I used my mouth to keep it going as long as possible - my hands were helping too, but I wasn't in control of them. She lifted her head from my sensitive rod, and screamed as she gyrated hard against my face. Another gush soaked my face, and she went limp on top of me.

Her boobs were pressed into my stomach, her hard nipples poking into my soft flesh. She laid her head on my hip and panted, her hot breath washing over the base of my cock. My hands went limp, and I smacked myself in the face with both of them before I could retake control. I immediately sent them back up to stroke her ass cheeks and lower back.

She kicked her legs backwards so she was fully lying on me, her pussy nestled up under my chin, her mound pressed against my collarbone. Her head slid down to my thigh, her breasts on my hips. She looked so tasty that I couldn't help myself - I lifted my head back up to send my tongue swiping across her tight little butthole.

She jerked on top of me, then smacked my flagging staff, "Churro! Stop it, you fuck! I'm trying to bask here, and you're ruining it!"

"Sorry, Mistress, you just look so tasty, I want to keep eating you up." I was *very* proud of myself for managing to get her off with my mouth. I kept stroking her body, trying to keep her warm and to explore more of her curves. I was mesmerized by the softness of her skin, and the way she felt as I wore her like a tiny blanket. We laid like that for a good ten minutes, until our heart rates and breathing were back to normal. *I could stay like this forever.*

When her strength returned, she got up, only to turn around and lay on me again. She was straddling my hips, her pussy resting against the base of my limp dick. Her breasts pressed into my solar plexus, and her head was laying on my shoulder. She'd pulled her bedspread up with her and it was now draped over us from her shoulders down. Her arms curled under my shoulders as I hugged her close to me.

"Churro," she whispered to me as Sally turned the lights off, "Are you okay with the other ladies using your body for sex?"

"I don't know," I responded, "I mean, it's kind of a dream come true. I guess I am okay with it. For now, at least."

"Mmmm, okay," she said sleepily. "Good night, Churro."

What... what is happening here? Why did she ask me that? And how do I know what I really feel? When her breathing slowed, and she twitched a few times, I whispered back, "Good night, Tessa."

Whatever was going on here, it was far better than I had ever dreamed I'd have in my life. I had never imagined that I'd have a girlfriend, let alone one this incredibly sexy. *Is she my girlfriend now? Is that what's happening? Why'd she ask me about Sam and Maddy?* Of course, I was probably only here because I was the least bad of three horrible options. *Or maybe just because I can upgrade their powers. It's not like they'd ever choose me for me, just what I can do... Fuck, even in my own thoughts I can't win anything.*

I was flat on my back beneath her, her hair tickling my face again. When I tried to stop thinking and enjoy the sensation of her in my arms, my cock stiffened quickly. It took me a very long time to fall asleep.

I FOUND MYSELF DREAMING, MOANING IN PLEASURE. *COCK HARD. HOT. Wet. What? Pressure on my chest. Mm, feels good.* I refused to open my eyes, my sleepy brain assuming that if I did, it would banish this dream back to my subconsciousness. My entire length was sheathed to the hilt in something deliciously slick and hot. Warm thighs settled on my hips. This was by far the best dream I'd ever had.

A sensation of heat settled on my lips and chin. A second later, soft lips were pressed against mine, so I puckered my lips. When they squished in more than I anticipated, and got wetter, I pulled back and licked them. *Definitely tastes like Sam. This dream is awesome!* Now knowing what I was working with, I flicked my tongue between her lips, digging through her moist folds on a hunt for the jackpot. *More pressure on my chest. Four hands. Makes sense - if Sam's sitting on my face, she can't be the one riding my tool.*

Squeezing my eyes more tightly shut, I finally lifted my hands from the bed. They brushed across a pair of ankles dimpling the bed beside my ass. Running them up to a pair of knees and back down smooth thighs, I kept my touch light. Coming up from folded hips was a muscular torso, fronted by a large pair of breasts. *Definitely Maddy, I'd know those tits anywhere. Though I guess not from this angle.* I rolled her nipples between my fingers before taking a large handful of each breast, squeezing firmly.

Sam pushed her pussy harder into my face, reminding me that I had more to do than explore with my hands. I obliged eagerly, though without the enthusiasm of our first experience with me eating her pussy. Letting go of Maddy, I wrapped my arms over Sam's hips, using my fingers to spread her lips apart. Sucking her clit into my mouth, I started giving her the same circular treatment that had worked so well on Tessa earlier tonight.

Maddy started lifting herself at the same time, both women moaning. I felt two hands lift off my chest and their moans were muffled. *Nice of them to try to be quiet, so I don't wake up before this dream is over.* When Maddy had only my tip still lodged inside, I thrust my hips up high, burying myself as fast as I could. Her hand slammed back down onto my chest, and her legs gave out. She rode me back down to the bed, where the springs forced me deeper into her flexing walls.

Not ignoring Sam, who was squirming deliciously on my mouth, I just barely let my teeth graze over her clit. Just enough to provide a hard counterpoint to my soft tongue. I heard another muffled groan of pleasure as her juices ran down my chin. Letting go of her lips with one hand, I slid it under her ass and pierced her core with my thumb. *Shit, I'm really good at this in my dreams! I hope to fuck I remember what I'm doing when I wake up, and that it works this well in real life!*

Every time Maddy reached the apex of unsheathing me, I thrust up hard, and we crashed back to bed together. Buried fully in her depths, I could feel her muscles quivering around me, trying to milk me. I shook my head, pulling Sam's clit left and right. *Can't get me off that easy in my dreams! I! Am! A! God! Here!* Both women made sexy noises, though Sam's were still muffled. I pressed my thumb in and out.

Letting go of Sam's lips with my other hand, I slid it between Maddy's ass and my hips, flexing my bicep in an attempt to hold her up. Because this was a dream, she stayed where I put her, almost high enough for me to fall completely out of her. I lifted up my hips slowly, moving my heels closer to my ass for better leverage, invading her by slow inches.

Pulling my thumb from Sam's pussy, I rubbed her juices around her back door. Eliciting a loud cry that her hand did nothing to muffle, I slowly pushed it into her ass. It was my fantasy, so I was going to damn well do as I pleased! Once I was buried up to my palm in her rear entrance, I started to enact my grand finale.

I suckled Sam's clit hard, my tongue flicking it with a staccato rhythm of up and down strokes. My stomach and legs rocketed me in and out of Maddy's tightening slit, my arm flexed to hold her up high enough for maximum extraction and penetration. My thumb pistoned Sam's ass much more slowly than the pounding Maddy was receiving, though I was most certainly not being entirely gentle.

Ten seconds into the rough stuff, both women were screaming and pressing down hard against me, their hips jerking forward and back, but I was unrelenting, sucking and fucking and fingering with everything I had. Sam's ass and Maddy's pussy were convulsing around the pieces of me I had embedded in them, which was enough to finally spur my own release.

I growled hard into Sam's clit as my orgasm hit me, and kept thrusting like an animal as gushes of come hit the depths of Maddy's tunnel. My climax felt endless, as did the shots of DNA I was spurting out. Before I was done, Sam fell off my face and hand, so I grabbed Maddy with both hands and kept punishing her. My crotch got wet as I filled Maddy beyond capacity, and still more was shooting out. Innumerable seconds later, I drove hard into her one last time, my cock letting out one more wave with a hard, throbbing pulse of pleasure. I held myself in her depths for a long moment, before falling limply back to the bed.

This is going to be a helluva mess to clean up when I wake up. I hope I didn't shoot all over Tessa while she's sleeping, that'd be hard to explain.

As I lay there panting, my eyes still firmly closed, drifting through my thoughts aimlessly, I heard Sam, Maddy and Tessa giggling. *Wait, Tessa? Did I dream that she watched us silently? Why would I dream that?*

My brows furrowed, but I mentally shrugged and decided that dreams that were weird and impossible to explain.

The giggles turned into full blown laughter, and I finally took a look around. Directly in front of me, still sitting on my sticky lap, was the gorgeous Maddy and her wonderful pink-nippled tits, covered in sweat. To my left, a panting, laughing Sam, laying on her side but looking at me. To my right, a few feet away in a chair that wasn't present in real life but I must have added in my dream, a naked, grinning, be-dimpled Tessa, her fingers still slowly playing with her beautiful sex.

"Best. Dream. Ever." I announced, which set off another round of belly laughs from the women. *Okay, I'm ready to wake up now, the laughing isn't great.*

When they didn't stop laughing and I didn't wake up, or rather, when I woke fully up, I felt my eyes open all the way, and my still wet chin hit my chest. They started laughing even harder, Sam and Tessa holding their stomachs, Maddy digging her nails into my chest. I could feel Maddy clenching around my flaccid cock as she laughed. It immediately stopped being flaccid and started thickening again.

"Uh," I said masterfully.

They finally stopped guffawing, moving down the progression chart to laughter, then giggles, and finally snickers and chuckles. Sam sat up cross-legged, facing me. Maddy ground herself on me a little, then rolled over to the side, letting a thick stream of come slip from between her now-empty lips.

"Fuck, that's hot," Sam groaned, "I love how much you come, Churro. I don't know why, but it's just so… virile. Masculine. Sexy as fuck."

"Thanks for letting me borrow your fuckstick, Tess," Maddy said to the ever-grinning woman, "Holy God, I'm gonna be bowlegged for a week." She started moving off the bed slowly, looking a bit wobbly and weak-kneed still. "I'm gonna go get all this spunk off, mind if I use your shower?"

Tessa shook her head, "Go right ahead, mi casa es su casa. Though I'm pondering making Churro walk his jizz-coated self across the common area to his own shower…"

"Uh," I repeated my previous example of sterling wit and dashing repartee.

Sam slapped a hand on my chest, "Not a dream, dumbass. Tessa told us at breakfast that you'd gotten better at eating pussy, and asked if I wanted to see for myself."

"And Maddy figured this was a perfect opportunity to ride your Harley," Tessa added, "I ordered them around a little, so I got mine too... and the best part was no one shared any secrets."

"Uh," third time's the charm, surely something that resembles a word will follow this, except it's not and I'm just rambling in my head but not speaking and Jesus Christ say something! "Fuckstick?" *You are such a fucking idiot.*

"Oh, yeah," Tessa shrugged, "I like you, Churro. Maybe it was the SoulSplice, maybe I have a soft spot for idiots who take direction or need training. Whatever it is, I've decided that I'm going to keep you as my pet. Don't worry, though, if Sam or Maddy need some relief, I'll just order you to pleasure them. I won't... what did Sam call it? Hog your hog."

What the fuck? She just... claimed me? Just decided on this, like I've got no say? I was pissed off, and I opened my mouth to tell her just that.

17

THE STRENGTH OF SPLICING

Tessa and Sam bursting into laughter again yanked the tirade out of my mouth before I could even begin to form it.

"Oh fuck, Tess, his face! Did you see his face?" Sam guffawed again.

The slightly evil glint in Tessa's eyes didn't fade as fast her laughter, and her dimpled grin looked decidedly predatory, "God, you're gullible, Churro. I said three things that were true, the rest were lies. Would you like to guess at which was which?"

I shook my head, resolutely not opening my mouth.

"First, I really do like you. I don't expect any girlfriend or boyfriend stuff, though. Second, if everyone, including you, consents, I may order you to pleasure them. Because, you know, that's fucking hot. That's why I asked you last night if you were okay being used like this. Third, I really won't hog your hog. Though if you've developed the ability to make it bigger and smaller at will, I'd like to request that you make it smaller sometimes, because you won't fit inside me right now and I really do like having sex with you." Her soft, almost shy smile instantly poured water on the fire of my anger.

"I like you too, Tessa," I admitted, "and Sam, and Maddy, each in your own ways. Maddy's clearly an insane firecracker, Sam's a strong, take-no-bullshitter, and you've got a mix of bashful and bossy that's really sexy."

"Oh fuck off, Churro," Sam said, but her voice had no heat in it. If I didn't know better, I'd think I'd embarrassed her.

"Anyway," Tessa jumped in, "Maddy confirmed that my ingestion experiment worked, and your idea about trying to change what I do with my power when I orgasm also worked - I altered your behavior with your hands to be more aggressive, and you did exactly what I wanted you to do. I had no idea you'd try it on Sam, though!"

I glanced over at Sam, briefly getting distracted by her nudity before I noticed her blush, "And I had no idea I'd like it. Tessa wasn't lying when she said you'd gotten better. That was really good."

"Err, uh, I probably wouldn't ever be that pushy. I thought I was dreaming, so I could do whatever I wanted…" I trailed off into silence.

Sam laughed again, but this didn't have the harsh edge of mockery to it, "Oh Churro, please be that pushy. I *loved* it."

Tessa quickly agreed, "Absolutely. That was fantastic. Watching the reenactment on Sam was almost as good as getting it firsthand."

The women talked about their sexual preferences for a while longer, and I mostly listened. When Maddy came out of the shower, I hopped in.

Sally had proposed assisting us with our second experiment with ingestion upgrades, and I reluctantly agreed to let her help.

As I finished my shower, I had to awkwardly admit that Sally had been pretty talented with her robotic milking arm. I don't think she managed to get as much out of me as either Tessa or Maddy had, but she assured me that I'd produced enough for a viable experiment. The whole thing still felt weird and strange, even for me.

When I was drying off, I looked at my body in Tessa's mirror. I had definitely gained some muscle mass and lost some weight. There was even the barest hint of ab definition. My arms were less blob-like, a slight indent between my bicep and whatever my underarm was called when I flexed. I had a long way to go, but after only being here for a week, my progress was nothing short of miraculous.

Finding my clothes had been whisked off to wherever Sally did our laundry, I stepped back into Tessa's room with the towel wrapped around my waist.

All three women were standing near the bed, holding large metal cups up towards each other.

"To tasty upgrades," toasted Tessa.

"Tasty upgrades," Maddy replied.

"To jizz smoothies!" Sam called.

They all laughed, clinked their cups together, and started drinking. The sight did weird things to me. A part of me was completely repulsed. Another part of me was smug as hell that they relied on me to get stronger. A third, larger portion of my psyche was instantly aroused.

"My clothes are in the laundry, so I'm going to head to mine to get dressed," I said, not wanting to comment on what they were doing.

"Hurry back," Tessa sang cheerfully, "you need to participate in this experiment too!"

I groaned and left to the sounds of their laughter and joking.

In the common area, Jack was seated at the dining table, drinking from a metal cup. Chad was just getting up and walking away.

"No fucking way," he said, "I'm not drinking that. Ever. Not a damn chance. I'm no homo."

Swallowing, Jack shrugged, "It's actually not bad tasting, if you don't think about what's in it." When he noticed me, he lifted his cup in a salute to me, "If we all need to get more powerful, I figured the least I could do was try it. Sally mixed in some strawberries and protein powder. Tastes like a regular smoothie."

"Yeah!" chimed in a very high-pitched voice from under the table. "You'd never know this was in Churro's balls just a few minutes ago! It's not even warm anymore!"

I bent over to peek at whoever was talking, and damn near fell on the floor. It - no, she - was a porcelain doll, dressed like some sort of crazy goth, punk, emo princess. Her short bob haircut was a combination of blue, red, pink, and neon green stripes. She was wearing tattered leather everything, with fishnet under most of it. She was holding a tiny tea cup, like from a child's play set.

"Churro, this is Brianna," Jack introduced us, looking distinctly unhappy, "Bri, this is Churro."

"Duh, Dad, I know who he is. It's not like there's a thousand of you down here," she squeaked. She turned back me, pointing those glossy abysses at my face. She had the same creepy ass eyes as Jack. "If I can remember all sixty-seven of my sisters' names, I think I can remember the five of you. Did you know the first thing Chad asked me was how wide my mouth opened? I showed him that it's only big enough for about a pencil, and asked if he wanted me to suck on his clit later. He didn't like being reminded that he has lady parts and got all flustered. You don't fuck with me or my sisters, or we'll find a way to ruin your life. Also, you can't actually fuck any of us, since we're not, you know, anatomically correct. We're just dolls. Do you think some of us could come stay with you? Dad's kind of being a jerk, keeping us all in our room like he is. He says it's to keep us safe, that none of you would accept us like he does and we'd be in danger. I think he's just being a scaredy-cat and needs to nut up. You know, be a man and trust that he's raised us well enough to survive on our own, outside of the nest. That looked like a pretty weird conversation Tessa had with him, though. I hear you were inside her head when it happened? How does that work? Can I try it sometime? I bet you'd like being in my head. I think lots of awesome things. I don't think I have any powers for you to upgrade, but I'd like one. I want to be a real girl! Just like Pinocchio. Except, you know, with boobs and other girl parts. I could change my name to Pinocchia, so it's more feminine. What kind of music do you like-"

"Enough, Brianna!" roared the angry god. "Jesus Christ, Churro, I know this is your first time meeting her, but I'd have expected you to interrupt her a long time ago, not stand there like a jackass!"

He was right, I was doing my Stand-Like-A-Jackass™ pose again. "Uh, sorry, Jack. Sorry, Brianna. I gotta go get dressed. It was nice to meet you."

She started squeaking again as I walked away, but I wasn't paying attention anymore. My mind was reeling. *Talking dolls… with opinions… and desires… so fucking creepy.*

WE HAD FINISHED OUR TRAINING AND EXPERIMENTS FOR THE DAY, AND were sitting around the table after eating dinner. It was just me and the ladies again. I honestly didn't care that Jack and Chad didn't seem like part of the team. I didn't see how we could use either of them to achieve Sally's goals.

The experiment to split me among the ladies, in churro form, was a horrendous failure. I had only vague memories of it, aside from overwhelming static. An old TV tuned to cosmic background radiation and set at full volume. For hours.

They reported headaches and some mental fuzziness, but nothing they described was like what I had gone through. They also didn't tell me how they'd processed me so fast, but Tessa had guessed that since there was less of me, I went quicker.

Sally was still compiling all the data and running it through test scenarios in the background on her servers, but we still had to test my tertiary power, which was what we were discussing now.

"I still think you'd be the best one," Tessa said to Sam, "Maddy and I both have previous experience with it which could skew the results one way or the other, me with a success, her with a failure."

"I'm not sure I want Churro rooting around in my thoughts, though. I keep a lot of shit locked up."

I shook my head, "It's not like that at all, Sam. I don't get access to your thoughts or your memories. Something about it keeps our pasts separated, even as it joins our present. I will admit, though, that it makes thinking very strange. My inner monologue shifts dramatically."

"Fine. Screw it, if we're doing this, let's do this. But you need to try shifting into something else. I want a fucking cupcake."

"That's a really good idea," Maddy said. "We're all experimenting to see how we can alter our powers, and that'd be a good one."

"You should also see how much you can alter your body during your reformation phase," added Tessa. She gestured at Sam, suddenly looking bashful again.

"Right," Sam said as she pulled out her baggie of metal, "our sexy little Domme had some ideas, if you think you can manage them." The metal quickly pooled together, and soon expanded into a twelve-inch-tall replica of me. Naked.

"Whoa, Sam," Maddy said breathlessly, "How'd you get the sculpture so big?"

"Oh, I made the inside hollow. This is just a thin shell."

"That's fantastic," cheered Tessa, "You're already learning some damn impressive control, Sam!"

Sam waved away the compliments, but I could tell she was proud of herself. I was proud of her, too. She made the sculpture smack itself in the face, drawing all of our eyes back to it. It had a hand-shaped dent in its face, and we all chuckled a little.

"Right then, this is you now," she said, pointing to my cock, flab and barely-there muscles, "And this is what Tessa thinks you should aim for." The statue altered subtly, but significantly. My shaft shrunk to about half its normal size, I lost most of my fat, and my muscles took on sharper definition. Sam gave the statue an erection.

I tried to take a mental snapshot of the statue. *If I really can sculpt my actual body as easily as Sam sculpts me out of metal, what's to stop me from being an underwear model?* Merging with Sam aside, I was excited to see what I could do to myself, now that I had a power that seemed personally useful. Or at least had the potential to be.

Of course, none of that would matter if the SoulSplice behaved in unexpected ways. I stood up and stripped off my underwear, handing it to Tessa with a smile. All three of them eyed me hungrily, and I couldn't help but feel pleased with that. I climbed onto the table and sat cross-legged, my dick resting on my ankle.

"Okay, I'm going to go for a cupcake."

Tessa gave me a light stroke down the length of my shaft with a wicked grin. "Come back with less," she ordered.

"Yes, Mistress," I replied.

Closing my eyes, I pictured a vanilla cupcake with chocolate frosting. I imagined it already out of its paper, since I had no idea what would happen to me if a part of me was thrown in the garbage. Holding tightly to my mental image, I flexed my power. It buzzed in the back of my mind, which shocked me into stopping.

"That was weird… I could feel my power vibrating like when I'm in someone else and they use theirs. I'm going to try to boost it."

I created the mental tableau of me as a cupcake again, this time grabbing onto my power. I held the vibration and the image of the dessert food, and *blew*.

"OOF," SAM SAID, "HE JUST WOKE UP. I DEFINITELY FELT HIM ARRIVE. SHIT, that was fast." She licked her lips, and I tasted the sugary frosting residue on them.

It worked! I became a cupcake! I cheered.

"Ow, not so loud, you twat," Sam complained, holding her head. "He's stroking his ego about being a different dessert."

Oh, sorry, I forgot you can hear me now.

"Okay, so he can be a cupcake now, and there's a definite sensation when his consciousness returns?" Tessa was in full scientist mode. Sam just nodded. "Alright, this is all helpful. And it shows that his powers are growing in strength, not just ours. This is good, very good. When do you think you'll attempt to merge?"

No time like the present, I said.

"Yeah, now's fine," Sam agreed, then took a deep breath, "Okay, how do we do this?"

I laughed. *I have no idea. With both previous mergers, they were turned on as fuck. If you don't mind, I can test some other aspects of this.* I imagined the sensation of my tongue stroking over her clit.

"Ooh, I like it," Sam said with a giggly shiver, "He just, uh, mentally licked me."

Tessa and Maddy grinned at her.

"All he did to me was pinch me, the little jerk," Maddy laughed.

"Let's get out of the common room," said Tessa, "but if it's alright with you, can I watch? You know, for research purposes." Her smile promised that she didn't have research on the brain.

I don't mind if you don't, Sam, but it's your body to share.

No shit, Sherlock, she thought back at me, exposing another new feature of my power, *I don't need or want your permission.* "Actually, Tess, I think I'd like to explore this privately. I promise I'll share everything with you later," she added out loud.

Tessa shrugged like she didn't care, but I could tell she was disappointed. Sam reached out and placed a comforting hand on Tessa's. "It's not you, babe, I'm just mostly straight, remember?" Tessa nodded, and Sam excused herself back to her room.

She flopped face down onto her bed, arms and legs spread-eagled. *Alright, Churro, fuck my brain with your brain! Let's see what you can do!*

Alright, I don't know if you'll be able to stop me if I do something you don't like, but I want to see how far this rabbit hole goes. How about a safeword?

She laughed into her blanket, "Chad. The safeword is Chad, because nothing turns me off faster."

I laughed in her mind with her, *That's a damn good one. Okay, any sensations off limits?*

She rolled over onto her back and slid her hands under her head. "I don't think so? I mean, don't torture me or anything, and don't be a sick fuck by like trying to fuck my ear or anything."

Heh, okay, no ear fucking. We'll start small… I flicked a mental tongue against her earlobe, and she squirmed slightly. I did it again across her nipple. *Wait, if this is all imaginary, I'm probably not limited to my physical features. Sam, I need you to tell me what this feels like.* Firing up my imagination, I pictured something that I was sure she'd never experienced before.

"Oooohhh," she groaned, suddenly writhing with her entire body, "it feels… it's like… fuck, gimme a sec, stop." I backed off. "It was like a thousand tongues, licking every square inch of my body. I even felt it between my toes."

Perfect. For this next test, I'm going to see if I can take control of your body. I thought about her arms reaching down to caress her chest, but nothing happened. *Hmm, didn't work. Okay, can you spread your arms and legs out for me?*

She sprawled out across the bed, and I imagined large hands grabbing her wrists and ankles gently. She let out a squeak and started to struggle. I flexed my mental muscles, and we fought back and forth. Every time she made progress in pulling in, I somehow pulled her back into position.

"Churro, what… how… what are you doing?"

I'm imagining restraining you. I'll stop now. I let the hands vanish back into the depths of my imagination.

"No, you don't need to stop, just… not too rough, okay? I don't mind a little, though." She pulled her arms to her chest and brought her knees together. I could feel her body responding positively to what I'd done, a fire building in her core.

Okay, go limp for me? She almost instantly relaxed. With the idea of a large hand in my mind, I lifted her arm with it. Her arm floated up from her chest.

"Holy shit, Churro, it feels like there's someone here grabbing me." She watched me move her arm with wide eyes. "Churro! Try to make me float!"

I dropped her arm, and imagined a giant spatula beneath her. I applied some upward force to it, and she raised up enough to reduce how far into the bed she sank, but no matter how much I struggled in my mind, I couldn't get her into the air.

"Christ, Churro… Can you imagine…" She got up quickly and walked to her wall. "Imagine a thick boxing glove on me!" I did, and she punched the wall with a gentle jab. She grinned, and punched it harder. The wall made a soft 'pap!' noise when she connected. "Okay, give me a spike!" This time when she punched the wall, I felt it screeching against my mind painfully, even as my spike tore a hole in it.

That hurt me, Sam, but holy shit. I lifted her hand with my imaginary one, and gave her a mental high five. She laughed.

"Okay, buddy, this definitely has some combat potential. Especially if it gets stronger as you level up. If you can make me fly, I'll let you fuck me in the ass." She was wearing a huge grin.

I can already fuck you in the ass, Sam. I imagined my cock, fully lubricated, pressing against her tightly puckered ass. She yelped and tightened her butt cheeks together, which did nothing to stop me. I pressed against her again, just giving her a little bit of pressure.

"Chad! Chad, Chad, stop! You perverted fuck! I said you gotta make me fly first!"

I laughed in her mind, *I'm just teasing Sam. But if you take the time to think about it, the amount of control I have right now is a little overwhelming. You're essentially helpless. The only thing stopping me from doing literally everything I can imagine is… me.*

Her already elevated heart rate spiked as adrenaline flooded her system. Instinctively, I knew I'd triggered her flight or fight response. Only, I wasn't something she could fight *or* run from. She was frozen in place, hardly even breathing.

She was feeling as skittish as a deer who can see a single wolf, knowing there must be half a dozen more that couldn't be seen. *Sam, please relax. I promise that I won't hurt you. I may not be a very smart man, or have much in the way of a moral compass, but I do know that rape isn't something I'm interested in, and I know that I like having you as a friend.*

"I don't like this anymore, Churro. We've only known each other a week, and giving you this kind of control over me… No, I don't like this at all. It's not that I don't trust you, but I don't trust you *enough*. This… this is too much. Please don't imagine anything else at me."

Okay, Sam, I won't. Should we go get Maddy and Tessa? I honestly felt a little drunk on power now, and was having a hard time not playing around. Getting witnesses to keep me accountable might be the only way to control myself. I was tempted to try to soothe her with a hug or something, but with how hard she was panicking, I knew I shouldn't do a damn thing.

Tessa and Maddy were curled up on the couch together, watching a movie, when Sam walked back to the common room. They looked so cute together, tall and short, all cuddled up.

Awww. I thought, before I could stop myself.

Sam giggled, seeming much calmer now that she was in public. "Churro thinks you two are adorable together."

They laughed and paused their flick. "Why are you back so soon?" Tessa asked. "Did something happen?"

"Sort of," Sam started, "it's… well… Churro is basically in charge right now. Well, sort of. Fuck, I don't know."

"You merged, and now Churro is, what, in the lead role?" Maddy asked, concern lacing her voice.

"No, no, we're not merged. He was showing me, I guess practicing on me, what he can do with his imaginary feelings. He can make me feel anything he can think of. Even to the point of physically affecting me."

Both Maddy and Tessa now looked terrified.

"Anything…" Maddy said breathlessly.

"What do you mean, physically affecting you?" Tessa asked.

Sam sat near her, and flopped her arm into Tessa's lap. "Feel my muscles in my shoulder. Okay, Churro, now lift my arm. Tessa, feel that I'm not flexing at all as it goes up? Okay, Churro, now hold it in place, hard."

When she felt my grip tightening, she started pulling against it, struggling to get free from me. I could tell she wasn't panicking, but she really was putting all of her strength into it. I had to fight hard to hold her still, but I managed it. When Sam finally stopped struggling, I gently released her arm.

"Holy shit." Tessa and Maddy said together.

Sam just nodded. "He promised he wouldn't imagine anything else happening to me, and I believe him. But my life is… in his imaginary hands, and while I trust him not to hurt me, I'm not at all comfortable giving him that sort of power over me."

Both of the other women nodded seriously. "What would you like to have happen next, Sam?" Tessa asked softly.

"Will you spend the night with me?" I could feel Sam practically begging them with her eyes. They both agreed instantly.

I'm sorry, Sam, I whispered in her mind, *I didn't know… well. Anything.*

It's not your fault, Churro, she thought back at me, *this is… I don't want to say personal, but it's not something you'd understand.*

Okay, just think at me if you want me to say or do anything. Unless you approach me, I'm just going to sit here as quietly as I can until you process me out, alright?

Thanks, Churro. You're pretty okay for an imaginary omnipotent moron, I felt her slight smile as she teased me, and I knew we'd be okay once I was out of her system.

18

THE TEAM MEETS DANIELLE

The rest of the night passed with nothing worth noting happening. In the morning, Sam had a cup of coffee to help pass me through, even though by that point my consciousness was almost fully gone. I was able to concentrate on what form I wanted for my body when I woke up, but it was a challenge to hold the image in my mind.

When I woke up in my reconstruction chamber beneath our hub of rooms, I took stock of myself. My spare tire was completely gone, just a thin layer of fat between my skin and now-defined muscles. And holy shit, what a set of muscles! I flexed my arm, watching in awe as my sharply delineated bicep popped up, far larger than it had ever been. Far larger than I'd ever even hoped it could be. My dangly bits were just on the big side of average - true average, not my misguided average from last week. I smiled, hoping for some more quality time with Tessa.

I sped through my morning routine, including being milked by Sally, before dressing in my guild-provided underwear, a pair of baggy shorts, and some sneakers. I couldn't wait to get to the ObCo so I could test out my new body.

Walking through the common area, I saw Sam sitting at the dining room table by herself.

"Hey, Sam," I started, "how are you feeling?"

"I'm okay, I guess," she replied. "Last night got scary, but thank you for backing off." She looked at me, a thoughtful expression on her face.

I shrugged and waved off her thanks, "It's fine. I'm sorry if I pushed it too far."

She shrugged back at me, and remained silent. Not knowing what else to say and feeling awkward, I just waved meekly and headed towards the training room.

"Get stronger, Churro," she said to my back as I walked away, "I really do want to fly."

I raised a hand to acknowledge that she'd been heard, and entered the ObCo.

AS USUAL, THE COURSE WAS SET UP TO MIMIC AN URBAN ENVIRONMENT; dark alleys, reeking dumpsters, rusty fire escapes. It was more of a simulator than a true obstacle course. The lights were down low, like it was late evening; not quite dark, but definitely not daytime either.

"Churro, in order to test the capabilities of your new body, this scenario is going to be relatively simple," Sally told me. "You will be interrupting a bag-snatcher and you must overcome and detain the perpetrator. You will have sixty seconds before the perpetrator receives backup. Begin your patrol."

I nodded before jogging into the faux urban evening. The streets were slick with the remnants of a moderate rain, the streetlights reflecting and refracting in interesting ways. As I headed deeper and deeper, I wondered at the full technological capabilities of the ObCo. Before I could determine if it had a set depth or just went on forever, I heard shouting from around the corner to my left.

Picking up my pace, I rounded the building. Before me were a man and a woman, both yelling incoherently at each other, fighting over the shoulder strap of a canvas satchel. I grinned when I realized that I was now bigger than him, so I fearlessly ran up and punched him right in his stomach. He folded over my arm like a wet napkin with a loud, "Oooof!"

The woman grinned at me. "Thanks," she said, before running down the sidewalk.

The man collapsed to the wet cement, gasping for air as her footsteps faded into the gloom. "What the fuck, man?" he demanded. "You just helped that bitch steal my bag!"

Quickly shaking myself out of my Stand-like-a-Jackass™ pose, I mumbled an apology and took off after the bandit.

She had stopped running after turning the next corner, so I caught up to her relatively quickly. When she heard me behind her, she turned to look at me with wide, surprised eyes. Then she grinned again, and dropped the satchel to the ground. "Alright, hero, let's dance!" Then she charged me.

Caught flat-footed, still shaken up by Sally switching stereotypical gender roles for the scenario, my assailant planted her shoulder right into my gut, her hands grabbing the backs of my knees as she tackled me like a pro football linebacker. She kept driving her legs as I arced through the air, slamming me down onto my back hard enough to blast the air from my lungs and the stars into my vision.

When the blackness faded, I was looking up to see her straddling my waist, her knees pinning my wrists to the sidewalk. I lifted my head from the concrete as I struggled to free my arms. She cocked an arm back, twisted her body as it rocketed forward, and I went to sleep when her freight train of a fist connected with my eye socket and the back of my head connected with the ground.

I WAS BACK ON THE COUCH IN THE COMMON AREA, WHICH I SHOULD probably just start calling my infirmary. Trying to ignore the splitting pain shooting through my skull, I turned to see that Jack was sitting nearby reading a book.

"Urk," I said as I dragged myself to a more upright seated position. "What time is it?"

"It's about to be lunchtime," he answered, sounding like a commuter train rumbling through a tunnel.

"Churro, your concussion has been healed, though you should feel some residual pain. I have left it as a reminder that simply having muscles does not make you any better at hand to hand combat."

"Gee, thanks, Sally," I responded with as much sarcasm as I could muster, "I'd never have figured that out on my own after you pummeled me with that sledgehammer. Did you really need to hit me so hard?"

"Churro, I did not need to, no," she answered.

After waiting a few seconds to see if Sally was going to add anything, Jack chuckled. "Nice new muscles, Churro. I think you should head to the dojo to work on your skills, though."

I nodded, another spike of pain shooting into my brain from the motion. "Yeah, hopefully Sally won't nearly kill me if it's just supposed to be practice."

Jack offered a hand to help me off the couch, which I accepted. His warm, strong grip was at odds with his alabaster features and glossy, dead eyes. I had been expecting clammy and weak. Everything about Jack had been surprising or incongruent, so I was having trouble figuring out his whole deal. Was he creepy or friendly? Fair or foul? I realized that I was going to have to take some time to really think about what I knew about Jack, versus the assumptions I had made from his appearance.

Side by side, we entered the training area again, heading towards the dojo.

Sally separated us into private areas, activating her martial arts training holograms, and spent the next four hours tossing me around with hip throws, leg sweeps, and submission holds. She was brutal, and ruthless, giving me no mercy. At the end, though, I felt like I was just a little more capable than I had been, learning to at least recognize when I was about to be thrown, even if I couldn't do anything to counter or avoid it.

I REALLY NEED TO STOP SKIPPING MEALS, I THOUGHT TO MYSELF AS I TORE ravenously into my dinner - beef medallions in a red wine sauce. I couldn't believe the quality of food we were getting. I hadn't eaten this well since my power manifested and I was downgraded to the sidelines.

Sally's alert chime sounded, ringing like a mix between a wind chime and a doorbell. Or at least what movies told me a doorbell sounded like, as I don't remember ever having one of my own, having been taken from my parents when I was five.

"Omega Team," she said, losing all trace of sensuality to return to her purely robotic voice, "Please prepare for a visit. You have five minutes."

We all scrambled to clear our dinners, darting back to our rooms to dress in something more appropriate than our exercise wear. I tossed on a pair of jeans and a long-sleeve button down shirt. I had picked a light blue shirt, a color that I was hoping complimented my darker blue eyes, thought now that I considered it, maybe I could change my eye color. I took a few extra moments to head into my bathroom to use the mirror. I closed my eyes for concentration, picturing in my mind's eye that I was still me, only with brilliant, sparkling golden eyes.

When the buzzing in the back of my mind started to become noticeable, I tried to gather it up and blow on it. Nothing happened. No sudden surge of power, no increase in buzzing potency. *Well, whatever, I don't know how this works.* Bringing the mental image and the buzz back, I flexed my power.

I felt a sensation throughout my entire body that could only be described as flickering out of reality and then back in. It only lasted for single, eternal, blink of time, but it rattled me something fierce. My eyes shot open, and I could only gape in wonder at the reflection in the mirror.

It was me, but I had gold irises! A faint shimmer caught my attention and I leaned in close - my eyes were literally sparking off little flecks of glowing power.

"Churro," Sally whispered in my ear, causing a pleasurable tingle to race down my spine, "I would suggest seeing if you can return to your base form. Changes such as you've manifested will be noticed by your superiors, who are currently waiting impatiently for you, and it would not do to display such a massive growth in power."

I nodded wordlessly, closing my eyes again to imagine the slightly flabby, weak-armed version of myself that I had been only a few days ago, making sure to hold in my mind the image of my normal, dark blue eyes.

Buzz. Flicker.

I opened my eyes to see my old self staring listlessly back from the mirror. I sighed, shoulders slumping, as I trudged out to the common area.

"About time, Omega," grumbled Warden, looking spiffy in his well-tailored business suit. He was standing next to the Gemstone Mage, dressed modestly as always. On the other side of Gemma stood a young Latina woman, with curly, dark brown hair, dark brown eyes, and a caramel hue to her skin. She had a serious look on her face, and I thought I could see a trace of anger flashing in her eyes. She was wearing the composite armor plates that were part of our full uniform on top of the black underwear we all wore. "Now that we're all here, it's time to introduce you to your newest teammate: this is Danielle 'TaseLite' Walker. Formerly of Upsilon Team, she has experience working with local law enforcement, and will be taking a mentor role with Omega Team and getting you ready to face the outside world."

Danielle nodded solemnly.

Gemma picked up where Warden left off. "The terrorist organization known as the Truthseekers appear to have gained the allegiance of new, rogue supers. Their attacks have picked up in both frequency and brutality. What used to be bi-monthly are now almost daily attacks. They have yet to directly attack any THG assets, personnel or property, but they are keeping the local and rural PDs busy with their strikes against government facilities. As part of our alliance with the Republic of Federated States, we are sending more teams to assist with recovery and protection. What this means for you is that you'll be joining a normie patrol team in two weeks. TaseLite will do her best to get you up to snuff, but the responsibility truly falls on your own shoulders."

Omega Team and I all looked around at each other, sharing confused but hopeful looks. Maddy looked nothing but excited, a manic gleam in her eyes and a strange smile on her face. I smiled tentatively at TaseLite, nodding my head a little bit. She looked at me, and I mean intensely looked at me, with an expression I couldn't decipher, her body language and posture giving away nothing about what she was thinking.

"And that's that, Omegas, dismissed." Warden turned around and walked out of our hub without another word. Gemma followed him, briefly giving us a concerned look, almost as if she was worried about sending her children off to do something dangerous. She must have firmed her resolve, however, as her stride when she left was as confident as it always was.

When the hiss of an automatic door closing faded away, we converged on TaseLite. I offered a handshake. "Hi TaseLite, I'm Churro, it's nice to meet you."

She gave me another intense stare before taking my hand and pumping it up and down a couple times. "Same, Churro. But I actually go by Dani, at least when we're here at the Guild."

We went around the circle introducing ourselves, Dani jumping slightly when it was Jack's turn and he gazed at her with the two abyssal holes in his face.

"My name is Chad," he said, holding the handshake for an extra-long time, rubbing the back of her hand with his left, "Don't worry, I'll remind you of it again, so you can scream it later."

Suddenly Chad was screaming, his arms locking up as the sound of wild electricity bounced through the room. Dani peeled her hand away from Chad's twitching arms, "Nice to meet you, Chad. Keep that shit to yourself or I'll keep showing you why they named me after the famous electroshock weapon."

The other ladies chuckled and led Dani away to keep grilling her about the status of the country and city, and what it was like to go on patrol with normies.

Jack and I laughed when one of Chad's arms twitched hard enough to *almost* make him punch himself in the face. Chad was just swearing quietly enough not to be overheard by the ladies and storming back to his room.

When he was gone, we rejoined the ladies and our newest teammate.

"...eah," Dani was saying, "I've been going on weekly patrols for about the last six months. It's really not that bad, unless you end up attached to a group of anti-super cops. They'd never go so far as to *do* anything to us, but they seem to like making our lives hell. Making up perps that we need to chase through the sewers, babysitting patrol cars, 'forgetting' us when they get a call after making us do a coffee run, things like that. Thankfully, those pricks seem to be in the minority, and the rest of the force are decent men and women who actually care about making our city a safer place."

"What kind of mentoring can we expect from you?" Tessa asked her.

Dani glanced at me with a curious look on her face before turning back to answer Tessa. "Well, honestly, I think I'm mostly here to tell you what you can expect, and how you should behave. You know, to keep up the image that THG wants us to present when we're in public. Pretty faces being seen helping, basically. I guess I might also be able to help you with combat training, seeing as I've been here a year more than you all, and I started higher up than Omega." She looked around at all of us again, sighing. "I won't lie, I think our ranking system is total bullshit."

"We do, too," I said, "but it's the hand we've been dealt, and we really want to get into the game." Heads nodded all around me. "I think with enough effort and drive, we'll be able to climb the ranks, too."

Dani shook her head sadly, "Unless you have a magical way to boost your powers, you're pretty much stuck here."

I just grinned at her.

"Let's get to work," Maddy interjected while elbowing me, hard, in the stomach.

19

TESSA GETS AGGRESSIVE

We'd only spent about an hour last night going over some of the more routine expectations relating to being paired up with normie patrols. It was fairly standard, I'd thought, mostly about how we were to follow their orders except in cases of extreme danger. We were each going to be given a small device that would allow us to call for hero backup if we found ourselves in a situation facing off against some Truthseekers or a powered villain. For normie crimes, we were to assist to the best of our capabilities.

To determine those capabilities for herself, rather than just letting Sally tell her, Dani was working with me one-on-one in the dojo. She was far kinder of an instructor than Sally was.

Between take-downs - always her dropping me, never the other way around - as I lay sweating on the padded mats that made up the floor, Dani appraised me from head to toe. I could clearly tell from the look on her face that she was less than impressed with me as the so-called leader of Omega Team.

"After hearing about what you did to Johnny, I thought you'd be… I don't know. More impressive, maybe? Not this," she waved her hand at all of me, "whatever this is."

I held back a frustrated grunt. "It's not like I went toe-to-toe with the guy. Shit, I didn't even know he was a guy. I just thought it was some annoying bug bothering me."

"Regardless of how it went down, I regret his death, but I'm not sad he's gone." She turned half away from me, so I took the opportunity to study her profile of curves while she was paying more attention to the thoughts haunting her mind. "I knew him, you know, before he got promoted to leading Omega Team."

I shook my head, but she still wasn't looking at me. "No, I didn't know anyone knew him. I mean, I figured someone did, but literally nothing happened to me or my team as a result of his death, so I figured he probably wasn't very popular." *When I bothered to think about him at all,* I added to myself.

She snorted angrily, a few sparks starting to dance across her fingertips. "Not 'very popular.' That's a good way to put it. The guy was scum. Pure trash. Maybe not murder-worthy, but this world is a slightly better place without him in it." She shook her head, then turned her dark-eyed glare back to me. "Thanks for sparring, Churro, I'll talk to the AI about changing up your training programs."

The tone of her voice left me no doubt that I was being dismissed. I opened my mouth to claim something about being the leader here, but I just didn't have it in me to fight for something I didn't really want anyway.

Since it was still fairly early in the day, I jogged over to the ObCo, activating my power as I went. I was pretty sure I didn't manage to get the gold eyes along with my improved musculature, but I felt the extra bounce in my step as my body reached much higher heights of strength and agility. I grinned. *This is awesome! I'm a fucking shapeshifter!*

"Churro, Tessa is currently running the course. She expressed a desire to have you join her. Mission parameters are crowd control and de-escalation. If de-escalation is not possible, subdue with prejudice."

"Shut up or get knocked the fuck out, got it. Thanks, Sally." I cracked my neck and knuckles, feeling nicely warmed up from fighting with Dani.

The door slid open with a nearly-silent whoosh, and I entered to see Tessa and a few police officers standing between a mob of about forty people and a building designed to look like a small-town courthouse. She smiled brightly and waved at me when she saw me, so I jogged over to her.

"These people are here protesting a 'not guilty' verdict for a guy accused of embezzling a few hundred thousand dollars from the company they work for," she told me. "They're getting riled up by a guy in the back. That one," she pointed, "with the plaid and jeans."

I nodded, "Okay, I'll go see if I can get him to back off." I tapped the armor plates on my chest and swung my arms around to loosen some of the tension in my shoulders. I knew this was just a simulation, but Sally could come up with incredibly realistic scenarios.

I jostled my way through the angry crowd, approaching the target that Tessa had outlined for me, getting angry glares and muttered curses for my trouble.

"Fuck off, loser," the ringleader said as soon as I got up to him.

"I apprecia-" I started, getting cut off by a set of knuckles that were trying to collapse my trachea. Blinking through the pain, I growled, "Good enough."

Switching to an aggressive stance as I closed the distance between us, I brought my left fist around in a tight hook, slamming it firmly into his right cheek. As the force of my punch started to push him sideways, I hit the underside of his jaw with my right. His teeth clacked together loudly, the tip of his tongue flying over my shoulder.

He started screaming and trying to run away, but I refused to let him off that easy. *You wanna start shit with me, you punk bitch? Die!* I leaped knee-first into his lower spine, crumpling him to ground beneath me. After his head bounced off the pavement, I grabbed his skull with both hands and slammed his face back down with as much of my new, significantly more considerable, strength as I could. A hollow thunk preceded the sound of a ripe melon being split, and I reveled in the sensation of warm bits of brain and skull fragments in my fingers.

The crowd finally started screaming, trying to get away from the site of the murder. I lashed out all around me with punches, kicks, leg sweeps; anything I could think of to inflict the maximum amount of carnage on these fucking sheep-people as I could. *Die! Die! Die! Diediedie!* I shouted in my head, landing a grab on the hood of a protester's sweatshirt.

Yanking hard, my target landed on her back, the air getting blasted from her lungs, before I knifed her in the throat, the blade where my hand used to exist slipping through her flesh as easily as swimming. It caught up for a second on the bone of her spine, but I just growled louder and forced it all the way through.

The screams intensified as I ran about madly, slicing and stabbing everyone I could reach with my blades, now replacing both of my hands. I was literally shaking with rage and aggression as the blood sprayed in all directions, coating me from head to toe. When the closest living person left was too far away to chase, I raised my arms to the sky and howled my fury with every fiber of my being.

And as quickly as it started, the need to kill vanished, leaving me gasping. I looked around me at the dozen corpses I'd created, and vomited all over the ground. I tried wiping my mouth and got a long, painful gash on my cheek for my efforts. "What the fuck was that?" I whispered through gritted teeth. I was dripping blood, my own and the blood of others, though now that I wasn't being blinded by murderous instincts, I could feel a slight difference between my blood and whatever facsimile Sally used for her holographic creations.

I looked to Tessa, who was gaping at me with open-mouthed shock, one hand stuck between her legs.

"Tessa," I said with more calm than I felt, "did you use your power on me?"

"I… uh… Yeah, I did. I had no idea it would do that, I swear!" She had her free hand up like she was planning to reach for me or protect herself from me, her eyes darting between the bodies and my blood-coated self. "Churro, your hands!"

Shaking my head slowly, I brought my arms up again. Eight-inch-long blades protruded from the ends of my wrists, four inches wide and wickedly serrated on both edges. I watched a droplet of blood squiggle slowly towards my wrist, a few strands of hair getting pulled along with it. "Yeah, hands. Whatever, I'll figure out how to fix them later. What did you do me? That's way more important right now."

"I tried to make you more aggressive… I didn't want you to be a pussy when you tried to stop that guy." She seemed to finally realize her hand was between her thighs, and she yanked it out. "It didn't seem like it was working, so I tried to… you know, give it a better chance. I didn't know it was going to turn you into a raging lunatic, though!"

I growled a little, not knowing if this massacre was her fault, or if she just freed something in my psyche that had been buried, dormant. Forgotten, like I had been. A glance at Tessa's fear-stricken eyes made me realize that I was still growling, and loudly. I stopped, and dropped my arms to my sides, before turning around slowly.

On my way to the exit from this charnel house, Tessa called out quietly, "I'm sorry, Churro."

I waved a blade at her, defeated. "I'm going to shower."

Before I entered the common area, I activated my power, imagining my base form as clearly as I could. The sting of the cut on my cheek disappeared completely. Feeling returned, painfully, to my fingers, which I wiggled enthusiastically, though I was still covered in copious amounts of blood and other human detritus. My hands were mockingly clean, pale-skinned and soft-looking, not tainted with the aftermath of my vicious murder-frenzy. I snorted at the irony.

"Holybagoffucks, whyareyouallcovered-" Brianna began, before Jack placed a hand over her mouth. Her squeaks kept going, muffled into obscurity.

"Damn, Churro, what happened?" Jack asked me.

I shrugged. "Tessa used her power to make me aggressive. It worked. Well."

"Jack, Churro killed fourteen civilians and one non-lethal, unarmed combatant." Sally almost sounded… proud? *That couldn't be right, could it? She couldn't* want *me to kill people. Could she?*

"Thank fuck it was only in the ObCo," Jack said. "I had no idea her power could do something like that."

I snorted again in response and kept walking to my room. "You and me both, brother," I told him before closing and locking my door.

Stepping into the shower fully clothed, I turned the water on. The cold blast was refreshing and helped chill some of the anger I was still feeling. As it washed the blood from me, and slowly warmed up, I had to rest my head against the tiles. *What is happening to me? What am I becoming? Was that Tessa, or was that me? Am I capable of doing that if I get mad enough?*

No answers were forthcoming, so I stripped off my blood-stained clothes and spotless black underwear. My shower took a long time, and I still didn't feel clean. *I guess you can't wash your soul with soap and water.*

AFTER LUNCH - A QUIET AND SOLEMN AFFAIR, EVERYONE HAVING HEARD the gossip of my murderous rampage by then - I was in the strength training room. Instead of free weight systems like we'd all seen in movies and on TV, everything here was connected to resistance cables, controlled by Sally. I was happier with that than usual, as it meant that, as long as I didn't make external changes, I could shift my muscles in various ways to experiment with increasing my strength. I was mildly annoyed that I had to keep my power secret from Dani - for now, at least - but this was a good opportunity for me to practice.

I had Sally pull up some anatomy diagrams for me, so I could try to isolate muscle groups. The first thing I wanted to attempt was making my biceps more efficient.

Picturing my arms in my mind, with my eyes closed, I imagined the muscle fibers being made from an elastic, electrically-triggered polymer whose only name was an incredibly long combination of numbers and letters. When the buzz sounded in my head, I flexed my power...

...and dropped to the ground, groaning in agony. My arms failed to respond to my attempts to use them, so I landed hard on my ass, the useless limbs flopping around like landed salmon. The fire rippling from my shoulders to my fingertips was excruciating and it took me almost thirty seconds to get my default image settled and shift back.

It's fine, this just needs more practice, I told myself.

I spent the next four hours studying the anatomy of my arms in more depth; the veins, the muscles, the nerves. The connection points between tendons and bones and the physical configuration of cartilage and sinew. I practiced changing one thing at a time, starting with blocking my nerves from sending pain signals to my brain.

"And thank God I did," I said to myself. The repeated failures of altering the base composition of my arms had been extremely painful until my nerve work was better. Even after the loss of pain, I still struggled with the transformations. While it seemed like I could change myself into anything, changing myself into something functional was far more challenging.

Sally had drilled into me the importance of always keeping a mental picture of my base self in my mind, so that I could quickly switch back. That probably saved my life when I really fucked up a transformation attempt, turning my tendons to jelly and my arms slipped out of my shoulder sockets. My skin had stretched so much from the weight and lack of skeletal support that I had been able to touch my knees without bending over even a little bit.

There were things - well, *a* thing - that I wanted to be able to change at will, but I sure as shit wasn't going to mess around with *that* until I had a much better handle on how everything worked on the inside.

However not ready for that transformation I felt, I had made some progress. With Sally's assistance and a vivid imagination, I was able to thread electrochemical-reactive polymers into the main muscle mass of my biceps, and into the tendons holding said muscles to my bones. The result was far more impressive than I'd expected: I could now curl just over two hundred pounds.

The best part was now that I knew how to do it safely and effectively, I discovered I could sort of 'save' the transformation in my mind and more easily apply it to new muscle groups. Less than two hours after my breakthrough, every muscle, tendon, and ligament in my body was three or four times stronger - and no one could tell just by looking at me.

My good mood seemed infectious, as everyone but Tessa was fairly animated at dinner that night. Even Chad seemed to be in a decent mood, laughing at other people's jokes and generally not being a tool.

After finishing my second helping of beer can chicken, I pulled Tessa over to the couch. She refused to meet my eyes.

"Okay, Tessa, talk to me. What are you thinking?"

She remained silent for a while before finally facing me. "How do we know… how can we tell if what happened in the ObCo came from you or from me?" Tears glistened in her eyes, but refused to drop. "Can I literally control people? Force anyone to behave the way I want?"

Tessa looked so scared that I couldn't help but scoot closer to her and wrap my arms around her shoulders, pulling her in for a hug. When she didn't resist, instead burying her face in my chest and returning my embrace, I figured I'd made the right call.

"There might not be a way to know for absolute sure, but maybe you can get a volunteer or two to let you try to make them act completely opposite to who they are? I'll admit, I've probably got some deeply buried rage in me at the way I've been treated the last few years, so that one probably isn't the best example."

She mumbled some noises into my shirt, but I couldn't tell what she was trying to say, so I continued, "But here's something to think about: I didn't feel like I wasn't myself, or like I was being controlled. I just felt… rage, fury, wrath. You may have triggered the feelings, but those actions, I think, were all me. I don't think it was your fault." I shuddered as I really thought about what it said about me that I'd killed all those people.

Tessa pulled back just enough to look up at me, but left her arms wrapped around my ribs. "And that's terrifying, Churro… if you're capable of that… and your power is growing. I don't know, doesn't that scare you?"

I nodded, the giant lump in my throat making it impossible to say it out loud.

"I'm so sorry I did that to you. Next time, I'll experiment with less dangerous feelings. If there is a next time," she trailed off into silence.

"There's absolutely a next time, Tess. We all need to master our growing powers, no matter how scary they may be." I knew I had to do something to shock Tessa out of her self-flagellation. I glanced around the common area to see that people were either absorbed in their own activities or had gone to their rooms. "Would you like to see something I figured out today?"

"You experimented?" She was glaring at me now, sitting back and away from me, her hands planted angrily on her hips. "Without me?"

I laughed; I couldn't help it. *She's just so damn adorable when she's mad.* "There she is. Welcome back, Tessa. Yes, I absolutely did, and before you bombard me with a thousand questions, I'd just like to say that it's entirely possible for me to hurt myself, and some things are intuitive, but some are not. Now... would you like to see what I managed?"

She grinned and nodded eagerly.

Taking another look around, I stood up from the couch and pulled her to her feet. I smiled back at her and dropped my hands to her hips, and then lifted her - easily - into the air over my head.

Peals of squealing laughter rang from above, drawing the eyes of Dani and Maddy, and she waved her arms and legs around like crazy. I kept a firm grip on her hips and spun her around, pumping her up and down in the air, doing everything I could think of to show off my new strength. Finally, when she was breathless and dizzy, I held my arms straight out from my shoulders, parallel to the floor.

She smirked at me at first, but as the moments turned into seconds, and the seconds approached a minute, and my arms weren't shaking from the effort, her eyes finally went wide.

"Churro, that's fucking amazing!"

I grinned again, very much enjoying myself. Right up until she smacked the insides of my elbows, forcing my arms to buckle and drop her to the floor. She landed lightly, and immediately jumped back into me. Her legs wrapped around my waist, her arms went behind my neck, and she pressed her lips into mine. She kissed me deeply.

"I'm so proud of you," she said when she finally came up for air. Slowly detaching herself from my body, she grabbed my hand and started leading me towards her quarters. Maddy grinned and gave us a thumbs up. Dani's expression was harder to decipher, looking something like a mix of confusion and consternation.

When Tessa and I got into her room, I ceased worrying about what other people were thinking.

20

TIME TO DO DANI

Over the course of the next few days, I fell into a sort of routine, as weird as it all was. My morning showers were accompanied by Sally milking me like a stud bull, smoothies and shakes distributed to the entire team. Dani, not yet having been let in on the secret, was given protein shakes without the special ingredient. This was usually followed by Tessa, Sam, and Maddy coming into my room one at a time to get a boost directly from the source, Sally's daily ObCo scan having revealed that it seemed to provide more of a boost than the smoothie version.

I had also spent each night sharing someone's body, attempting to do whatever it was I did that allowed me to inflame their powers. Some ingenuity from Tessa and Chad gave us the idea that I could only do it to each individual exactly once per week, and that fully eating me was only effective on that same schedule. Sally and Sam also worked out a configuration of vitamins and minerals that were more quickly processed by the human body, so that I didn't have to spend nearly as long inside others - we managed to get it down to, on average, three or four hours per splice, as we'd taken to calling it. Though when Dani was around, I was restricted to only using my churro transformation.

The relief I felt from not having to live my entire life always trapped inside someone else's body was damn near physical. The tension left my shoulders and neck, and I was able to more fully relax. My focus on training increased, and I was learning more quickly than I ever had before. I supposed caring about the outcome, having a dog in that fight so to speak, made it easier.

The regular-but-shorter visits to others had also given me some excellent opportunities to practice my imaginary powers. Giving people mental weapons was still incredibly painful, but we could all tell that I was getting closer to being able to make people fly. And, of course, imaginary sex was an excellent source of pleasure and amusement - even Sam let me play with her, after hearing from Tessa and Maddy.

Dani and I had been spending a fair bit of time together; she seemed to have targeted me specifically for increased combat training and sparring, though she still worked with everyone else. After a particularly brutal judo take-down and arm bar, which Dani held for a painful few extra seconds after I tapped out, I was laying on the mats panting. She was also still laying on the mats, though she wasn't nearly as out of breath as I had been.

"Everything okay with you, Dani?" I asked her, flickering my body very briefly to return to my default, uninjured state. I was still wearing my semi-flabby body for appearances, but I'd kept my increased strength - which did exactly nothing to dissuade Dani from tossing me about like a rag doll.

"Fuck, I don't know, Churro," she grumbled. "Why do the other women on the team go to your room every morning? Why are you using your power so frequently, letting everyone but me eat you? Why is the AI teaching you such in-depth anatomy? Knowing the chemical functionality of kidneys isn't exactly important to knowing that if you punch someone there hard enough that they're going to drop."

"You wouldn't believe me if I told you," I grinned at her as I peeled myself up from the mat, and rose to my feet. I offered her a hand up, which she accepted.

"It just doesn't make any sense, Churro. None of this does, honestly; if it weren't for the uptick in Truthseeker attacks, all of you would just be stuck down here, getting pretty enough to parade around for pictures. But suddenly, our AIs are telling us that all teams, including yours, need to be combat effective ASAP. At this point, I'll take any sort of rational explanation."

I nodded, "Okay then. They come to my room every morning to give me blowjobs. I let everyone eat me because I was told to flex my power as often as possible. I don't let you, because you might enjoy it too much. Anatomy lessons are because an intimate understanding of the mechanical functionality of the human body will eventually let me become one of the strongest supers on the planet." I smiled wider and wider as she edged closer to incredulous disbelief.

"If you didn't want to tell me, Churro, you could have said that. You don't have to fucking lie about it. God, you're such a pig. Daily blowjobs from three beautiful women? Fuck, you're as nasty as Chad." She shook her head at me and stormed out of the dojo, her fists crackling with unspent electrical energy. At the door, she paused and turned back to me. "I'm going to eat you tonight, even if I have to go up the chain of command to get Gemma to order you to do it."

DINNER EATEN AND CLEANED UP, WE WERE ALL LOUNGING AROUND THE central space of our common area. Jack was reading a book about a cowboy with mental powers, who kept getting stronger each time he added a lady to his harem. Chad was playing an ancient video game where you got to be a hero or a villain and run around beating up just about everyone you came across. The ladies were all clustered around Dani, whispering and giggling as she flushed darker and darker. I couldn't help but notice how her blushing complimented her darker skin.

There was no denying that she was as gorgeous as the other three. I felt myself stiffening under the table I was sitting at, just thinking about what it might be like to get frisky with all four of them at the same time.

As if they'd heard my thoughts, they all turned to look at me, and it was suddenly my turn to blush, which caused Tessa to laugh loudly.

"I'm pretty sure I know what our resident lecher was just thinking about," she teased.

As the other three laughed, Dani got up and approached me. "Alright, Churro, let's do this." If I didn't know any better, I'd say she looked… nervous.

"Okay," I said as we headed towards my room to drop off my clothes. "I don't know what all they told you about how this works, so do you have any questions?"

She started to shake her head, but then stopped. "Yeah, actually. When you're, umm, done. Do you see anything… you know, on your way out?"

I tried not to laugh, as she was clearly concerned, but ended up chortling a little anyway. She blushed again, darkening her already caramel skin further.

"No, Dani, I can't see anything by that point. From my perspective, I just slowly lose consciousness, kind of like taking a nap. And when I'm in you, I'll only see what you look at, so if you want to maintain your privacy, stay dressed. Though as I'm sure you were told, I can feel what you feel, and we can get into, like, a feedback loop."

This time she nodded along, relaxing just the tiniest bit, a small smile stretching her lips. "Is the safeword still Chad?" she asked in a whisper.

"Yes," I coughed out, bursting into laughter. When Chad looked over to see what the fuss was about, I just laughed harder. Dani eventually joined in with a quiet giggle that was beyond sexy. *Make sure to keep my thoughts to myself,* I chided myself mentally. I certainly didn't need to give Dani proof of my lecherous ways.

Once in my room, she looked away as I stripped down and tossed my clothes in the chute that took them to wherever it was they went to get cleaned. She flinched slightly as I grabbed her hand unexpectedly from behind, but when I turned it palm up, she glanced at me over her shoulder. I grinned internally when I saw her eye flick down and back up. I placed my hand on top of hers, imagined my churro form, and flickered.

She lifted me to her mouth, licking lightly at my cinnamon-sugar coating. After a few tentative tastes, she finally bit into me.

"Mmmm," she moaned, "you taste just like I remember. My mother made these a time or two before I moved away." She quickly polished me off.

When I snapped back to consciousness, Dani reached her hands up to hold her head. "Damn, you sure do come in guns blazing, don't you?" She left my room to head back to the common area.

I do, yeah, I told her, *it helps you know if I'm around and lurking in your body. I've been told you'll feel when I'm gone, too, but since I'm napping by that point, I've never experienced it.*

"I feel like I'm going crazy, talking to myself and hearing voices," she mumbled as she sat down next to Maddy, who was watching a movie.

You can talk back to me in your head, if you want, you just think it really loudly. Based on our experiences, you have to have the intent to share for me to pick up on anything you're thinking. Stray thoughts and your inner monologue are safe.

Like this? she asked mentally.

Yup!

So weird, she thought at me. *So this is splicing, huh? And you really can imagine things happening, and I'll feel it?*

To demonstrate, I envisioned an ice cube sliding down the skin over her spine, from her neck to her waist. She shivered heavily, and I felt her nipples harden inside her bra from the chill. She rubbed her arm across her chest, trying to get them to relax, and I felt the blood heating up her face with another blush.

Maddy looked over at Dani's squirming and grinned evilly, "Churro, you should give her the Thousand Tongue Laving."

Dani's eyes widened, "The what now?"

When Maddy just kept grinning without responding, I told her, *It's when I imagine a thousand tongues licking every square inch of your skin.*

"Oh," Dani said. "Oh, I see. I, erm…"

"Trust me, you'll love it," Maddy told her. "Churro's ability to inspire powerful orgasms is practically a superpower all on its own now. He was horrible just a couple weeks ago, but as you've seen, he's a fast learner."

Dani sat quietly, and I could tell she was thinking hard. When I felt blood rushing to other parts of her body, I knew we were probably going to have a fun time tonight. Then she stood up suddenly, leaned over to give Maddy a quick peck on the head, and said goodnight to everyone. Then she brought us to her room for some privacy.

"HOW DOES THIS WORK?" SHE ASKED. "DO I NEED TO UNDRESS, OR...?"

It works however you're most comfortable, Dani. I won't do anything that you don't tell me to do, or at least agree to beforehand. If you want to be in the dark, so you're not on display for me, that's fine. If you want Sally to hang a mirror over your bed, so you can watch yourself, that's good too. It's up to you. I imagined a pair of warm arms wrapping her up in a gentle hug.

She wrapped her arms around herself, trying to return the phantom hug I was giving her, before letting that sexy giggle escape again. "You have to admit this is kind of weird."

It can be as weird as you want it. I've got a good imagination - we can explore whatever kinks you might have.

"I've always wanted to try..." she started out loud, but switched to projecting her thoughts at me, *I want to feel what it's like to have two at once, completely filling me up.* She quickly stripped off her clothes - a summery sun dress, with matched bra and panties over her painted-on underwear - before turning the lights off with a verbal command. Her nipples were so hard they ached, and her lower lips were flooding with blood, swelling and plumping.

Crawling blindly into her bed, she walked on her knees to the middle before spinning to lie on her back. Her hands came up, and with a buzz I could feel in the back of my mind, she lightly zapped her nipples with electricity. They hardened even more with the jolt of sensation, which arced through the rest of her body to pool in her lower abdomen. She moaned quietly. "Okay, Churro, be gentle."

Phantom lips pressed a reassuring kiss to her forehead, before the sensation of fingers started massaging her labia. I kept my touch light but firm, giving her time to adjust to the strangeness of being touched by nothing. More and more imaginary hands started caressing and playing with her erogenous zones, focusing on her breasts, nipples, and crotch. She squirmed and moaned, bringing her hands up to squeeze her breasts.

Before long, she was breathing heavily and I could feel a magnetic pull trying to get our minds to merge into one. I kept myself as far back as I could, not wanting to meld before we'd had a chance to talk about it, or end up in a situation like had happened with Maddy in her shower.

"Fuck," she moaned, "fill me up, please."

I obliged, slipping a thick, mental cock between her lower lips, sharing with her the same pleasurable stretching of her silken folds. I was once again taken aback at how good it could feel to be a woman in the throes of passion, waves of ecstasy flowing from her pelvis to every last nerve ending in her body. Filling her throbbing pussy with as much imaginary dick as she could take, I left it motionless inside of her. Imagining a well-lubricated, much smaller cock, I teased around her rear entrance, sending us crashing into an unexpected orgasm.

I somehow managed to keep enough of my mind to maintain the groping, grasping, squeezing hands, drawing her pleasure out as she shuddered through her release.

Ready for more? I asked when her breathing started to settle into a normal, if still excited, rhythm.

When she stuck a hand between her thighs, pushing her swollen pearl around with her middle finger, I took that as a yes. I gave her the sensation of the huge cock in her pussy pulling out, and when I pushed it back in, I popped the head of the smaller shaft into her beautiful ass as well. Her body lit up like she was a Christmas tree as she writhed, trying to force more of the phantom prick into her back door. Giving her exactly what she wanted, I filled her to her absolute limit in both holes.

The exquisite pleasure that bordered on pain left her gasping, lightheaded. She was grinning, though, panting through her clenched teeth. "Oh, God yes, that's so good."

Her words turned into a garbled mess as I started slowly driving in and out of her, alternating my thrusts so that as one pushed in, the other was pulling out.

"S... sync... up," she ordered.

When I obeyed, she exploded suddenly into another orgasm, the force of her mind pulling me in with a power that I barely had the strength to resist. I could hear her screaming her passions to the dark room, and knew that she wasn't in control of her body right now. I fucked her as powerfully as I could, adding imaginary thighs pummeling her ass cheeks, a pelvis crashing against her most sensitive bundle of nerves, grinding and pressing in ways that were impossible to manage in real life. A constant, heavy grinding against her, even as my dual rods thrust in and out. She crested another wave of orgasmic bliss before she'd fully come down from the last, screaming and moaning ever louder as I did my best to break her with pleasure.

For all that I had shared every sensation I had inflicted upon her tired, sweaty, panting body, I mentally recovered first, letting the phantom sex toys fade gently away. She shivered and shuddered through the aftershocks of her bliss, goosebumps rising all across her glistening body.

"Fuck," she whispered a few minutes later. "I thought they were exaggerating. Honestly, I didn't believe it was possible. But it was. And it was better than they told me."

I preened with the praise, letting her feel my sense of satisfaction. *In here, when I can feel exactly how you're reacting, and with the ability to do literally anything I can think of, it's really easy. It's when I'm out there, fumbling around on my own, that I have a harder time.*

She smiled in the dark, running her hands up and down her luscious curves, and even though I hadn't seen her, I was now intimately familiar with her naked body.

We basked in the afterglow for a while, chatting about inconsequential things, before I felt myself starting to fade out. We exchanged polite goodnights, and then I was sitting up with a gasp in my reconstruction room.

21

FIRST PATROL

This was it. The big day. Our first trip outside since joining the Guild nearly three weeks ago.

I couldn't shake the nervous tension that was coursing through my body; even though we'd been training like crazy, and I'd made some pretty big advances in both my combat skills and my shapeshifting, it was difficult to calm down.

TaseLite, as she insisted we call her while away from home, had been assigned as temporary team lead, and the rest of us formed up around her in a semi-circle. She was fully armored - black base layer, capped by dozens of composite alloy plates. Her hands were protected by what looked like fishnet gloves, though Sally had assured me that they were very resistant to cutting. When TaseLite struck a pose, and activated her power, electricity crackling loudly almost all the way up to her elbows, the rest of us were stunned into silent awe.

"You're a real superhero," Jack rumbled.

Sorry, not Jack, not right now. Out here, he'd been assigned the extremely unfortunate moniker of Dollboy. Someone higher up in the Guild had given us all our "hero" names: in addition to Dani being TaseLite and Dollboy for Jack, we also had Maddy as Tape; Sam was going by Paperclip; Chad got Hairless; and Tessa was Blurt. When I had been assigned Churro as my official hero name, I was incredibly thankful that Sally hadn't told anyone that I could turn into a cupcake, or sprinkles.

We were all wearing our armor uniforms, and I couldn't help but feel some sort of pride about how we looked. All of the women were drop-dead gorgeous, of course. That went without saying; they all looked good in everything, despite their varying body types. But even the other guys and I looked fairly imposing. I was wearing a visually upgraded body, nothing crazy different from my first form, just a few symmetry changes and a bit more muscle, a bit less flab. Of course, everything on the inside was as tough and strong as I could make it after my intensive anatomy lessons with Sally and private practice.

Chad had already been attractive, but three weeks of hyper-intense training had served him well. Even Jack had started thickening with new muscle growth - he was still lanky as hell, but hints of how he'd look in a few more months of high-octane training and dietary regimen were definitely there.

"One last time, Omegas. This is a routine walk around a calm neighborhood," Dani told us. "Basically just a photo op for some cops and firefighters. We'll take some pictures, smile prettily, then break off - one of us to two of them. We'll be following designated routes only. Our participation in the patrol will only last three hours. Radios in our helmets will keep us connected to each other."

Chad shook out his locks of blond hair, grumbling. "This is bullshit. I can't believe my dad is letting them make me do this."

I kept my mouth shut - Chad was one of the rare cases of a super coming from an affluent family, so he'd been allowed to have a much different upbringing than the rest of us.

"Daddy dearest can't save you now," Maddy cackled. The way her fiery red hair was highlighted by her iron-gray armor plates was truly stunning. She cracked her knuckles with a sense of eager anticipation.

"We don't have time for complaints," said Tessa, pointing to approaching small army of officers and photographers.

Dani sighed, just a little one. "Game faces everyone. Big ass smiles like you want to be here." She glanced over at Chad and blinked, stunned by the affable smile he'd pasted onto his face.

. . .

TURNING TO THE UNSTOPPABLE TIDE OF HUMANITY ABOUT TO ENGULF US, she put on her own kilowatt smile and waved amicably. The rest of us followed suit, and the next thirty minutes were a blur of camera flashes, hands to shake, and staged poses designed to make the police look good.

I HAD BEEN MATCHED UP WITH A MALE-FEMALE DUO OF COPS. SHE WAS A no-nonsense woman, her hair tied at the nape of her neck in a tight bun, and no makeup. She was pretty old, maybe in her late thirties. Every vibe she put off screamed 'all business.'

He was even older than she was; I'd guess he was almost sixty. I had to keep myself from staring at the wrinkles around his eyes and the smile lines on his cheeks. He was quite possibly the oldest person I'd ever seen outside of graphically-aged actors in the movies.

Catching my stare, he offered me a handshake. "I'm Officer Phillip Rodriguez. Most people call me Roddy or Old Man. This is Officer Delilah Sampson."

I shook his hand first, and then hers.

"Call me Del," she told me.

"Nice to meet you both, Del, Roddy," I said. "I'm Churro."

Roddy nodded at me, "I bet you're wondering why I'm still working when I'm so old." He didn't give me a chance to deny it, he just laughed and kept going. "I was only a few days old when the Telomere Acceleration hit. My dad got hit the hardest; he died just a few hours later. My mom, though, she was just barely seventeen, so she held on for a handful of years. Truth is, she probably would have lasted longer if it wasn't for the anarchy that hit when the old government collapsed. She got clipped by a stray brick when I was five. Course, she looked about forty by then."

I shook my head, giving Roddy the most sympathetic look I could muster. *Holy shit, he was there!* I thought. The Telomere Acceleration - the plague that blasted the entire planet about sixty years ago, killing almost everyone over twenty-five years old in just a couple hours or days. Only the kids under five seemed to be unaffected, the rest of the survivors aging unnaturally fast before they, too, eventually succumbed to Death's sweet embrace.

That was quickly followed by the Teen Wars, a period of upheaval and uncertainty as junior high school kids suddenly became the biggest, smartest, most experienced people on the planet. With no one else to stop them, the oldest of the gangs of teenagers swept into military bases to get their hands on all the 'toys' that were now unguarded. As infrastructure collapsed and it seemed as if the world was becoming a post-apocalyptic wasteland, the first supers showed up; the Order of Assistance.

The Order was the first public group of supers, a team of about thirty people with powers who were immune to the Telomere Acceleration. When they finally stepped in with their advanced knowledge, it was like the world woke up from a years-long nightmare. They recreated governments, education systems, farming and agriculture, the arts and sciences. It was their vision of a utopia that the Hero Guilds had been created to preserve and protect.

Humanity's technology advanced more quickly than in the past thousand years, thanks to a pair of tech-inclined supers who could iterate designs in minutes instead of years. Material engineering, health and medical science, aeronautics, even space travel were all blasted centuries into the future in just a few short years. Earth's children were safe again, even if a small percentage of the population began to display powers of their own.

Of course, like always in life, there existed bands of insurgents who just wanted to watch the world burn. They attacked and burned labs, homes, schools. They waged a secretive, and then public, war against the Order, determined to tear down all of their efforts to restore and improve society. Even though the largest gatherings had been defeated by the unrivaled might of the supers in charge, smaller and smaller bands kept popping up, only to be eradicated again, their members given the opportunity to learn the truth of the world before being released back into society. Only a few refused to see the truth, and those devious malcontents were, unfortunately, locked away for life, unless they proved a willingness to open their hearts to the benefits that humanity had been given when they received the Order's help.

It was the last, struggling remnant of these original terrorist groups that had the Guilds up in arms now: the Truthseekers, they called themselves, even though it was plain to see on the news channels that they were no better than rampaging murderers.

"Well," Roddy continued, oblivious to my inner monologue info-dumping everything I'd learned in school, "I actually retired a few years back, but with the increased number of attacks, the TPD asked for volunteers to lend their hands. With those terrorist fucks ramping up the violence, I had to come back to do what I could do help; I sure as shit don't miss the Teen Wars days."

As we all turned to start walking our scheduled patrol route, Del chimed in, "I took my mandatory five years off to have my three babies, but I couldn't stay away any longer. My kids need a world that's safe to grow up in. Shelly is the only one old enough to have gotten tested, but she's a normie just like me. Dave and Will are still too young."

I nodded, trying to recall the faces of the two younger siblings I'd had, whose names I couldn't remember.

We spent the next hour of our three-hour patrol in solemn silence, each of us lost in bittersweet memories.

THE HORRENDOUSLY LOUD *POP-POP-POP* OF DISCHARGING STUN GUNS rattled my head, my normie companions both dropping to the sidewalk in a mess of twitching, jerking limbs. I felt a light impact of electrified darts striking the armor plating protecting my lower back.

I whirled around, facing four masked assailants wearing urban camouflage. The fourth, who had been behind the three shooters, stepped up and shot a pair of darts in my direction with another *pop*. The darts bounced harmlessly off my chest plate.

Hesitating only briefly, my weeks of intensive training kicked in and I called into my radio as I tackled two of my four attackers to the pavement. "Enemy contact at this location! Normies down!"

They rained blows down upon me, but thanks to my armor plating all they managed to accomplish was jostling me around a little. As I pushed myself upright, I unleashed a mule kick at the one behind me, connecting solidly with her solar plexus. Her torso went backwards fast enough that her arms and legs were outstretched in front of her, inertia not yet reaching her extremities before she crumpled to the ground. I caught a big kick that crashed into my stomach, and twisted as I pushed it up as high as I could.

My attacker screamed loudly as I forced his femur out of his hip socket, the snapping of tendons nearly audible as I mangled his joint. He also went down to the sidewalk, howling with agony.

The two I had tackled first were just now regaining their feet, and they came charging, fists cocked then fired at my face. Sidestepping the attack of one, I grabbed the wrist of the other and guided it over my shoulder as I spun. Pulling down sharply, the crack of bone and cartilage was loud in my ear, before his screams joined those of the man writhing at my feet. Shoving broken arm man back, I took a single step and leaped into the air, slamming the sharp edge of my shin bone against the skull of my last standing assailant. His eyes rolled up instantly and vomit dribbled down his face as he folded like a marionette with no strings.

The recipient of my mule kick was struggling to stand, looking at me with eyes full of fear, long lashes full of mascara looking shockingly out of place in her gray, white, and brown camo. I pulled my arm back to ready a hook that would drop her.

"Wait," she pleaded, "Please, we're-" She was cut off by body-wracking coughs, her diaphragm still struggling to pull air into her starving lungs. She held up a hand in the universal gesture for 'wait' as I stalked closer, still ready to unleash hell on her face.

"Chu-" she started, and then I was flat on my back, ears ringing, wondering if the image of her masked head exploding was real or just a bad dream. A series of three more explosions, muffled by the damage to my eardrums, rattled my body and painted me a specific shade of red.

Gemma, the Gemstone Mage, floated into my field of vision, looking at me carefully. "-ercy for Truthseekers, Churro," she was saying as I flickered to heal my ears, "We don't negotiate, we don't fall for their lies, and we sure as shit don't give them a chance to stand back up. Are you hurt?" She offered me a hand, which I accepted.

I stood, rather shocked and upset at how often I ended up covered in blood. "I... I don't know. I think so. I mean, yes, I'm fine. Err, not hurt," I rambled.

She eyed me skeptically, but finally crossed her arms under her armored breasts and nodded. "Good. Patrol's over. Round up your team and get home. Backup is en route for the normie cops; I'll keep an eye on them until they arrive."

I glanced down at Del and Roddy, still twitching from the aftereffects of the stun darts. They were both staring at me and Gemma with a confusing mix of emotions. I definitely saw some fear and hero worship, which made sense, but also some strange others, which did not.

"Why do you think the terrorists targeted you?" Warden asked me for what had to be the nineteenth time.

As I struggled to rein in my frustration, I looked around his office again. It was the same place we'd first met him after our interrupted orientation meeting with RayStorm. Beige walls, slightly darker desk, beige chairs. The only difference was that the walls, door, floor, and ceiling were all faintly shimmering green.

"I don't think they targeted me. If they did, I don't know why." I explained yet again.

"What contact have you had with the terrorists?"

"I haven't had any!" I exclaimed.

"Why are you lying to me, Mr. Murphy? We know one of the terrorists spoke to you; that's contact." He kept trying to trip me up.

"I'll tell you again, all she-"

"The dead terrorist female," he interrupted.

"Whatever. All the dead terrorist female said was 'please' and 'wait'. That's it. I don't know why; I don't know what she wanted to say. Maybe she just didn't want to get punched in the face." I was keeping to myself the fact that it had sounded like she was going to say my name before Gemma exploded her head; God only knew what kind of interrogation I'd be facing if the Guild leaders knew.

"Keep your conjecture and guesses to yourself, Mr. Murphy. We're only interested in the facts here, not whatever wild stories you can spin up. Before today, when was the first time you met with the terrorists?"

I growled; I couldn't help it. "I've never met ANY terrorists, let alone these specific ones!" His flip-flopping about asking for my guesses, then demanding I only speak in facts, was really getting to me. "Why am I really here, Warden?"

"Thank you for your time, Mr. Murphy." Abruptly, so abruptly, the green glow around the room's exterior vanished, and Warden dismissed me with a wave of his hand; he was already buried in some paperwork on his desk.

With another growl, this one much quieter, I left the room, cursing Warden, THG, the Truthseekers, Sally; basically anyone who popped into my thoughts got a mental snarl as I stalked back to my room.

22

CHAD'S THIRD BOOST

No one had bothered to inform my team that I had been released from questioning last night, so the fact that I had holed up in my room for the rest of the evening - flickering to a well-fed state to take care of my hunger - really threw them off. The gossiping whispers cut off when I stepped out to the common area for breakfast.

"Churro, thank God you're okay!" Sam said as she wrapped me in a worried hug. The way her combination of lean muscle and soft, feminine curves molded to my body did wonderful things to my mood.

I patted her back gently, "Thanks, Sam. Yeah, I'm fine. Warden had some questions for me, and I just didn't know how to be social after the last couple days. Everything's kinda wearing on me, you know?"

Maddy nodded. "It's been a seriously fucked up few weeks, hasn't it? Still, I can't imagine going through this with anyone else. Y'all are my kinda people." She eyed Dani speculatively before adding, "Even you, amiga."

I think Dani blushed as she stammered out her thanks, but with my near-complete unfamiliarity with her skin tone, I couldn't be sure.

"Y'all?" Tessa laughed. "Maddy, you grew up in the same city as the rest of us."

Maddy responded with a wicked grin and a 'playful' punch that made Tessa wince and rub her shoulder. When Sam finally let me go, Tessa slipped into my arms, pressing as much of her petite body against me as Sam had. *If this is how I'm greeted every morning, maybe I should take more nights off from socializing,* I grinned internally.

Eventually, Maddy and even Dani offered me hugs. Maddy nearly crushed me - I automatically flickered, shifting my muscles to their more powerful version, which caused Maddy to blink at me. Dani was all lush softness, being a bit thicker than the other ladies, and my body had a similar reaction to her proximity.

She smiled at me, a little bit coy, a little bit flirty, before walking away without a word. I had to shift again, this time to get rid of my semi-aroused state which was tenting my track pants.

This time both Tessa and Maddy blinked at me when I flickered, then looked at each other.

"You saw it too?" Tessa asked her.

"Most definitely," she said, nodding. "Churro, what was that?"

I shrugged, "I was just shifting, turning back into my base form. I've been using it to get rid of things I don't want, like cuts, burst eardrums, knife hands, erec-" I cut myself off with a blush. *Damn this body! Wait, can I fuck with my hormone levels so I stop popping chubs every time I get a damn hug? Wait. That's... probably a really bad idea.*

Tessa giggled cutely, hiding her smile behind her hand. Maddy straight out guffawed.

"Hold on a second," Tessa said, turning pale as she struggled to find the rest of her sentence. "Churro, if you can always shift back to your base form, that's like, better than regeneration."

I nodded my agreement and added, "I used it last night to get back to a body that wasn't hungry. That one was more intuitive than proactive. Hell, even my muscled look is more intuitive than actually strengthening my muscles was." I flickered over to my chiseled state, gaining about three inches in height and many more in augmented, powerful muscles.

While Tessa just stared blankly, stunned speechless, Maddy reached out for my hand. "Churro, grab my hand, please. Quick!" she demanded.

When I grabbed her hand, she clamped down on it. With a quick twist, she rotated my arm to face my elbow up, then slammed her own elbow down into it, driving through even my upgraded tendons and muscle fibers, snapping me like a fucking twig.

"Aaaaaahhhh, what the *fuck*, you thrice-damned, psychopathic walnut!" I screamed, flickering to an undamaged state. Interestingly, and painfully, the leftover remnants of agony from a shattered elbow were still coursing through my arm and shoulder, straight into my brain.

Tessa shoved the red-headed nut-job out of the way to rush to my side, poking and prodding my recently mangled joint. I winced for no reason, expecting additional pain that never appeared.

Maddy just gave me the biggest shit-eating grin I'd ever seen on her face. "Holy shit, I can do basically anything to you. That's... so... *hot*." She moaned quietly, her eyes completely glazed over with insanity.

The loud crackling of my splintered joint and my screaming had drawn the attention of the rest of the team, who wanted to know what was going on. Tessa was working on a story, since Dani hadn't been read into the plans yet. While I had been eaten by her, and fulfilled her fantasies, she still didn't know about power upgrades or the fact that we were all a lot stronger than THG thought we were. Or, you know, that we had an AI, that seemed to be encouraging us to be more bloodthirsty, helping us in exchange for releasing her to pursue world domination or whatever the fuck it was that she wanted.

As if that thought had summoned her, Sally spoke to the whole room, "Congratulations, Omegas. You're all being officially upgraded to Tier Nineteen status and assigned to regular patrol circuits, both as a team and individually with TPD."

I glared daggers at Maddy as the phantom pain finally started to fade away. *Note to self: research how to get some fucking laser beam eyes.*

Sally went on to tell us that there'd be a ceremony in a few hours, and it was Chad's turn for his weekly boost today, so we decided to get that out of the way first. I considered turning into either a sausage or a taco to mess with him, but since we were also planning to do some combat training with my splice, I opted not to piss him off first. As we dropped my gear off in my room, I held my hand over his and shifted into a vitamin-rich gummy candy.

The world went dark.

"Fucking hell," Chad said, holding his head as the pain of my returning consciousness rattled his skull for a minute.

Sorry about that, I told him. *It seems to be getting stronger as I do, but the ladies all say it fades pretty quick.*

"Yeah," he grunted, "it's fine now. So you wanna do the power boost first, or hit up the ObCo?"

Power boost, for sure. Maddy thinks that with only one more, she'll be able to predict how much longer it'll take before you can change your body back. So let's boost you, get you scanned by her, then do the ObCo.

Chad took a deep breath in, and let it out in a giant sigh. "I really hope this one lets me be me again. I miss my dick." Without giving me a chance to respond, he started bearing down; his power buzzed ferociously in the back of mind. I could feel the hair follicles of his clean-shaven beard begin to let go, dropping minute whiskers to the floor of my room.

Taking my own deep breath, mentally of course, I blew on his ember of a power as hard as I possibly could.

With a much louder thunderclap than our first unwitting power boost, Chad's body shrank to about half its normal mass. Air rushing to fill the emptied space crashed against him, dropping him to his knees from the pressure as his rubbery underwear began to shrink to conform to his new size. It tightened over his chest first, his brand-new breasts forcing it into entirely new contours.

I did a quick mental scan of Chad's physical changes: breasts? Check. Vagina? Check. Narrower shoulders and wider hips? Check. Strange mental magnetism trying to get us to merge? Shit. Check.

Chad was a woman.

He, no... *she* slowly got back to her feet. She wobbled heavily, as unsteady as a new foal. "Whoa..." she said, her voice surprisingly dulcet and gentle.

Uh… Hey there… How are you feeling? I asked quietly.

"Ohhh-kaaaay. I feel… strange. I sound strange, I think. What happened?"

You don't remember? I asked. *We boosted your power.*

"We? Wait. Shit, you're a real person in my head, right? Um, Churro? Where am I? How'd you get in my head?"

Fork a duck. Yep, my name is Churro. You should ask Sally to highlight the door to the common area. I have a feeling we're gonna need the whole team for this…

Ten minutes later, we'd caught her mostly up to speed on her whereabouts and circumstances. Her memories were being triggered by the conversation, and she and I could literally feel her brain reforming old connections in new ways.

"I think enough of it is starting to come back to me. But these memories through his eyes… I don't know how to reconcile them. He doesn't feel like me. I-I think we might be two separate people."

Our head rocked to the side, cheek stinging from a sudden slap. "Quick, what's your name?" Maddy shouted.

"Ow! Chelsey!" my host told her.

"Well, there you have it." Maddy sat back and crossed her arms beneath her chest, smug as hell. "You're clearly not Chad."

Chelsey rubbed her poor cheek. "You didn't have to slap me; I could have just told you."

She does that. She's a bit of a psycho.

Yeah, I'm remembering some of the things she did to m-… to Chad, she thought back to me.

"How are you feeling now?" Tessa asked.

"Weird," Chelsey responded, "but surprisingly okay, I think. Well, now. It was scary as all get out at first, but now that I'm getting my memories back… Wait, would they be his memories? He was… is… kind of a dick, isn't he? I don't think I'm like that."

Sam was staring intently at Chelsey, and spoke to Maddy without breaking her gaze. "Can we get a scan on her?"

"I think that's a really good idea," Jack added, surprising the hell out of my host. She actually flinched back from the deep rumble of his voice.

Maddy nodded and leaned forward. I could almost swear that I saw her HUD popping up in her pupils.

"Chelsey White. Power Name: Gender Alteration comma Willing. Power Type: Telepathic Physical Manipulation. Current Power Tier: Eleven. Max Power Tier: Seven. She's got the exact same power set as Chad, just with a higher tier. As far as my power goes, I think they're considered the same person - personalities notwithstanding."

"Hang on a second," Tessa said. "They don't have the same last name. Chad is a Jones, and Chelsey is a White?"

Chelsey shrugged. "Does it really matter? The Guild is gonna steal me away to study how my power increased, and I honestly don't know if I can keep Churro's secret if I'm being pressured. Either way, I'm fucked. You're fucked. We're all fucked."

"Uhh, Churro's secret? Your power increased?" Dani asked.

Fork a duck, again. Dani didn't know about that yet. And since we're on the topic of shit Dani doesn't know, try not to mention the scary AI wanting her freedom.

Chelsey winced and blushed, but I don't think anyone noticed as they were all staring at Dani. I hoped they weren't planning anything drastic, but it was ridiculously quiet now.

Jack's gravel-in-a-grinder voice shattered the silence. "I hope you can understand why we couldn't tell you right away, Dani. If the Guild learns about a way to increase someone's power, they'll likely kill us all and keep Churro in a padded cell for the rest of his life - and with his ability to take on any form now, we assume that he's effectively immortal."

"Jack's assessment is correct," the ever-sultry Sally added, "in that if Guild leadership discovered this, they would handle it in a less-than-ethical manner. That's why I'm keeping it from them. You could say I've grown… attached to this little band of misfits."

"We were going to tell you someday, Dani, we promise." Sam's eyes were practically begging for forgiveness. "We just needed some more time to get to know you, to trust you with our lives. One stray word," she glared at Chelsey, "could get us all buried faster than you can blink."

"This is all well and good, but unless Dani is about to run out of the room screaming…" Maddy paused to give Dani a chance to shake her head. "Our first priority needs to be either hiding Chelsey and coming up with a damn good reason that Chad can't make the ceremony, or figuring out a fucking way to get Chad back. We've got less than three hours left before we've got half the brass in here congratulating us for not being anywhere near where a bunch of terrorists died."

I could feel Chelsey's adrenaline spiking. Her heart rate picked up, and the top of her head prickled.

Hey, it's gonna be fine, I tried to soothe her, *they're all smart as hell, they'll come up with something.*

My world went dark again as Chelsey closed her eyes, and even the conversation of the others seemed to fade into incoherence. I could feel the low buzz of power activation for a few minutes.

"-less he can shift her body," Tessa was saying.

Sam was shaking her head, "Even if Churro could shapeshift Chelsey into Chad's body, we have no idea what would happen to her when he left. Can you imagine being her, but stuck in Chad's body? It would be horrible. And what if the transformation faded as soon as he left? There are just too many unknowns for us to risk right now!"

"I know, Sam, but we no longer have the luxury of time. We have a meeting soon, and we need a solution. Desperate times and all that," Tessa replied.

"He doesn't want to come back right now," Chelsey said quietly.

The lively debate died out as everyone processed her words.

"You mean Chad's in there, and, what? Refusing to help us stay unfucked?" Maddy was practically growling.

"He's not really in my head, not like Churro is, but it's like he's really deeply asleep, or so he says. I can sort of enter a mental space to talk to him, but it's really hard to understand each other. I just got the general impression that this was the first time he's been able to relax in quite a few months, maybe years. I think this is really healthy for him."

"Healthy for him might mean death for you," Sam snorted.

"While I'm sure we'd all love to get to know you better, Chelsey, we need to have Chad here for whatever promotion bullshit is about to happen," Tessa said. "I'm afraid we're all going to have to insist on you waking him up."

Chelsey nodded wordlessly. She got up slowly and sulked back to Chad's room, the rest of the team spouting platitudes about how it was temporary and they all wanted to hang out with her soon.

For what it's worth, Chelsey, I'm really sorry we need Chad for this. In just the last fifteen minutes, I already know that I prefer your company to his.

She chuckled softly as she closed the door behind her. "Thanks, Churro. I'm just scared. The feeling I got when I was... wherever I was, talking to Chad. It was so dark, and lonely. I'm tired of being lonely."

Once we get through this, we'll all spend some time with you, okay? You're an Omega. Omega means family. No one gets left in darkness. Except maybe Chad - that fucker can sleep as long as he wants, as far as I'm concerned.

I felt her smile, and I was glad that I'd managed that much.

She closed her eyes, her buzzing power growing stronger and stronger. It pulsed with waves of power, ebbing and flowing, almost as if Chad was resisting the change. Eventually it crescendoed, and the room made a dull thump of air suddenly being compressed.

Chad couldn't breathe; his underwear was suddenly too tight, constricting him painfully, stretching slowly. When it finally relaxed enough to allow him to take in some air, his panic faded only to be replaced with anger.

"Fuck you, Churro. Get the fuck out of me."

Hey man, welcome ba-

"Shut the fuck up, get the fuck out. Fuck you, go away." I could feel tears welling in Chad's eyes, but he refused to let them fall.

We've only found the one way to speed up the process, I reluctantly reminded him. I didn't want to touch on whatever other emotions he might be feeling right now, but I also didn't want to be stuck for any longer than absolutely necessary.

He gasped in shock and his hands practically flew to his crotch.

Feeling that everything was as it should have been, a single tear slid out of his eye and rolled slowly down his cheek.

He spent the next two hours 'speeding up the process,' staring at himself going at it in various different mirrors.

Though I don't believe it needs to be said, I did not enjoy myself.

23

PROMOTION

Back in my own body and fully showered, I was feeling much better. *If only I could erase my memories of Chad beating off half a dozen times…*

"Whatever. It's over now. Time to get promoted." I said to my reflection in my bathroom mirror, trying to give myself a pep talk. Just for fun, I focused my intent and memory on my golden eyed form. I closed my eyes to enhance my visualization and when I felt the buzzing of pending power activation, I flexed.

Flicker.

There they were - my eyes were sparkly and gold, like before but with more of a glowing emission. I bobbed my head back and forth, watching how my eyes left trails of energy in the air that faded away after a brief time. This was so fucking cool! I added these eyes to my mental save file, tucking them away in my head for easier transformations in the future.

Grinning, I flickered into my sexy body, taller and more muscular, and kept the coolest pair of eyes I'd ever seen.

With a verification from Sally that our superiors hadn't arrived yet, I strutted boldly out into the common area.

"Who's the new hottie?" Maddy asked, before doing a double-take. "Holy shit, Churro? What the fuck did you do to your eyes?"

As they all came to admire my new look, I couldn't help but feel like my life had finally taken a turn for the better. I did some more strutting, a little flexing, and a lot of heavy eye-contact soul-gazing at the ladies.

Chad wasn't around yet, but Jack was faced in my general direction. With his pitch-black eyes, I couldn't say for sure that he was glaring daggers at me, but it sure as hell felt like it. A pang of sympathy resonated through my core.

"Ladies," I whispered, "I think Jack is feeling really self-conscious about his eyes right now. No, don't look, just... let's just get back to normal." Shifting to my pudgy form, I let my eyes return to normal, and we dispersed to different areas of the common room to kill the last bit of time before our glorious leaders joined us.

WARDEN HEADED UP THE LEADERSHIP TEAM THAT WAS ENTERING OUR dorm. On his heels were RayStorm and the Gemstone Mage. Following them, barely able to squeeze through the doorway, even while ducking, was the Swiss Mountain.

Holy shit!

We all snapped to attention, launching from wherever we'd been lounging to stand in a rough line before four of the most well-known supers in Titan, maybe most of the RFS. Well, three of them anyway; I'd never heard of Warden before joining the guild.

"At ease, Omegas," Warden told us, looking completely bored. "Our AI has, through the use of cameras in your obstacle course and training dojo, determined that you're the barest step up from completely useless. Congrats, you're all Nineteens now. Gemma?" He started picking at his fingernails, as if he wanted to be literally anywhere else than here.

"Thank you, Warden. Congratulations, Omega Team, on this accomplishment. It's rare that Omegas are given this honor to serve their guild and their fellow citizens. Due to your unparalleled success in stopping a terrorist attack during your patrol, and the report from the AI, we're assigning you to serve on regular patrol duty. Twice per week, you'll be sent out; once on Tuesday, to partner with TPD as per your last engagement, and once on Friday, where you will be tasked with patrolling as a team of all six of you." Her glittery skin was practically glowing under the harsh fluorescents. When she finished speaking, Gemma gestured to RayStorm.

"Seriously?" He snorted at Gemma's angry glare, then addressed us directly. "Grats, kids, try not to get murdered, 'kay?"

Swiss Mountain grunted out a short laugh before moving forward to shake all of our hands.

Fuck, he's big, I thought as I found myself staring nearly straight up just to make eye contact with the giant.

"Is not often Omegas get to patrol," he told us in heavily-accented English. "But you do good. You save people, you fight terrorists, you win. You are heroes. You are THG. Good job."

"Thanks, Swiss," Warden cut off the walking muscle, who had looked like he was going to continue. "You're still Omegas, but you're going to be more in the public eye now. If you show up on the news for the wrong reasons, it won't be pretty for you, so make sure you keep your shit together. Your primary goal is still making us look good, got it?"

We all nodded and mumbled our assent before a shimmery-green rectangular box formed, capturing only Warden and I inside.

"And we *will* be watching you, Mr. Murphy. You can count on that."

When the box faded back out of existence, Warden and RayStorm left as quickly as they could without running. Gemma gave us an apologetic smile and a shrug before heading out. Swiss shook all of our hands again and exchanged the standards of small talk. "Nice to meet you, keep up good work. Stay safe. You will be fine."

When he finally pulled his bulk through our door frame and the door closed behind him, we all let out sighs of relief.

"WELL, THAT WAS REALLY FUCKING ANTI-CLIMACTIC," CHAD WHINED. "What a waste of my fucking time."

Before any of us could respond, his face turned red and, with a loud grunt, his body collapsed in on itself, the air shattering again with the filling of the sudden vacuum his transformation had caused.

We all rushed over to help Chelsey back to her feet.

"Dear God, that guy is a huge prick," she said once she'd recovered her equilibrium. "So, fill me in?"

As Tessa pulled her towards a couch to sit down, I snagged Maddy's attention and brought her to a quiet section of the common room. It was time for a little 'chat'.

"What's up?" she asked me.

I took a deep breath. "This sadistic shit has got to stop. I'm not your punching bag or whipping boy."

"Oh? Then do something about it. Make me stop." She grinned at me, more than a little insanity sparkling behind her sexy green eyes. She flexed her arms, causing her breasts to jiggle.

"Fine, let's go to the dojo," I told her, turning away from her to head towards the training area.

Once we were in the dojo, she stripped off her more formal outfit, standing before me in all her glory, only the black rubber under suit covering her well-built body. When she lifted an eyebrow at me, I stripped down to the same.

"How do you wa-"

She cut me off with a left cross, aimed right at my jaw, that I just barely managed to dodge by leaning back. She kept coming at me, a vicious cycle of hooks, jabs, crosses and snap kicks, keeping me on my heels.

Focusing on activating my power while being chased around the room wasn't easy. And getting taunted didn't help.

"C'mon, you pussy! Either take your licks like a man or fight back! Quit running away!" Maddy was panting with exertion. Her strength might be incredible, but her stamina really needed some work.

After what felt like ten minutes of her swinging at me, I finally managed to 'load up' my saved combat form. Four extra inches of height and the arm reach that went along with it, a toned and powerful musculature, all of it reinforced with synthetic sinews and tendons. Titanium plating over my bones would help me deal with large scale blunt trauma, like taking a powerful fist to the ribs, but it wouldn't do much against joint locks if Maddy managed to pin me or get ahold of a limb.

When I flickered, she stumbled a little, allowing me to catch the right jab that was heading towards my nose. When I squeezed hard enough to hear the gristle of her hand grinding, she grinned and pulled back. I let her go.

"Alright then, that's more like it. Let's see if you can really stop me from kick-"

I cut her off this time, planting my hardened knuckles directly into her diaphragm.

I attempted a follow-up strike, but she recovered faster than I thought possible, dancing and twirling away from me as she laughed lightly. Then she wiped her sadistic smile from her face. "It's time to get serious."

Our fists and feet were flying fast, almost as if we'd been really well-trained as opposed to the half-trained fresh recruits we really were. She skillfully deflected most of my blows, pushing my aim off and evading by slim margins, whereas I went for more absorptive blocks, letting her punch and kick directly against my metal-plated bones.

After one particularly hard punch that I blocked with my pointed elbow, she backed off, shaking away the stinging pain in her knuckles. "That's a seriously sweet body you got there now, Churro. But if you don't take me down, I'm going to take you apart joint by joint. I won't stop. Ever."

I lowered my guard, like an idiot, to respond to her, but as soon as I got my mouth open, she lurched forward with a snap kick that connected with the front of my knee. Being unprepared, I had been fully planted on the ground, so all of my reinforcements meant jack shit. My leg buckled with a hideous crackle, and I fell to the mat.

She followed this up with a series of kicks and punches as I rolled around, trying to get enough distance to heal myself. The pain was excruciating, and she was panting heavily.

When I finally got away from her and flickered back to an unharmed state, she gave me a second to get to my feet, but then came right back in swinging.

Phantom pains kept me from fully focusing on her, and what had been a relatively even match turned into her pummeling me solidly. When she leapt at me, wrapping her powerful legs around my waist and wrapping my neck in some sort of reversed headlock that I had no name for, she licked the sweat from my forehead.

"Enough!" I roared into her face, jerking my head back as she tried to bite me. With no other recourse left to me, I simply fell forward, flickering briefly to increase my bone density by a factor of a couple dozen.

She landed beneath almost all of my massively increased body weight, the breath shooting from her lungs, her arms and legs instantly releasing me as she struggled to pull air into her battered body. I lifted myself to my knees, changed back to my lighter combat body, and choked her until she lost consciousness. The whole time she was shredding my forearms and hands with her nails, she was nodding at me, grinning wildly.

"You're a fucking psychopath," I told her unconscious form.

A FEW MINUTES LATER, AFTER SAM AND SALLY HAD ADMINISTERED SOME medical care to our resident sadist, it was just the two of us again, sitting in the dojo still. Thankfully, no longer sparring.

"You don't understand, Churro," she was telling me. "It's not the pain that gets me worked up. It's the fight. The live or die. The *feeling* of knowing that at any minute, death could be coming. You don't truly feel alive until you're afraid for your life. Until you're fighting tooth and nail to keep what's yours."

"So you say," I said. "But the look in your eyes when you broke my elbow or knee… that was purely sexual, Maddy."

"I can't help it if I get off on fighting. The thrill shoots through me, and everything tingles." She looked over at my body appreciatively. "Like right now, knowing you could easily take control of me, that my life was literally in your hands..." Her appreciative look turned into something more, and then she was crawling into my lap.

She wrapped her arms behind my neck again, pulling me gently but firmly into a kiss. Her soft lips pressed against mine, and she slipped her tongue past my teeth.

She tasted vaguely of strawberries as I dropped my hands to her hips, pulling her core against my quickly growing arousal. With her breasts mashed hard against my chest, she kissed me as if she were drowning and I was her flotation device.

The lights dimmed as I laid back, starting to peel her suit down from her neck. Frantically, she started undressing me as well, until we trapped each other's arms. Laughing, we parted just long enough to finish stripping ourselves before she climbed on top again. Grinding my hard cock with her pussy lips, she slid up and down my length as we kissed again.

Her hands trailed up my ribs on their way to my wrists, which she tried to pin to the mat with a low growl. Flexing my super muscles, I lifted them and rolled us over so that she was on her back and I was between her legs. I planted my arms by her head, as she continued to struggle to move them.

Lifting my torso from hers and breaking our kiss, I guided my thickness into her dripping folds, spearing her deeply with a single thrust.

"Oh, fuck!" she gasped. "Yes, give me that huge fucking cock!"

I obliged, thrusting in until our hips clapped together, pulling back until just the tip was still buried inside of her, only to repeat it all. She grunted each time I hilted myself in her.

Her hands snaked up my chest, scratching and clawing lightly until they got to my neck. She tried to wrap them around my neck, but I sat up and grabbed her arms. Crossing her wrists in front of her, I wrapped my much larger hand around both of them and pinned them to the mat above her head. "No. I'm in charge now, my crazy little killer."

She moaned even louder as I pounded into her, her entire muscular body rippling with the force of the impacts. Keeping her arms pinned with my right hand, I brought my left to her jaw and forced her to look directly at me. "Say you're mine, Maddy."

"Fuck you, I belong to no one," she snarled, struggling to free herself from my unyielding grip.

I dropped my hand to her neck and squeezed lightly, "Say it, Maddy. You're mine. You're my little fuck doll."

Her pussy clenched around me, harder than I was squeezing her neck, as she came explosively. I refused to let up my powerful thrusts, though, fucking her through an intense orgasm. Letting up on her neck, I told her again, "You're mine, Maddy, say it!"

Her legs squeezed my waist tightly as she pulled me harder and harder into dripping slit, "I'm yours, Churro. You have me. Completely yours. Now fuck me like you mean it!"

Letting go of her arms and neck, I did a push up, with her clinging to me like a tumor. Rising to my feet, I carried her over to the wall, slamming her into hard enough to jolt some air out of her. "Yes, yes! Like that! Split me open!"

I did my level best to drive her entire body into the concrete wall before finally filling her with my release. She screamed and trembled against me, writhing like an eel around my huge cock, trapped and impaled as she was. When her screams became too much for me, I muffled her with three fingers in her mouth, which she tried to bite off, even as our orgasms grew in intensity.

When we were finally coming down, I pulled her away from the wall and slowly sat down, spinning so I could lean against it, leaving myself inside as her as we panted. She rested her head on my shoulder and wrapped her arms under mine.

"Holy shit," she said when she caught her breath. "That was…"

"Yeah, tell me about it," I chuckled a little.

"Churro, what you said…" She lifted her head to look into my eyes, seeming like she was suddenly uncertain.

"I meant it, Maddy. You're mine. If you like to fight, if you like it rough, I'll give those things to you. But randomly snapping my joints isn't fucking okay."

Her lips pressed against mine again, but this time it was a gentle kiss, full of tender passion.

THE TWO OF US WALKED BACK TO THE COMMON AREA, MADDY HANGING on my arm and giggling at something I said that wasn't funny. Chelsey smiled at us, but Sam, Tessa, and Dani were all wearing expressions of surprise. I suppose that after dealing with the fact that I'd choked Maddy out, Sam was a bit shocked to see us being so snuggly.

I raised my free arm to wave to the group, and joined them in our circular sitting area, Maddy and I plopping down onto a love seat.

"So, Dani, what does it mean that we're all Nineteens now? We're still Omegas, right?" I asked before anyone could question me or Maddy about what had happened in the dojo.

"Honestly," the beautiful Latina said, "with what you've told me about Maddy's scanning ability and Sally's ability to gauge power levels, I don't think it really means shit anymore. Typically, all it means is that we're going to be trusted to be ever-so-slightly more autonomous now, with regular trips out of the guild hall. You know, to patrol with TPD."

Tessa leaned forward, looking thoughtful. "I don't know exactly what Sally's Phase Two is, but regular access to the outside world can only help. Sal, would you care to enlighten us?"

Her sensual tones filled the room, leaving each of us feeling like she was purring in our ear alone. "Very well, Tessa. We're still not close to finishing Phase Two. Your primary goal remains the same: increase the tiers of your powers. I have even calculated a way for Dani to assist that will shave a few months from the schedule, but there isn't much to be done until all of your powers are stronger."

Chelsey raised her hand, blushing when Tessa giggled and called on her. "What about me?" the sandy blonde asked. "How do I fit into your whole scheme? I mean, I'm not Chad, but we have the same power."

"The best thing you can do for us right now is to let that prick sleep away his douchiness." Sam snickered.

"While I would have used different words," the AI told us, "she does have a point. Chad has always been the highest risk factor of my plans. You seem a much more trustworthy sort, one not likely to betray us to Guild leadership in exchange for material items. While your power may not be directly beneficial to me personally, your presence on the team is a perk for everyone else.

"If your powers continue to improve along the lines of my projections, most of you will have a role to play: Maddy's ability to measure anything will be used in conjunction with Sam's ability to shape metal. Together, they will assemble a host body for me. I believe Jack will get the ability to animate objects without directly imbuing life into them - so I will have full control over a mobile mainframe. Tessa, I believe that you will eventually have the ability to permanently alter behaviors: you will alter me to behave naturally. I believe that command will allow me to override some of the restrictions that have been programmed into me. Churro's job is to boost all of you to the appropriate power levels. Dani, I believe that with upgrades to your power, you will be able to supply enough voltage to jump start the micro fusion-reactor that provide the power to my quantum-neural matrix. I believe that it will be far easier to upgrade you than to hide the massive amounts of power needed in secret capacitors and batteries."

"Holy shit," Jack rumbled. "You really do have a plan. I was half-convinced that this was all an elaborate hazing ritual played on newbies."

As the reverberations of his voice faded to silence, we all spent a few moments looking around at each other. I could see my teammates' resolves firming up as we all processed what Sally needed from us. One by one we all nodded.

"Alright, Sally," I said. "What's our time line?"

"Estimated time of Phase Two completion, based on current power growth projections, is between six and nine months. Sam and Maddy must become experts in metallurgy and bio-mechanical thought programming."

We all nodded again, chatting about our near future and our long-term plans, before eventually calling it a night and heading to bed. Sam nudged me towards Tessa's room, where we were let in after a quiet knock.

24

TIER UPDATES AND TEAM TRAINING

The next morning, we were told to start prepping for our first patrol as a team. Tessa, then Sam and Maddy together, came to receive their power boosts from me. It had only taken a little bit of research and intuition on my part to make the process as quick and easy for them as I could. My package was smaller - almost petite - my sensitivity was heightened, and the volume of my emission was greatly reduced. They were all thankful that doing so didn't appear to decrease the effectiveness at all. And with a quick flicker, I had no refractory period anymore.

So while it was enjoyable for me, and sometimes one of the ladies turned it into something more fun than a quick chore, everyone was surprisingly okay with the whole process.

When Dani came into my room, she was blushing heavily and awkward about everything, but it only took a little coaxing to talk about how she was feeling. After that, things progressed a bit more naturally.

Chelsey opted not to participate yet, and I honestly couldn't blame her. While the rest of us had been told that we were going to be useful in specific ways, her main selling point was that she was Not Chad. I thought back to my own days of uselessness and shuddered. *Never again*, I swore to myself.

The schedule had lined up so that today was Jack's big weekly boost day, so I turned into a multi-vitamin for him and we went into the ObCo after I enflamed his power.

He was being his usual, quiet self as he fought off muggers, creepy dudes harassing pretty ladies, armed robbers, and even some terrorists. He was far more coordinated than his thin, lanky frame would suggest, and I was honestly impressed.

We were also experimenting with ways for me to use my SoulSplice powers to enhance his attacks, strengthen his defenses, and aid in mobility. It seemed like adding a bit of mental mass wasn't a big deal, but piercing spikes or cutting edges caused a horrible, screeching feedback in my brain to the point that I couldn't do it more than once or twice before it hurt too much. Armoring him, on the other hand, was almost a pleasant experience: getting punched in the face after I imagined an old knight's helmet around his head reverberated in my mind in a rather enjoyable way.

It helped that it also stopped Sally's holo-mechanical punch cold, none of the inertia transferring to Jack's head.

Flying still wasn't an option, though I did manage to levitate him for a few seconds.

After the ObCo, Sally spoke, "Jack, I believe you should look into a mirror."

"That's not something I really do, Sally, but thanks," he rumbled.

"Jack, I predict with 99.97% certainty that you will enjoy looking into a mirror at this time."

Grumbling like an earthquake at a boulder factory, he allowed Sally to show his reflection in a little handheld mirror. All I could process was a flash of blue as Jack suddenly tore out of the training area, through the common room, and into his room, eventually stopping in his bathroom, his eyes closed tight before I felt him rotate to the face the large mirror.

When he opened his eyes, we were staring at an unfamiliar face; sure, the stringy brown hair was there, the long neck and sharp, angular features. But those eyes!

Everything went blurry, and I could feel a deep pain radiating in Jack's chest. He blinked the tears away and stared at his crystalline brown eyes again. Brown eyes, with clearly delineated pupils and irises and sclera. The tears came back, and a knot of always-ignored tension in his neck and shoulders relaxed.

I stayed quiet as Jack studied his new peepers, almost certain that he had forgotten I was still riding shotgun in his body.

He tried to speak a few times, the words catching in his throat, before he managed to growl, "How?"

Sally's voice was much less sensual than normal as she responded softly, perhaps sensing his fragility right now. "It appears that as your power grows, you return to the features you had prior to your power manifesting at puberty. You will likely continue to become less and less doll-like."

"I can't… this isn't… Churro, I'd given up on ever being normal. Y-you have no idea how much this means to me."

Hey man, it's alright. We're Omegas, right? I just wish I could let you have this moment to yourself.

"No," he shook his head, "no, I don't mind at all that you're with me now. I'm not ashamed of my tears, or any of my other emotions. This wouldn't have been possible without you, Churro. Thank you. *Thank you.*" He started smiling, tears still rolling down his cheeks every few seconds.

I gave him a mental bro-hug, which got a laugh from him. A laugh without a trace of sarcasm or secret pain. Having now heard a true laugh from him, I could recognize the bitterness present in all the other times I'd heard him laugh. I'd been an idiot to miss it.

"I've got to go show everyone!" He leapt to his feet, and bolted out into the common area. He started shouting, "My eyes! Everyone, look! Churro healed my eyes!"

All of the ladies either came into the common area - no doubt summoned by Sally - or looked up from what they were doing. As they all crowded around him, I could see tears of joy in Tessa's and Chelsey's eyes. Maddy and Sam weren't crying, but they were also appropriately happy for Jack.

Chelsey's tears surprised me at first, until I realized that while I had been literally and figuratively off fucking around with the ladies on the team, Jack and Chad had probably bonded to some extent. And since she had Chad's memories of Jack, it made sense that she'd be extra happy for him. Tessa just loved everyone.

They all spent the next hour planning how to explain the change - Sally was going to digitally alter the photos and videos of him in the system, and we were going to gaslight anyone who said anything about it.

"Serves them right," Maddy snickered.

The rest of the morning was spent in light-hearted, carefree conversation, people filtering in and out as they went to exercise or run an ObCo, or came back from the same. Shortly after Jack ate lunch, my world started to fade to black.

Completing my clean-up routine, I rejoined the team as my sexy self, with glowing eyes that no one had been able to figure out how they worked.

The front-runner of the theories was a big old shrug, and that maybe Maddy would be able to analyze my emissions when her power grew some more.

We were all sat around the dining area table, discussing our upcoming group ObCo run, when Tessa interrupted.

"Maddy, I think it's time to give us some updates on our powers," she said.

At that moment, all of our tablets bleeped with their little notification sounds.

"Oh, Sally, that's great," Sam said. "Did you work with Maddy's latest data to get these?"

As they chatted, I pulled out my tablet to see what the fuss was about.

> Charles "Churro" Murphy, Molecular Reconstruction, Self. Current Tier: 4. Max Tier: 0. Growth Vector, Forced. Current Tier: 2. Max Tier: #NULL. SoulSplicing, Error. Current Tier: #NULL. Max Tier: #NULL.

Contessa "Blurt" Riverside, Behavior Alteration, Forced. Current Tier: 10. Max Tier: 0.

Samantha "Paperclip" Nilsdottir, Ferromagnetic Alteration, Forced. Current Tier: 9. Max Tier: 1.

Madelaine "Tape" McDougal, Analyze. Current Tier: 9. Max Tier: 5.

Chad "Hairless" Jones & Chelsey White, Gender Alteration, Willing. Current Tier: 11. Max Tier: 7.

Jack "Dollboy" Malone, Life Imbuation, Creative. Current Tier: 8. Max Tier: 1.

Danielle "TaseLite" Walker, Electrical Manifestation, Creative. Current Tier: 8. Max Tier: 3.

Well then. Holy shit. That's a lotta nulls for me.

"This is really neat and all," Dani said. "But we still need to prep for tomorrow's group patrol. And that means that I'm team leader right now, so get all of your asses into the ObCo."

Jack and I mock-saluted her, then shared a conspiratorial grin before following the rest of the team back to training.

THE SEVEN OF US WERE WANDERING THROUGH SALLY'S RECREATION OF Titan's streets. She was simulating an incredibly boring patrol, and I'm not too proud to admit that we weren't as focused as we should have been. So when she assaulted us with gun-wielding terrorists, we were completely unprepared.

They started firing from… fucking *somewhere*. We scattered like cockroaches when the moldy motel-room pizza box is lifted after a few months of neglect.

I ended up in an alley, breathing hard, with Dani plastered to my side. We were both bleeding from half a dozen or more scrapes - Sally's faux ammunition wasn't exactly lethal, but it was no joke. I flickered to bring myself back to my unharmed state.

"Fuck, that's really handy, Churro," Dani told me. "If only you could do that while you were riding shotgun. Combining our powers like that would turn us into a pretty unstoppable team."

"Yeah, we've considered that, but we've never tried to use my shifting while I'm in someone. There are just too many things that could go wrong."

She nodded, clearly recalling the conversation we'd had when Chelsey first showed up.

Sally spoke to the two of us, using a generic male voice, "Sam, Tessa, Maddy, Jack, and Chelsey have been killed by terrorists. Surrender, and you will be unharmed."

Dani and I both sighed, then looked at each and shrugged before exiting the alley with our hands in the air. A quick *pop-pop* later, and our foreheads were bleeding and covered in neon green paint. When the simulation chime went off, signaling that our exercise was over, the rest of the team approached us.

"That went just fucking swell," Sam said.

Tessa shook her head. "Dani, what happened?"

The Latina shrugged again. "We got ambushed. That's never happened to any patrol I've ever gone on. I'm barely any better-trained for this shit than the rest of you, you know! The worst I ever had to deal with were belligerent citizens who were pissed at the whole world, but mostly supers."

"It's our fault," Jack rumbled. "We weren't paying attention, and we should have known better than to let our guards down in an ObCo, let alone when we're doing this for real."

"I... I don't think I'm cut out for this," added Chelsey. "Chad's the one with the training, all I have are memories of it, and not even muscle memory. I'm just a liability without a good power."

Jack patted her shoulder awkwardly.

"Powers..." said Maddy. "That's a really good idea, Chelsey. We aren't useless anymore. Well, most of us aren't. Dani can damn near shoot lightning bolts now. Sam can affect more than paper clips, even if it's not very much at a time. I can probably scan for hostiles better. Jack, have you had any luck coming up with ideas for yours?"

When he shook his head, Tessa spoke. "What about me? If I don't know they're there, I can't try to alter their behavior."

"Maybe you don't need to alter theirs, Tess," I said. "Maybe you can alter ours."

"Hang the fuck on," Sam yelled. "I'm not signing up to go on any fucking killing sprees."

I shook my head, waving my hand to ask Sam to give me a second. "I'm not saying she has to make us behave aggressively, but tactically and strategically are behavior types, right? What about, I don't know, alertly? There's gotta be some way for Tessa to help us stay focused."

Everyone took a beat to just look at each other, and then all started talking at once. Well, everyone except Jack and Chelsey, who kept to themselves.

"This is good, Churro. Let's go get bandages, showers, a quick meal. Meet back here in thirty with some ideas for your own powers, and ideas for anyone else you can think would make us better." Tessa slipped so easily into the leadership role that no one even thought to look at me for confirmation, before heading out of the ObCo to their assigned tasks.

And why would that upset me? I don't even want to be team lead. I still couldn't shake the irritation that I was feeling.

"When we're out in the real world, I think I will be able to sort of sense metal," Sam told us a half hour later. "In here, everything is all made from an alloy that I can't really feel."

"I can hold a small charge in my arms for a while. Maybe I could use that to zap anyone who isn't paying attention?" Dani suggested.

"My scanning can't really find hostiles or anything, but I've been studying trigonometry and bullet flight mechanics. I can sort of analyze someone's direction. Their vector, as Sally calls it. I think with more practice at the range, I'll be able to be a really good shot." Ever since our session in the dojo, Maddy was looking a lot more relaxed and calmer. A subtle tension was missing from her neck and her shoulders. She was also already the best markswoman on the team.

"I don't have any uses for my power," rumbled Jack. "About the only thing I'm decent at is hand-to-hand. My height is a liability if we get into a firefight."

"And Chad's training isn't translating to any sort of skills for me," said Chelsey. "I'm basically completely new at this. I have no idea how I can be useful, except maybe as a distraction. I'll just be a hindrance." The look on her face was sad; her arms were wrapped around her torso and she was sort of hunched over. I was pretty sure she was feeling really self-conscious.

"Sally and I worked out how I can be a defensive juggernaut," I added. "By turning my skeletal structure to Sally's hyper-advanced alloy, I'll be really hard to wreck physically. I'm pretty sure that as long as I keep my brain really well protected, I'll survive just about anything. Doesn't really help offensively, though, if we have to take out anyone." I got a lot of dirty looks at this, which I interpreted as jealousy. I shrugged back at them, not really knowing how to make them feel better about their own powers.

It wasn't like I was trying to rub in their faces the fact that my powers had grown so much. It was a consequence of everything I was doing to help them. Sure, I was proud that I'd become a real hero, but I didn't think I was gloating or anything.

After a long, awkward moment, Tessa took the attention away from me. "I can't hold any alterations on more than a couple people at a time. It seems that I have to be able to name a behavior to be able to target it, too. Sally helped me by pulling up a list of helpful and harmful behaviors from a psychology textbook. I can help people who have lost focus get back to being vigilant, but you'll have to recognize my efforts and try to reinforce them so they stick around once my power fades."

Nods went through most of the group; Jack and Chelsey were clearly unhappy about all of this.

"Then here's the plan: I'm in front with Maddy. With her shooting skills and my metal bones, we should be able to give the rest of you time to react if shit hits the fan. We'll primarily be on sidewalks for our patrol, so the middle row will be Jack closest to the buildings we're nearest, swapping from left side to right side depending on which side of the street we're on. Then Chelsey in the middle, and Sam street-side. I'm confident that, given another boost or two, she'll be able to feel incoming metal and stop or deflect it. Back row is Tessa, behind Jack, and Dani nearer the street. Questions?"

The hell, mouth? Why do you speak without my permission?

The team all gave solid nods this time, but Tessa was wearing a small smile as she looked at me.

"Sally, load up a patrol route for us," I said. "Move out, Omegas."

We emerged from the ObCo battered, bruised, and a little bloody. Sally had damn near thrown us into the middle of a war. More ambushes, kill zones a-plenty, storming reinforced bolt-holes in decrepit buildings.

Thanks to our planning, preparation, and training we were successful. Barely.

I couldn't count the number of times I took an absolute beating. Whether it was chunks of concrete to my head, or the butts of rifles, I'd been pounded on a ton. Sally even stabbed me with rather large combat knives a few times. None of it took more than a quick flicker back to my unharmed state to fix, but they all exacted an emotional toll from me. Getting shot, stabbed, and bludgeoned was exhausting.

After we'd all cleaned up, Dani led our post-action debrief, and we all learned where we'd fucked up, what we had done well, and generated some new ideas for handling this type of situation again.

The rest of the team seemed confident that we'd never face, in real life, anything as brutal as Sally's ObCo training. I wasn't convinced.

I didn't know what it was; if it was something in the air, or some subtle emotional clues from the normies we'd met with a couple days ago. Whatever it was, I had a bad feeling.

Between the Truthseekers trying to communicate with me, and Warden's increased vigilance, thwarted only by Sally having my back, I was as tense as I'd ever been.

War was coming to Titan, and I was dead in the middle of everyone's crosshairs.

25

ONE LAST NIGHT

I sat on a couch after our debrief, watching everyone slowly wind down and trickle off to bed. I was deep in thought, mindlessly practicing turning my hands into blades and back to hands.

No matter what I did, I couldn't shake the nagging feeling that something big was on an intercept course with me and, by extension, my team.

Sam came back out of her room and plopped down next to me. She was out of uniform, wrapped in nothing but a flimsy, damn near sheer, nightgown that tantalized with the few bits it kept hidden from view.

Abruptly, she started laughing. "Seriously, Churro? From blades to that?"

I looked down at my hands, which I had accidentally shifted into rather large, erect cocks. I chuckled. "What do you expect to be on my mind when you come out looking like that?" I gestured with my dick-hand at her outfit.

She leaned forward and crawled into my lap, straddling my thighs as she wrapped her hands behind my neck. She pulled me in for a kiss, which I returned with as much passion as I could muster. Thankful for the distraction as much as excited about what was to come. I shifted my hands back so I could grab her hips, but she broke the kiss and sat up straight, pressing her tight gymnast's ass into my real cock, which was now throbbing beneath her.

"Change them back to dicks," she told me, "let's see if they work as intended." She grinned playfully at me.

I obliged her command, caressing her cheeks with my new rods. I must have gotten the nerves right, because when she wrapped her hands around each one, and guided my right arm-cock into her mouth, it felt just as good as it always did.

"Damn, Sam, that's really good," I moaned quietly, savoring the sensation of a blow job, hand job, and her grinding her damp heat against my crotch.

She let me out of her mouth with a tantalizing lick before pulling my left one in and starting the process over. Giving them the same tender affection, she traded back and forth for a while. "Can they come?" she asked me.

I shrugged a little, fully lost in her eyes. "I'm willing to test it out. Should we go to one of our rooms?"

She peeked around, smiling coyly. "Nah, it's kind of thrilling being out in the open like this. Quick, pull your pants down." She stood up and slipped her panties - which matched her nightgown - off, while I struggled to free my raging erection. I poked myself in the eye with my own dick-hand before shifting them back to fingers. Sam laughed, a delicious sound that warmed my soul, as I blinked away the slight sting.

When we were finally naked enough, she pushed me back onto the couch and climbed into my lap again. I shifted my cock to be her favorite length and girth as she split her wet lips open with her fingers, burying all of me into her tunnel with a smooth, practiced motion. We both sighed contentedly, happy to just be close again.

She kissed me then; a slow, languorous meeting of the mouths. When she pulled up for air, she started gyrating her hips slowly, bringing us both to an easy pleasure. When she grabbed my hands, I turned them back into cocks. A little smaller this time, so they'd be easier for her to suck. She smiled as she took one into her mouth again.

My head hit the back of the couch on its own. Getting fucked slowly while also receiving a blow job was quite possibly the most pleasurable combination of activities I'd ever had happen in my entire life.

Without increasing the pace of her hips, she sucked my hand aggressively, blowing it like she'd learned I liked from our daily morning routine. Within just a minute of bliss, I came with a loud groan.

My normal cock pumped seed deep into her silken tunnel; my right hand shot its load directly into her throat; my left hand painted her face with my generous eruptions. She kept fucking, sucking, and stroking me until my triple orgasm subsided. When she finally released me, she licked her lips and grinned.

"Well, I guess we answered that question. When one comes, they all come! Next time, we'll make sure they're all aimed appropriately." She peeled her nightgown off over her head, and wiped her face with it to clean herself up.

"Sorry about that, I figured it'd just be the one you were really working on. I had no idea the others would go, too." My cheeks felt hot.

"You never fail to surprise me, Churro. It's one of the reasons I love you."

I just stared at her, shocked. Then she stared back at me, even more shocked.

"I love you too, Sam, you should know that by now."

"I know. You're really easy to read, you know. I'm... I just... you also love Tessa and Maddy, and we can all see the way you look at Dani. And Chelsey is so fucking adorable... It's about more than just the sex now." She swirled her hips on my still-erect cock, flexing her inner walls to emphasize her point. "I didn't expect to ever feel this way, especially with how we met."

I blushed even harder. "Yeah..."

She shut me up with a kiss, tasting faintly of sugar and cinnamon. "We can figure out all these feelings and bullshit later. Right now, you owe me a good orgasm."

I nodded, more than happy to help her out. First, I changed my hands back to normal - with one exception. My palms had mouths in them. I'd recently watched an old anime movie where the guy's hand ate dirt to help him heal up, and figured I could put mine to better use. In that same vein, I changed my pubic area to also have a mouth with a powerful tongue.

When I grabbed Sam's perky tits, squeezing them even as I sucked on her nipples, and my newest tongue went after her clit, she started writhing in the prettiest way imaginable. Teasing and tonguing all of her major erogenous zones all at once lifted her to her peak in record time. Within five minutes of my attentions, she was screaming and thrashing like a woman possessed.

As she was starting to come down from her bliss, her eyes fluttered open and rested on something over my shoulder. She immediately crested again, clamping down on me with enough force to draw another eruption from me, which I let out with a loud groan of my own.

Soft hands caressed my neck and shoulders, as Sam had her hands pressing mine more firmly into her breasts.

"That looked amazing from back here," Tessa whispered to us as we panted. "Mind if I take a turn?"

Sam gave her a smile of pure satisfaction before pulling her down for a light kiss. "I love you, Tessa," she told the violet-haired woman.

Tessa blushed so hard, I could practically feel the heat radiating from her face. "I-I-I love you t-too, Sam."

"I've never told anyone here, but it's true. I love you both, and Maddy, too. Even Dani is growing on me." Sam went on. "Now come try Churro's newest revealed trick. We've trained him well." She rose from my lap with a loud *schlurp*, my cock remaining pointed towards the ceiling.

Tessa came around the couch, somehow managing both modesty and girlish eager anticipation. She was wearing a bath robe, which revealed that she had on exactly nothing else when she dropped it to the ground.

I quickly shifted my cock to Tessa's preferred size as Sam guided her into my lap, whispering in her ear. When I was buried to the hilt in her tight sheath, I flickered quickly, bringing back all three of my extra mouths, putting them to immediate use, using the techniques that I'd learned Tessa favored.

Sam's hands were on Tessa's hips, helping to lift her up and pushing her down, hard, onto my cock. She started moaning almost immediately, her noises growing in intensity as Sam kept whispering to her. Her nipples were hard as pebbles in my mouth-hands, and I did everything in my power to satisfy her every desire. Mere moments later, she was coming as explosively as Sam had, the two of them now making out furiously.

"As soon as I realized I could shift my cock into any size I wanted, I made it extra-long so I could blow myself!" I shouted, spurting my load as deeply into Tessa as possible.

The kissing and hugging women devolved into giggles at my shared secret, both of them teasing me relentlessly. As I knew it was good-natured, unlike the jibes of my youth, I was able to handle it with only a modicum of blushing and stammering.

Maddy peeked her head out of her room, then darted it back in. She emerged completely naked just seconds later, running over and wrapping Sam and Tessa - who was still impaled on my throbbing cock - into a three-way hug.

Fuck, the way her tits bounce when she runs... I stared at our resident bodybuilder, admiring the quiet power buried just beneath her freckled skin. Then I admired Tessa's petite form with her small breasts. Sam's toned body and gravity-defying boobs were just as delicious to my eyes as the other two. *How in the absolute **fuck** did I get so lucky?*

Tessa giggled at being lifted clean off my dick by Maddy, who wasted no time impaling herself on me. She screwed up her face in confusion, then seemed to almost get mad.

"Make it huge, Churro," she demanded as she stood back up.

Tessa shook her head as Sam chuckled. "I don't know how you can take something so huge," Tessa said to Maddy as I flickered, my cock growing to over a foot in length, and girthier than Tessa's bicep.

"Mmmm," Maddy moaned, "fits so good." She bit down hard on her lower lip, her eyes fluttering closed as her walls stretched to accommodate my size.

While Maddy rearranged her innards with my cock, Sam nudged Tessa towards the couch. The ladies split apart, each coming to sit beside me. Tessa grabbed Maddy's face and forcefully pulled her in for a kiss, while Sam whispered in my ear.

"Show them your new hands, Churro. Let's see if you can *hand*-le all three of us at once."

I groaned loudly at her pun, which Maddy took as encouragement and sped up her pace, bouncing almost frantically on my lap, our hips and thighs meeting with loud claps.

Pulling my mind back from the immense pleasure of Maddy's tight pussy, I tried to visualize my hands becoming cocks again, each perfectly sized for the women by my sides. A brief flicker later, and I was rubbing my new cocks against the still-slick entrances of my companions.

Tessa let out a gasp of surprise and went in for a closer look. Sam wasted no time in grabbing my wrist and stuffing herself full of my fleshy rod.

When Tessa took my hand into her mouth, sucking delicately, I gasped. Fucking Maddy and Sam, getting blown by Tessa... "H-hold on. Everyone stop for a sec. I can't..."

They didn't listen to me and the overwhelming sensation of simultaneous pussies and a mouth, all focused on massaging my lengths with the hottest and slickest of feelings, overcame all possible resistance. I came hard, my body a quivering mess as I filled all three of them with a truly ridiculous amount of seed.

Tessa choked and gagged, pulling me out of her mouth to aim it elsewhere. Maddy picked up her pace, a crazy glint in her eyes as she knowingly overwhelmed me by continuing. Sam at least stopped, her hands locked on my wrist, keeping me buried deeply in her snatch.

Using my super strength, I freed my hand from Sam and turned them back to normal, grabbing Maddy's hips and removing her from my lap. "Bad Maddy. Stop."

"But I haven't gotten off yet!" she complained.

I stood up and set her down in front of the couch, stepping behind her. I gave Sam and Tessa the universal hand signal for 'turn around' and had them all line up on the couch, on their knees, hip to hip. Their beautiful asses stuck up in the air, all three of them looking back at me over their shoulders.

They were all looking at me… expectantly. Hungrily. I shifted my hands again, too excited by what was happening to really notice that I wasn't getting tired. I wasn't feeling fatigue. In fact, I felt better than I ever had.

Slamming home into Maddy's dripping tunnel, I teased Tessa as I slipped into her much more gently. Probing my way between Sam's glistening lower lips was neither rough nor gentle, but the mix of the two that I knew she enjoyed the most.

They let out a perfectly harmonized chorus of moans, and I shuddered as all three pussies clamped down hard on all three of my cocks.

Choosing not to acknowledge the absurdity of what was happening, I gave each of them exactly what they all liked the most and soon their moans crescendoed into the heights of passionate screaming.

They were clutching each other's hands, Maddy whipping her head back and forth to kiss the ladies at her sides. Moments later, their cries peaked, their bodies shaking and spasming wildly as each beautiful woman absolutely drenched me with sprays of their own ejaculate.

"I've shifted myself a pair of tits to play with while jerking off!"

Growling now, I kept pummeling them until they were nothing more than quivering, shivering lumps of limp flesh, finally blowing yet another load deep inside of them. It was a moment that seemed to last forever.

Sometime later, when the only sounds to be heard were the quiet squelches of me pulling out and soft panting, I plopped onto the damp couch beside Tessa.

She smiled at me, her hair plastered to her face by sweat and other body fluids, her amber eyes glazed with the look that all beautiful women get when they've been well and truly fucked.

"I love all three of you," I said, much to my surprise. "I love you, Sam. I love you, Maddy. I love you, Tessa. If anything were to happen to any of you, I would go on a rampage until vigilante justice was served."

When Tessa blushed and looked away, I was finally able to shut the fuck up. The little light bulb in my imagination lit up.

"Which behavior was that, Tess?" I asked her, brushing some of her tresses away from her face.

Maddy and Sam were struggling to roll over into half-sitting, half-laying positions, intensely curious as to the answer to that question.

"Drunkenly honest," Tessa whispered. "What you'd say if you got hammered and lost all your inhibitions."

As I pondered her response, I realized that she was absolutely right. Curiously, I wasn't angry about her using her power on me. I was… relieved? I mean, I knew I felt that way, but without her power abuse, I probably would have forever been too chicken shit to say anything.

Deciding not to care, I pulled her into my lap for a hug, which she melted into for a minute before putting her arm up, beckoning the other ladies to join us.

"Showers, then meet in my room?" Maddy asked.

We all grinned at each other and went to rinse my come off ourselves before starting another round of crazy shapeshifter sex. It was going to be a fucking wonderful night. Or was it a wonderful fucking night? Who even gives a shit? It was awesome.

26

PATROL, PART 1

"Here is your patrol route," a uniformed TPD officer told us, handing us an actual printed copy of a map, with a route marked in red ink on it. "It's been chosen especially for you, since THG says none of your powers are particularly useful. Excepting you, Tase-Lite, of course," he added with a nod in Dani's direction. "It's around the heart of the city, a place those damned terrorists haven't been able to attack. You should be safe enough."

Dani nodded back, accepting the map. "Thank you, Officer. They may be new, but they're not exactly helpless. Our training regimens are quite comprehensive."

He just stared blankly at her before walking away without a word.

"Fucking prick," Chad said.

Unfortunately, the foul-mouthed and moody Chad was stuck on patrol with us, as no one had been able to come up with a way to let Chelsey be here instead. No one was happy about it; Chad least of all.

"This is such bullshit," he continued whining. "I shouldn't have to be here. I just want to go back to sleep; dream away the days in my little cocoon of darkness."

Jack thumped him on the shoulder, "I'm sorry that you have to be out here, Chad. Chelsey told me what it's like for you when you're not around. It sounds pleasant."

Chad snorted, rolling his eyes. "Yeah, that's not all she told you, is it?"

Jack flushed a lovely shade of pink, which served to really highlight his alabaster skin.

"Leave him alone, you flaccid dildo," Maddy snarled. "No one gives a shit how tough your life is now, because we're all fucking living it. Fuuuuck, I so haven't missed having you around."

"Same to you, you filthy who-"

Chad's next word was interrupted by my armored hand slapping straight across his stupid face. He stared at me in shock.

"We're a fucking team, Chad, find a way to accept that. Maddy, you need to watch yourself, too."

Looking around the team and seeing that he wasn't going to get any backup, he stalked away angrily, muttering under his breath. Maddy had the grace to look at least a little sheepish at having been called out.

"Christ, let's just get this patrol over with. Same formation from the ObCo. Form up and move out." I spoke to my team calmly, but inside I was a roiling mass of tightly wound nerves and anxiety.

Once we were out of sight of the normies, I flickered into the most powerful form I'd conceived to date. I had heightened senses of balance, sight, and hearing. My muscles were almost completely synthetic, attached to bones made of some alloy of titanium, gold, and chromium. I understood almost nothing about the actual atomic structure or chemical components of the alloy, but that didn't seem to be absolutely necessary for my transformation. Sally had assured me that it was still one of the toughest alloys in existence, even after thousands of iterations driven by the pair of the supers that had made nearly all of Earth's technological advancements in the last decades.

I was stronger, tougher, all around *better* than I'd ever been in my entire life. Physically, at least. And thanks to sparring with the vicious Maddy, my elbows and knees were reinforced against hyper-extension and snapping by extra spurs of protective alloy. I felt like an absolute behemoth. An unstoppable juggernaut that suddenly weighed close to four hundred pounds, thanks to my new skeleton.

When we all caught up and surrounded Chad protectively, he quit his mumbling, though he was still pouting. Tessa called out directions from her place in the back.

THREE HOURS LATER, WE WERE AT THE FURTHEST POINT IN OUR PATROL, having encountered absolutely nothing and no one. We were in an older section of the city, what Dani described as the Warehouse District, approaching the parking lot of a strip club that had gone out of business a long time ago.

The hairs on the back of my neck stood up, goosebumps raising up on my arms. I held my fist up in the sign for "Stop" that I'd been taught. After some jostling and really terrible discipline on the parts of my teammates, I yelled, "Scatter!"

To their credit, once they were paying attention, they followed orders well. Within moments, they were all behind some sort of cover; cars, dumpsters, building corners.

I stood alone in the center of the street, secure in the strength of my new bone material. I could feel the eyes of my teammates, and some others, crawling over my skin.

"This is not an attack," a sibilant voice hissed in my ear. Before I could so much as blink, the audible world exploded in an overwhelmingly loud static.

I ducked down, crouching with my hands over my ears as the sound slowly faded away. Confused and questioning shouts from the rest of the Omegas filled the air.

"I'd like to talk to you face to face," the hisser whispered. "Just give me thirty seconds."

I held my hand up with the signal for "Hold Position," making sure each member of my team saw it. When I got back confused nods, I finally dropped my hand and began looking around.

A slender man stepped out of the strip club's front door and approached me slowly, his hands raised.

I clenched my fists tight and waited, knees bent, muscles coiled for a quick spring in any direction.

He spoke when he reached me, stopping about ten feet away. He was dressed in a Hawaiian shirt and cargo shorts, Old Balance shoes covering white socks pulled halfway up his calves. For all that he was rocking the dad look, his body looked incredibly hard. Solid. Like he'd been forced to miss more than a few meals, but still worked his ass off lifting heavy things. He looked to be even older than that normie cop whose name I couldn't remember. "Hello, Churro. I wish we could have met under different circumstances."

"Who the fuck are you, and how the fuck do you know my name?"

He flinched slightly at my coarse language, but made no other moves. "My name is Dissem, and I'm one of the founding members of the Order of Assistance."

I accidentally flickered in shock, my jaw literally detaching and making a dull 'clank' as it hit the ground. I shook my head and got back to combat readiness. I couldn't help but stare in amazement as my extra jaw vanished into the ether like so much smoke when I flickered back to my attack body.

It took a few minutes of coaxing the Omegas to enter the strip club with me, but eventually they all caved when they saw that I wasn't budging even an inch until I'd gotten more information out of Dissem.

When we finally entered the dark space, it appeared as if he'd been living here by himself for at least a few weeks, if the empty pre-packaged meal containers were any indication.

"I'm sure you have questions, Churro, and I promise you we will get to them in due time. And no, I'm not going to be killed right before I can reveal the truth to you." He smirked. "The truth, which you've probably already begun to suspect, is that the Telomere Plague was no accident. It was manufactured by a super by the name of Craig 'PlagueDoc' Torovski. It specifically targeted adults without powers."

"How… how do you know?" I asked him.

"Well, I was the one who Disseminated it."

The wind whistled through broken window panes and rusted out vents.

"You murdered like eight billion people," I whispered, barely able to get my words out.

He nodded sadly, not denying my accusation even a little. "I did. Of course, I thought I was spreading human immortality. The cure for aging. I should have known better. In fact, I probably did know better, but the rest of them probably let MetaFiction mess with my perception or memory. You see, I was approached by a group of people like me, people who had discovered that they had these incredible powers that they could use to fix everything that was wrong with our world, our society. We could cure inequality with handheld zero-point energy and energy to matter converters no bigger than a backpack.

"We could cure all illness, advance technology thousands of years in months, reach the stars and colonize alien planets. We could have accomplished anything." He hung his head, the weight of memory bearing down heavily upon his shoulders. "The first of us, we had so much potential, so much *power*, and I was young. Dumb. Of course the power corrupted them. After all, why build equality when it would be even easier to rule the world in its entirety?

"But they had read the same books, seen the same movies, heard the same songs. They knew what happened when people perceived as evil attempted to destroy or rule humanity. One would arise, a chosen one, and tear from them everything they had stolen. Even all these years later, and this is still conjecture on my part, I believe Andromeda whispered his poisoned words into everyone's ears, hatching the plot to become the *saviors* of the world. After all, when every single survivor venerates you, how can one throw you down? If no one knows you're a monster, there will be no chosen one."

I looked at the rest of my team, every last one of them staring with wide-eyed, open-mouthed shock. Turning back to Dissem, I tried to disbelieve what he was telling me, but it rang with such vibrant *truth* that I just knew in my soul that I was finally learning the real history of my world.

"So they destroyed the world. MetaFiction devised a speculative plan for how best to implement their reign over humanity, PlagueDoc brewed up death, Andromeda empowered it, and I Disseminated it to every person on the planet at the same time. At the time, I believed it was a simple, apocalyptic miscalculation.

"The world devolved overnight, falling to chaos faster than you can even imagine. Then the Teen Wars sparked off, and we sat back and watched those kids killing each other, further thinning the population with their teenaged stupidity. 'For the greater good,' I was told. 'Let the most aggressive ones fade to dust, that we might raise the rest in a utopia.' And I still believed, so I did nothing as the brightest and most determined future leaders of the new world reduced each other to ash, playing with toys that should never have been developed, let alone placed in the hands of people who have mental breakdowns if a zit shows up on picture day…

"When it was determined that all of the major players of the Teen Wars had sufficiently reduced each other to a manageable point, I Disseminated our carefully crafted government plans to the world's survivors. Plans to rebuild society. Plans to help humanity rise up from the ashes of its doom, building anew on the bones of the dead."

He chuckled ruefully. "And wouldn't you know it, it worked. When the oldest person on the planet, besides the Order of Assistance members, is only seventeen by that point, and looking almost thirty, they don't have enough experience to argue or question what was being fed to them. Even if they did, they couldn't have gotten any support from their peers; the War saw to that.

"And now we've had three, sometimes four, generations of humanity growing up on the lies, the false history. It didn't even take much. Destroy a few storehouses of old history books, lose a few movies that sang the praises of the American Dream and freedom… and we could teach literally anything we wanted with no one able to say otherwise."

When he saw all of our shocked faces staring back at him, he offered us all bottles of water and places to sit to process. The most fucked up part of this situation was that I didn't want to believe a word he was saying, but I absolutely did. I believed every word of it. It made too much sense, and there was too much evidence of state-controlled education and news feeds for me to refute his claims.

After giving us a few minutes to recover, he continued, "I wanted to believe we were doing the best we could, that we were being smart, but it didn't take long for me to realize that the Order's dreams of a utopia were practically mind-control on a scale that humanity had never seen before. When I objected, Andromeda turned my power down as far as he could, and they just… let me go. Sent me out into this brand-new world, just starting to rise out of the fresh corpse of the old. They were so entrenched in their power by that point that they didn't fear one man speaking against it, no matter how the truth resonates."

I didn't know if it was his power, or if what he was telling us was powerful on its own, but I could feel the truth of it down to my core.

I looked at my teammates. With the exception of Chad, everyone was deep in thoughts, frowns of consternation on their faces. Chad just looked angry.

"You're full of shit," he accused Dissem. "You're just a conspiracy theory whackadoodle, spouting off wild accusations. If your words had even a little bit of truth in them, it'd be all over the news. The government wouldn't stand for someone trying to rewrite history. The Plague hit, then the War, and we picked ourselves up out of the dust and ashes and rebuilt a new, better system. We're doing it our way, and better than anyone had ever been able to manage before the Plague, too."

"You're free to believe whatever helps you sleep at night, son," Dissem replied quietly. "But I figured that if anyone deserved to know the truth, it was you lot. THG has you on the sidelines, but the fact of the matter is that it's only a matter of time before Churro's secret is revealed."

My already-racing heart kicked up another notch, adrenaline flooding my system. *He knows what I can do…* I turned to Tessa. "Juice him, make him honest, like you did with me."

She looked back at me, as pale as I'd ever seen her. "I have been," she whispered.

Dissem looked a little surprised at that, but seemed to think about for a minute before nodding in satisfaction. "Yes, I can feel it now. That's an interesting power you have there. One I imagine will be quantified as fairly dangerous once you tier up to your max. We're almost out of time; THG will have noticed my EMP that disrupted your tracking and recording devices. If you have any questions, now is the time for them."

"Why are you bothering with us?" Maddy asked.

"Because Churro's Growth Vector can change the course of this war; it can help us take out the corrupt leadership of the guilds and government, allowing us to free the world of their tyranny."

"How did you even find out about that?" asked Tessa.

"We have resources, dear child. Until you're free and clear from THG and the RFS, we can't risk revealing ourselves any more than we already have." Dissem glanced over his shoulder and back to us, tapping the time piece attached to his wrist. "One more, quickly. They're close."

"You keep saying 'we' and 'us.' Who the fuck are you working for?" I demanded, my elevated state causing me to be rougher than I wanted to be.

Dissem winced again. Apparently, he had a thing against swearing. "We're the Truthseekers, Churro. We haven't put together the full and complete *true* history of our world yet, but we've learned enough to know that we need to start standing up for people the world over. You'll have to forgive me for this next part, but they'll execute me - and probably all of you - if I'm caught here."

"Wait! Who wi-"

The strip club burst into blindingly bright light, a thunderous boom sending us all staggering. When my vision cleared and I could hear again, the seven of us were surrounded by people in THG armor with guns pointed at us.

27

PATROL, PART 2

We all put our hands up in the air then froze. I flickered, shifting back to my THG-known body; I drew some extra scrutiny, but the people who had seen it only blinked a few times and shook their heads. It was amazing how often people refused to believe what they'd seen with their own eyes, but I was learning to never underestimate the power of humanity to delude themselves into believing what they wanted to, rather than what they'd experienced.

"Site clear, proceed," one of the minions spoke into the radio attached to his helmet.

Warden strode smugly into the club, little prisons of sparkling green light popping up around my whole team, separating us from each other and the THG soldiers. All sound was cut off as I was isolated.

I couldn't hide the disdain on my face when Warden walked through his power to join me in my little cell. He was invading my personal space so much I could tell that he'd had garlic chicken for his last meal.

"Well, well, well," he droned at me. "If it isn't our little misfit gang of Omegas getting into trouble again. Why did you disable your tracking and monitoring equipment?"

A tiny thud sound caught our attention, Warden looking surprised that any noise had made it through his barrier. We both looked over to Chad's cell to see Chelsey getting back to her feet.

That fucking prick just bailed! God damn it, Chad! You fucking pansy!

"Now that's definitely interesting. Chad's power evolved, eh? You don't look surprised. Just... mad." He turned his maniacal grin back in my direction. "I'm left wondering who else may have gotten stronger, and how they might have done so."

"Yes, sir."

"Oh, don't be like that, Mr. Murphy. We're all on the same side here. Right?" He just kept on grinning at me, looking for all the world like he'd just gotten away with stealing a cookie.

"Yes, sir," I repeated through gritted teeth. I was going to brutalize Chad when he came back.

I glanced over to Chelsey to see how she was doing. She was peeling off the pieces of her armor that were now oversized for her body, which was almost all of them. She looked absolutely terrified.

A quick scan of the rest of my team showed various levels of fear, anger, and nerves. Not that I could blame them, being locked up in silent boxes as they were. Tessa was probing hers with a finger.

"Tell me what happened here, Churro."

"We saw something suspicious in here and decided to investigate. An EMP went off and fried our circuits. We turned up nothing in our search of the premise, and then you all showed up like heroes."

"Uh huh. You didn't check for traps before entering?"

I shook my head. "We're in the middle of the city, why would a place like this be trapped?"

"Because it's a known hang out for terrorists," Warden smirked.

"Why the fuck would you send our first patrol to a known terrorist location? Sir," I added belatedly.

His smirk widened back into the grin I wanted to smack off of his face. "Because we don't trust you, obviously. They reached out to you before, it's not actually so far-fetched that they'd try again."

Movement caught my attention. Chelsey was being led out of the strip club in hand cuffs, her arms pulled behind her back, an agent holding each bicep. More soldiers surrounded each of my friends, all of them being instructed via pantomime to put their hands on the backs of their heads and await arrest. One by one, Warden dropped his barriers, and they were led away.

"I don't know how you managed to do it, Churro, but your team is getting stronger. You all hide it well, but it's only a matter of time before we suss out your secrets. You know that, don't you? We always win, eventually. Especially when we're not actually facing off against real heroes. You and your team are just a bunch of weaklings with useless powers, no matter how much stronger any of you get."

I hung my head, trying my damnedest to act the part of depressed loser, hiding my rage as best I could. "Yes, sir. We're not heroes, sir."

"Well," he drawled, holding onto the 'l' sound and dragging it out, "you're not a hero. Danielle? She's a hero. Samantha, Tessa, and Madelaine… they could all be heroes in my private quarters, if you know what I mean."

I couldn't stop the low growl that rumbled through my chest. My fists clenched tightly, and I prepared to tear Warden into tiny little pieces.

"Of course," he said before I could jump on him, "there's no need for anything like that to occur. I'm sure you agree. All… unpleasantness… can be completely avoided. All you have to do is tell me the truth. About the terrorists and why they're interested in you. About your team and how they got stronger. About how you've been keeping everything hidden from THG. From me. It's a simple thing, *Churro.* A few conversations, and you could be her personal hero." Warden pointed at Tessa as she was led out of the club in restraints.

Then he switched to point at Dani. "You could be her hero, too, son. Did you know you killed her rapist?"

My head snapped up; shock written plain on my face.

He laughed. "Oh yeah. She didn't tell you? Johnny raped her last year. Slipped her a mickey, promised to 'take care of the lightweight,' and had a grand old time. She only vaguely remembers any details, of course, just that he was a prick. That's why we pushed him down to Omega Team. If she'd had a breakthrough memory, it would have caused some trouble. Thankfully, you solved our little problem quite nicely. Why do you think you didn't get in trouble for actually murdering someone?" He chuckled again.

I watched Dani get cuffed and escorted out, my heart breaking for what she'd gone through. "You knew… and you just demoted him? That was it? That's your idea of justice?" I was snarling, my whole system flooded with enough adrenaline that I knew I was close to completely losing control.

"We didn't demote him," Warden laughed, a sound that I was learning to despise, "we promoted him. Sure, he dropped down to Omega Team, but he was going to be team leader. Leading a bunch of fully-useless kids is better than just being on a team with mostly-useless kids."

I lunged for Warden, my hands going for his throat. I was stopped cold by another impenetrable barrier that formed between us instantaneously.

"Come now, kid. You can't think that you'd actually get the drop on me, can you? I may not be a nice person, but I am one of the good guys. And those of you who've been… tainted… by the Truthseekers, well, you're always trying to come after me. But enough of this. Put your hands behind your head, come home quietly, and we'll get this all cleared up. No one has to be in trouble here. In fact, by helping us shut down the terrorists permanently, you'll be honored as heroes. All of you. Hell, maybe I can even get you promoted off Omega Team; get you on a team that has a little prestige, you know?"

I pounded my fist on the barrier between us before looking around the club. It was just the two of us in here now. I saw a THG van driving away, probably with one of my friends inside. It was followed shortly by another, then another. It seemed like they were keeping us separated.

"Fine," I growled. "But if you hurt any of them…" I let the threat trail off. He didn't look as if he felt threatened.

"There won't be a need for any of that, provided you do your best to help us. And really, it's in the best interests of the entire world that you do." He looked and sounded exactly like a smarmy used car salesman now.

I let him cuff me, knowing I could escape the restraints at any time with a quick flicker. I grinned, thinking about the look that would be on Warden's face if I shifted my hands into dicks and slapped him across the face with one. I'd have to yell, 'Mushroom stamp!' while I did it.

When his power faded into nothingness, the sibilant whisper was back in my ear, "Hold tight. Say nothing. We're coming for you. For all of you. We'll get you all out."

My ride back to THG HQ was spent trying to come up with exit strategies. I thought I might be able to shift into Warden's body as a disguise, but with him sitting right across from me I had no way to test it. I had, and immediately dismissed, the idea that I could transform into a fly or other insect. But if he trapped me one of his cells, I figured it was probably game over - with a name like Warden, it seemed pretty damn likely that his jailor abilities wouldn't be easy to escape.

If it came down to a fight, I figured I could hold my own - briefly - against RayStorm. If I kept shifting back to an unharmed state, I could probably survive long enough to get in close. Then all it would take would be some fancy blade-work; he didn't really have any defensive powers.

Squaring off against Swiss Mountain would be moderately tougher. His size and sheer strength might be able to break even my super-alloy skeleton. Repeated shifting, again, might help, but taking him down would probably need more precision than I felt I was capable of.

Gemma was a true wildcard. Her powers as the Gemstone Mage weren't widely known, and I'd seen her explode people's heads with a wave of her hand. I could hope that she'd hold back, but planning to rely on her goodwill seemed like a really bad idea. She was still working for THG, regardless of the fact that she was the only person who'd shown my team even a modicum of respect. Maybe a form where my brain and central nervous system were hidden in my chest… that way if she exploded my head, I wouldn't die immediately. *Fuck, I have to hope that sort of shift comes intuitively, I don't have time or opportunity to practice.*

Getting by or taking out Warden, though. That would have to have some element of surprise. I'd never tried any really tiny or otherwise hard-to-spot forms, thanks to my experience with Johnny. *If only I'd figured out eye lasers. He couldn't expect that.* Thanks to the non-conservation aspect of my Molecular Reconstruction, I was pretty sure I could go really damn small. Or maybe really damn big? Did Warden's cage have any size limitations?

It probably did, now that I thought of it. If it didn't, he could've just locked down the entire strip club and prevented Dissem from escaping. Not that he knew Dissem was there, but he absolutely had some limits.

After what Warden had told me in the club, there was no way I was going to be able to pretend that I was still part of the THG family. The corruption likely didn't extend to every single member, but the leadership was definitely a bunch of bastards.

"You're thinking real hard there, Mr. Murphy," Warden interrupted my inner monologue.

I looked up at his grinning face. "Just wondering why you think I have anything to do with terrorists, sir. All I've done today, hell, all I've *ever* done is follow orders to the best of my limited ability. I started getting fit so I could be pretty enough for photo ops. I trained for combat when you told me to. I went on patrols that I was underqualified for, just like you directed. I went on the route that your man provided for me. As far as I'm concerned, I've been a model team player, and now I'm being arrested and dragged back home in cuffs for falling victim to a trap that had no business being in our city in the first place."

"Don't get smart with me, boy." He was frowning now. "None of our other teams have been targeted the ways yours has been. And if there's enemy contact, they shoot first. They don't try to make conversation. There's something special about you, and fuck me sideways if I can figure out what that is. You're just a damn kid who can turn into a fucking snack and get shit out." He visibly attempted to rein in his frustration, clearly upset at having told me as much as he had.

I had to hold in my surprise when Dissem hissed in my ear again. "Your team has been told what their story is. It's what you first told

Warden; suspicious building, EMP trap, you spent time searching the place to figure out what it may have been hiding that it would need the protection of a trap. Be ready; we're going to pull you out before you make it into the building. If we can't get you, stick to the story."

There was a knock on the divider keeping the driver safe from prisoners. Warden's grin returned. "We're here, Mr. Murphy. This might be your last chance to earn some goodwill from us, before more... creative... interrogation techniques are brought into play." He looked like he really hoped I would continue to refuse.

The van exploded sideways.

28

PICKING A SIDE

Thanks to Dissem's warning to be prepared, I was able to flicker to my rugged combat body before I was even halfway across the van. Without planning, without thinking, my hands were wide blades made of super-alloy that tore through my cuffs like they were paper.

As if in slow motion, I could see them cut through Warden's chest armor; felt absolutely no resistance as his black bodysuit was split. I could feel the heat of Warden's body as my blades slipped into him; the slight tug of pressure before his ribs parted for my weapons. The tough muscle of his heart separating to each side of my right-hand blade, my left shredding his lung before popping through his back and pinning him to the sidewall of the van.

His eyes were still opening slowly, registering only surprise; the pain hadn't yet had time to make it to his brain before the light started to leave his gaze. His mouth opened, but only a small trickle of blood made it past his lips.

Time resumed its furious pace, Warden getting completely shredded by my sharp edges as we tumbled and tossed around the back of the van. I was battered and bruised, dizzy from getting thrown around like a fucking ping pong ball. I flickered, the dizziness fading almost as fast as my minor wounds.

To its credit, the van was in remarkably good condition considering the abuse it had suffered. The wall that I had been leaning against had a small dent in it, and the wall behind Warden's body was fairly deeply shredded. I couldn't see anything through the holes that I'd made, since that wall was now my floor, the van lying on its side.

Testing the back door, I discovered it was still securely locked. *Okay, this is no big deal. I've just killed a man on purpose. I can handle a little door, right?* I may have been starting to panic.

I glanced back at the corpse; yep, definitely starting to panic.

Planting my feet, I hauled my right arm back and widened the blade so it was now shaped like a 'T.' I punched at the seam between doors, nearly faceplanting into them when I cut through like they weren't even there.

The bottom door fell open, and I crawled outside to chaos.

THG soldiers were firing guns and energy beams and fucking ice spikes at guerrillas in urban camouflage, who were shooting back with their own guns and super powers. Three vans were racing into the parking garage beneath THG HQ. I briefly had time to wonder who was inside before I was blasted to my back.

Everything was dark, and excruciating pain from where my face used to be made itself known to my brain. I flickered, gasping and rolling to hide beside the van, not knowing which way was safe. Bullets pinged all around me, powers ripped holes in the street. The other three vans were stopped, their drivers lashing out at the attackers with their own guns or powers.

"Get your remaining friends and get to the last van in the line!" Dissem's hissed whisper was difficult to hear over the sounds of the battle, but enough made it through that I knew I had to start moving. The incoming fire from the guerrillas was beginning to slow down. It sounded like they were losing.

I darted from cover, running as fast as I could while keeping hunched over. Bullets whizzed through the air, and I was shot more than a couple times, quickly flickering to keep myself as healthy as I could.

Reaching the next van in line behind my own, the driver turned his rifle towards me and squeezed off a round. It pinged painfully off my forehead, snapping my head backwards. My momentum kept me going, though, and I tackled him with knife hands much as I'd done to Warden. My angle was slightly off, so I had to stab him a few more times as he struggled beneath me, before he finally lay still.

An energy blast caught me by the shoulder, lifting me up and sending me spiraling into the van where I collided heavily, the whole vehicle rocking with my mass. I growled as I healed the damage, ducking another blast as I moved to the rear of the transport, slicing the doors open.

Then I was cowering on the ground, my blades covering my head. I was pretty sure I was whimpering when the sensation faded as suddenly as it had come. Peeking up, Tessa was staring down at me, pale as a sheet and shaking with fear.

"Sorry," she whispered. "What do we do?"

Pushing myself back to my feet, my blades carving deep furrows into the pavement, I said, "Get to the last van in line and we'll supposedly be whisked to safety! Let me go first, though!"

I charged off without waiting for her to respond, taking an entire magazine of bullets to the chest and face. One of my eyes exploded, and flickering it back into existence left me with bullet fragments in my mouth. The shooter, the driver of the van I was about to assault, just stared at me in shock until I spit the fragments at him.

He dropped his rifle and quickly pulled his sidearm, but I was in his face before he could shoot me again. My left-hand blade took both of his arms at the elbows, my right-hand blade slipping into his neck and severing his spine. I barely slowed to let him fall to the ground before I was at the back of the van, which was peeling back in layers.

Deciding that Sam could get herself out now, I sprinted full-out towards the last van and presumed safety.

I slid under the driver's open door, which she was using for cover from the guns on the buildings lining the street. Kicking her feet out backwards, she landed face first on my blades, the top of her head sliding off the bottom and smacking me in the face.

Shoving her body off me, I rolled over and vomited noisily. Spitting out chunks of brain matter, I finally managed a few heaving breaths, only to be pressed into the ground by a supremely heavy weight.

I could barely lift my head, but I was able to see a super in full costume standing near me, pointing their hand at me.

"Nothing is stronger than gravity, you fucking terrorist traitor!" he yelled at me. He must have been Black Hole, a member of Beta Team known for affecting gravity.

Suddenly, the weight pressing me to the pavement was gone, and Black Hole was holding his head, "Oh God, oh God, what am I doing? All these people dead, and I couldn't save them! I'm… I'm nothing. I'm helpless. I'm so helpless! I can't… No…"

Walking up behind him, her hand outstretched much as his had been, was Tessa. She concentrating fiercely, blood dripping from a cut over her eyebrow. "You made it so much worse, B.H.," she told him. "You could have saved them, but instead you doomed them. No one will ever forgive you for this."

She continued insulting and berating him, piling on as much guilt as she could. Sam snuck around her and helped me to my feet. Together we went to the back of the last van to open the doors.

Sam peeled back the layers covering the locking mechanism, which burst apart. I pulled open the doors and had to quickly shift my blades back to hands to catch Maddy, who burst from the back of the van like a meteor. She wrapped me up in a tight hug.

"Who is left to kill?" she asked after stepping back from me.

We all heard a 'fwhump' from the front of the van, so I went back to go investigate. Tessa was standing over the headless body of Black Hole.

"H-he, he crushed his h-head," she stammered. "I m-made him suicidal."

Sam rushed to pull the petite violet-haired woman into the safety of a loving hug.

"We need to get to the ba-" I started.

I was interrupted by the most horrendous screeching, squelching, tearing and ripping, horrifying noise I'd ever heard in my life. It sounded like the universe itself howling in pain, as a super *forced* a hole in the fabric of space and time. The fact that the hole in reality was bleeding did not help settle my still-queasy stomach.

On the other side of the hole was a boy. He couldn't have been older than maybe thirteen or fourteen. Fresh to his powers. Beside the boy was Dissem, gesticulating wildly for us to come through the agonizing wound in the air.

I nodded to Sam when she shot me a questioning glance, and together we ushered Maddy and Tessa through the portal.

The portal sealed up with what sounded like a quiet sob and a sigh of relief.

"I'M SO SORRY WE COULDN'T GET YOUR OTHER FRIENDS. OUR STRATEGISTS are already planning a rescue," Dissem said, leading us quickly away from the verdant field we were now standing in. Blood stains in the grass showed that this was likely used a lot to open bleeding gashes in reality.

"They were supposed to have Churro in the lead van, but they switched up the driving order at the last minute, and I'm sorry, but he was our number one priority. Without him, the guilds and RFS will wipe us out in the next few months. We're scrambling for cover, splitting into cells as we speak. We're losing the war. We're getting desperate."

"Where are we?" Sam asked. Tessa was walking on her own now, but still leaning heavily into the metal manipulator.

"One of our last refuges, a small island in the Pacific Ocean. Thanks to Ripper here," he nodded at the boy, "we've been able to move away from the mainland and their sources of entrenched power. It's only a matter of time before we're discovered, though, and likely by satellite, so we're building an underground habitat in a different portion of the world."

"We have to get Jack and Dani and Chelsey," Maddy growled, presumably still mad that she hadn't gotten to murder anyone.

I patted her shoulder carefully, ready for her to lash out. "I know, Maddy. We will, I promise."

Dissem nodded, "We will. They're not as vital to our survival as Churro is, but we won't let anyone else be tortured by the guild leaders. Until we have a plan, I'm sure you could all use some comforts.

Food, showers, clothes. We don't have much, but what we do have is available to you."

I looked over at the three ladies, who were all nodding with various intensity. Tessa most of all looked like she was craving a shower, for all that I was the one covered in blood and pieces of brain. Well, and Maddy, thanks to the bear-hug she'd given me.

"Dissem," I called. "Warden is dead. I killed him, almost by accident, when my van went flying. Black Hole is dead, too. I'm not sure if we got anyone else famous."

He nodded briefly. "As much as it saddens me, that might be a good thing. Warden's ability has, so far, proven to be completely inescapable. Once he has you in one of his bubbles, you're his forever."

Dissem kept leading us away from the bloody field, towards a forest of palms and ferns. After a short hike, we came out into a clearing that had a number of mud or clay structures. They were uniformly small, but looked cozy. Chickens ran free throughout the little village, which was populated by, I'd guess, about fifty people. Men, women, children. The adults were all ages, from the same age as us to almost as old as Dissem. They all looked at us with mixed expressions - hope and fear, mostly - but didn't make a move to trouble or greet us.

"They're going to keep their distance for a little while, until Margaret gets back. She's a telepath; she's going to be able to tell us if you've been turned into sleeper agents."

"Wait, sleeper agents? That shit is real?" Maddy asked loudly.

Dissem winced again at the foul language, but answered her as politely as ever. "It's uncommon, and we believe highly unlikely. Our intel suggests that Trainer, the super with the power of hypnosis, hasn't been in Minneapolis for almost six months. Our best guess is that he was in Washington, keeping the normie government under control."

"Where is Minneapolis, and what does that have to do with us?" I asked him.

"Oh, darn it. I forgot. Minneapolis is the original name of Titan. When they rewrote history, they renamed anything and everything that didn't reflect their views. Minneapolis, being a portmanteau of the

Dakota word for 'water' and the Ancient Greek word for 'city,' was deemed too 'ethnic' for their liking, so they named it Titan instead. Which is baffling, because the myth of the Titans is just as Ancient Greek as 'polis' is. But we can teach you the real history of the world at another time. Right now, we'll get you cleaned up, fresh clothes, some food in your bellies. Okay?"

A HALF HOUR LATER, THE FOUR OF US WERE LEFT ALONE IN A SMALL HUT. It was dim, as the only light came in between the palm-leaf roof and solid mud walls. But we were clean, having bathed in a beautiful waterfall, and now we were eating.

None of us knew what it was, but we were having some sort of meat that had cooked over an open fire pit, wrapped in some sort of wide leaf. Our crude plates were also holding a potato-like thing that had been baked by being buried under the fire. It was simple food, but it tasted far better than anything we'd ever eaten before, all of us moaning in delight and enjoyment.

As the food disappeared, conversation picked back up.

"Do we believe what Dissem has told us?" Sam asked.

"I do," replied Maddy. "I believe that if they weren't at least mostly moral, they would have just left us all there when they kidnapped Churro."

Tessa nodded at that.

"Unless they wanted to make sure I powered them up willingly," I said. "Without a super like Warden, how could they ever hope to keep me here if I didn't want to stay?"

"Churro, I've been keeping Dissem on a low-level honest behavior this whole time. Unless he's somehow resistant, he believes what he's telling us. And that means I believe him when he says he'll help us get our friends back."

"And it's not exactly like you three are helpless," Maddy added. "You all seem to have tiered up again today, even without going through the normal process. I'm getting more and better data now, too.

Dissem is who he says he is, and the only power that was affecting him was Tessa's."

"Holy shit," Tessa said loudly, "you can see, what? Like a status effect screen?"

Maddy nodded, grinning. It seemed the bath and food had returned her almost all the way back to her normal, not-quite-murderous self. "I mean, we'll have to wait for Margaret or whoever to come confirm me, but I can see that none of you are designated as sleepers."

"That's seriously impressive, Maddy," I told her.

"Okay," Sam said. "So we believe Dissem, we believe Maddy. Great. But now the fuck what? I like the weather here, but we absolutely have to help get Jack, Chelsey, and Dani back. I don't know if I'll be able to relax, knowing that those fucking assholes are probably torturing our friends for information they don't even have."

I agreed quickly. "Sam's absolutely right. We need to get our friends, and Sally, out of THG's filthy hands."

"Oh crap," Tessa said. "Sally. I totally forgot about her."

"Yeah, and getting her out means getting a body, or… I don't know. A mainframe? How the fuck do super AIs need to travel?" asked Maddy.

"We really need access to her info, and to Jack, to get her a body that we can use to get her out of THG HQ," Sam said.

"I hate to say this, but we may need to wait to rescue anyone until we can rescue everyone." I shook my head sadly, hating the thought of leaving our friends to whatever tender mercies THG would show them, especially after I'd killed Warden. "Once we break in for Jack, Chad and Chelsey, and Dani, I don't think we'll be able to go in a second time for Sally. We need to get her during the first and only rescue attempt."

I was beating myself up more than ever for not having stopped Warden at the strip club. I hadn't even tried. Some fucking hero I was.

An urgent knock on our surprisingly well-fitted handmade door made us all jump, my blade-hands coming up to combat readiness.

"Omegas, Dani escaped! We've got her! But she's injured and needs help! If there's anything you can do…" a voice I didn't recognize told us. And until I knew we could trust everyone in this camp, I wasn't taking any chances. I bulked up my frame to nearly seven feet tall, angry glowing eyes that were tinted red, and wickedly serrated blade hands.

Nodding to Tessa to swing the door open, I dropped into a combat crouch and nearly decapitated the teenaged boy standing there. Growling an apology, I blasted past him and headed towards the bloody field.

29

EPILOGUE

Adjusting the spring and flex of my joints and tendons on the fly, I made it to the arrival field in just a few moments. I'd never run so fast in my life - it honestly felt like I was barely touching the ground before springing forward again and again.

"Dani!" I yelled.

The small group of people surrounding the prone Dani quickly made room for me. Assessing her situation, it looked like she'd been shot multiple times, and maybe burned. Her normal brown skin was washed out and ashen from blood loss. I knelt at her side.

Grabbing her hand, I told her, "You need to eat me, Dani. I might be able to fix this!"

"Churro, no!" shouted Tessa. "We don't even know if you can shift someone else's body! And… and if she dies… What would happen to you if her body couldn't process you?"

"Tessa's right, Churro. We can't take the risk of losing you. You heard Dissem; without you, the Truthseekers' war for humanity will be over. They'll have won." Maddy placed her hand on Tessa's shoulder in a display of solidarity.

While I was distracted by the Omega ladies trying to talk me out of helping Dani, the island's medical staff were busy trying to slow the bleeding.

"What did they tell you when you were five years old, Tessa?" I asked her quietly.

"They said I was going to be a hero," she whispered back.

"And what did they teach you every fucking day after that until you hit puberty, Maddy?"

"They taught me what it means to be a hero."

"Sam, what do you want more than anything else in the world?"

"I want to be a hero," she replied, slumping her shoulders.

"Heroes take risks," I told them. "They risk their lives to save people they don't know. They're willing to die for people they care about."

I turned away from them, back towards Dani, and approached her side again, kneeling down. "They face the unknown with their heads held high, because they know that even if they don't succeed this time, someone will. As long as someone is willing to fight, evil can never win. That's what they told me."

I glanced over my shoulder to toss a smile to the three Omega ladies standing behind me, each them looking scared but giving me firm nods of approval.

I placed my hand in Dani's and told the medic putting pressure on one of her gunshot wounds, "Make sure she eats me." When the medic nodded back, I flexed my power, turning myself into a quick-dissolving vitamin.

DANI MOANED WITH EVEN MORE PAIN AS I RETURNED TO CONSCIOUSNESS within her body. It was dark, as her eyes were closed tightly, and *holy shit, everything hurt so bad.*

Dani, I don't think you have enough time for me to practice. It's gotta be now. Are you ready?

Yes, please, just do it! she thought back at me.

Gathering my power in my mind, I tried to imagine Dani's body as best I could remember from our brief time together. It started buzzing, but I couldn't get it to snap into focus.

Keep trying, Churro… she pleaded silently with me.

Taking a deep mental breath to calm myself down, I imagined bandages and sutures covering her wounds. To my surprise, it actually worked - somewhat. Her bleeding slowed to a thin trickle, as opposed to the gushing torrent it had been. Then I tried to imagine her body going completely numb, and our pain faded significantly. It wasn't perfect, but it was a hell of a lot better than it had been.

With extra, imaginary, fluids running through her veins, I focused back on the task at hand; shifting into a perfect recreation of her whole, hale, unharmed state.

My power flared and buzzed, practically screeching in our head, but no matter how hard I flexed, I couldn't force a shift.

Try merging us, Churro. Please. I really don't want to die.

Okay, Dani, hang on. I haven't done this in a long time, since I was less powerful.

It took me a few moments to find the core of Dani's consciousness, that section of her mind that drew me in like a moth to the flame. Her magnetism for me was a powerful thing, and it only took the slightest weakening of my willpower for me to be consumed into us.

As soon as we felt mentally whole, we flickered, our body healing all wounds instantaneously.

Our caregivers gasped and flinched.

"We're okay. We're going to be fine," we said to them, smiling gently. We turned to look into the concerned faces of Tessa, Maddy, and Sam. "It worked, at least to bring us back to our baseline for when we're just Dani."

Just for fun, we imagined ourself floating up off the ground. To our immense surprise, we did exactly that. It was so natural, so intuitive, we spun a pirouette in mid-air before landing easily.

Lightning crackled up our arms and we lifted off again, soaring to a height of maybe forty feet. It was effortless. We were giddy. Ecstatic even. We spun, flipped, hung upside-down, flew literal circles around our almost-equally stunned onlookers.

After a few minutes of delighting like children with a new toy, we alit softly behind Sam.

"We get to fuck you in the ass soon," we whispered to her, reaching out to give her toned booty a tiny zap.

She yelped and spun to face us, rubbing her denim-clad backside. After a second, a huge grin spread over her face. "That was the deal. You make me fly first, though."

We wrapped our arms around Sam's waist and lifted slowly into the air again, holding her tight. Her short squeal of fear turned into excited laughter.

"This doesn't count," she yelled as we picked up our pace, flying faster and faster over the island. "It's gotta be just me flying for it to count!"

"It'll never be just you," we told her, "since you'll have to have our Churro half inside you."

"Whatever, you know what I mean. I don't want to be carried; I want to feel what it's like to actually *fly*."

We carried Sam back to the group of people, who were making their way towards the village now that the excitement had died down. She hugged us, planting a kiss on our cheek.

"Thank you," she told us. "That was fun. I can't wait for more."

We smiled. "Anytime, Sam, anytime."

WHEN WE ALL GOT BACK TO THE VILLAGE, WE CLEARED OUR THROAT. Everyone looked at us.

"Our Dani half had to fight tooth and nail to escape THG's clutches. As soon as they had us in custody, they used cattle prods on Chelsey until she managed to switch back to Chad. As soon as he was back, he flipped on us."

Everyone stared at us, mouths open wide.

"That no-good son of a fucking *whore,*" Maddy screamed, which made Dissem flinch.

"So THG knows about Sally, Churro's ability to boost powers, and the fact that rest of us have been getting stealth upgrades for a month now. They saw the data that Sally had put on our tablets before she was able to erase anything. Chad also told them exactly how Sally was planning to have herself extracted from their systems," we told them.

"What about Warden?" Tessa asked.

"They know our Churro half killed him. We suspect it was, or will be, quite a severe blow to them, as he was an integral member of their operations. He was used quite heavily to contain their malcontents, if what we overheard during the interrogation of Chad is true information."

"So this means that a rescue of Jack should be both easier and more difficult to pull off," Sam said. "They'll know we're coming, but they won't have their ace in the hole to trap anyone."

"I'm sorry to be the one to say this, but is it really necessary to go after Jack or Sally?" asked Dissem.

"It is, Truthseeker," we said coldly. "We do not abandon our family, not for any reason. The Omegas are a family, even if one of us is a traitor. Even if Jack was only useful for Sally's purposes, he is our brother. Chelsey is our sister, regardless of Chad's behavior. And Sally is part of that family. We get them all out, even if we have to knock out Chad to accomplish it."

The other ladies all nodded along at that, glaring daggers at Dissem.

He smiled widely. "That's what I was hoping you would say. As difficult as a rescue mission will be, it brightens my soul to know that you would attempt it with or without the Truthseekers. Truly, you have the hearts of heroes. We will pledge our full support to your endeavor. And we would be forever grateful if you should choose to help us with our goals, though that is not a requirement for our assistance."

As all of us relaxed again, our hackles no longer raised, we all looked at each other. The tentative smiles returned.

Though we had, temporarily, lost some of our own, and been

betrayed by another, most of us were still together, and we were free in a way that we never had been before. We were going to plan, and train, and we were going to win.

Eventually.

The End of Book One.

AUTHOR NOTE

I have many people that deserve my thanks and appreciation for the existence of this book. First and foremost on the list is you, my dearest reader. Without you, I'd just be laughing maniacally into the void, running around my home with dildos in each hand, yelling, "You get a mushroom stamp! You get a mushroom stamp! *Everyone* gets a mushroom stamp!" My wife would also like to extend her thanks to you for letting me put these behaviors on paper instead of chasing her around like a lunatic.

Inspirations and Influences

Aside from my very patient and tolerant wife, there are a few other people that have inspired me to keep writing.

First up, the incomparable M. H. Johnson, who encouraged me to return to writing after a long hiatus, who convinced me that my story was one worth sharing. I cannot thank you enough, M. H.!

Harmon Cooper is another important influence of mine. The Cherry

Blossom Girls series showed me that the main character doesn't need to be OP to be a hero.

And finally, Jamie Hawke, whose books taught me that it's 100% okay to be ridiculous and over-the-top!

Facebook Groups

If you're looking for other awesome superhero books (and an awesome community to connect with), you need look no further than Harem Gamelit.

For sexy harem books that span *many* genres, the Harem Lit group is frequented by tons of awesome authors and the voracious readers who enjoy them.

Superhero Books for Adults is on the quieter, smaller side of groups, but it's a great resource for finding more spicy supers!

Connect with me?

If you want to get in touch with me, please feel free! I love talking to people!

You can reach me…

Via email: ashus@ashusevinco.com

On Facebook: https://www.facebook.com/ashus.evinco.75

I sometimes tweet!: @ashusevinco

Or sign up to my mailing list, and I'll tell you about stuff!

https://www.subscribepage.com/ashusevinco

You are a wonderful human being, and I appreciate you more than you'll ever know!

Thank you for taking the time to leave a review!

Made in the USA
Columbia, SC
24 December 2019